# A NECESSARY EVIL

India, 1920: The fabulously wealthy kingdom of Sambalpore is home to tigers, elephants, diamond mines, and the beautiful Palace of the Sun. But when the Maharaja's son and heir to the throne is assassinated in the presence of Captain Sam Wyndham and Sergeant "Surrender-not" Banerjee, they discover a kingdom riven with suppressed conflict. Prince Adhir was a moderniser whose attitudes — and romantic relationship — may have upset the more religious elements of his country, while his brother — now in line to the throne — appears to be a feckless playboy. As Wyndham and Banerjee desperately try to unravel the mystery behind the assassination, they become entangled in a dangerous world where those in power live by their own rules, and those who cross their paths pay with their lives . . .

# SPECIAL MESSAGE TO READERS

# A NECESSARY EVIL

## ABIR MUKHERJEE

ISIS
LARGE
PRINT

First published in Great Britain 2017
by
Harvill Secker
an imprint of Vintage

First Isis Edition
published 2018
by arrangement with
Penguin Random House UK

A catalogue record for this book is available
from the British Library.

ISBN 978–1–78541–596–8 (hb)
ISBN 978–1–78541–602–6 (pb)

Published by
F. A. Thorpe (Publishing)
Anstey, Leicestershire

Set by Words & Graphics Ltd.
Anstey, Leicestershire
Printed and bound in Great Britain by
T. J. International Ltd., Padstow, Cornwall

This book is printed on acid-free paper

In loving memory of my father-in-law,
Manharlal Devjeebhai Mistry,
*Bapu*

For Sonal,
for everything

You can't make an omelette without breaking heads.

# CHAPTER
# ONE

## *Friday 18 June 1920*

It's not often you see a man with a diamond in his beard. But when a prince runs out of space on his ears, fingers and clothes, I suppose the whiskers on his chin are as good a place as any.

The massive mahogany doors of Government House had opened on the stroke of midday and out they'd glided: a menagerie of maharajas, nizams, nawabs and others; all twenty of them draped in silk, gold, precious gems and enough pearls to sink a squadron of dowager countesses. One or two claimed descent from the sun or the moon; others from one of a hundred Hindu deities. We just lumped them all together and called them *the princes*.

These twenty were from the kingdoms closest to Calcutta. Across India there were more than five hundred of them, and together they were rulers of two fifths of the country. At least that's what they told themselves, and it was a fiction we were only too happy to endorse, just so long as they all sang "Rule Britannia" and swore allegiance to the King Emperor across the seas.

They processed like gods, in strict order of precedence, with the Viceroy at their head, into the

1

blistering heat and towards the shade of a dozen silk parasols. On one side, behind a solid red line of turbaned soldiers of the Viceregal bodyguard, stood a scrum of royal advisers, civil servants and assorted hangers-on. And behind all of them stood Surrender-not and me.

A sudden burst of cannon fire — a salute from the guns on the lawn — sent a murder of crows shrieking from the palm trees. I counted the blasts: thirty-one in total, an honour reserved solely for the Viceroy — no native prince ever merited more than twenty-one. It served to underline the point that in India, this particular British civil servant outranked any native, even one descended from the sun.

Like the cannons, the session the princes had just attended was purely for show. The real work would be done later by their ministers and the men of the Indian Civil Service. For the government of the Raj, the important thing was that the princes were *here*, on the lawn, for the group photograph.

The Viceroy, Lord Chelmsford, shuffled along in full ceremonial regalia. He never seemed quite comfortable in it, and it made him look like the doorman at Claridge's. For a man who normally resembled a malnourished undertaker, he'd scrubbed up pretty well, but next to the princes he appeared as drab as a pigeon in a field full of peacocks.

"Which one's our man?"

"That one," Surrender-not replied, nodding towards a tall, fine-featured individual in a pink silk turban. The prince we were here to see had been third down the stairs and was first in line to the throne of a kingdom tucked away in the wilds of Orissa, somewhere to the south-west of Bengal. His Serene Highness the Crown Prince Adhir Singh Sai of Sambalpore had requested our presence — or rather, Surrender-not's presence. They'd been at Harrow together. I was here only because I'd been ordered to attend. It was a direct command from Lord Taggart, the Commissioner of Police, who claimed it was a request from the Viceroy himself. "These talks are of paramount importance to the government of the Raj," he'd intoned, "and Sambalpore's agreement is vital to their success."

It was hard to believe Sambalpore could be vital to anything. Even finding it on a map — obscured as it was under the "R" of "ORISSA" — took a magnifying glass and a degree of patience that I seemed to lack these days. The place was tiny, the size of the Isle of Wight, with a population to match. And yet here I was, about to eavesdrop on a chat between its crown prince and Surrender-not because the Government of India had deemed it a matter of imperial importance.

The princes took their places around the Viceroy for the official photograph. The most important were seated on gilded chairs, with the lesser figures standing behind them on a bench. Prince Adhir was seated to the Viceroy's right. The princes made uncomfortable small talk as the furniture was adjusted. A few tried to slip away but were shepherded back into position by harassed-looking civil servants. Eventually the photographer called for attention. The princes duly ceased their chatter and faced forwards: flashbulbs popped,

3

capturing the scene for posterity, and finally they were given their freedom.

There was a spark of recognition as Crown Prince Adhir spotted Surrender-not. He extricated himself from a conversation with a rotund maharaja wearing the contents of a bank vault on his person and a tiger skin on his shoulder, and made his way over. He was tall and fair skinned for an Indian, with the bearing of a cavalry officer or a polo player. By the standards of the princes around him, he was dressed rather plainly: a pale blue silk tunic studded with diamond buttons and tied at the waist by a golden cummerbund, white silk trousers and black Oxford brogues, polished to a shine. His turban was held in place with a clip studded with emeralds and a sapphire the size of a goose egg.

If Lord Taggart was to be believed, the prince's father, the Maharaja, was the fifth richest man in India. And everyone knew that the richest man in India was also the richest man in the world.

A smile broke out on the prince's face as he walked over.

"Bunty Banerjee!" he exclaimed, his arms held wide. "How long has it been?"

*Bunty* — I'd never heard anyone call Surrender-not that before, and I'd shared lodgings with him for a year. He'd kept that particular *nom de guerre* a secret, and I didn't blame him. If anyone at school had seen fit to christen me *Bunty*, I'd hardly be advertising the fact myself. Of course Surrender-not wasn't his real name either. It had been bestowed upon him by a colleague when he'd joined the Imperial Police Force. His parents

4

had named him Surendranath: it meant king of the gods; and while I could make a fair stab at the correct Bengali pronunciation, I never could get it quite right. He'd told me it wasn't my fault. He'd said the English language just didn't possess the right consonants — it lacked a soft "d", apparently. According to him, the English language lacked a great many things.

"An honour to see you again, Your Highness," said Surrender-not with a slight nod.

The prince looked pained, the way the aristocracy often do when they pretend they want you to treat them like ordinary folk. "Come now, Bunty, I think we can dispense with the formalities. And who is this?" he asked, proffering me a jewel-encrusted hand.

"Allow me to introduce Captain Wyndham," said Banerjee, "formerly of Scotland Yard."

"Wyndham?" the prince repeated. "The fellow who captured that terrorist, Sen, last year? You must be the Viceroy's favourite policeman."

Sen was an Indian revolutionary who'd been on the run from the authorities for four years. I'd arrested him for the murder of a British official and been all but declared a hero of the Raj. The truth was rather more complex, but I had neither the time nor the will to correct the story. More importantly, I didn't have the permission of the Viceroy, who'd declared the whole matter subject to the Official Secrets Act of 1911. Instead, I smiled and shook the prince's hand.

"A pleasure to meet you, Your Highness."

"Please," he said affably, "call me Adi. All my friends do." He thought for a moment. "Actually, I'm rather glad you're here. There's a matter of some delicacy that I wished to discuss with Bunty, and the opinion of a man with your credentials could prove most valuable. Just the ticket, in fact." His face brightened. "Your presence must be divinely inspired."

I could have told him it was inspired more by the Viceroy than by God, but in British India that was pretty much the next best thing. If the prince wanted to talk to me, it at least saved me from hanging around eavesdropping like an Indian mother on the night of her son's wedding.

"I'd be happy to be of service, Your Highness."

With a click of his fingers, he summoned a gentleman who stood close by. The man was bald, bespectacled and nervous — like a librarian lost in a dangerous part of town — and though finely dressed, he lacked the swagger, not to mention the jewellery, of a prince.

"Alas, this isn't an appropriate juncture for such a discussion," said the prince as the man hurried over. "Maybe you and Bunty would care to accompany me back to the Grand where we can discuss matters more comfortably."

It didn't sound like a question. I suspected many of the prince's orders were similarly framed. The bald man performed a low bow before him.

"Oh good," said the prince wearily, "Captain Wyndham, Bunty, I'm pleased to introduce Harish Chandra Davé, the Dewan of Sambalpore."

Dewan means prime minister, pronounced by the Indians as divan, like the sofa.

6

"Your Highness," said the Dewan, grinning obsequiously as he straightened up. He was sweating; we all were, except, it seemed, the prince. The Dewan glanced quickly at Banerjee and me. He reached into his pocket, pulled out a red cotton handkerchief and proceeded to mop his glistening forehead. "If I may have a word in private, I —"

"If this is about my decision, Davé," said the prince testily, "I'm afraid it is final."

The Dewan gave an embarrassed shake of his head. "If I may, Your Highness, I very much doubt *that* would be in alignment with His Highness your father's intentions."

The prince sighed. "And *I* very much doubt my father would give two figs about the whole show. What's more, my father isn't here. Unless he or the Viceroy has seen fit to elevate *you* to the position of Yuvraj, I suggest you follow my wishes and get to work."

The Dewan mopped his brow once again and bowed low before backing away like a whipped dog.

"Bloody bureaucrat," the prince muttered under his breath. He turned to Surrender-not, "He's a Gujarati, would you believe, Bunty, and he thinks he's smarter than everyone else."

"The trouble is, Adi," said the sergeant, "they often are."

The prince afforded him a wry smile. "Well, in terms of these *talks*, and for his own sake, I hope he sticks to my orders."

From the precious little I'd gleaned from Lord Taggart, the talks related to the establishment of something called the Chamber of Princes. It might have sounded like the title of a Gilbert and Sullivan opera, but the Chamber of Princes was His Majesty's Government's latest bright idea to assuage the growing clamour from the natives for Home Rule. It was billed as an Indian House of Lords — a powerful Indian voice in Indian matters — and all the native princes were being invited, in the strongest terms, to join. I could see a certain twisted logic to it. After all, if there was one group in India more out of touch with the popular mood among the natives than us, it was five hundred or so fat and feckless princes. If indeed there were any natives who were on our side, it was probably them.

"Might I ask your position?" I asked.

The prince laughed coolly. "Absolute eyewash, the whole bally lot of it. It'll be nothing more than a talking shop. The people will see right through it."

"You don't think it will happen?"

"On the contrary," he smiled, "I expect it'll sail through and be up and running by next year. Of course, the big boys — Hyderabad, Gwalior and the like — won't join. It would compromise the fiction that they are real countries, and I'll be damned if Sambalpore signs up. But the others, the little fellows — Cooch Behar, the smaller Rajputs and the northern states — they'll practically beg for entry. Anything to aggrandise their own positions. I'll say one thing for you British," he continued, "you certainly know how to appeal to our vanity. We've surrendered this land to you and for what? A few fine words, fancy titles and scraps from your table over which we bicker like bald men fighting over a comb."

"What about the other eastern principalities?" asked Surrender-not. "From what I understand, they tend to follow Sambalpore's lead in most things."

"That's true," the prince responded, "and quite possibly they will this time too, but only because we bankroll them. Given the choice, though, I expect they'd all be in favour."

On the far side of the gardens the military band started up and, as the familiar strains of "God Save the King" drifted across the lawns, princes and commoners alike stood and turned to face the band. Many began to sing, though not the prince, who for the first time looked somewhat less serene than his title suggested.

"Time to beat a retreat, I think," he said. "From the look of it, the Viceroy's winding up to give one of his celebrated speeches and I for one don't plan on wasting any more of this fine day listening to him . . . Unless you'd rather stay?"

I had no objections. The Viceroy had all the charisma of a wet rag. Earlier in the year I'd had the pleasure of sitting through one of his speeches at a passing-out parade for new officers, and I had no great desire to repeat the experience.

"It's settled then," said the prince. "We'll stay for the rest of the song and then be on our merry way."

The final notes of the anthem faded away and the guests returned to their conversations as the Viceroy strode towards a dais that had been erected on the grass.

"Now's the hour," the prince exclaimed. "Let's go while there's still time." He turned and headed up the path, back towards the building, with Surrender-not at his side and me bringing up the rear. Several civil service heads turned towards us in consternation as the Viceroy commenced his address, but the prince paid them as much attention as the proverbial elephant does a pack of jackals.

He seemed to know his way around the maze that was Government House and after passing through serried ranks of turbaned attendants manning several sets of doors, we exited the residence, this time down the red carpet on the main stairs at the front of the building.

Our premature departure seemed to have taken the prince's retinue by surprise. There was a flurry of activity as a bull of a man dressed in a scarlet tunic and black trousers frantically barked orders at several flunkeys. From his uniform, bearing and the decibels emanating from his throat, the man might have easily been mistaken for a colonel of the Scots Guards. If he hadn't been sporting a turban, that is.

"There you are, Shekar," exclaimed the prince.

"Your Highness," replied the man, with a peremptory salute.

The prince turned to us. "Colonel Shekar Arora, my aide-de-camp."

The man was built like the north face of Kanchenjunga and sported an expression that was just as icy. His skin was bronzed and weathered and his eyes were a startling greyish green. Together they pointed to a man of the mountains, a man with at least some Afghan blood in his veins. Most striking, though, was his facial hair, which he wore in the style of the Indian warriors of old: his beard close cropped and his moustache short, waxed and turned up at the ends.

"The car has been summoned, Your Highness," he said in a clipped tone. "It will be here shortly."

"Good." The prince nodded. "I've the devil's own thirst. The sooner we get back to the Grand, the better."

A silver open-topped Rolls-Royce pulled up and a liveried footman ran over and opened the door. There was a moment's hesitation. There were five of us including the chauffeur — one too many. In normal circumstances we could have managed three in the back and two in the front, but the prince didn't seem the type who dealt much with normal circumstances. In any case, this was hardly the sort of car for such an unseemly crush. The prince himself suggested the solution.

"Shekar, why don't you drive?" Another command couched as a question.

The hulking ADC clicked his heels and made his way round to the driver's side.

"You can sit back here with me, Bunty," said the prince as he made himself comfortable on the red leather banquette. "The captain can sit up front with Shekar."

Surrender-not and I both did as requested and the car immediately set off, up the long gravel driveway between the rows of palms and manicured lawns.

* * *

The Grand Hotel was situated mere minutes from the East Gate of the residence, but for security reasons, only the North Gate was currently open. The car sailed through and almost immediately came to a halt: the roads east from there were closed. Instead, the ADC reversed and headed down Government Place and onto Esplanade West.

I turned around in my seat to better face Banerjee and the prince. I wasn't used to sitting in the front. The prince seemed to read my thoughts.

"Hierarchies are odd things are they not, Captain?" He smiled.

"In what way, Your Highness?"

"Take the three of us," he said, "a prince, a police inspector and a sergeant. On the face of it, our relative positions in the pecking order seem clear. But things are rarely that simple."

He pointed towards the gates of the Bengal Club, which we were passing on our left. "I may be a prince, but the colour of my skin precludes me from entering that august institution, and the same goes for Bunty here. You, though, an Englishman, would have no such problem. In Calcutta all doors are open to you. Suddenly our hierarchy has changed somewhat, no?"

"I take your point," I said.

"But that's not the end of it," he continued. "Our friend Bunty is a Brahmin. As a member of the priestly caste, he outranks even a prince, let alone, I fear, a casteless English policeman." The prince smiled. "Once more our hierarchy changes, and who is to say which of the three is most legitimate?"

"A prince, a priest and a policeman drive past the Bengal Club in a Rolls-Royce . . ." I said. "It sounds like the opening to a not very amusing joke."

"On the contrary," said the prince. "If you think about it, it is actually *most* amusing."

I turned my attention to the road. The route we were taking was in completely the opposite direction to that of the Grand Hotel. I'd no idea how well the ADC knew the streets of Calcutta, but first impressions suggested about as well as I knew the boulevards of Timbuktu.

"Do you know where you're going?" I asked.

The ADC shot me a look that could have frozen the Ganges.

"I do," he said. "Unfortunately the roads towards Chowringhee are closed for a religious procession. We are therefore required to take an alternative route through the *Maidan*."

Though this seemed an odd choice, it was a pleasant day and there were worse ways of spending it than cruising through the park in a Rolls-Royce. In the rear, Surrender-not was in conversation with the prince.

"So, Adi, what is it you wanted to talk about?"

I turned in time to see the prince's features darken.

"I've received some letters," he said, fiddling with the diamond collar button on his silk tunic. "It's probably nothing, but when I heard from your brother that you're now a detective sergeant, I thought I might seek your advice."

"What sort of letters?"

"To be honest, calling them *letters* affords them an importance they hardly deserve. They're just notes."

"And when did you receive them?" I asked.

"Last week, back in Sambalpore. A few days before we left for Calcutta."

"Do you have them with you?"

"They're in my suite," said the prince. "You'll see them soon enough. Although why aren't we there yet?" He turned irritably to his ADC. "What's going on, Shekar?"

"Diversions, Your Highness," replied the ADC.

"These letters," I asked, "did you show them to anyone?"

The prince gestured towards Arora. "Only to Shekar."

"And *how* did you receive them? I take it that one doesn't just post a letter to the Crown Prince of Sambalpore, care of the royal palace?"

"That's the curious thing," replied the prince. "Both had been left in my rooms: the first under the pillows in my bed; the second in the pocket of a suit. And both said the same thing . . ."

The car slowed as we approached the sharp left turn onto Chowringhee. From out of nowhere, a man in the saffron robes of a Hindu priest leaped out into our path. He was little more than an orange blur. The car came shuddering to a halt and he seemed to have disappeared under the front axle.

"Did we hit him?" asked the prince, rising from his position on the back seat. The ADC cursed, flung open

14

his door and jumped out. He hurried round to the front and I saw him kneel over the prone man. Then came a thud, the sickening sound of something heavy connecting with flesh and bone, and the ADC seemed to collapse.

"My God!" exclaimed the prince. From his standing position, he had a better view of the situation. I threw open my door, but before I could move, the man in saffron had stood up. He had wild eyes between dirty, matted hair, an unkempt beard and what looked like streaks of ash smeared vertically on his forehead. In his hand an object glinted and my insides turned to ice.

"Get down!" I shouted to the prince while fumbling with the button on my holster, but he was like a rabbit hypnotised by a cobra. The attacker raised his revolver and fired. The first shot hit the car's windscreen with a crack, shattering the glass. I turned to see Surrender-not desperately grabbing at the prince, trying to pull him down.

All too late.

As the next two shots rang out, I knew they would find their mark. Both hit the prince squarely in the chest. For a few seconds he just stood there, as though he really was divine and the bullets had passed straight through him. Then blotches of bright crimson blood began to soak through the silk of his tunic and he crumpled, like a paper cup in the monsoon.

# CHAPTER
# TWO

My first thought was to tend to the prince, but there was no time, not while there were still bullets left in the assassin's gun.

I rolled out of my seat and onto the roadside just as he fired a fourth shot. I couldn't say where the bullet ended up, only that it hadn't passed through me. I dived back behind the Rolls's open door as the assailant fired once more. The bullet struck the car just in front of my face. I've seen bullets rip through sheet metal as if it was no more than tissue paper, so it seemed a miracle when this one failed to penetrate the door. Later, I'd learn that the prince's Rolls was plated with solid silver. Money well spent.

I shifted position, expecting a sixth shot, but instead came the wonderful click of an empty gun. That suggested a revolver with only five chambers or an assassin with only five bullets, and though the former was rare, the latter was unheard of. I'd never yet met a professional killer who skimped on ammunition. Taking my chance, I pulled my Webley from its holster, rose, fired, and missed, the bullet splintering the trunk of a nearby tree. The attacker was already running.

On the back seat, Surrender-not was kneeling over the prince, trying to staunch the flow of blood from the man's chest with his shirt. At the front of the car, Colonel Arora rose unsteadily to his feet and put one hand to his bloodied scalp. He'd been lucky. His turban seemed to have absorbed much of the blow. Without it, he might not have got up quite so quickly — or at all.

"Get the prince to a hospital!" I shouted to him, as I sprinted after the attacker. The man had a head start of about twenty-five yards and had already made it to the far side of Chowringhee.

He'd chosen the location of his attack well. Chowringhee was an odd street. The opposite pavement was one of the busiest thoroughfares in town, its boutiques, hotels and colonnaded arcade packed with pedestrians. This side, however, open to the sun and bordered only by the open expanse of the *Maidan*, was generally deserted. The only people on this side of the road were a couple of coolies, and they weren't exactly the sort who came running to help at the sound of gunshots.

I chased after the assassin, narrowly avoiding several cars as I raced across the four lanes of traffic. I'd have lost him in the throng outside the whitewashed walls of the Indian Museum if it hadn't been for his bright orange robes. Firing into the crowd was too dangerous. In any case, taking a shot at someone dressed as a Hindu holy man in front of so many people would have been madness. I had enough to worry about without instigating a religious riot.

17

The assassin dived into the maze of lanes that ran off to the east of Chowringhee. He was in good shape, or at least better shape than I was, and if anything, the distance between us was lengthening. I reached the top of the lane, tried to catch my breath and shouted at him to stop. I didn't hold out any real hope — it's not often that an assassin armed with a gun and a good head start does the decent thing and heeds such a request, but to my surprise, the man did just that. He stopped, spun round, raised his gun and fired. He must have reloaded on the run. Pretty impressive. I threw myself to the ground in time to hear the bullet explode into the wall beside me, sending shards of brick and powder into the air. I scrambled to my feet and returned fire, again hitting nothing more than air. The man turned and fled into the labyrinth of streets. He turned left into an alley and I lost sight of him. I kept running. From ahead of me came a strange rumble: the sound of massed voices and the rhythmic beating of drums. Emerging from the lane, I turned the corner onto Dharmatollah Street and came to a dead stop. The wide thoroughfare was jammed with people, natives to a man. The roar was deafening. Voices were chanting in time with the drums. Towards the head of the throng was a monstrous wheeled contraption, three storeys tall and resembling a Hindu temple. The thing was moving slowly, pulled along by a mass of men hauling ropes a hundred feet long. I searched frantically for the assassin, but it was no use. The scrum was too thick and too many of them wore saffron shirts. The man had disappeared.

18

# CHAPTER
# THREE

"How the hell am I supposed to explain this to the Viceroy?" roared Lord Taggart, slamming his fist down on his desk. "The crown prince of a sovereign state is gunned down in broad daylight while in the presence of two of my officers, who not only fail to stop it, but also allow the assassin to escape *scot-free!*" The vein in his left temple looked ready to burst. "I'd suspend the pair of you if the situation weren't so serious."

Surrender-not and I were seated in the Commissioner's ample office on the third floor of police headquarters at Lal Bazar. I held Taggart's gaze while Surrender-not concentrated on his shoes. The room felt uncomfortably hot, partly due to the roasting the Commissioner was handing out.

It wasn't often he lost his rag, but I couldn't blame him. Surrender-not and I had been working together for over a year now, and it was fair to say this wasn't exactly our finest hour. Surrender-not was probably in shock from witnessing the death of his friend. And as for me, I was suffering from what felt like the onset of influenza, but which I knew heralded something quite different.

After losing the assassin, I'd made my way back to the *Maidan* to find the Rolls gone. Other than tyre marks on the concrete and some broken glass, there was precious little sign that anything had taken place. I'd scoured the grass verge, though, and found two shell casings. Pocketing them, I'd hailed a taxi and set off for the Medical College Hospital on College Street. It was the closest medical facility to the scene and the best in Calcutta. Surrender-not would have been sure to take the prince there.

It was all over by the time I arrived. The doctors had tried frantically to stabilise him, but the moment the bullets struck, the prince was as good as dead. There was little else to do but return to Lal Bazar and break the news to the Commissioner.

"Tell me again how you lost him."

"I chased him from Chowringhee," I replied, "through the back streets as far as Dharmatollah. I couldn't shoot at him there on account of the crowds. Once in the alleys, I loosed off a shot or two."

"And you missed?"

It was an odd question given that he already knew the answer.

"Yes, sir."

Taggart looked incredulous.

"For Christ's sake, Wyndham!" he erupted. "You spent four years in the army. Surely you must have learned to shoot straight?"

I could have pointed out that I'd spent half of that time in military intelligence reporting directly to him. For most of the rest of the time I'd sat in a trench and done my damnedest to avoid being blown up by German shells that came out of nowhere. The truth was that in almost four years, I'd hardly shot anyone.

Taggart regained his composure somewhat. "Then what happened?"

"He continued running towards Dharmatollah Street," I replied, "where I lost him in some religious procession — thousands of people pulling some monstrous contraption."

"The Juggernaut, sir," said Surrender-not.

"What?" asked Taggart.

"The procession that Captain Wyndham got caught up in, sir. It's the *Rath Yatra* — the progress of the chariot of the Hindu deity, Lord Jagannath. Each year his chariot is pulled through the streets by thousands of devotees. At some point, the British confused the name of the god with his chariot. It's from him that we derive the English word *juggernaut*."

"What did he look like?" asked Taggart.

Surrender-not looked perplexed. "Lord Jagannath?"

"The assassin, Sergeant, not the deity."

"Lean, medium height, dark skin," I said. "Bearded, with long, matted hair that looked as though it hadn't been washed in months. And he had some strange markings on his forehead: two lines of white ash, joined at the bridge of the nose, on either side of a thinner, red line."

"Does that mean anything to you, Sergeant?" asked Taggart. When it came to native idiosyncrasies, the Commissioner, like me, had long since learned that it was best to ask one of their own.

"It has a religious significance," replied Surrender-not. "Priests often wear such markings."

"Do you think the assassin might have something to do with that religious procession?" asked Taggart.

"It's possible, sir," replied Surrender-not. "It may have been more than simple coincidence that he ran straight into the crowd on Dharmatollah."

"He was wearing saffron-coloured robes," I added. "There were a lot of them wearing saffron in the crowd."

"So this might have been a religious attack?" surmised Taggart. He seemed almost relieved. "God, I hope so. Anything's better than a political motive."

"Then again, the robes may have been a disguise," I cautioned.

"But why would a religious extremist want to kill the Crown Prince of Sambalpore?" asked Surrender-not. "In the time I knew him, I'd hardly have described him as religious."

"That's for you and the captain here to find out," said Taggart. "And let's not discount the religious angle. The Viceroy would prefer to hear that this is a religious attack and has nothing to do with his precious talks. Sambalpore brings with it almost a dozen other princely states and the Viceroy hopes this momentum will persuade some of the more recalcitrant middle-ranking kingdoms to sign up." He took off his spectacles, wiped them with a handkerchief and replaced them gently onto his face.

"In the meantime, you two are going to catch this assassin and you're going to do it in double-quick time.

The last thing we need is a bunch of these maharajas and nabobs leaving town on the pre-text that we can't guarantee their safety.

"Now if that's all, gentlemen," he said, rising from behind his desk.

"There's something else you should know, sir," I said.

He looked at me wearily.

"What should I know, Sam?"

"The prince had received some letters that seemed to be troubling him. That's why he wanted to meet Sergeant Banerjee today."

His face fell. "You've seen these letters?"

"No, sir. Though the prince informed us that he had them at his suite at the Grand Hotel."

"Well, you'd better get over there and retrieve them then, hadn't you?"

"I was planning on doing so immediately after briefing you, sir."

"And what else are you planning on doing, Captain?" he said tersely.

"I'd like to interview the prince's ADC and also the Dewan of Sambalpore, a chap called Davé. It looked like there might have been some tension between him and the prince. And I want to get a sketch of the attacker made up. We can get it in to tomorrow morning's papers, both English and native. If he's still in the city, hopefully someone will know where he is."

Taggart paused, then pointed to the door.

"Very well," he said. "What are you waiting for?"

★ ★ ★

At the opposite end of the corridor from Taggart's office was a room that, it was rumoured, had the best views south over the city. It should have been occupied by a senior officer, but on account of the good light, it had been allocated to a civilian, the police force's resident sketch artist, a diminutive Scotsman by the name of Wilson.

I knocked and entered to see a picture window and walls covered in pencil-sketches, the vast majority of them head-and-shoulders portraits of individuals, mostly men and mostly native. In the centre of the room, in front of an inclined desk, sat Wilson. He was a grizzled chap, with the pugnacious attitude of a terrier and a passion for beer and the Bible, indulging in the latter on a Sunday and devoting most other evenings to the former. Indeed, it was the coming together of the two that had led him to Calcutta in the first place. And after a round or three, he'd happily tell you his life story: of how, in his younger days, his ambition had been to drink his way from one end of the bar to the other in the Bon Accord public house in Glasgow, something he never quite managed without being hospitalised. In hospital he'd found God, and God, in what I presumed must have been a joke, had told him to come to Calcutta as a missionary, a task for which he was temperamentally unsuited, his eagerness for a punch-up being rather at odds with the missionary ethos, and in the end he'd parted ways with the brethren and somehow ended up sketching for the Bengal Police.

24

"It's no' often we see you up here, Captain Wyndham," he said, with a grin on his face. He rose to his feet. "And the ever-faithful Sergeant Banerjee too! What a pleasure this is. Have ye come tae admire the view?"

"We've come in search of a good artist," I said. "Do you know of any?"

"Aye, very funny. Now tell me what ye want."

"We need a sketch done. An Indian chap, and we need it urgently."

"You're in luck, boys," he said. "Indian chaps are my forté. What's your man done, by the way?"

"He shot a prince," said Surrender-not.

"That's quite serious." He nodded sagely. "So where's your eye-witness?"

"You're looking at them," I said.

He raised an eyebrow, then laughed. "You two? You were on the scene when the big cheese got knocked off?"

I nodded.

"And you let the shooter get away? My word, Wyndham, a wee bit careless that, no? What did old Taggart have to say about it?"

"He was philosophical."

"Aye, I'll bet he was. I'm sure he had some choice philosophical words for you. Swears like a docker does that one when he's angry."

"And how would you know?" I asked.

"His office is down the corridor, man. I can hear him! Call yourself a detective, man? I'm surprised he's no' got the two of you on traffic duty, checkin' the licences of rickshaw *wallahs*. Anyway, ye better get on wi' describin' the chap. I've got better things tae do, even if the two o' you huvnae."

I started on the description, the beard, the ash on the forehead. Eventually Wilson shook his head. "So you got given the slip by a priest? Good show, gentlemen. I wish I'd been there tae see it."

"The man was armed," said Surrender-not loyally.

"Aye, and so was yer boss, here," he replied, pointing a charcoal-smeared finger at me.

In between the running commentary, Wilson sketched away, adjusting the subject's hair or eyes in response to our comments. Finally I was satisfied.

"That's not bad," I said.

"Right," he nodded, "I'll get this tae the papers."

"I want both English and Bengali," I said, "and see if there are any Orissa papers published in town."

Wilson's face soured.

"I'm an artist, remember? You two clowns are meant tae be the detectives. You find out about the Orissa papers. In the meantime, I'll get this out tae the usual suspects."

"Thank you," I said and turned for the door.

"Good luck, Wyndham," he said. "And Sergeant Banerjee, you really should stop hanging' around wi' the likes of the captain here. It'd be a shame tae see a talent like yours wasted on inspecting bullock carts."

Surrender-not was silent as we sat in the back of a police car on the short journey from Lal Bazar to the Grand Hotel, his face as long as the bar at the Bengal

Club. Not that I was much in the mood for conversation myself. Failing to prevent an assassination doesn't naturally lend itself to pleasant discourse.

"How well did you know the prince?" I asked eventually.

"Well enough," replied Surrender-not. "He was in my brother's year at Harrow, a few years senior to me. I caught up with him some time later when we were both up at Cambridge."

"Were you close?"

"Not particularly, though at school all the Indian boys gravitated to one another to some degree. Safety in numbers and all that. Adi may have been a prince, but to the English schoolboys he was just another *darkie*. I fear that those days made a deep impression on him."

"You don't seem to have been scarred by the experience."

"I was a decent bowler," he mused. "Boys tend to look past the colour of your skin if you can deliver a good off-cutter against Eton."

"Any idea why someone might want to kill him?"

The sergeant shook his head. "I'm afraid not, sir."

The car passed under the colonnaded facade of the Grand Hotel and came to a stop in the courtyard outside the main entrance. A turbaned footman came smartly over and opened the door.

We made our way along an avenue of miniature palms, and into a glittering marble lobby smelling faintly of frangipani and furniture polish. At the far end of the spotless floor stood a mahogany desk manned by a native receptionist in morning coat and moustache. I showed him my warrant card and asked for the prince's room.

"The Sambalpore Suite, sir. Third floor."

"And what's the room number?"

"It doesn't have a room number, sir," he replied. "It's a suite, sir. The Sambalpore Suite. It is permanently occupied by the State of Sambalpore."

I couldn't read his expression, what with his nose being so far in the air, but I got the impression he thought me an idiot. It's always galling when a native talks down to you, but rather than remonstrate, I bit my tongue, thanked him and passed him a ten-rupee note. It paid to be on good terms with the staff at the best hotels in town. You never knew, one day one of them might feed you some useful information.

With Surrender-not in tow, I headed for the stairs, wondering exactly how much it might cost to permanently rent a suite at the Grand.

The door was opened by a manservant in an emerald and gold uniform.

"Captain Wyndham and Sergeant Banerjee to see Prime Minister Davé," I said.

The servant nodded, then led us towards a sitting room located at the far end of a long hallway.

The Sambalpore Suite was even more opulent than I'd imagined, finished in gold leaf and the white marble that seemed as common in Calcutta as red bricks are in London, its walls decorated with oriental artwork and tapestries. The whole exuded an elegance you didn't often find in a hotel room, or at least not the type that I frequented.

Half a dozen doors led off the hallway, which suggested that the Sambalpore Suite was significantly larger than my lodgings. The rent was probably steeper too.

Leaving us at the entrance to the sitting room, the manservant retreated and went in search of the Dewan. Surrender-not took a seat on a gilded sofa embroidered in golden silk, one of those French ones, a Louis XIV or whatever, that are better appreciated from a distance than by sitting on them. I walked over to the windows and took in the view across the *Maidan* to the river beyond. To the south-west, only a few hundred yards from the hotel, I had a clear view of the spot where the crown prince had met his end. Mayo Road had been closed, the area roped off and a couple of native constables posted as sentries. Meanwhile, other officers were on their hands and knees, carrying out the fingertip search I'd ordered earlier, though I doubted there'd be much to add to the two shell casings I already had. I was no expert, but I'd seen my share of shell casings and I'd not come across this type before. They looked old. Probably pre war. Possibly pre twentieth century.

Surrender-not was mute on the sofa behind me. He was never exactly talkative — that was one of the things I liked about him — but there are various sorts of silence, and when you know someone well enough, you learn to discern the differences between them. He was still young, and though he'd killed a few people himself, some of them in order to save my own hide, he'd not yet experienced the trauma of seeing a friend gunned down before his eyes; of having to look on impotently as their lifeblood slowly drains away.

I, however, had experienced it far too many times and as a consequence, felt nothing.

"Are you all right, Sergeant?" I asked.

"Sir?"

"Would you like a cigarette?"

"No. Thank you, sir."

From the corridor came the sound of raised voices. They grew louder then stopped abruptly. Moments later the door opened and the Dewan, his face ashen, walked into the room. Surrender-not stood to meet him.

"Gentlemen," he said, "you don't mind if we dispense with the pleasantries. As you can imagine, today's events have been most . . . trying. I would be grateful for any assistance you could offer in terms of the repatriation of His Highness Prince Adhir's remains."

Surrender-not and I exchanged glances.

"I'm afraid that's not something we'll be able to help with," I said. "Though I'm sure the prince's body will be released to you as soon as is practicable."

That didn't seem to go down well with the Dewan, though it did bring some of the colour back to his cheeks.

"His Highness the Maharaja has been informed of the tragic news and his orders are that his son's remains be repatriated to Sambalpore without delay. There is to

**30**

be no post-mortem and on no account should his body be further desecrated. The request has already been forwarded to the Viceroy and is non-negotiable."

He seemed a different man from the lackey who'd been introduced to us at Government House earlier. Somewhere between then and now, he'd found time to grow a spine.

"Naturally," he continued, "His Highness is anxious that the perpetrator or perpetrators of this heinous act are apprehended and punished with the utmost haste, and, in the interests of Anglo-Sambalpori relations, we ask to be kept fully informed of the progress of your investigation. A note to this effect has already been dispatched to the Viceroy and will no doubt be communicated to your superiors."

"With regard to the investigation," I interrupted, "there are some matters on which we would appreciate your help."

The Dewan directed us to the sofa, while he took a nearby chair.

"Please," he said, "carry on."

"Your disagreement with the crown prince this afternoon. What was it about?"

A shadow passed across his features, then vanished in an instant.

"I had no disagreement with the Yuvraj."

"The *Yuvraj?*" I asked.

"It's the Hindi term for crown prince, sir," volunteered Surrender-not. "Technically he was the *Yuvraj* Adhir Singh Sai of Sambalpore."

"With respect, Prime Minister," I continued, "both the sergeant and I witnessed the altercation. There was clearly a disagreement over some aspect of the negotiations with the Viceroy."

"He was the Yuvraj," the Dewan sighed, "and I am a mere functionary, employed to enact the wishes of the royal family."

"But in your capacity as Prime Minister, surely you are also an adviser to the royal family? It appeared that your advice was at odds with the prince's views."

He smiled awkwardly. "The Yuvraj was a young man, Captain. And young men are often headstrong — a prince more than most. He was opposed to Sambalpore acceding to the Viceroy's request to join the Chamber of Princes."

"And you disagreed with him?"

"If age affords us one gift," he continued, "it is a degree of wisdom. Sambalpore is a small state, blessed by the gods with a certain natural bounty, which means it has often been the subject of covetous glances from others. Let us not forget our history. Your own East India Company tried, on more than one occasion, to annex our kingdom. A state such as Sambalpore needs friends, and a voice at the top table. A seat in the Chamber of Princes would afford us such a voice."

"And what will happen now?"

The Dewan pondered the question. "Obviously we will withdraw temporarily from the talks. Then, after a suitable period of mourning, I will discuss the matter once more with the Maharaja and," there was an almost imperceptible pause, "his other advisers."

"Have you any idea who might want to assassinate the Yuvraj?"

"Certainly," he replied. "Those leftist radicals: troublemakers in league with the Congress Party. They would do anything to undermine the royal family's hold on Sambalpore. The chief of the Sambalpore militia has been ordered to arrest the ringleaders."

"Did the prince mention to you that he had received certain letters recently?"

The Dewan's brow creased. "What sort of letters?"

"We don't know," said Surrender-not, "but they seem to have unnerved him."

"He never mentioned any letters to me."

"He mentioned them to Colonel Arora," I said.

"In that case," replied the Dewan, "it is a matter for the colonel to explain."

He pressed a brass button on the wall beside him. A bell sounded and the manservant returned.

"*Arora sahib ko bulaane,*" said the Dewan.

The servant nodded and left the room.

Moments later, the door opened and in strode the ADC. He wore a fresh turban and sported a purple bruise the size of a hand grenade on the side of his head. He looked less formidable than before, as though the assassination of his master had physically knocked a couple of inches off him.

"Sir," he said.

"How's the head?" I asked.

He raised a large hand to his swollen face. "The doctors do not believe there has been any fracturing of the skull," he said in a measured tone.

"That's something to be thankful for," said Surrender-not.

The Sikh glowered at him, before regaining his composure. "How can I help you, gentlemen?"

"We need to ask you some questions about the attack," I said, directing him to a sofa.

It seemed, though, that the colonel preferred to stand. "You were there," he replied. "You saw everything I did."

"Still. We need your version of events."

"For the record," added Surrender-not by way of explanation, pulling out a yellow notebook and pencil from his breast pocket.

"What would you like to know?"

"Let's start from the beginning," I said. "When we left Government House, why did you choose that particular route back to the hotel? It was hardly the most direct."

The ADC paused and licked his thin lips before answering. "The direct roads were all closed for the *Rath Yatra*. You saw as much."

"But why go through the *Maidan*?"

"It was a route I am familiar with. The Yuvraj and I have driven it many times before. He liked to drive through the park."

"And what happened as you reached the end of Mayo Road and the turning onto Chowringhee? When did you first notice the assassin?"

The colonel tensed. "I only saw him as he stepped onto the road in front of the car. He must have been hiding behind one of the trees. Naturally, I braked as quickly as I could. I didn't think the car had struck the fellow but he went down so I assumed we had hit him. Now I only wish I had accelerated and run the swine over."

"Then what happened?"

"As you saw, I got out of the car to check if he was hurt. He was lying prone beneath the car's radiator. I bent down to see if he was all right. That's when he turned and struck me. The next thing I remember is hearing the shots."

"Did you see what he hit you with?"

He shook his head. "It was something solid, at any rate."

"We didn't find any object left at the scene," I said.

The colonel fixed me with a stare. "I assume he took it with him."

"Did you recognise the attacker?"

"I had never seen him before," he growled. "Rest assured, though, I shall never forget that face. I will take his image to my funeral pyre."

His face coloured. I felt some sympathy for him. The shame of what had transpired would live with him for the rest of his life, and possibly into his next one.

"Now, Arora," said the Dewan, "the captain mentioned some letters that the Yuvraj claimed to have received recently. Do you know anything about them?"

"Sorry?" He looked distracted. Maybe he was still reliving the events of earlier in the day.

"The notes he mentioned in the car," I clarified.

"Yes. He showed them to me."

"Do you have them?"

He shook his head. "His Highness kept them."

"What did they say, exactly?" I asked.

"I don't know. I couldn't read them. They were written in Oriya. Neither the Yuvraj nor I speak Oriya. Few people at court do. Business is conducted in English or sometimes in Hindi, but Oriya? Never."

"But it's the language of the local area, is it not?" asked Surrender-not.

"Yes," he replied, "but it's not the language of court."

"Didn't the prince ask you to have them translated?" I asked.

The colonel shook his head. "He did not, and I had forgotten about them until he mentioned them in the car earlier today."

"He seems to have obtained a translation from someone," I said.

"Yes," agreed the ADC, "but not through me."

"Could it have been someone at the palace?" I asked.

He smiled thinly and looked to the Dewan before turning his gaze back to me. "Discretion is a quality in short supply at the palace."

"Have you any idea who might want the Yuvraj dead?" I asked.

The ADC stroked his neatly trimmed beard. "I would not wish to speculate. That may be a question more suitable for the Dewan to answer."

"Mr Davé has already given us his thoughts," I said. "I asked *you*."

He shook his head. "I cannot think of anyone."

"I take it you'll be returning to Sambalpore?"

36

The Sikh looked out of the window and nodded slowly. "I have been so ordered." He turned to me. "I must answer for failing in my duty to the Yuvraj."

"Captain Wyndham, you will appreciate that we both have urgent matters to attend to," interjected the Dewan. "If there's nothing further . . ."

"I'd like to search the prince's rooms, if I may."

The Dewan looked at me as though I was mad. "That is out of the question," he said firmly.

It isn't often that an Indian has the nerve to decline the request of a British police officer, and I didn't have time for such games.

"If you prefer, Mr Davé, I can be back here in an hour with two warrants," I said. "One granting permission to turn this whole suite upside down, and the other for your arrest on a charge of obstruction."

The Dewan looked down and shook his head. "Feel free to do your damnedest, Captain," he replied in measured tones. "For one thing, you will find that this suite is officially recognised as the sovereign territory of Sambalpore. And as for arresting me, may I suggest you speak to the Viceroy before you take actions that may result in a premature and regrettable conclusion to your career."

# CHAPTER
# FOUR

It was just before nine in the evening and I was sitting on a chair on the veranda, contemplating the day's events with the assistance of a bottle of Glenfarclas. Surrender-not sat beside me, staring out at the darkened street and doing a passable impression of a Carmelite nun.

Some considered it a bad show — a *sahib* sharing lodgings with a native. Others put it down to eccentricity. Either way, it wasn't something that bothered me. Surrender-not viewed the world with an optimism I'd lost, and with an eastern sensibility that challenged my often preconceived English notions. I found his presence refreshing, and those that didn't like it could frankly go to hell.

"What's on your mind?" I asked him.

"I was thinking about Adi Sai," he replied, "and how one cannot cheat one's destiny."

"You think it was his destiny to be murdered today?"

"If it was written in his stars that it was his fate, then there was nothing he or anyone else could have done about it."

It was a quintessentially Hindu view of the world.

"Maybe you should have mentioned that to Lord Taggart," I said. "You might have saved us a grilling."

"I'm serious," he replied. "And it looks like his fate followed him from Sambalpore to Calcutta."

I didn't know about fate, but I agreed there was a chance his attacker had followed him here. I sipped slowly at my whisky. "How do you think the assassin knew where to strike?" I asked.

"How do you mean, sir?"

"How did he know that we were going to take the route through the *Maidan*? I mean, we didn't even know we were going to take that route. We only took it because the direct route to Chowringhee was closed. How did the assassin know to wait at the bottom of Mayo Road?"

Surrender-not turned to face me, suddenly animated. "You don't think —" He broke off mid-sentence.

"That Colonel Arora was part of the plot?"

"He *was* the one who chose the route. He could have tipped off the attacker."

"I don't think so," I said, shaking my head. "From the sound of the blow with which the man struck the Colonel, I think he's lucky to be alive."

"Then how *did* he know we were going to take Mayo Road?" asked Surrender-not.

"Maybe there were several assassins covering *all* the routes," I said. "It's been done by terrorists before."

Before I could give it much more thought, there was a knock at the door. Behind me I heard Sandesh, our manservant, pad barefoot down the hallway. The front door opened and my stomach leaped as I recognised the voice of the new arrival. It had been a while since I'd last heard it, and things between us were *complicated* to say the least, but even now, it acted like electricity on my synapses.

I knocked back the whisky, took a deep breath and returned to the living room just as Sandesh showed our visitor in.

She wore a sleek black silk dress and a choker with a diamond at its centre, and to me, she was the most beautiful thing in all of Bengal.

"Miss Grant," I said. "This is a pleasant surprise."

I meant it too.

I'd first met her while investigating the death of her former employer. We'd even been close for a while. But there had been a slight misunderstanding, which had rather derailed things. I didn't blame her for it, though: I imagine most women would go off a man who'd accused them of complicity in murder. I had of course tried to explain that I hadn't *technically* accused her of anything; but it's difficult to resurrect a romance by resorting to technicalities.

Not that the whole thing had affected her much; indeed, she'd come out of it smelling of roses, or at least smelling of whatever expensive perfume she wore these days. She'd made quite a bit of money out of the whole affair, had invested it in the stock of a jute company, and was now rumoured to be worth a pretty rupee. She was smart that way. Smarter than I was, at any rate.

The money had done a lot for her. Not only did it allow her to dress as elegantly as she deserved to, it had also gone a long way to removing the one stigma that her looks and charm could never overcome: her part-Indian blood. Not that her being an Anglo-Indian had ever been an issue for me.

I directed her to the sofa.

"Surrender-not was saying, just the other day, that we don't see enough of you," I lied. It wasn't the first time I'd put him on the spot, but I considered it an essential part of his training. A good detective needs to be able to think on his feet, after all.

"Talk of the devil," I said as he entered the room.

"Oh yes, Miss Grant. A-absolutely . . . Just the other day," he stammered from his position near the door.

"Can I offer you a drink?" I asked. "There's not much of a selection, I'm afraid. We've whisky, and there's some gin somewhere. Neither Surrender-not nor I much care for it, but we always seem to get through it at a fair rate of knots. It's odd as we don't get many lady callers — not unless you count the housekeeper, of course, and she swears she never touches the stuff. I suspect she's more of a champagne drinker. As, I suppose, are you these days," I said, gesturing to the diamond-studded choker round her neck.

"Whisky's fine," she said, turning to Sandesh, "*ek chota peg.*"

"One for me too, Sandesh," I added, "but make mine a *burra*. Anything for you, Surrender-not?"

"I better not," he replied, still hovering near the door.

Sandesh nodded and made for the drinks cabinet.

"A quiet night in for you both?" asked Annie, fanning herself gently with a newspaper she'd picked up from the coffee table.

"Absolutely, Miss Grant," I said. "Surrender-not's mother wanted him to meet some girl tonight, but the boy's not particularly keen on settling down just yet. He's told her he can't make it because I've got him working night and day on a case."

Surrender-not smiled weakly.

"As a result we're keeping a low profile."

"And what do you think his mother makes of you calling her son *Surrender-not*?" she replied. "For pity's sake, Sam. You could at least *try* to pronounce it properly."

Surrender-not and I shared a look.

"Well, if he doesn't like it, I suppose I could always call him Bunty."

"What?" said Annie, perplexed.

The sergeant's face reddened. "Surrender-not is fine," he said hastily.

Sandesh brought over the drinks, then retreated quietly from the room, pressing the switch on the wall activating the ceiling fan as he went.

"Anyway, Miss Grant," I said, "as you can see, Bunty and I are both very busy. Is there something we can do for you, or have you just popped round to enjoy the sparkling conversation?"

She took another sip of her whisky, a substantially larger one this time. "Actually, I came round to ask you to stop interfering in my affairs."

I feigned a look of innocence that could have graced the face of St Francis of Assisi. "I'm afraid you'll have to explain, Miss Grant, as I've no idea what you're talking about."

She didn't look wholly convinced. "So you haven't been talking to Mr Peal about me?"

"Who?"

"Charles Peal — the solicitor."

"The name doesn't ring any bells." I shrugged.

"Well, *he* seems to know *you*, Sam."

"Old fellow with a big nose?" I asked, as though suddenly struck with inspiration. "Now you come to mention it, I think I might have come across him in the Calcutta Club once. Nice enough chap, I suppose — if you like that sort."

"He mentioned you'd spun him some story about me. Apparently the phrase *suspicion of complicity to murder* was used more than once."

I puffed out my cheeks and scratched the back of my head. "That's a shocking accusation. I only talked to him for about five minutes."

"And in that time, you managed to sully my reputation? How did my name even come up?"

"He said he was an acquaintance of yours."

"Oh really?" She folded her arms. "He told me you seemed to know that he'd taken me to dinner a few times. Are you spying on me, Sam?"

"Of course not," I said. "I expect Surrender-not must have mentioned it to me. He knows pretty much everything that goes on in this city." This wasn't strictly true. Surrender-not didn't have a clue what went on in the brothel next door, never mind the rest of town.

The truth was I had quite a few paid informers across town, from rickshaw *wallahs* to shopkeepers. The doorman at the Great Eastern Hotel just happened to be one of them.

"If you don't mind," said Surrender-not, "I really should be getting on." And he left the room with rather more haste than seemed either appropriate or helpful.

"So, old Charlie Peal's keen on you, is he?" I asked.

"I don't see why that should be any business of yours, Captain Wyndham," she replied.

"It isn't," I said, "but if you ask me, he must be at least fifteen years older than you. What is he, forty?"

I thought I noticed the faintest of smiles on her face.

"He told me he was thirty-five."

Charlie Peal was a bigger liar than I was.

"And you believed him?" I said. "I can get Surrender-not to check, if you want?"

"That won't be necessary, Sam," she said, taking another sip.

It was time to take the initiative.

"And what are you doing going to dinner with someone as dull as that?" I asked. "I've met corpses more lively than him. I only talked to him for five minutes and it felt like I was physically ageing. You carry on seeing him and before you know it you'll look sixty."

"So you were doing me a favour, besmirching my reputation, were you?"

44

"As I said, I didn't do anything ... But you're welcome."

She paused, then held out her glass. "Aren't you going to offer me a top-up?"

I took the tumbler from her and walked over to the drinks cabinet.

"There's another reason I'm here," she said as I refilled the glasses.

"And what might that be?" I asked, with my back still turned towards her.

"Adi Sai."

I turned around as calmly as I could.

"What do you know about him?"

"I heard he'd been shot today. That you were with him when it happened."

"How did you come to hear that?" I asked, passing her drink to her.

"Come now, Sam," she said. "Do you think Surrender-not's the only one who knows what goes on in this city? I've got contacts at the *Statesman*. They're running a picture of the assassin in tomorrow's paper."

"So you've come to check that I wasn't hurt?" I asked. "I'm touched."

"No," she said firmly. "I've come to ask you what happened. Adi was a friend. We were introduced last year at a party. I've met him and other members of the family a few times since then."

That the prince might have been a friend of Annie's was not something I wanted to hear. "You know I can't tell you anything."

"You can at least tell me when the funeral is."

"Why?" I asked.

"Because I'd like to attend."

I shook my head. "There'll be no funeral in Calcutta. All I know is that the body's being repatriated to Sambalpore as soon as possible."

She didn't stay much longer. Just long enough to finish her drink, walk to the hall and kiss me on the cheek. I closed the front door behind her and slowly breathed out.

# CHAPTER
# FIVE

That night, I lay awake on my bed in the turgid heat.

My head felt thick, like fog. My eyes watered and my nose ran, and overlaying everything, the constant throbbing at the temples, an incessant drumbeat of pain.

A casual observer might think I was coming down with a cold, but the initiated would know. These were the first symptoms of opium withdrawal.

I should point out that I'm not an addict or, to use the vernacular, an opium fiend. *Fiend* — even the name has a certain malevolence to it, something that I've never felt applied to me. My usage was purely medicinal.

They say opium, if taken in moderation, is difficult to become addicted to. This was one of the reasons it was my drug of choice after the war. So it was a shock the first time I experienced withdrawal. To be fair, the symptoms tended to subside over a period of a week or so, after which my head cleared and I could function normally once more. As such, while the after-effects weren't pleasant, I judged my condition to be manageable.

I lay there and forced myself to concentrate. I replayed Adhir's murder in my mind. Dissecting it. Analysing it. Was there anything I could, or should, have done differently? I turned over. But sleep wouldn't be coming soon, and so I got up, pulled on a shirt and headed for the door. Surrender-not was in the living room, sitting in the dark. No doubt he too was re-living the murder in his head.

"I'm going for a walk," I said.

He stared at me with that hang-dog expression of his, but said nothing. It wasn't as though he was ignorant of my situation — you would have to be a particularly useless policeman to spend a year living in the same digs as someone without realising that their fondness for midnight walks might be for reasons other than exercise, but we never discussed it.

Calcutta's Chinatown was Tangra, a rats' nest of lanes and dirt roads to the south of White Town. It was a hinterland of seedy buildings, dormitories and dilapidated factories hidden behind high walls and spike-topped metal gates. There wasn't much to see during the day, just another shabby suburb, distinguishable from the other non-white areas only by the fact that most of the hoardings were in Chinese. At night, though, Tangra transformed itself into a hive of *shebeens*, street kitchens, gambling houses and opium dens. In short, it housed all the things that made living in a sweltering, crumbling metropolis of several million people worthwhile.

I ordered the taxi to stop beside a boarded-up shop and handed the driver a few crumpled notes. Crossing an open drain, I headed down an ill-lit alley that was deserted save for a pack of mongrel dogs and a mound of rotting refuse that smelled worse than the drain.

A door opened up ahead, spilling a shaft of greasy yellow light into the rubble-strewn *gullee*. A man stumbled out, silhouetted against the glare, and staggered past without looking up. The door slammed shut and the alley plunged once more into darkness. I kept walking, heading for another door a hundred yards further along.

I knocked twice and waited. Eventually it opened a crack, just wide enough for an eyeball to stare out.

"What you want?"

"Lao Yin sent me," I said.

"Who are you?"

"A friend."

"You wait."

The door closed. I waited.

I'd never met Lao Yin, but I knew about him: most of the Imperial Police Force did. He was rumoured to be a representative of the Red Gang, a Shanghai-based criminal organisation that specialised in opium, prostitution, gambling and extortion. And with that sort of pedigree it was natural that they exercised a degree of political control too. Lao Yin was in Calcutta to manage the supply side of their opium operations and his name opened many doors in Tangra, including, I hoped, this one. Minutes later I was being ushered through the doorway, along a narrow passageway and through to a small room lit by hurricane lamps where the plaster flaked from the walls onto a floor scattered with dirty mattresses. The sweet, earthy scent of opium smoke hung in the stifling air.

Two of the mattresses were occupied, both by Orientals. Both lay on their sides, one pulling at an opium pipe, the other seemingly passed out.

An elderly Chinese woman entered. From the lines on her face, I guessed she wasn't far off eighty but her movements were still spritely.

She smiled and pointed to an empty mattress.

"Please make comfortable," she said softly. "I bring afeem."

I settled onto the mattress, lay my head on a smooth, porcelain pillow and waited until she returned with the opium tray. On it sat the pipe, lamp, opium resin and a collection of tools used to cook the O.

I tried to relax as she sat cross-legged on the floor and set to work, warming the ball of opium over the flickering candle flame. Just being in the presence of the O seemed to ease my symptoms. The woman teased and pulled the ball as I looked on, almost hypnotised. As it heated, the ball softened and transformed into a viscous state and then began to evaporate. She placed it into the saddle of the pipe and handed it to me. I took the first pull. The tendrils of O worked their magic, infiltrating first my lungs, then through the capillaries into my bloodstream. I heard the crack of the old woman's bones as she stood up, then the sound of her footsteps. I took a second pull, then a third, and felt my nose begin to itch and a million nerve endings across my body seemed to fire in unison. I shut my eyes as the whole world gradually contracted to the area inside my skull.

# CHAPTER
# SIX

## Saturday 19 June 1920

It was another stupidly stifling day — overcast but sweltering. "Calcutta Weather" they called it. The monsoon rains were coming, you could feel it, yet the clouds were still to break. Surrender-not and I were in the Wolseley, crossing the pontoon bridge over the river.

Our destination, the Hotel Yes Please, was a no-star dive located partway down a cobbled street missing half its cobbles. A stone's throw from Howrah station, the area was popular with native travellers of limited means needing a place to stay, and the street was dotted with lodging houses and dubious-looking eateries. From outside, the Yes Please looked a cut above the others, which is to say that it had a pot plant beside the door and a sign above it that was still legible.

Leaving the Wolseley parked some way down the street, Surrender-not and I headed for the entrance. The air stank with the God-awful smell of ammonia and dung that indicated a tannery was located not far upwind. A number of Chinamen sat on the veranda of the building opposite, engrossed in that oriental version of dominoes that seems to fascinate them. Their presence confirmed what my nostrils had suggested. In

Calcutta, where there was a tannery, there were Chinamen. They had a virtual monopoly in the city's leather trade, since the locals, Hindus in the main, would have nothing to do with the slaughter of cows, and their Mohammedan neighbours weren't overly keen either.

We crossed over the open sewer by way of a strategically placed slab, then up a short flight of stairs into the dimly lit lobby. At one end, behind a metal grille, sat a plump, middle-aged woman. Beside her, a reed-thin joss stick in a metal holder released a stream of incense which battled in vain against the stench from outside.

She looked up — a moon face with the slightly oriental features that many Bengalis seemed to possess. Her dark eyes were tinged with *kohl* and in the centre of her forehead sat a red dot the size of a ha'penny.

"Mrs Mitter?" I enquired.

Her face lit up. "Yes. You received my message?"

"You have information as to the whereabouts of the man we're looking for?"

"*Hā.*" She nodded. "He is lodging here for last two-three days. Here for the *Rath Yatra*, or so he said. Odd no? Why come to Calcutta for *Rath Yatra* when real temple to Lord Jagannath is in Puri?"

"You're sure it's him?"

"Most sure," she snorted. "Though sketch in the paper was hardly work of art. You maybe should get Asit Haldar or one of the Tagores to do next one."

"When did you see him last?"

"This morning only. When he returned from taking breakfast." She brandished a native newspaper. "I had paper open to page with his picture when he passed on way to his room."

"How long is he registered to stay?"

"Let me see." She donned the pair of spectacles that were suspended from a chain around her neck, then opened the large, hard-backed ledger with a marbled cover which sat on the desk in front of her. "Scheduled departure is today. Check out by eleven o'clock."

"Less than two hours," said Surrender-not.

"Which room is he in?" I asked.

She smiled. "You are forgetting something, no, Inspector *sahib*? Newspaper clearly states there is substantial reward for any informations leading to his capture."

"We haven't captured him yet," said Surrender-not.

"He is upstairs only," she shot back, "and newspapers says information *leading* to capture, not *led* to. My information is *leading* to his capture, no?"

We didn't have time to argue. Besides, I'd learned that it was futile to do so. Engaging in an argument with a Bengali woman was generally a hiding to nothing.

"Very well," I said, pulling out my wallet, extracting a ten-rupee note and placing it in the gap between the grille and the counter. "Now what room is he in?"

She looked at the note as if I'd just blown my nose with it. "That is hardly substantial, *sahib*. What do you expect me to do with ten rupees, celebrate with a box of *ladoos*?"

54

"Right." I sighed, pulling out another ten. "That's all I have."

"Shame," she replied. "I would happily have told you for sixty."

I looked to Surrender-not. "Open your wallet, Sergeant."

"But . . . Yes, sir." He sighed, handing over two crisp twenties.

"Room twenty-three." Mrs Mitter smiled, sweeping up the notes. "It is on second floor. You want master key?"

"As long as there's no extra charge," mumbled Surrender-not.

"Please," I said as she held out a ring of keys.

I took the keys and headed for the stairs with Surrender-not half a pace behind me.

We reached the second floor and crept down a corridor illuminated solely by light from a window at the far end. Number 23 was about halfway along. I drew my revolver as Surrender-not knelt down and quietly pushed the key into the lock. As he was about to turn it, a shot rang out. A bullet blew a hole in the door about a foot above his head. The sergeant threw himself to the floor, taking the key with him. I stepped back, drew my revolver and took aim.

"Police!" I shouted. "Open up!"

Another two shots rang out and two more holes punctured the door, sending a shower of splinters flying.

I dived for cover.

From inside the room came the noise of scraping furniture, then the smell of burning.

"What's he doing in there?" asked Surrender-not.

"Either destroying evidence or attempting to burn the place down. You know what to do," I shouted to Surrender-not and threw him my revolver. The sergeant nodded as I left the relative safety of the wall and launched myself at the door. I crashed into it with as much force as I could muster and achieved precious little for my trouble other than a bruised shoulder. In response, another bullet came blasting through the wood only inches from my head. I flung myself back behind the wall and prepared to try again.

"Wait, sir!" shouted Surrender-not. "Let me try the key again!"

He threw the gun back to me and snatched the key from the floor. Dropping to his belly, he inched his way to the door. The smell of burning was growing stronger. He reached up, slotted the master key into the lock and turned it with a click. Anticipating another shot, he quickly dropped flat on the floor, but no shot came. We looked at each other. I nodded and he gently reached up and pulled down the door handle. I kicked it open and crouched down. Inching forward, I scanned the room: a bed, a desk, a wooden *almirah* and a wastepaper bin on fire. No sign of our suspect, though. At the far end, a set of French doors had been flung open. I raced over to them, just in time to see a man sprinting along a balcony that ran the length of the building.

"Put that fire out!" I shouted over my shoulder as I raced after the suspect. The man had made it to the end of the balcony and, with his revolver, smashed another set of French doors and dived into a different room. I reached the shattered door in time to see him disappear into the corridor beyond. I loosed off a shot, more out of frustration than in the expectation of hitting him, and pursued him into the hallway and up a flight of stairs, bursting out onto the roof only a dozen or so paces behind.

The man ran to the edge, no doubt hoping to make his escape across the rooftops, but was stopped by a three-foot-high coil of barbed wire which ran between the hotel and the building next door.

Dead end.

He turned and I got my first good look at his face. It was the man who'd shot the prince. Same beard, same wild eyes, same markings on his forehead.

"Drop the gun and raise your hands!" I shouted, aiming my revolver at his chest.

The man's eyes darted left and right, frantically searching for a way out. Then, still holding his revolver, he slowly raised his arms.

"I said drop the gun!"

He looked up, as though suddenly noticing it was still in his hand.

For an instant, he looked at me and smiled, then he lowered the revolver to his temple and fired.

It was a risky thing to do. Shooting oneself in the head is harder than you might think. The cranium is tough and sometimes you just end up blowing out part of your skull rather than your brains. But I guess he was lucky. He was dead before he hit the floor.

I walked over, knelt down and put my fingers to his neck. Then I picked up the revolver that lay beside him.

"You shot him?" gasped Surrender-not from somewhere behind me.

"He shot himself," I said, returning to my feet.

"But why?"

"I suppose he figured it was better to die from a bullet to the head than face the hangman's noose. Regicide's a serious offence . . ."

"Where does that leave us?"

"I don't know," I said slowly, examining the dead man's revolver. It was an antiquated thing with only five chambers and a trigger that folded in. "We needed to interrogate him. As it is, we still know absolutely nothing about who he was or what his motives were. Let's hope we find something in his room. Did you manage to put out that fire?"

He grimaced. "Yes, sir. Though I'm not sure it was in time to save anything."

The building was soon crawling with khaki-clad officers of the Howrah police. They covered the assassin's corpse and prepared it for transport to the Medical College Hospital morgue, where it would likely lie next to the body of the man he'd murdered less than twenty-four hours earlier, proving yet again that the universe has a sense of humour.

Surrender-not and I were back in the assassin's room, looking for anything that might shed light on his identity. A team of officers would carry out a finger-tip search later, but for now the two of us made a start going through the dead man's few possessions. The room was spartan, the *almirah* was closed and the bed had been made. If it wasn't for the burned-out wastepaper bin and a door that now resembled a Swiss cheese, you'd have been hard pressed to guess that anyone had actually stayed there.

Surrender-not opened the *almirah*. In one corner of the cabinet was a small, saffron-coloured bundle tied to a long bamboo stick. Surrender-not brought it over to the narrow single bed. Unpicking the knot he opened up the cloth and spread out its contents.

A pair of underwear, a vest, some *betel* nut, a small ball of what looked like opium resin and a flimsy booklet printed in some eastern language. The man had obviously believed in travelling light. I flicked through the pamphlet before tossing it over to Surrender-not.

"What do you make of this?"

Surrender-not studied it intently, and I took advantage of his distraction to pocket the opium.

"I'm no expert," he said finally, "but the text appears to be Sanskrit. It could be some sort of religious tract."

"Really?" I said, as he returned the pamphlet. "You're a Brahmin. Can't you read it?"

"I'm not a very good priest," he replied, "which is why I joined the police force."

I walked over to the burned-out bin, picked it up and placed it on the desk. With one finger, I sifted through the remains of what looked to have been a sheaf of papers. All that was left now was a pile of ashes.

"Whatever he was burning, he certainly did a thorough job of it," I mused. "He's destroyed pretty much everything."

"Maybe not everything . . ." said Surrender-not. He was on his hands and knees under the desk. He brought something out and placed it on the desk. It was a scrap of paper, seemingly torn from the corner of a newspaper. I guessed it had either been lying there for days or, more interestingly, fallen to the floor when the assassin threw all the other papers in the bin. I picked it up and examined it closely. One side was smudged with some sort of grease and covered in eastern type. This was a different script from that of the booklet, and while I was certainly not an expert in Indian languages, it obviously wasn't Bengali, lacking the sharp angles and straight lines that characterised that particular typeface. It didn't look like Hindi, either. This text was far more rounded, full of curls and squiggles. I turned it over: more of the strange writing above a picture of something. It was hard to tell exactly what, as the paper was only a corner scrap, torn from a whole sheet of newsprint. In amongst the foreign type, however, there was one thing I did recognise — the English characters "NGER 99K". They meant nothing to me. Whatever had preceded it had been ripped off and, I guessed, consumed by the flames in the bin.

"Can you do any better with this, Reverend?" I said, passing the scrap to Surrender-not.

He peered at it, then shook his head. "Looks like a South Indian language to me, sir."

"What about the stuff on the back?"

"There's something familiar about it, sir. I just can't remember what."

"That's very useful, Sergeant," I said. "Any thoughts on the grease stains?"

His brows knitted in concentration.

"Residue?"

"Smell it."

He lifted the scrap to his nose.

"Oil of some sort. Smells like the stuff we use to oil our revolvers. Do you still have the gun, sir?"

I removed it from my pocket and handed it to him. He opened up the chamber and smelled it, then nodded.

"It's possible that the revolver was wiped with this paper."

"Not *wiped*," I said. "*Wrapped.*"

"What?"

"My guess is the gun was wrapped in a sheet of newspaper, from which this scrap was torn."

"Why would a holy man wrap a gun in newspaper?" asked Surrender-not. "Was he trying to protect his clothes?"

"The man's head and body were covered in ash. I don't get the impression he was the type to be overly fastidious about the state of his under-garments."

But Surrender-not's observation was valid. Why wrap the gun in newspaper? And why had the assassin stayed on in the city after he'd completed his task? They were good questions. And as yet I had no answers.

There came the sound of wailing from the corridor, and a moment later, the sari-clad figure of Mrs Mitter appeared.

"*Hai Ram!*" she exclaimed. "Look at all this damage! Who will pay for it?"

"You've got the reward money," Surrender-not ventured.

"Are you mad? There is over two hundred rupees' worth of damage. Look at the door . . . and the furnitures! And why did you set fire to my waste bin?"

"That was the work of your paying guest," I said.

"And where is *he*?" she questioned.

"You might say he's checked out early."

"*Someone* must pay for all this," she asserted, sweeping her hand over the general carnage.

"I'll tell you what, Mrs Mitter," I said, "you help us identify the man and I'll see what I can do about expediting any claim for compensation you might have."

"You want to know the fellow's name?"

"That would be a start."

"It's in the book," she said. "The guests' register. He signed upon arrival. I will bring it." She took another despairing look at the room then headed back down to the lobby.

I walked out onto the balcony and lit a cigarette. Below me, the assassin's body, wrapped in a white sheet, was being transferred by two police orderlies into a waiting ambulance. Surrender-not joined me.

"I want the man identified," I said. "Whatever is written in the register is probably a false name. Nevertheless, check it out."

"Yes, sir," he replied.

"And get the Fingerprint Bureau to take a set of his prints at the morgue."

According to Surrender-not, Calcutta was where the science of modern fingerprint detection was born. He claimed it was two Bengalis — one a Hindu, the other a Mohammedan — who'd done the work. Of course the classification system they'd devised bore not their names, but that of their supervisor, Edward Henry. He'd gone on to receive a knighthood and become commissioner of Scotland Yard. I wasn't sure what had become of his two subordinates.

Mrs Mitter returned holding the large, hard-backed ledger. She put on her spectacles and proceeded to thumb through the pages.

"*Hā, ei-tho*," she said, looking up. "This one." She passed over the book and pointed to a name scrawled in black ink. It read *Bala Bhadra*.

"Is that a Bengali name?" I asked.

She let out a snort of derision. "Maybe you ask your friend?"

I turned to Surrender-not.

He shook his head.

"Balabhadra is the brother of Lord Jagannath."

# CHAPTER
# SEVEN

"So you let him shoot himself?"

It was an hour later and we were back in Lord Taggart's office. Our efforts in tracking down the killer hadn't done much to redeem us in the Commissioner's eyes.

"It was rather difficult to stop him, sir," I replied, "seeing as he had a loaded gun in his hand."

More to the point, I was quite glad he'd fired at himself rather than at me.

"You're sure this was the man who murdered the crown prince?"

"Yes, sir. His revolver is being tested as we speak. We should have confirmation as to whether it was the murder weapon within twenty-four hours."

The Commissioner pondered this.

"And there's nothing to suggest a wider political dimension?"

"We've no way of knowing if this was a one-off attack by some disgruntled fanatic or the start of something more serious, sir."

Taggart removed his spectacles and pinched the bridge of his nose.

"Have you any theories, gentlemen?"

I'd been expecting the question, but that didn't make it any easier to answer. I had some ideas, though not much more than speculation and postulation and half-baked premises, and nothing that was remotely reasoned through. Still, Lord Taggart wanted answers and it was my job to give him some.

"We've several theories, sir," I replied, "but nothing concrete."

"Let's hear them anyway."

"First, and most likely at this stage, the man was a religious fanatic who bore a grudge against the crown prince. The problem is we don't know why he'd do that."

"Who knows why religious fanatics do anything?" replied Taggart. "That's why they're called fanatics. Besides, the fact that he shot himself rather suggests he wasn't exactly playing with a full deck, Sam."

Surrender-not coughed gently. Taggart turned to him.

"You have something to add, Sergeant?"

"If I may, sir, there may be some . . . problems with that theory."

"Such as?"

"There are some loose ends, sir. When cornered, the assassin burned some documents in a wastepaper bin before trying to escape. It would suggest he was attempting to destroy something incriminating. Their destruction took precedence over his attempt to flee, which could imply a wider conspiracy."

Taggart thought for a moment. "Did you manage to retrieve the documents?"

"No, sir," replied Surrender-not. "By the time we gained access to the room, they were little more than ash."

"So, at this stage, your theory is purely conjecture?"

"Yes, sir."

"There's also the letters, sir," I added. "The ones the prince wanted to show us."

"Did you get hold of them?" asked the Commissioner.

"Unfortunately not, sir," I replied. "We questioned the Dewan and the prince's ADC. The Dewan claimed to know nothing about them. The ADC stated that he'd been shown them in Sambalpore but that they were in a language he couldn't read. We requested permission to search the prince's rooms but the Dewan refused. He was quite implacable on the subject. He said the hotel suite was sovereign Sambalpori territory."

"So you've no letters either," he grumbled. "The Viceroy is deeply concerned about this whole episode. Nothing is to be allowed to derail the current talks. Given the sensitivity, you'll need to come up with something more than a bin full of ashes if I'm going to justify keeping the case open."

"There is one other thing, sir," I said. "We found a scrap of newspaper in the assassin's hotel room. It had traces of gun oil on one side. We believe it was used to wrap the revolver."

"And?"

"I think it might have been a package, sir. Someone delivered the gun to the assassin for this particular killing. It's imperative we keep digging."

The Commissioner sighed. "It's not enough, Sam. The Viceroy wants the matter concluded. Unless you can come up with something concrete, loose ends or not, I'm going to have to close the case."

Surrender-not and I trudged silently back to my office.

*Loose ends.*

The Commissioner employed them as throwaway words — as though the letters and other indications of a deeper conspiracy were to be tossed to the breeze and forgotten about.

But I couldn't just forget about them; they would lodge in my brain like stones in a shoe. I fretted over them with the compulsion of an alcoholic going after his next drink. Because to me they represented truth untold and, by extension, justice denied.

I was keen on justice. Always had been, but more so these days after the war. One thing it had taught me was that there was precious little justice to be found in this world, and anything I could do to further its ends was probably a good thing.

"Right," I said, taking my seat. "The man wants something tangible. So let's give it to him."

From my desk drawer, I pulled out a folder and extracted the scrap of newspaper and the pamphlet Surrender-not suspected was a religious text.

"We need to get these translated," I said.

Surrender-not was peering at the scrap of paper — the side with the picture and the English characters "NGER 99K".

"May I see that, sir?"

I handed him the scrap and he examined it.

"I know what this is!" he exclaimed, beaming like a Frenchman in a wine cellar. "I was sure I had seen it before."

"Well?"

"It's an advertisement for a sewing machine, sir. A SINGER 99K, to be precise." Then his face fell. "I'm not sure that takes us any further forward, though."

I thought for a moment. "Maybe it does —"

Before I could continue, there was a knock at the door. Surrender-not rose to open it. In front of him stood our *peon*, Ram Lal. He was an old bird of about sixty, with grey hair, stubble, and the kind of pronounced stoop that comes from a life spent sitting on a stool, waiting for messages to deliver. Despite his years of service, Ram Lal had never quite managed to master English, and my conversations with him generally descended into a quagmire of pidgin Bengali, sign language and a fair degree of shouting and pointing.

"Inspector Captain *sahib*," he said, saluting. "One *chitee* is coming." He handed me a small white envelope. There was no stamp or postmark. I ripped it open. Inside were two sheets of paper with a few lines scrawled in blue ink. The script was foreign, unintelligible to me, but I knew where I'd seen it before: the scrap of paper with the Singer advertisement.

I passed them to Surrender-not. "You know what these are?"

A smile broke out on his face. "The warning notes sent to Prince Adhir? Maybe the gods are smiling on us."

"Who gave you this?" I asked the *peon*.

"*Kee?*"

"I don't have time for this," I said. "Surrender-not, ask him in Bengali."

"*Ke tomaké eita dilo?*"

"Desk sar-gent."

"Get down there and speak to the desk sergeant," I said to Surrender-not. "Find out who delivered this."

The sergeant nodded and headed for the door with the *peon* at his heels.

I picked up the scrap of paper with the sewing machine advertisement again, then lifted the telephone receiver. It took a few calls to obtain the number I was looking for, but I had a hunch, and with a bit of luck, this scrap of paper, together with what I assumed were the letters the crown prince had received before his death, might just be enough to convince the Commissioner to keep open the case.

Surrender-not returned ten minutes later with a native constable in tow. The man had a nest of wiry black hair and a toothbrush moustache.

"That's not the desk sergeant," I said.

"No, sir. The desk sergeant was of little help. The letter was delivered by a street urchin, probably paid a few *annas* for his trouble. This is Constable Biswal," he continued, "originally from Bhubaneswar. I thought he might be able to help decipher our letters, sir."

**69**

"Very well," I said, passing the envelope to the constable. The man extracted the two sheets, read them quickly, then nodded.

"Oriya," he said.

"The language of Orissa," Surrender-not added. "It's what most people in Sambalpore would speak."

"Most people?" I asked.

"The common folk," he said. "As Colonel Arora confirmed, they don't speak it at the royal court."

"Can you translate them?" I asked the constable.

"Yes, sir." He smiled. "They both bear the same message: *Your life is in danger, leave Sambalpore before the twenty-seventh day of Ashada.*"

"When is that?" I asked.

"Yesterday," replied Surrender-not.

I was alone in the office when the telephone rang. It was the call I'd been waiting for — a lady by the name of Miss Cavendish from Singer Sewing Machines' Calcutta office. I thanked her for returning my call, then asked what I needed to know.

"Can you tell me in which Orissan-language newspapers you most recently placed advertisements?"

"That's a most obscure question, Captain Wyndham," she said in prim and matronly tones. You could almost smell the talcum powder down the telephone line. "I would need to telephone our representative office in Cuttack. May I call you back?"

"Of course," I said. "I look forward to it."

Next I summoned Ram Lal from his stool in the corridor.

"Find Banerjee," I said. "Tell him to come to my office."

He smiled, displaying a few remaining teeth, then nodded his head in that curiously Indian fashion. "Many Banerjees is downstairs, *sahib*. Which one you want?"

"Surrender-not Banerjee. The sergeant."

"Ah, Surendranath *babu*." He grinned. "*Ṭhik āchē*."

Surrender-not arrived just as Miss Cavendish called back.

"Captain Wyndham? I have that information for you. It appears we only place advertisements in two Orissan-language newspapers. I'm afraid, however, that the pronunciation of their names is quite beyond me. If it helps, I can spell them for you."

"Please do," I said, grabbing a pen and notepad as she slowly spelled out the names. The first was titled the *Dainik Asha*. It was the second, though, that brought a smile to my face. The *Sambalpore Hiteishini*.

"When were the advertisements last placed?" I asked.

"They're weekly papers," she replied. "The most recent issues would have gone out last Monday."

I thanked her and replaced the receiver, then passed the notepad over to Surrender-not.

He read it and grinned. "So there's a chance the assassin was dispatched from Sambalpore."

"It looks that way," I said, "but we need to be sure. At the moment, all we really have is conjecture. A piece of newsprint, which we *think* was used to wrap what we *believe* was the murder weapon, which *likely* came from a newspaper printed in Orissa, *possibly* in Sambalpore."

"But taken in conjunction with the warning letters to the Yuvraj, surely it points to a connection to Sambalpore?"

"I want copies of last Monday's editions of both papers," I said. "Find that advertisement and, more importantly, match the writing on the other side. Then find out the radius of the paper's circulation. Start with the Sambalpore whatever-it-is."

"Yes, sir." He nodded.

"In the meantime," I said, picking up the letters, "I'm going to speak to Lord Taggart again. Let's give him what we've got."

# CHAPTER
# EIGHT

"So what do you propose to do now?"

Lord Taggart was staring out of the French windows of his office at a sky the colour of a dreadnought.

"I want to go to Sambalpore," I replied.

"Out of the question, Sam," he said as he turned to face me. "It's not British territory. We have no jurisdiction there."

"But the crime was committed on British territory, sir. We have a duty to follow the trail. If it led to France, you'd have no hesitation in dispatching me to Paris, expecting at least some cooperation from the Sûreté."

"Sambalpore isn't France, Sam. It's worse, if anything."

"I appreciate that, sir," I said, "but it's a tiny feudal kingdom whose heir to the throne has just been assassinated. I'd have thought they'd welcome our assistance."

"Look, Sam," sighed Taggart, "if it were up to me, I'd let you go. In fact, I'd bloody order you to go. But there's the Viceroy to consider. With all the brouhaha over the new Chamber of Princes, this case has become a political issue. All he wants is to chalk it down to fanatics and sweep it under the carpet."

That was understandable. The Viceroy might be the most powerful man in India, overlord to hundreds of millions, but in the grand scheme of things, he was just a functionary who took his orders from Whitehall. All he was really interested in was keeping his nose clean and serving out his time as Governor-General without the Raj collapsing around him. With any luck he'd be relieved in a few years and then posted to a billet where the natives were less troublesome. That was the thing about viceroys, they might assume the mantle of demigods, but in truth, since the time of Lord Curzon, the only thing that's really mattered to any of them is to keep the plates spinning until they can move on. No one wants to be remembered as the man in charge when the music stopped — the man who lost India. But that wasn't my concern. Everyone has their own priorities. The Viceroy's was the avoidance of anything that might rock the ship of state; mine was getting to the truth, and I wasn't about to give up on this case now, just because the Viceroy might deem the results unpalatable.

"There might be another way, sir . . ."

There was a knock on the doors of the Commissioner's office and Surrender-not was shown into the room, looking like an errant schoolboy summoned to the headmaster's office.

The Commissioner looked up, lifting his spectacles from the desk.

"Sergeant Banerjee, reporting as ordered."

"Good, good," said Taggart, peering at Surrender-not over the top of his spectacles. "Well, come in, lad." He gestured to the chair next to me. "Now, Sergeant . . ." Taggart made a show of reading some papers on his desk. "I understand that you were a close friend of the late Crown Prince of Sambalpore."

"I wouldn't say we were close, sir. He was my brother's friend."

"No, Sergeant," continued Taggart, "you *were* close friends. Very close friends. Indeed, that is why I think it appropriate that you accompany the prince's body back to Sambalpore as a representative of the Imperial Police Force."

"Me, sir?" spluttered Surrender-not.

"Yes. Captain Wyndham informs me that he wishes to accompany you, though he will be going in an *unofficial* capacity."

"I'll be on holiday," I said.

"It's only fitting," continued the Commissioner, "seeing as you both were instrumental in hunting down his attacker. But you, and not the captain, are the official representative. You should note that you are there solely to pay our respects at his funeral, and, let me stress, not in any investigative capacity. Is that clear, Sergeant?"

The sergeant swallowed hard.

"Captain Wyndham is the senior officer, sir. Shouldn't he be the representative?"

"As I said, *you* were the prince's friend, you should be our representative. Besides, I have more faith in you obeying my orders than I do the captain. And I repeat:

you are in no way to treat this as an extension of the inquiry into the prince's murder. Do I make myself clear, Sergeant?"

"Yes, sir. Absolutely, sir."

"So you're on holiday?" said Surrender-not.

We were back in my office, me sitting behind the desk, him pacing the floor like an expectant father.

"I've always wanted to see Sambalpore," I replied.

"But you hadn't heard of the place two days ago, sir. You looked it up in the atlas."

"Now now, Surrender-not," I said. "Just because I didn't go to Cambridge doesn't mean I don't know my geography. Anyway, I hope you're looking forward to your role as the official representative of the Imperial Police Force."

"Official representative . . ." Surrender-not rolled the words around his tongue as though trying them out. "Official representative," he repeated, then shook his head.

"It's a great honour," I said. "Your mother will be proud. Maybe I should telephone and tell her the good news? I'd have thought a son who's an official representative should be able to attract a much better calibre of girl than a mere sergeant, not to mention commanding a significantly larger dowry. You play your cards right and you may never have to work again . . . Not that you need to work now."

He stared at me.

"I still don't understand why the Commissioner would choose me," he queried. His look turned to one

76

of consternation. "You *are* all right with this, aren't you, sir?"

"Of course I am," I replied.

Taggart would have to make a report to the Viceroy, and after the fallout from the Sen case, it was fair to say that the man wasn't entirely convinced that I was pulling wholeheartedly for the side. Any mention that I was off to Sambalpore might set alarm bells ringing. This way, Taggart could truthfully tell him that Surrender-not had been dispatched as the emissary of the police force, conveniently leaving out any mention of my name.

"You deserve it," I said.

"Right," he said. "I suppose I should liaise with the Yuvraj's ADC and find out the plans for the repatriation of his body."

"And quickly too," I added. "I rather formed the impression that the Dewan wasn't keen on wasting any time getting it back to Sambalpore."

"I take it you intend to keep investigating while we're down there, in spite of what the Commissioner had to say?"

"All I heard was him order *you* not to investigate. He didn't say anything about me. Besides, I'm going to have to do something to keep myself occupied while you're off hobnobbing with the Maharaja."

"You could always invite Miss Grant along, sir," he said.

"I hardly think that would be appropriate, Sergeant," I replied, "inviting an unmarried woman on holiday."

His ears turned a nice shade of crimson. "I didn't mean to imply . . . I mean, I . . . you did say that she knew the family and wanted to pay her respects, sir."

When I thought about it, though, it wasn't such a terrible idea. And it would also get Annie away from old Charlie Peal for a few days, not that Surrender-not needed to know any of that.

"I think you've got enough to do without worrying about Miss Grant and her social calendar," I said. "Now get to work, Sergeant."

"Yes, sir. Sorry, sir," he said as he turned to leave.

"And Surrender-not," I called after him, "don't forget to follow up on the ballistics test on the revolver and identifying which of the two newspapers that scrap was torn from. You might be the official representative to the court of Sambalpore, but you still have your day job."

"Yes, sir," he said and smiled.

I waited till he'd left, then picked up the receiver and dialled Annie's telephone number. The maid answered after an inordinately long delay, only to tell me that the *memsahib* of the house was out.

"Tell her Captain Wyndham telephoned and please ask her to call me back before six p.m." I left my number and hung up.

Soon after, Surrender-not stuck his head round the door.

"It appears the Yuvraj's body is being repatriated tonight on the ten p.m. train," he said, before disappearing once more.

As it transpired, Annie called back within the hour.

"What can I do for you, Sam?" she said.

There was no point in procrastinating. "I was calling to invite you to Sambalpore for a few days. You said you wanted to pay your respects to the prince's family, and Surrender-not is attending the funeral as the police force's representative."

"And you?"

"I'm visiting in a personal capacity. I just thought it might be nice to take a break from Calcutta," I said. "I've never seen a maharaja's palace before. I hear some of them are quite fancy."

"And your visit wouldn't have anything to do with the investigation into Adhir's assassination, would it?"

"I've no authority down there."

"That's not an answer, Sam."

"Yes it is."

There was silence, punctuated only by the crackling of the line and the sound of traffic in the street below my window. I found myself sweating, and not just from the humidity.

"So you want me to accompany you to Sambalpore?" she asked finally. "Isn't that rather forward?"

"You wouldn't be accompanying me," I said. "You're a friend of the family and you'd be going for your own reasons. We'd just be making the trip down together. What do you say?"

"When do you leave?"

"The prince's body is being repatriated tonight. The train leaves Howrah at ten o'clock."

"You don't give a girl much notice, do you, Sam?"

"I'd have thought that after hanging around with the likes of Charlie Peal, you might appreciate a bit of spontaneity," I replied. "No doubt he'd have given you two weeks' notice and requested a written response in triplicate."

"Very funny, Sam," she said.

"So you'll come?"

Once again there was silence and I felt my heart thumping in my chest.

"You'll just have to wait and see, won't you, Captain Wyndham? But a word of advice . . ."

"Yes?" I said.

"Don't hold your breath."

# CHAPTER
# NINE

The first fat droplets fell that evening from low scudding clouds. Flashes of lightning scarred the sky.

The monsoon. Far more than just rain, it sustained life, brought forth the promise of new birth, broke the heat and vanquished drought. It was the country's saviour, India's true god.

It had been building for some time now. The staccato showers that always preceded it had come and gone, and the barometer, thermometer and anemometer all pointed to this being the real thing. The natives at least were in no doubt. They rushed out into streets and turned their heads skyward.

The rain began to fall more rapidly: a growing percussion on the rooftops as the wind picked up, swaying the trees in the street and carrying the scent of marigolds on its breath.

How does one explain the monsoon to someone who's never experienced it? As we left our lodgings it fell as a curtain, a sheer veil of water that dropped suddenly and continued for hours. It took only seconds to be soaked to the raw.

Surrender-not looked heavenward. "It's auspicious to commence a journey during the rain," he said. "At least that's what my father thinks. He'd say the gods are smiling on us."

"You're sure they're not laughing at us?" I asked. "Anyway, I thought you said he wasn't religious?"

"He's not," he replied, somewhat enigmatically.

The short trip between the veranda and the waiting taxi was enough to leave us drenched.

"Howrah station," I ordered the driver.

"*Hā, sahib*," he said, nodding. He started the engine and began to navigate his way through the tempest in the direction of the river.

The approaches to Howrah Bridge were bad at the best of times. Tonight the scene resembled one of those paintings of Napoleon's retreat from Moscow. Men, animals and vehicles jammed the narrow artery. There were bullock wagons laden with sodden goods, rain-lashed, *lunghi*-clad farmers, their baskets balanced precariously on their heads, and semi-naked coolies pushing old carts overloaded with produce, all competing for space with trucks and omnibuses. All were headed towards the same destination — the huge building on the far shore, lit up by arc lamps and looking more like a Roman fort than a railway station.

Our taxi inched across the bridge as the lightning flashed ever closer. On both sides, a flotilla of small boats and steamers plied the channel between the Armenian *ghat* and the ferry terminal on the opposite shore.

We reached the Howrah side as the clock on one of the station's towers struck half past nine. The taxi pulled to a halt and a red-shirted coolie hurried over and flung open the door. His face was creased and grey with stubble, and on his head sat a dirty white turban.

"I carry your luggages, *sahib*?"

"How much?"

"Eight *annas*."

"Too much," I replied. "Four."

"Six," he shot back, wrestling the case from my hand. "*Kon platfrom*?" he asked.

"Platform one," said Surrender-not, emerging from the cab.

"*Platfrom* one, very good, *sahib*," said the coolie as he turned and plunged into the crowd of commuters with our cases on his head.

Walking into Howrah station was akin to entering Babel before the Lord took issue with their construction plans. All the peoples of the world, gathered under the station's soot-stained glass roof. White, native, oriental, African; all jostled for space in the crowded ticket hall, as farmers, pilgrims, soldiers and salarymen fought their way to the platforms in the hope of passage to their desired destinations. Whatever else it might be, Howrah station was not for the faint hearted.

A white man could, should he choose to, spend his days in Calcutta living in pretty much splendid isolation, without ever having to deal with any natives other than his servants. But Howrah station was like a watering hole in the savannah, where all animals from the highest to the lowest were forced to congregate cheek by jowl, the one place in the city where an

Englishman, by necessity, had to confront India at its rawest.

The place smelled of fish, fresh produce and damp clothes. Underpinning it all was the smell of smoke from the engines, and the constant chorus of the hawkers touting their wares. Cries of "*Komla Lebu*" and "*Gorrom Cha*" competed with the continuous announcements from the station Tannoy — vital information intoned in English and Bengali, and incomprehensible in both.

Platform one, often reserved for VIP trains, was situated on the far left of the concourse: cordoned off by velvet ropes and brass stands, it was an oasis of calm in the maelstrom. Waiting there stood a handsome locomotive and train of six carriages, each painted in green and gold and embossed with the Royal Seal of Sambalpore, a leaping tiger under a crown.

Back on the concourse, to the sound of barked orders, a cortège of sepoys in dress uniform, with an English officer at their side and a coffin on their shoulders, progressed solemnly through the crowd. The casket was draped in the Union flag and garlands of flowers and was flanked by the Dewan and Colonel Arora.

A hush descended as the cortège passed by and people touched their hands to their foreheads in reverence for the dead. As the crowds parted, I caught sight of a man in civilian clothes and my blood froze. He might have been out of uniform but the moustache and the pipe clamped firmly at the corner of his mouth were unmistakable. Major Dawson, chief of Section H and head of the military's intelligence operation in Bengal. At least I assumed he was the head. It's hard to be sure exactly who is in charge when you're dealing with secret policemen. As far as I could tell, Dawson ran the show, which made it all the more surprising to see him here, watching the cortège of a dead man pass by.

He hadn't spotted me, which was just as well. Our relationship was somewhat fractious. He suspected me of meddling in Section H's affairs and I suspected him of having tried to kill me at least once. If he spotted me boarding the train, it was a pretty safe bet that the Viceroy would know about it before bedtime, and that might present some problems for Lord Taggart, given how fastidiously he'd avoided mentioning my participation in this little jaunt to Sambalpore in his report.

I crouched down and pulled at Surrender-not's shirt. He spun round angrily, probably thinking that someone was trying to pick his pockets. It was a fair assumption to make. More money was stolen from pockets in Howrah station every day than went missing from Calcutta's banks in a year. His expression changed when he saw me, though.

"Are you all right, sir?"

"Dawson," I whispered, gesturing towards the intelligence officer.

Surrender-not looked over, then dropped to a crouch. "What's he doing here?"

"Good question."

"He's not in uniform. Do you think he might be going somewhere?"

"I doubt he's off on his holidays, Sergeant," I said, "but whatever he's up to, it could make things rather uncomfortable if he sees me here. You'll need to distract him while I slip on to the train."

"What should I say to him?"

"I'm sure you'll think of something."

Surrender-not swallowed hard. "Very well." He nodded, stood up and made his way through the crowd towards the major. Soon he was within ten feet of the man and trying to attract his attention.

"I say, Major Daws —"

He was cut off in mid sentence as a farmer the size of a barn barged into him, sending him flying. As if on cue, another gorilla of a man hurried over. Both men positioned themselves squarely between Surrender-not and the major and made a rather splendid show of helping the sergeant back on to his feet. I turned to see Dawson's reaction, but he'd gone, disappeared into the crowd. I didn't hang about trying to find him. Instead, I stood up and rushed towards platform one.

# CHAPTER
## TEN

I reached the gate on the heels of the military cortège. Our coolie was already there, remonstrating with a railway official. He pointed to me and eventually the guard deigned to let him through.

The Dewan was discussing something with the officer in charge of the pall bearers. He then spoke briefly to an assistant who nodded and led the cortège down the platform towards the fifth carriage.

"Prime Minister Davé," I called out.

He turned and stared as though slapped in the face by my very presence.

"Captain Wyndham? I was not informed that you would be accompanying us. I was under the impression that your colleague, Sergeant Banerjee, was to be the representative of the Imperial Police Force."

"That's correct, sir," I said. "I'm attending in a personal capacity. I wished to pay my respects at the Yuvraj's funeral."

He eyed me suspiciously.

"Very well," he said. "It is only fitting, I suppose. I understand you and Sergeant Banerjee were responsible for apprehending the Yuvraj's killer. The Maharaja may wish to meet you."

"We tracked him down, at any rate," I replied. "He preferred to shoot himself rather than be apprehended."

The Dewan forced an awkward smile. "I am informed that he was most likely a religious zealot of some kind. Who knows what goes through the mind of a man like that?"

I could have told him that in this case, the last thing was a bullet from a rather old revolver, but he didn't seem the type to appreciate the insight.

He called to Colonel Arora, who was talking to a uniformed native who had descended from the train. The colonel broke off his conversation and marched smartly over.

"Captain Wyndham," he said, "a pleasure to see you again."

"The captain will be travelling with us," said the Dewan. "Please arrange a berth for him."

"As you command, Dewan *sahib*," said the colonel. "Captain, if you'll come with me."

"So you have decided to journey with us to Sambalpore," said Arora as I took my leave of the Dewan and accompanied him down the platform.

"I thought I might like to see a genuine Indian maharaja in his native habitat, as it were."

"Really, Captain?" He smiled. "I wouldn't have pegged you for an anthropologist."

"I'm not," I replied. "Though I confess, I have recently discovered an interest in South Indian languages that I never knew I possessed. You might say I'm going to Sambalpore to indulge my curiosity in the written word."

Arora kept his eyes trained firmly ahead. "Well, I hope your time with us is most productive," he replied.

The colonel stopped at the entrance to one of the carriages and gestured for me to board.

I climbed the iron steps into a walnut-panelled and thickly carpeted cocoon that seemed more like the lobby of some rather exclusive cinema than the vestibule of a railway carriage.

An impeccably tailored attendant in a green and gold uniform came over, his hands clasped together in *pranaam*.

"Let's find you a berth," said the colonel. He conversed briefly with the attendant, who, after a moment's hesitation, turned to me.

"Follow me please, *sahib*."

I left the colonel and accompanied the man along the corridor, past several compartment doors polished to a shine.

"You are liking our train, *sahib*?" he asked.

"It's certainly better than the eight-fifteen to Paddington," I replied.

The attendant kept his opinion on that to himself and continued down the corridor.

"This cabin is unoccupied, *sahib*," he said, stopping at one of the doors and sliding it open. "Do you require anything else?"

"I assume my colleague, Sergeant Banerjee, also has a cabin in this carriage."

"Yes, *sahib*. The officer is in the next cabin."

"There may be a third person joining us," I said, "a woman. She'll need a cabin too."

"I shall make the arrangements, *sahib*."

"And please tell the sergeant to join me once he is aboard."

I entered and closed the door. The compartment smelled of rose oil. To one side, a bed — a real one not a bunk — was set against the wall. Beside it, a chair furnished in purple velvet and a rococo writing desk, with fluted flourishes giving the impression that it had melted slightly in the heat. Opposite the bed stood a walnut-lacquered wardrobe and a door that led to a water closet complete with marble basin and enough gold fittings to make the *Orient Express* look like a cattle transport.

Outside the window was a different world. On the platform opposite, a native family had set up temporary residence. The elder child, a girl of about five, her hair tied in pigtails, watched with rapt attention as a hawker played a tune on a tin whistle. The younger one, a half-naked boy of about two with a black string around his belly and *kohl* around his eyes, stared at me, then quickly hid his face in the *anchal* of his mother's sari. I watched as the woman put her efforts into laying down some makeshift bedding on which the children would sleep. Meanwhile, her husband looked out forlornly at the rain tumbling from the platform roof onto the waterlogged tracks.

Slipping off my jacket, I threw it on the bed and went into the bathroom to wash my face. The water was cold, properly cold, which was something of a miracle in Calcutta, and the towel felt like a cloud of sandalwood.

There was a knock on the door and, after a suitable pause, Surrender-not entered looking like he'd just gone three rounds with Jack Dempsey. His left cheek was beginning to swell and his wire-framed spectacles sat awkwardly on his face.

"Are you all right, Sergeant?" I asked, directing him to the easy chair.

"I think so, sir."

"Good work, by the way. Your distraction certainly did the trick. Dawson took off like a scalded dog when he realised you'd spotted him. I expect he hightailed it out of the station as soon as those goons accosted you."

"Yes, sir," he said ruefully. "Rather solid chaps."

That was the thing about Section H's native operatives. They tended to be soldiers in *mufti*, drawn from the ranks with promises of better pay and rapid promotion. The problem was, these six-foot bruisers from Chandigarh and Lahore didn't exactly blend seamlessly with the Bengali population. It was like using wrestlers to infiltrate a gang of jockeys.

He removed his spectacles and began to bend them back into shape. Without them, his eyes looked curiously small. "Judging by the size of his minders, sir, I think you may have been correct in your supposition that the major was not off on holiday."

"I don't think Dawson takes holidays," I said. "I doubt he even sleeps."

"You think his being here has something to do with the Yuvraj's assassination?"

"It's possible," I said, "though if he was here in an official capacity, why not turn up in uniform? And why scarper so quickly?"

"He might have been here for something else. Maybe they're tracking terrorists?"

I considered this. Howrah station was the city's gateway. Most people coming to Calcutta naturally passed through it.

"Perhaps," I replied, "though it would have to be important for him to turn up in *mufti*. He's hardly a field operative."

A whistle blew on the platform outside. I glanced at my watch. Ten p.m. on the dot. Surrender-not replaced his spectacles.

"You didn't happen to see Miss Grant out there?" I asked.

He seemed somewhat thrown by the question.

"I wasn't really looking, sir."

"Of course," I said, and something twisted in the pit of my stomach as I realised Annie wasn't coming. I told myself it was probably for the best, that this way, I'd be able to concentrate on the case without distraction, but it was still a bitter pill to swallow.

With a gentle lurch the train shunted forward and out of the station, slipping into the night past the marshalling yards and rain-sodden houses of Howrah.

Surrender-not stirred.

"If there's nothing else, sir, I'll make my way to my cabin."

That suited me. I needed to think, to make sense of Dawson's presence on the concourse, though that wasn't the only reason I wanted some time to myself. After agreeing to meet in an hour to track down some supper, he left and I locked the door behind him.

The cabin was suddenly quiet. I took my suitcase and set it down on the bed. Snapping open the locks, I removed the shirts and other camouflage that sat on top, to reveal a varnished wooden case with a silver handle and delicate ivory detailing. Fashioned from a deep mahogany, it had a silver lock in the shape of a dragon's head. The handle continued the motif. The case was a thing of beauty and I took a moment to admire it. But it was nothing when compared with its contents.

Extracting a small silver key from my pocket, I placed it in the lock and turned. The mechanism clicked softly and sent a slight shiver up my spine. I lifted the lid and stared: a lamp, a ceramic pipe bowl, a selection of thin needles and tools, and, of course, a shortened bamboo opium pipe with carved porcelain end pieces. All sat snugly on a red velvet bed. It was a travelling opium kit and I'd fallen in love as soon as I'd spotted it in an antique shop near Park Street. I knew I had to have it, for no other reason than that I'd never seen anything like it. I'd never entertained any thought of using it — that is until I'd spotted the ball of opium resin in the dead assassin's knapsack. Even now, I wasn't sure exactly why I'd brought it along. I'd never prepared my own opium pipe before. It was a complicated business that took a degree of skill and training and I certainly wasn't about to master it on a moving train. What's more, bringing it with me was a risk. What if my suitcase should be damaged and its contents revealed? It was a compromising possession for a police officer, even one who was technically on holiday.

I realised then that I'd packed it because I couldn't bear to be parted from it. The recognition hit me like a punch in the face. I quickly closed the case and covered it with clothes, then took out a fresh shirt, trousers and the half-empty bottle of Glenfarclas I'd tucked in with them.

Changing out of my damp clothes, I poured a measure into a cut-glass tumbler that sat on the writing desk. I sat down and took a sip. Outside, the rain continued to lash down, and now and again a twinkling light in the window of a dwelling passed gently by.

This would be my first visit to a native state. In fact, it would be my first real trip anywhere in India. As journeys went, it wasn't a bad start and if this train was anything to go by, Sambalpore seemed the sort of place I might get used to. And yet I felt uneasy. Annie's no-show had dampened my spirits somewhat, and more importantly, the sight of Major Dawson on the concourse had unnerved me. I couldn't shake the feeling that his presence was somehow linked to the Yuvraj's assassination. Since we'd received the warning notes that had been sent to Adhir, I'd felt certain that the trail led to Sambalpore. But Dawson's appearance on the platform had raised another possibility: that Section H or their masters were somehow involved. Sambalpore's accession to the Chamber of Princes was, after all, a key part of the Viceroy's plans. Was it possible that someone in the India Office had sanctioned the prince's removal in the belief that his replacement would prove more amenable to the Viceroy's wishes?

My stomach lurched as the implications of that sank in. The political assassination of a prince was an endeavour that wouldn't have been undertaken lightly. If Section H were behind this, it was a certainty that getting to the truth would be dangerous and nigh on impossible. Worse still, if Section H were involved, being on a train heading to Sambalpore would take me directly away from the answers rather than towards them.

I took another sip and watched the night slip by. My thoughts turned to the warning notes. They were written in Oriya and had been delivered to the prince inside his palace. Even if there was a British angle to the conspiracy, someone with a knowledge of the local language had still deduced enough about a plot to have tried to warn Adhir, and the chances were that that someone was in Sambalpore. Finding them had to be my first priority.

An hour later, Surrender-not knocked on my door. He was dressed in black tie and patent leather shoes with a shine that could have kept ships away from rocks.

"Are you off to the opera?" I asked.

"I thought you wanted to go looking for the dining car, sir?" he asked.

"Yes," I replied, "but we're not attending a state dinner."

"It's a state train." He shrugged. "Do you want me to change?"

"No." I sighed. "Let's go. I'm hungry."

The sergeant opened the connecting door at the end of the carriage. The rain was still coming down and a torrent poured from the roof into the gap between the two bogeys. I jumped quickly across the space between the footplates and stumbled inside the next carriage with Surrender-not close behind.

The lounge car was dominated by a mirrored bar and a large black Steinway which no one was playing. In front of it were dotted a dozen or so armchairs finished in green leather, and small polished ivory side tables. Around one such table sat the Dewan and a silver-haired European gentleman, who, judging by the cut of his dinner jacket, was probably English. He looked around sixty, with the face of a field marshal and the manner of a banker. He examined me coldly, as a doctor might do a leper, then returned to his conversation, leaving Surrender-not and I to continue our progress through the train.

The dining car's walls were panelled in dark, varnished wood and the windows were framed with thick curtains of purple velvet tied back with golden pelmets. It was empty, save for a jacketed waiter arranging cutlery and Colonel Arora sitting at one of a half-dozen tables draped in white napery, with a single orchid for company. His face set hard, Arora stared out of the window, concentrating on the blackness beyond. There was an intensity to his expression that suggested his thoughts weren't particularly pleasant. As far as I was concerned, that was no bad thing. You can learn a lot by disturbing a man when he's lost in introspection.

I called over to him.

"Colonel."

He turned and stared, and for a moment, there was anger visible in his eyes. I held his gaze, trying to fathom its meaning. He must have realised and immediately his expression changed — his emotions reined in.

He gave a curt nod. "Captain, Sergeant."

"You don't mind if we join you?"

"Of course," he replied politely, "please do."

The cutlery clinked softly as the train passed over a set of points.

The waiter broke off from his polishing and came over.

"May I bring you an aperitif?"

It seemed rude to refuse.

He returned with two flutes of champagne on a silver tray.

"I think there's time for a spot of supper," said Arora, consulting his watch. He turned to the waiter. "What have we tonight?"

"Pea and mint soup, wild boar pot roast, and for dessert: Eton mess."

"Good, good," said the colonel.

For the train of an Indian royal family, the food sounded decidedly English.

The waiter departed and I turned to the colonel.

"Who's the Englishman with the Dewan in the lounge car?"

"That," replied Arora, "is Sir Ernest Fitzmaurice, board director of the Anglo-Indian Diamond Corporation and, so he tells us, firm friend of the kingdom of Sambalpore. We've had a long and florid relationship with Anglo-Indian," he continued. "The company is the purchaser of almost ninety per cent of our diamond production. When the East India Company was trying to strangle the state into submission, it was Anglo-Indian Diamond who broke the embargo, smuggling out our produce when no other English company would touch us. It's Anglo-Indian's money that's paid for Sambalpore's schools and clinics, not to mention the Maharaja's cars."

Possibly the wine, too, I thought, judging by the rather fine Gran Cabernet Franc that accompanied the meal and the velvet Jurançon served with dessert. The conversation was cordial, with the colonel reeling off tales of Sambalpore's history and the resistance of its rulers to the invading Mughals. Eventually we rose to return to our compartments.

"Don't get too comfortable, Captain," said Arora. "In a few hours we shall reach Jharsugudah, where we shall have to change trains."

"The Sambalpore royal train doesn't go to Sambalpore?" I asked.

"It can't," replied the colonel. "You British do not allow broad-gauge railway tracks to be laid in the native states. The India Office is scared that if it did, it might assist us in transporting troops and heavy guns, which we might then use against you."

"That's absurd," I said.

"Of course it is," he replied. "But it's also a fact. So at Jharsugudah, we will change to another royal train on the narrow-gauge line, which will take us the last fifty miles to Sambalpore."

Sure enough, two hours later, the train pulled into a cordoned-off platform at Jharsugudah railway station and I walked out into a stiflingly humid night. There was no rain, though, and the tracks looked dry. It seemed we'd outrun the monsoon.

The train that would take us on to Sambalpore was a miniaturised version of the one we'd just alighted from and we boarded it without ceremony or fanfare. Further down, the guards lowered the Yuvraj's coffin and I watched as they carried it across, laying it to rest in the forward-most carriage before readying the prince for the final leg of his journey home.

# CHAPTER
# ELEVEN

## *Sunday 20 June 1920*

I gave up on sleep as the dawn rays pierced the slatted shutters of my compartment window. I knew from the atlas that our toy train was puffing its way across the Deccan, the high plateau that rises from the Gangetic plain and forms most of southern India. The carriage rocked gently and the temptation to lie abed would have been compelling had it not been for Surrender-not knocking on my cabin door.

"Sir? Are you awake?"

I pulled myself off the banquette, flipped the latch on the compartment door and slid it open.

"There you are," he said.

"Where did you expect me to be?"

"What?"

"What is it, Sergeant?" I asked, running a hand through my hair.

"Colonel Arora says we'll be arriving in Sambalpore within the hour. I thought you might appreciate the advance notice."

"What time is it?" I yawned.

"Almost half past five," he replied.

I walked over to the window and lifted the shutter fully. The dawn revealed a landscape starkly different from that of Bengal. In the space of a few hundred miles, verdant jungle had given way to an alien landscape of desiccated scrub and dusty brown earth. Skinny trees passed by in the half-light, deciduous and dull and nothing like the tropical palms of Calcutta.

"Shall I see you in the dining car?" he asked brightly. "The chef is preparing a South Indian breakfast, *idlis* and what not."

My stomach lurched. The natives seemed to consider it a mortal sin to serve any meal, even breakfast, without the addition of half a pound of spices. That was all well and good, but there are times when all an Englishman really wants is a slice of toast and a cup of tea.

"You carry on," I said. "I'll give it a miss."

I closed the door and dressed, as outside the sky brightened and the parched land came into focus. The monsoon might have reached Calcutta, but Orissa was still as dry as a Baghdad summer.

At a quarter after six, the train pulled into Sambalpore, and into a station that looked like it had been transported from somewhere in the Cotswolds: golden sandstone walls, slate roof and a provincial calm. Even the clouds were grey enough to be English. Only the heat felt Indian.

We shuddered to a halt. Outside the window stood a line of stern-faced soldiers and sombre officials. I retrieved my suitcase, made my way out of the compartment, and headed down the narrow corridor, meeting Surrender-not, clad in full dress uniform, en route. We descended onto the platform in time to see a phalanx of guards board the carriage containing the Yuvraj's coffin.

The Dewan stood nearby, flanked by the Englishman, Fitzmaurice. Both looked on as the coffin was brought down on the shoulders of the guards. Colonel Arora waited a distance apart and saluted as the body of his former master was carried along the platform towards the station concourse. There, behind a wooden barrier and among a crowd of natives, stood a pale, dark-haired man, busily scanning the faces coming off the train. That he was British was evident from his complexion and also his clothing: morning coat, tie and pinstripe trousers — the full regimental dress of the Foreign Office. His face brightened as he noticed Surrender-not's uniform and he began to stride over.

"You must be Sergeant Banerjee," he said rather stiffly, offering an outstretched hand.

"That's correct," replied Surrender-not, shaking it. "And may I present Captain Wyndham, also of the Imperial Police."

A cloud of confusion passed across the Englishman's face.

"I'm sorry? The cable contained only the notification of *your* arrival. No mention was made of any British officer. There must be some mistake."

"There's no mistake," I interjected. "I'm here in a personal capacity. To pay my respects. Does that present a problem?"

He looked me up and down and ran a hand through his hair.

"No, no. Not at all," he replied with a haste that suggested the opposite. "It's a pleasure. The name's Carmichael. I'm the Resident here. His Majesty's representative to the Court of Sambalpore."

"So you're the ambassador?" asked Surrender-not.

"Oh, nothing quite so grand."

"Nevertheless," continued the sergeant, "it was good of you to come and meet us personally."

"Not especially," he replied. "There really isn't anyone else."

The crowd inside the station parted silently as the Yuvraj's coffin was borne out towards a waiting carriage. A great collective groan, a noise like that of a wounded animal, came from outside. It sounded like half of Sambalpore had turned out to receive their dead prince.

"We had better wait until things quieten down," counselled Carmichael. "It's not far to the Residency, but the roads will be jammed. The journey here was nightmarish. If this is what it's like today, I dread to think how many people are going to turn out for the funeral tomorrow."

"He was a popular man, then?" I asked.

"Oh, good gracious, yes," he replied. "All the royals are. Worshipped like gods. The whole town is in a state of shock." He scanned the concourse. "I say, there's a tea stall over there. How about a cup while we wait?"

He led the way across the bustling concourse. The stall itself was little more than a wooden plank balanced atop what looked like two bicycles welded together and draped in garlands of orange marigolds. The counter was painted blue and on it stood a stack of small earthen cups and several metal utensils. To one side, atop a makeshift brick stove, sat a bashed tin kettle with a long curved spout, and behind that stood a crumpled old native in a red turban. He held an almost identical pot and was busy pouring steaming, caramel-coloured tea from one vessel to the other.

"*Teen chai,*" ordered Carmichael loudly, holding up three fingers of one hand for good measure. The old man nodded and retrieved three of the clay cups from the stack, setting them out carefully before pouring equal measures of the tea into each one.

Carmichael paid the *chai wallah*, who then handed us our cups with a care that suggested he were passing us the Holy Grail. I raised mine to my lips and sipped slowly. I noticed the Dewan and Fitzmaurice exit the station and climb into a waiting Rolls-Royce.

"That chap, Fitzmaurice," I asked the Resident. "Do you know him?"

"Yes indeed." Carmichael nodded, quickly swallowing his tea. "I've met him several times. Sir Ernest's a very fine gentleman."

"He's not staying at the Residency?"

Carmichael made a curious face. "Not these days. The last few times he's stayed at the palace as a guest of the Maharaja."

"He comes here often, then?" asked Banerjee.

"Oh yes, quite often. At least he has done this year. Before that he tended to come once a year for the

Maharaja's annual shoot. A splendid affair that is. Even the Viceroy sometimes attends. Last year we bagged half a dozen tigers, a couple of black leopards and Lord knows how many chinkara."

"And recently?" I asked.

"What?"

"You were saying that recently Sir Ernest has visited more often?"

"That's right. He's been here several times over the past six months."

"Any idea why?"

Carmichael thought for a moment. "I'm afraid I'm not at liberty to say. Confidentiality, you understand?"

"Well, unless he's coming to take the air," I said, "I assume it has something to do with diamonds."

"Very astute of you." Carmichael grinned.

You didn't have to be Sherlock Holmes to make the deduction. He was the director of a diamond company and the kingdom of Sambalpore appeared to have more diamonds than Ali Baba and his forty thieves.

The station emptied gradually. Finishing the tea, Carmichael led us out towards a waiting Austin that looked like it might have been the oldest car in India. A faded Union Jack hung limply from a metal rod on the bonnet. A native driver stood beside it, polishing the headlights with a grimy rag.

"Apologies for the state of the transport," said Carmichael. "It's no Rolls-Royce."

"I wouldn't worry," I said. "The last journey the sergeant and I took in a Rolls didn't exactly end well. Though I'd have thought the India Office would have provided you with one for appearances' sake. Keeping up with the Joneses, and all that."

"Alas, no," said Carmichael ruefully. "The days of trying to impress the Maharaja and his ilk with displays of wealth went out with the East India Company. Since then we prefer to influence the princely states with displays of power. No point in buying fleets of Rolls-Royces when you can achieve the same effect with a few cannon and a crate of Lee Enfields. Which is fair enough, I suppose, though it does mean I have to be driven around in this thing."

"The price of Empire," said Banerjee, shaking his head as he took his seat next to the driver.

The journey through town was arduous, creeping along choked narrow lanes of nondescript houses. In the distance, upon a hill, sat the royal palace.

"The *Surya Mahal*," said Carmichael. "The Palace of the Sun, seat of maharajas of Sambalpore since . . . well, not that long really. They only built it about sixty years ago. After the Mutiny, at any rate. Before that, the maharajas preferred the security of the old fort down by the river. This part of the world was a pretty dangerous place until the early eighteen hundreds. Local rulers, Mughals and Marathas all fighting each another *and* us, of course.

"Luckily for Sambalpore, at the time of the 'fifty-seven Mutiny, the then ruler, the Rajah Veer Surendra Sai, was canny enough to see which way the wind was blowing. Unlike other native princes, he chose to back the East India Company — even sent some of his own troops to aid in the relief of Lucknow — and very well he did out of it, too. Expanded lands, the title of Maharaja and the gratitude of the India Office. Of such things are dynasties created."

The car finally approached the gates of the British Residency, a large walled compound, inside which stood a rather drab-looking two-storey building, with a balcony running the length of the upper floor and a bare flagpole on the roof.

"No Union Jack?" I asked.

Carmichael's face reddened. "I'm afraid not. Moths, you see. We've requested a replacement from Calcutta, but, as I told you, we're not high on the India Office's list of priorities."

"I wouldn't be so sure," I replied, thinking of the Viceroy's designs for the Chamber of Princes. "From what I hear, all that might be about to change."

The interior of the Residency was no less ordinary than the exterior. Indeed, there are town halls in the most unassuming corners of England that are more impressive than His Britannic Majesty's Residency in Sambalpore. Still, be it ever so humble . . .

In the ill-lit, camphor-smelling entrance hall, Carmichael took his leave, entrusting us to the care of his manservant, a shifty-looking native dressed in a white shirt, loose, draw-string trousers and bare feet.

"Munda will show you to your rooms," said Carmichael. "There's a basin, soap and a bucket of clean water in each so that you can freshen up. Please be ready and down here in an hour as we have an audience with the Maharaja and it wouldn't do to be late."

The manservant led the way up a flight of stairs and along a corridor with bare, whitewashed walls. He opened a door and ushered me inside, then shuffled off down the corridor with Surrender-not in tow.

The room was as plain as the rest of the building: a single bed, a wardrobe, a chair, a desk with a hurricane lamp sitting on it, and a picture of George V on the wall. Still, it was clean, and in India you couldn't really ask for much more.

Closing the door, I put down my case and sat down on the bed. I lit a cigarette, took a long pull and marvelled at the fates that had led me to this bare room in Sambalpore, pursuing a case against the wishes of the Viceroy and in a place where I had zero authority. As starts went, it hardly seemed auspicious, despite Surrender-not's father's views about the rain.

Still, just being in Sambalpore felt like progress. The obvious task was to track down whoever had sent those warning notes to Adhir. I had certain suspicions in that regard, but how exactly I was going to pursue them when I was technically on holiday was something I hadn't yet worked out. That, though, could wait. My immediate concern centred on what I was going to say to the Maharaja.

# CHAPTER
# TWELVE

The sun was high in the sky. You couldn't see it, but you could feel it, and the air smelled charred, coated with dust.

The old Austin wheezed its way towards the palace through the swirling currents of small-town India: the hawkers with their carts, their hoarse voices beseeching custom; the thin farmers sitting cross-legged in the shade of knotted and twisted pipal trees, imploring the townswomen to take a look at their produce, everything from bitter gourds to watermelons, all laid out on brightly coloured sheets.

"So what do you know about our illustrious ruler?" asked Carmichael.

"Not much," I replied.

"In that case," he said enthusiastically, "I should give you the potted history."

I had the feeling he had the whole thing down pat.

"The Maharaja — Rajan Kumar Sai — aged seventy-six and ruler of Sambalpore since 1858. Born into a poor, but high-caste, farming family, he came to the throne when, on the advice of his soothsayers, the previous maharaja adopted him on his deathbed as his heir, in an attempt to avoid falling foul of the old Doctrine of Lapse."

Carmichael read my expression.

"The Doctrine of Lapse," he explained, "was enacted by the then Viceroy, Lord Dalhousie. It allowed the East India Company to annex any princely state whose ruler died without a legitimate male heir or was deemed to be *manifestly incompetent*."

"And what constituted manifest incompetence?" I asked.

That was for the Company to decide." He grinned. "Through it, they acquired some of the mineral-rich kingdoms that might otherwise have remained in less *forward-thinking* native hands. It's proved pretty handy for the India Office, too. It allowed us to get rid of the old Gaekwad of Baroda on the pretext that he'd tried to poison his British Resident's grapefruit juice."

"So why wasn't Sambalpore annexed when the old maharaja died?" asked Surrender-not.

"Ah," said Carmichael, "you must remember that this was 1858, the year after the Mutiny. London had just stripped the East India Company of its hegemony and the whole of India was in flux. Power had shifted from the money men of the Company to the civil servants of the India Office, and stability rather than profit was the new order of the day. The former maharaja had supported the British the previous year and it was felt that it was better to have a steady ally in Sambalpore than to take on more lands that needed administration. It was one of those curious twists of fate. Had the old maharaja died five years earlier, or

**110**

indeed five years later, the kingdom probably wouldn't exist today."

The driver braked sharply as a skeletal grey cow wandered lazily into the road. He manoeuvred the car around the lumbering animal, which paid us scant attention as it chewed on a mouthful of cane leaves.

"The current maharaja has overseen the modernisation of Sambalpore," continued Carmichael, "though his reforms have not extended into the political sphere. Power is maintained in the hands of the Maharaja and his sons."

"How many sons does he have?" I asked.

"Until the tragic assassination of the Yuvraj, he had three recognised heirs to the throne, sons borne by his official wives. Those borne by his concubines have no claim to the throne."

"Concubines?"

"He had a hundred and twenty-six of them as at the end of last March," Carmichael continued, "and two hundred and fifty-six offspring, not counting the three official princes. We receive a copy of the kingdom's annual financial report. It's all set out in a note to the accounts."

"Tell me about the princes," I said.

"The only three children with a recognised claim to the throne were the Yuvraj Adhir Singh Sai, now deceased, and his brother, Prince Punit, aged twenty-nine, both sons of the Second Maharani, and their half-brother, Prince Alok, aged eighteen months, son of the Third Maharani. You may recall the newspaper reports last year of the Maharaja ordering

**111**

his swimming pool to be filled with champagne to celebrate the child's birth."

"Siring a child in your seventies is a cause for celebration, I suppose," I said. "Are we sure the Maharaja is the father?"

"Oh yes," replied Carmichael. "Other than the Maharaja and his legitimate sons, the only other men who would have been within fifty feet of the Maharani in private would all be eunuchs. For such an old roué, the old man is remarkably strict about these things.

"It's not all vice, though; the Maharaja has his virtues too," he continued. "He's overseen the development of Sambalpore from an illiterate feudal society to one with health and education levels on a par with those in Calcutta or Delhi. He's brought electricity to the kingdom, though it's limited mainly to Sambalpore town, and agricultural practices have been modernised, though he still owns most of the land. And he's paid for it all with funds generated from diamond sales."

"Lucky for such a small place to have such a source of revenue," I said.

"Sambalpore's a lucky place," he replied. "Before diamonds it was opium. The kingdom used to do a roaring trade back in the day. The East India Company couldn't get enough of the stuff for export to China. It's past its peak but they still produce a bit, even today. They say it's for use in medicinal preparations, but rumour has it that some of the officials turn a pretty penny supplying it to the black market."

I felt a shiver pass through me. A bitter-sweet pang of expectation.

"Anyway, the Maharaja's got a decent track record," he continued, "especially for a man who's always seemed more drawn to the lights of London and the fleshpots of Paris than he has to managing the affairs of state. The irony is that every time he wants to travel anywhere, he needs to apply to Delhi for his passport."

"Why?" asked Surrender-not.

"It's the law," said Carmichael. "None of the princes can leave India without the permission of the Viceroy."

"It sounds like they're under virtual house arrest," I said.

Carmichael smiled. "I suppose they are, in a manner of speaking."

The car turned a corner. Ahead rose the *Surya Mahal*, the Palace of the Sun. It was three storeys tall, four if you counted the shaded gardens on the roof, and painted bright yellow. Built in the Mughal style, with an arched facade and balconied, latticed windows, it seemed concocted more out of light and air and flights of fancy than of brick and stone. It was imbued with the most delicate of architectural features that made our own colonial buildings look bloated and ponderous.

A guard with more important things on his mind waved us lazily through the gateway without bothering to check our identification. Not that that was particularly unusual. In India, being white and in a car was enough to get you into most places, but in light of recent events, I'd have expected security around the royal family to be stiffer.

**113**

The Austin stopped beside a set of stairs leading up to a double-storey entrance arch. A footman with a face that seemed carved from mahogany appeared and opened the door. Carmichael acknowledged him with a nod and the man reciprocated, displaying none of the usual bowing and scraping that one expects of native attendants receiving a *sahib*.

"We have an audience with His Highness," said Carmichael.

"Yes, Mr Carmichael," replied the man impassively. "This way please. You are expected."

We followed him past two large wooden doors embellished with carvings of foliage and into an entrance hall dominated by a chandelier suspended from a ceiling several storeys above. There we were handed over to the care of another attendant who led the way down a marble corridor that smelled like a rose garden and stretched into the distance. At the end, we passed through another set of doors and were deposited into the care of a third official who continued the tour.

"I didn't expect a relay team would be required to take us to the Maharaja," I said.

"Don't worry," Carmichael replied, "you'll be able to rest soon enough. His Highness likes to keep *Indian time*. We're likely to be kept waiting a while before he sees us."

The final attendant led us into the sort of room King Midas might have decorated if he'd had the money. French furniture sat under gilded mirrors and golden foliage. In the centre, a glass table rested on the backs of four silver elephants, and reflected the light from a Baccarat chandelier.

As we sat down, a set of doors at the far end opened, and out walked Fitzmaurice in the company of a finely dressed native. He seemed preoccupied and might have walked past without noticing us had Carmichael not called after him.

"Sir Ernest; it's good to see you, sir."

The businessman brusquely returned the compliment, then made his excuses and followed the native out.

We went back to waiting. As the minutes passed, a series of unpleasant thoughts flashed through my head. I couldn't shake the sight of Dawson on the platform at Howrah. Would the Maharaja suspect British involvement in the death of his son? And if so, how would he react to meeting the men who'd been at his son's side when he'd been murdered?

My hands were shaking, maybe from a rush of adrenalin, or possibly from an absence of opium. The doors opened and an attendant in an emerald-green *kurta* walked over.

I braced myself.

"His Highness will see you now."

# CHAPTER
# THIRTEEN

I was expecting a jewel-encrusted ruler reclined on silk cushions, perhaps fanned by flunkeys with oversized peacock feathers in a throne room the size of the Albert Hall. The reality was rather different. The room we entered was no larger than the average study, with bookcases arranged along one wall, French doors which opened onto landscaped gardens, and an unmistakable hint of mildew in the air.

At one end, behind a gilded desk, sat the Maharaja, grey-haired and crumpled in a Savile Row suit and a starched white shirt whose collar hung loosely round his thin neck like a noose waiting to be tightened. He appeared preoccupied with some papers. On the wall behind him hung a tapestry depicting some gruesome scene from what looked like Hindu mythology: a bejewelled prince locked in combat against a double-headed demon. Above it were two arched windows covered with latticework screens. To his right stood the Dewan and on the left, Colonel Arora and a turbaned attendant.

The Dewan whispered in his ear and the old man looked up. Day-old silver bristles pockmarked his chin and his red, raw eyes betrayed his grief. I imagine the death of a child will do that to a man, even one who's sired over two hundred others.

"Mr Carmichael," he said impassively.

"Your Highness," replied the Resident, "may I introduce Captain Wyndham and Sergeant Banerjee of the Imperial Police Force. They are here to convey the Force's condolences and pay their respects. I am given to understand that Sergeant Banerjee was a friend of the Yuvraj."

There was a flicker in the old man's eyes. "You knew Adhir?" he asked Surrender-not.

"Yes, Your Highness. We were at Harrow together, though he was closer in age to my brother."

"Sergeant Banerjee and Captain Wyndham are the officers who tracked down and apprehended your son's assassin," interjected Colonel Arora.

The Maharaja stared hard. "I am in your debt, gentlemen," he said. "Do you have any idea what drove this man to commit such an act?"

"I'm afraid not, Your Highness," I replied. "The man chose to take his own life rather than surrender to us. But there is evidence to suggest he may have been dispatched from Sambalpore."

The old man sat up straighter.

Beside him, the Dewan stirred. "If I may, Your Highness —" he started, but the Maharaja cut him off with a motion of his hand.

"*Dispatched?* You suspect someone sent him to murder my son?"

"The investigation is not yet complete," I clarified, "but we understand the prince had received notes warning him that his life was in danger. Those notes were left in his room here at the palace."

The old man became suddenly animated. "You think the culprits are here? In Sambalpore?"

His exertions set off a sudden fit of coughing. As he doubled over, an attendant rushed to his aid, but the Maharaja waved him away.

"Quite possibly."

"Can you find them?"

"Your Highness!" protested the Dewan. "The British have no jurisdiction here. I fear their involvement would set a worrying precedent. In any case, Major Bhardwaj has been working on a similar theory and has already arrested a suspect."

Beside the Maharaja, Colonel Arora shifted awkwardly, as though blind-sided by the news. I caught his eye, and though it was only for an instant, I could tell what he was thinking.

"If I may, Your Highness," he intervened, "I understand that Captain Wyndham is a former Scotland Yard detective, and that he is currently on leave from the IPF. Perhaps he would care to provide us with the benefit of his experience in a purely personal capacity? Possibly as an adviser to Major Bhardwaj and his officers?"

The Maharaja remained silent, but his emotions played out on his face. The thought of British intervention in the affairs of his kingdom was doubtless anathema to him, but this was the murder of his son, and that meant the normal rules didn't apply. Then there were those two magic words — *Scotland Yard*. I

**118**

never ceased to be amazed by the store people placed on that particular establishment, believing in the omniscience of its officers the way that tribal people do in witch doctors. Not that I was complaining.

He cleared his throat. "We deem it expedient to extend an invitation to the captain, and to his colleague, of course, to observe and, should he so wish, advise Major Bhardwaj's investigation in a personal capacity. We would, of course, consider it a great service to the kingdom and would provide whatever comforts the captain and the sergeant would require during their stay."

"I'd like permission to interview individuals, Your Highness," I said. "In conjunction with your own officers, of course."

Something caught my eye. A glint of reflected light coming from the screened window above the tapestry. It shimmered for a second, then disappeared.

The Dewan vehemently shook his head. "That would be completely inappro —"

But the Maharaja cut him off. "You shall have a free hand, Captain, including the authority to interrogate whomsoever you wish."

"In which case, the sergeant and I would be most honoured to assist in any way we can, Your Highness."

He smiled thinly through grey lips. "Then it is settled. Colonel Arora will see to your accommodation and act as your liaison with the relevant officials. I trust, Captain, that you will be able to get to the bottom of this quickly. Time is short. Often shorter than we expect."

# CHAPTER
## FOURTEEN

"Well, that went rather well," said Banerjee as we followed Colonel Arora back towards the antechamber.

"Yes, I thought so too," replied the ADC. "What say you, Mr Carmichael?"

The Resident's face, however, appeared to register several conflicting emotions at once. He exchanged glances with the colonel.

"Captain, may I have a word in private?" Then, turning to the ADC, "A room please, Colonel," he said, with the authority of the Foreign Office in his voice.

Arora nodded, then opened the door to the antechamber. I followed Carmichael in.

"Close the door, please," he said, his back to me. For a moment, he stood, drumming his fingers on a side table. Then he turned around. He seemed to have aged ten years.

"I must say, Captain," he began, "this is most peculiar. First your unannounced arrival and now this."

"Is there something you wish to tell me, Mr Carmichael?" I asked.

He hesitated for a moment.

"I had hoped to avoid it, but given the circumstances . . ." He fished a pressed handkerchief from his pocket and dapped at his forehead. "I feel I ought to give you the lie of the land, so to speak. The royal court is a dangerous place, Wyndham. The politics are positively Byzantine. Loyalties can shift tremendously quickly. Now with the Yuvraj's assassination, I fear the game may become even more cut-throat."

"You make them sound like a band of pirates," I laughed, "rather than the rulers of one of our trusted Indian allies."

There came a noise from somewhere behind the wall, immediately drawing Carmichael's gaze. The colour drained from his face.

"Listen to me, Captain," he said, his voice dropping to a whisper. "The Yuvraj isn't the first member of the family to have met with an untimely death. You should be careful who you trust."

With that, he walked over to the door, opened it and beckoned to Banerjee and Arora.

"Well, if you'll excuse me, gentlemen," he said, "I must be getting back. I should wire Calcutta and inform them of developments." He turned to the ADC. "I trust you will see to it, Colonel, that the captain and the sergeant make it back to the Residency this evening. My wife is keen to meet our friends from Calcutta."

"You may rest assured, Mr Carmichael," said Arora, "I shall ensure that Captain Wyndham and Sergeant Banerjee are returned to you by six o'clock."

Carmichael gave me a nod, then turned and trudged off, looking like a man with all the cares of the empire on his shoulders.

"So. Where would you care to start?" asked the ADC.

"Perhaps you could tell us about this Major Bhardwaj whom the Dewan mentioned," I said.

"He's the head of the local militia," he replied dismissively, "essentially our chief of police. But don't be fooled by the rank, Captain. The man has no military training."

"Is he good at his job?"

"He's good at arresting people. Whether they're the *correct* people is a matter of conjecture."

"We'll need an office," I said as I pondered his response, "somewhere private to work from. Preferably in a different building from Major Bhardwaj and his men; and close to the palace, too, if possible."

"That should not present any difficulties," he replied. "In Sambalpore, nothing of any importance is far from the palace . . . except, of course, the diamond mines. They're about thirty miles upcountry. Come, we should be able to find you a billet that meets your specifications."

He led the way through the palace and out into an immaculately landscaped garden that would have looked at home in Versailles. Arora made for a gravel path that bisected the sweeping lawns. "The *Gulaab Bhavan*, the government administrative building," he said, "is located on the other side of the palace gardens. It's a short walk."

The gardens seemed a popular venue. A number of English women, matronly types in starched uniforms and sensible shoes, walked the greens, each with several

**122**

small Indian children in tow. Others sat on benches, primly reading to their charges. Still more ambled along the paths, each accompanied by a male attendant immaculately turned out in an emerald-green uniform and stiff fanned turban, and each pushing a large pram.

"The royal offspring," explained Arora. "At the last count, His Highness has sired two hundred and fifty-eight children, not including his three heirs."

"Mr Carmichael seemed to think the number was two hundred and fifty-six," queried Surrender-not.

The colonel smiled. "Two more have been born since the last accounts."

"That's a lot of children," I said.

"His Highness has always shown great interest in sexual theory and practice."

"It appears he certainly hasn't neglected the latter," I said.

"That much is true. I understand the kingdom of Sambalpore is the largest single customer of your Dunley Perambulator Company. In the last year alone, I believe we have purchased over two dozen of their contraptions."

"How does a military man like yourself come across that sort of information?" asked Banerjee.

"Oh, it's all in the accounts," replied the colonel nonchalantly. "We may be a sovereign state, but the India Office *babus* in Delhi require us to keep very detailed records. You'll be surprised at what's in there."

The *Gulaab Bhavan*, or Rose Building, turned out to be a rather handsome three-storey residence with a pink stucco exterior and vines creeping up its facade. The rear of the building was not quite as pretty as the front, dominated as it was by several sets of garage doors, some open to reveal a surfeit of headlights, polished metal and chrome bodywork.

"The ground floor houses the royal fleet of cars, an engine shop and accommodation for the engineers and chauffeurs," explained Arora. "Each car has its own designated team, and His Highness insists that the chauffeurs are all Italian. He believes them to be the best drivers in the world. Our offices are on the upper floors."

Outside, two natives, stripped to the waist, were busy buffing a dark blue Rolls-Royce to a shine. It was a special model: the passengers would sit in an enclosed compartment and the driver up front in the open. As if the separate compartment didn't afford privacy enough, there were thick blue curtains drawn over the windows.

"The *purdah* car," explained the colonel. "It's used by the maharanis. The windows are covered to protect their modesty."

"They're allowed to leave the harem?" I asked.

"Oh yes," he replied matter-of-factly. "The maharanis have quite busy lives. Even the concubines are allowed to use it occasionally."

"Where do they go?"

"All sorts of places: picnics up in the hills or trips to bathe in the river — the Mahanadi, which runs through Sambalpore, is considered holy. The Lord Jagannath is said to have taken the form of a log and travelled along it, down to Puri on the coast. And of course, the First Maharani uses it most mornings when she goes to the temple for her prayers."

Beside an open doorway sat a rotund sentry who paid us not the slightest notice as we passed. The interior was cool and quiet. It may have lacked the grandeur of the palace, but it was elegant enough, with marble floors and whitewashed walls dotted with photographs of the maharaja in a multitude of poses: His Highness on a grand throne; His Highness sitting on an elephant that appeared to have been dipped in a vat of gemstones; His Highness taking tea with King George; even one of him sitting on a scale, literally assessing his weight in gold.

"The majority of the kingdom's affairs are administered from this building," said Arora. "The Dewan's office is on the first floor, along with the Cabinet room and the other advisers' offices. They used to be scattered all over town but His Highness decreed that they all move here, for the sake of *efficiency*, though most of the advisers can't stand each other. Almost all of them still run their affairs from town and just keep vacant offices here. Other than the Dewan and his retinue, the place is generally empty unless there's a Cabinet meeting. We should have little trouble finding you an office."

The man was as good as his word. He led us up to the second floor where he opened the first door we came upon, craned his neck and peered inside.

"Is this acceptable?" he asked, opening the door wider.

The room was significantly larger than my office at Lal Bazar, with more than enough space for the two leather-topped desks it contained, and possibly a tennis court besides. It was plusher than my office, too, in that the walls were freshly painted and chairs upholstered. The rug on the floor just seemed excessive.

I looked at Surrender-not. "It'll do," I said. "But before we get too settled, I'd like to interview the man your Major Bhardwaj has arrested. As soon as possible."

The colonel thought for a moment, then gave the sort of curt, sharp nod that military men specialise in. "Very well. Give me some time to speak to him and I'll arrange it."

Arora took his leave while I took in the view from the window. Velvet lawns and an avenue of trees led down to the banks of a wide river which I presumed was the Mahanadi, though no gods or other logs seemed to be floating past today.

"Well, this is rather nice," said Surrender-not from behind me. I turned to see him making himself comfortable behind one of the desks.

"Best not get too cosy, Sergeant," I said. "I've a feeling we're going to find ourselves kept quite busy while we're here."

"Not if this suspect they've arrested really is the brains behind the assassination," he replied.

"And on what basis do you think they've arrested him?" I asked.

He straightened in his chair. "Pardon, sir?"

126

"Think about it. What proof do you think they could have? The assassination took place in Calcutta. The assassin killed himself there. Any evidence he had of a link to Sambalpore probably went up in flames back in his hotel room. Hell, *we're* only here on a hunch. Now given all that, I must say I'm looking forward to understanding exactly how the good Major Bhardwaj has cracked the case so quickly."

# CHAPTER
# FIFTEEN

The old fort stood on a rocky outcrop overlooking the Mahanadi, separated from the *Surya Mahal* by several miles and a thousand years. Its austere stone walls and pockmarked battlements were a stark rebuke to the light, playful architecture of the palace.

We were seated in the back of an old Mercedes Simplex, with Colonel Arora and his driver up front. The colonel had apologised for the car. It was almost ten years old and the suspension creaked. Even so, it was considerably more comfortable than Carmichael's Austin.

"I had hoped for something more modern," the colonel had said, "but His Highness insisted we use the Mercedes. He believes it to be a lucky car. Do you know what *Mercedes* means?" he asked.

I hadn't a clue. But then I hadn't gone to Cambridge.

"It's Spanish," replied Surrender-not. "Commonly used as a girls' name."

"Very good," the colonel nodded, "but it literally means *godsend*. His Highness believes you to have been sent here by god."

I recalled his son, the Yuvraj, saying something similar when we'd first met. Half an hour later he was dead.

"They say the old fort is haunted by the ghost of a Mughal general," continued the colonel, twisting in his seat. "We used to have a lot of bother with the Mughals a few hundred years ago. The general was captured and held prisoner in the fort's dungeon before being blinded and put to death. On nights when the wind is blowing from the east, his soul is reputed to walk the corridors, searching for a way home."

As the car approached the gates, Arora pointed to a small window, high up in the fort's walls. "Our prisoner is being held up there, I believe."

"Not in the dungeon?" I asked.

He threw me a disappointed look. "We aren't barbarians, Captain. What did you expect — the Black Hole of Calcutta?"

The driver brought the car to a halt in a dusty inner courtyard. Leaving Arora, we were taken inside by a soldier and led up three flights of a narrow spiral staircase into a small, sparsely furnished chamber. In one wall was a slit of a window, through which fell a shaft of light. The soldier went to find Major Bhardwaj.

From the window two temples were visible on the opposite bank of the river. Set inside a walled compound, the first was a large, white, marbled structure with a *shikara*, the sculpted steeple common to Hindu temples, two storeys high and covered in carvings. A distance away stood the ruins of a smaller, simpler edifice. As I watched, the blue Rolls-Royce with the covered windows approached the larger temple and came to a stop outside its walls. Before I could see anything more, the door behind me opened and in walked Major Bhardwaj.

The major was rather heavy set, with a military moustache and a demeanour as jolly as a mortuary. He certainly didn't seem overjoyed to see us.

"Gentlemen," he said curtly. "Colonel Arora has informed me of your credentials. I understand you wish to interview the prisoner."

"The Maharaja also wishes it," I clarified.

"Very well," said the major sourly. "This way please."

Bhardwaj led us to a solid wooden door partway along a stone corridor and gestured with a nod to the guard who stood outside it. Retrieving a large iron key from a ring on his belt, the man proceeded to unlock the door and hold it open for us. Colonel Arora had been right. They certainly weren't barbarians. The room was clean and comfortable and even sported a view out across the river. It could have been a decent hotel room if it wasn't for the bars on the window and the guard at the door. If that was the first surprise, the second was arguably greater.

A young woman in her twenties, her hair cut short, turned and rose from her seat at the desk where she had been writing. She was dressed in a plain blue *kurti* and white *churidaar* trousers, and she stared at Surrender-not quizzically through eyes tinged with *kohl*. She didn't much look like a hardened terrorist. If anything, she looked like a princess. Or at least she might have done had she some jewellery on her.

"Are we in the right room?" I asked.

Major Bhardwaj gave a slight laugh. "Oh yes, you can be assured of that. This woman has caused more trouble in the kingdom than anyone since the time of the Mughals."

"And does she have a name?"

"I have a name," she responded sharply, "though I fail to see what concern it is of yours." She turned towards the major before continuing. "Or have matters reached such a stage where the officers of the Anglo-Indian Diamond Company are now allowed to interrogate a subject of Sambalpore?"

"I assure you, miss," I replied, "I've nothing to do with the Anglo-Indian Diamond Company."

"And what about your friend?" she said, gesturing towards Surrender-not. "Why is he dressed like he's just stepped off a steamship?"

I looked over at Surrender-not in his dress uniform. He had that look on his face — the one he always got when introduced to a beautiful woman — or any woman really — a cross between a new-born puppy and a frightened child. There was something about women that left him as mute as a fish. Not exactly an ideal state of affairs given we were here to question the girl.

"His name is Banerjee and he's a policeman," I replied. "And he has nothing to do with them either."

She stared hard at me, as though trying to divine my intentions.

"And you? Who are you?" she asked.

"My name is Sam Wyndham," I said, "and I'm on holiday. Now I think it's only fair that you tell me *your* name."

She remained silent.

"Her name is Bidika," replied Major Bhardwaj. "Shreya Bidika. She is a teacher at a school in Sambalpore, but do not be fooled, she is also one of the leading agitators against the Maharaja."

"A pleasure to meet you, Miss Bidika," I said.

She ignored the pleasantry.

"So if you are not here on behalf of Anglo-Indian Diamond," she said, "what business have you with me? Let me guess — you're a lawyer that the Dewan has invited to our little kingdom to ensure that everything is above board and that justice is done."

"Not quite," I said. "I'm a detective. The sergeant and I have some experience with murder cases and His Highness the Maharaja thought it might be nice if we checked in on you."

"Yes, the father of our nation can be quite caring in that way," she said acerbically.

"I'm told most of his subjects are quite happy."

"Most of his subjects were raised to revere him as a god. How are they supposed to voice displeasure with a deity?"

"You don't seem to have a problem with it. Don't you regard him as a deity?"

"Well," she smiled thinly, "his venality is certainly godlike; however, gods don't suffer from senility."

"And your Congress friends think Sambalpore would be better without him? Is that it?"

"I'm not a Congress-woman," she said vehemently. "The Congress Party has a policy of non-interference in the governance of the princely states."

"So does the British government," I replied, "and yet, here I am and here you are too. Maybe both parties have a rather elastic definition of what constitutes *non-interference*?"

She smiled, and I noticed a slight relaxation of her shoulders. I sat down on the bed and gestured for her to resume her seat. Surrender-not remained standing awkwardly near the door.

"Do you know why you've been arrested?"

"Not officially."

"But you have a fair idea?"

"I would imagine it has something to do with the assassination of the Yuvraj in Calcutta."

"And do you have any knowledge of that crime?"

"None at all."

"But you don't deny that you'd like to see the back of the royal family."

"Not at all, but that cause is hardly going to be furthered by the death of the Yuvraj."

"No?" I asked, genuinely surprised.

"Of course not. If you had any knowledge of Sambalpore, you would know that. Besides, it can only happen when the people wake up. When they are educated."

"*Educated?*" scoffed Major Bhardwaj. "And how, Miss Schoolmistress, do you *educate* the people with your lies?"

"We speak the truth," she retorted. "We open the people's eyes."

"How?" spat the major. "By pouring poison into their hearts? Believe me, you and your kind will get what's coming to you."

Miss Bidika turned back to me. "As you see, Mr Wyndham, dissent is tolerated here about as much as it is in British India." The corners of her mouth turned up in a bitter smile. "At least there you have the semblance of due process. How ironic that we should be oppressed more by our own kind than by you."

"Is that why you had the crown prince murdered?" I asked. "A blow against oppression?"

"I told you. I had nothing to do with his murder."

"Well, unless you can prove it, I fear for your chances," I said. "I understand the kingdom of Sambalpore isn't particularly sold on the merits of habeas corpus."

She shook her head and sighed. "What would we have to gain from the Yuvraj's death? Whatever his faults, he was still a far better prospect as maharaja than his father. He, at least, knew things had to change. He might not have liked what we had to say, but he would listen. Now what do we have to look forward to? The continuing rule of an enfeebled old man who every day becomes more in thrall to his priests and astrologers? And when he dies, the accession of his second son, a man made in his father's image who spends most of his time hunting or womanising." She paused to remove a stray strand of hair from her face. "Believe me, Mr Wyndham, whoever murdered the

Yuvraj has set back the cause of progress in Sambalpore by many, many years."

That came as a shock. Revolutionaries were supposed to view the assassination of royalty as rather a good thing. The history books tended to be quite clear on that point. I didn't remember reading of Cromwell shedding a tear over the severed head of Charles I, or Lenin lamenting the freshly murdered Romanovs. Nevertheless, I had to keep going. I pulled a mortuary photograph of the assassin from my jacket pocket and showed it to Miss Bidika.

"Do you recognise this man?"

She shook her head.

I looked at her. "You're positive?"

"Yes."

She betrayed no hint of subterfuge, but as I went to return the photograph, I noticed Major Bhardwaj staring at it. The colour had drained from his face.

"Do *you* recognise him, Major?" I asked.

"What?"

I held it closer for him. "Do you recognise the assassin?"

He looked away quickly.

"No."

"You're sure?"

"I'm positive. He simply reminded me of someone . . . a priest I once knew."

"A priest?" I asked. The first time I'd seen him, with his saffron robes and the ash-marked forehead, I'd mistaken him for a holy man myself. "You're sure he's not the man you knew?"

"I'm sure. That man died a long time ago . . . but . . ."

"But what?"

"The resemblance is strong."

"Could he be a relative?" I asked. "A son, maybe?"

The major shook his head. "The man was an ascetic. In keeping with tradition, he had renounced the world to search for god. He had no children, as far as I know."

I felt the major was holding something back.

"This is the man who shot and killed your Yuvraj," I said. "You are positive you don't recognise him?"

"Yes," he said vehemently, "I have told you as much. Now, have you any more questions for the prisoner?"

It seemed I wasn't going to get any more out of the major for the present. As for his prisoner, I'd heard all I needed to from her.

"Not for the moment. What about you, Surrender-not? Anything to add?"

"N-nothing."

"Very well," I said. "That's all for now. Thank you, Miss Bidika, for your time."

She nodded. "Time, Mr Wyndham, is something I appear to have a surfeit of."

"I wouldn't be too sure of that," snorted the major as he ushered us out of the room. "Wheels are in motion, my dear lady."

Back in his office, I asked Bhardwaj what he'd meant.

"Her fate has yet to be formally decreed," he replied, "but what would you expect the sentence for treason and murder to be?"

136

"I was under the impression that the death penalty had been outlawed in the princely states."

The major smiled. "That much is true . . . and yet —"

"And yet what?" interjected Surrender-not.

"Prison regimes can be harsh," he replied, "especially for a woman."

"What's the nature of your evidence against her?" asked Surrender-not.

Bhardwaj shot him a disgusted look. "She's a known agitator. We have the pamphlets she's been circulating. All manner of seditious nonsense."

"With respect," said the sergeant, "sedition is not the same thing as conspiracy to murder."

"No?" questioned the major. "In my book they are merely different steps along the path to the same destination: the overthrow of the legitimate government of Sambalpore."

"Who will decide her fate?" I asked. "The Maharaja?"

"It will be a decision for the Cabinet, but yes, the royal family's opinion will be taken into account," he replied.

We left Bhardwaj and headed back down to the car. Colonel Arora stood leaning against it, smoking a cigarette.

"And what did you make of our little firebrand revolutionary?" he asked as the car headed back towards town.

"You didn't think to mention the prisoner was a woman?" I asked.

He grinned. "I thought that might surprise you. She's a feisty young thing . . . pretty, too, and from a good family. If it wasn't for her politics, she might have been chosen for the Maharaja's harem."

"Would she have had a choice in the matter?"

"Of course," he replied, "but it is considered a great honour, not to mention that it's security for life."

"Security?"

"Absolutely. His Highness's concubines are often simple village girls. They are grateful for the comfort and security of the zenana."

"And what happens when the Maharaja loses interest in them?"

He looked at me as if the question were ridiculous.

"Why would anything happen to them? They continue to live in the harem for the rest of their lives. After all, they are still women of the palace and they and their offspring are looked after accordingly. Indeed, I would imagine their lives probably become easier once their name stops appearing on the royal bedroom roster.

"Do you think she's behind the assassination?" he continued.

Carmichael's words echoed in my head and I hesitated over exactly how much to tell him. Arora may have been the one to convince the Maharaja to allow us to investigate, but he was still a member of the Sambalpori royal court and no doubt he had his own agenda.

138

"I think it might be worth doing a little more digging before we pronounce the case closed," I said. "What did you make of her, Surrender-not?"

"She's very beautiful," he replied, staring out at the Mahanadi River, which flowed gently on our left.

"Anything else?" I asked.

"Hmm?"

"Maybe your analysis of what she had to say?"

"Yes, sir. Sorry, sir," he said, refocusing. "She didn't strike me as a killer."

"Beautiful women are just as capable of plotting murder as anyone else," I reminded him.

"But still, sir . . ." His voice trailed off. He was brooding again.

"Come on, Sergeant," I said, "spit it out."

"It's nothing," he said, shaking his head. "Just something she mentioned got me thinking . . . She's wrong, you know."

"About what?" I asked.

"Ra."

"What?" I said blankly.

"The Egyptian god, Ra, sir," he said. "She said that gods don't suffer from senility. But by certain accounts, Ra did. They say that in his old age he became convinced that mankind was laughing at him."

"Fascinating," I said. "Is that important?"

"I don't know, exactly."

The colonel, though, seemed interested. "What happened?" he asked. "What did he do about the mockery?"

"It's a rather unpleasant story," sighed Surrender-not, "but essentially, he sent his two daughters to put the entire human race to death. They'd have succeeded, too, if one of them hadn't got drunk."

"Well," said the colonel, "maybe there is a lesson in there for all of us. Let us hope that our own god-king has no such ideas."

I nodded. "Let us indeed." But it struck me there was another lesson to be drawn from the tale of Ra and his daughters, and that was to never underestimate the power of intelligent women to commit even the darkest of deeds.

Surrender-not turned to address the colonel. "What will happen to her?"

"I expect she'll be made an example of, as the French might say, *pour décourager les autres*."

"*Made an example of?* How exactly?" asked Surrender-not.

The colonel looked away, focusing on a hill on the far side of the river. "Trust me, Sergeant, you don't want to know."

# CHAPTER
# SIXTEEN

The light was failing and the humidity clung like sackcloth. The car stopped at the gates of the Residency.

"I'll pick you up at nine tomorrow," said the colonel, then gave his driver the order to move off without bothering to wait for a reply.

I turned to Surrender-not.

"Come on."

We trudged back into the compound, past a native lowering a faded Union Jack, the rusted metal pulley creaking as he pulled on the halyard rope. As for the flag itself, the thing had more holes than a golf course. I guessed Carmichael had decided that flying a moth-eaten flag was preferable to flying no flag at all. I wasn't sure I agreed.

There was no sign of the Austin so I assumed our host was out somewhere. In any case, the front door was open and we made our way inside and up to our rooms.

I closed the door, peeled off my shirt and wiped at the perspiration on my chest with a *gamcha*, the thin cotton towel favoured by the natives and which is, to all intents and purposes, practically useless for soaking up anything. After managing merely to smear the sweat over my body, I gave up and instead splashed tepid water from the basin onto my face.

The familiar ache had started. For now it was restricted to my upper arms, but it wouldn't be long before it spread — first to the muscles of my back, then my chest and thighs, and finally into my bones. Behind it would come the fog — descending at first like a fine mist on my synapses, then swelling, congealing, solidifying, its grip tightening like a fist inside my skull which would eventually crowd out all thoughts but one. Opium.

The process from initial symptoms to full-blown withdrawal would take a while — days, probably — but once it had started, the only real way to stop it was a hit of O. For now, though, it was important to make use of what time I still had. I lay down on the creaking bed, then got back up and fished a crumpled packet of Capstans from my trouser pocket. Lighting a cigarette, I returned to the bed. An old newspaper advertisement extolling the virtues of tobacco on the intellectual process came to mind. *Smoke Ogden's to stimulate the brain.* That was good, because I needed to think things through and was grateful for all the help I could get — but I smoked the thing down to the fag end without any noticeable uptick in my cognitive processes. Still, cigarettes were only the first weapon in my armoury. Maybe it was time to bring out some heavier artillery. The suitcase was sat on a small chest in one corner of the room. I brought it back to the bed, snapped open the locks and lifted the lid. Instinctively, my eyes were drawn to where the opium travelling kit lay sleeping under its blanket of shirts, but I ignored it, instead pulling out the half-empty bottle of Glenfarclas. The supply would need to be managed carefully. There was precious little of the stuff available in Calcutta, and from what I'd seen of Carmichael's budget, I doubted decent malt of any description had made it to the Residency since before the Mutiny.

Taking a glass from beside the wash basin, I poured myself a single measure, took it back to the bed and sipped. The conversation with Miss Bidika troubled me. She'd assumed I was a representative of the Anglo-Indian Diamond Corporation. Was that simply because I was a *sahib*, or was there something more to it?

There were other things, too. Nothing significant, just odd. The first was Major Bhardwaj's reaction to the photograph of the dead assassin. The man had reminded him of a dead priest, he'd said. Then, when I'd asked him who would decide Miss Bidika's fate, the major had demurred — a Cabinet decision, taking into account the royal family's opinion. But the Maharaja was a god to his people, and in my experience, gods don't tend to delegate such decisions to committees.

When further sips didn't help, I knocked back the rest and poured another. A single measure of whisky is generally a false economy. It's better to start off with a double and save yourself the trouble of a refill. The second glass proved more useful. It occurred to me that Prince Adhir's brother, Prince Punit, would, as the new

Yuvraj, have a say in the running of things. It stood to reason that the Maharaja, at his age, might seek the opinion of his second son. Was that what Major Bhardwaj had been alluding to?

That particular deduction deserved a celebratory third measure, and I'd have poured it, had it not been for a knock at the door.

I opened it, to find Surrender-not standing at the threshold.

"What do you think they'll do to her?" he asked. He looked like a pint-sized Atlas with the burdens of the world on his shoulders.

"Who?"

"Miss Bidika."

"Come in," I said and sighed.

"I'm not disturbing you, am I?" he asked, walking in.

"Bit late to worry about that now."

I pointed him to the chair next to the desk. "I was about to have a drink, as it happens. You want one?"

"No, thank you." He eyed me suspiciously. "Your first one of the evening?"

I checked my watch. It had just gone six o'clock. Technically speaking, the first two had therefore been consumed while it was still afternoon.

"Yes," I said with the conviction of the righteous.

He ignored the chair and continued to stand. "Do you think they're going to charge her with complicity in Adhir's assassination?"

I poured myself that whisky.

"It certainly looks that way. She seems to be a thorn in the side of the royal family and I fear dissent is about

**144**

as welcome here as leprosy. Whether she's guilty or not, I'd imagine it suits their purpose to charge and convict her."

"And then what? Execute her?"

"They can't, not legally, anyway. I expect they'll lock her up, but I wouldn't put money on her coming out any time soon."

He fell silent, but it didn't take a clairvoyant to work out what was going on in his head. He was a hopeless romantic and Miss Bidika was a damsel in need of assistance. Rescuing her was the sort of thing he dreamed of, even if speaking to her afterward might prove a challenge.

"Do you think she's guilty, sir?"

"I doubt it. And the Maharaja doubts it too. He wants the real culprit caught. Why else would he agree to our involvement over the objections of his Dewan?"

Surrender-not nodded solemnly.

"So, Sergeant," I continued, "where should we begin?"

"You're the senior officer, sir."

"I'm on holiday, remember? And seeing as you're the one on the clock, you may as well earn your pay."

He extracted his notepad and pencil from the breast pocket of his shirt. "I suppose we return to first principles."

"Absolutely," I said, taking a sip of whisky. "And that means?"

"Motive," he said. "Who stood to gain from having the Yuvraj murdered?"

"Leaving aside Miss Bidika and her group of malcontents, who else could stand to gain?"

"Religious hot-heads?" he replied. "The assassin was dressed as a *sadhu*, a Hindu holy man. Maybe the prince was murdered as retribution for something he'd done to offend them?"

"It's possible," I replied. That the assassin took his own life suggested a degree of fanaticism which, outside of the Balkans, tended to be the preserve of the overly religious. But what exactly might Adhir have done? "We should ask Colonel Arora about that."

Surrender-not scribbled down the point in his notebook.

"Now, who else?" I asked. "Anyone closer to home?"

He tapped the pencil lightly against his teeth. "The most obvious beneficiary is his brother, Prince Punit. With Adhir out of the way, Punit becomes Yuvraj and next in line to the throne."

"Do you know him at all?" I asked.

Surrender-not shook his head. "No, he wasn't schooled in England. Second-son syndrome. His father sent him to Mayo College in Rajasthan. They call it the Harrow of India."

"We should interview him as soon as possible. Anyone else?"

"Not that I can think of."

"What about us?" I asked.

Surrender-not looked at me blankly. "We didn't kill him, sir. I'd have remembered."

"No, *us* as in the British government. Dawson was on the concourse at Howrah. Maybe Section H got rid

**146**

of Adhir, hoping it would smooth the path to Sambalpore's accession to the Viceroy's new talking shop?"

He looked sceptical. "Would the Viceroy sanction such a thing?"

It was a fair question. The Viceroy was, after all, about as dynamic as last week's lettuce. Yet the fact remained that Major Dawson *had* been at the station last night, and I doubted he was there to greet his mother.

I walked over to the window and rested my glass on the sill.

"Back in Calcutta, you suggested the Yuvraj might have developed a rather jaundiced view of the British from his time at school. What was behind that?"

Surrender-not rubbed his chin. His words, when they came, were guarded. I sensed he wanted to tell me everything but was conscious that what he had to say might give offence to an Englishman. Indians often did that, walking a conversational tightrope between speaking the truth and what they thought we wanted to hear.

"Well," he began, "of course there were the usual things, the name-calling and such, but I think what he really objected to was the fagging duties. He was a prince and saw himself as above all of that. I think the English boys knew this and made it worse for him."

I had some sympathy for the dead prince's point of view. Having to warm a frozen toilet seat for some stuck-up sixth-former every morning could, I imagine, very easily lead to a hatred of everything English for the rest of one's life.

"And do you know if he ever acted on this anti-British sentiment?"

He shook his head. "I've no idea. I hadn't seen him in years until two days ago."

The conversation was interrupted by a knock at the door.

"Captain Wyndham?" It was Carmichael's voice.

The door opened slightly and the Resident put his head round.

"I don't want to disturb you. I just wanted to say that dinner will be served in an hour. We have some other guests joining us tonight."

"Including that Fitzmaurice chap from Anglo-Indian Diamond?" I asked.

Carmichael gave an embarrassed laugh. "No, no. I believe he's dining at the palace tonight. No, our guests are of a different sort, but interesting nonetheless. The first is a Mr Golding, the kingdom's chief accountant. If there's one man who can give you chapter and verse on Sambalpore, it's him. Fabulous chap. Very keen on crosswords. He has me save copies of the *Statesman* for him, just so he can have a crack at the cryptic.

"And the other is a gentleman called Portelli. An anthropologist, and rather well regarded in those circles, apparently . . ." He tailed off. "Right then, I'll see you both in an hour." He closed the door behind him. Banerjee and I listened as his footsteps faded down the corridor.

Surrender-not looked grave, still probably preoccupied with the fate of Miss Bidika. I attempted to lighten the mood.

"Have you ever met an anthropologist before?"

"Not since Cambridge, sir."

"I knew one once," I said. "An old fellow by the name of Hogg who'd spent years living with a tribe in the Amazon. He gave a talk at a Salvation Army Hall in Whitechapel, illustrated it with a dozen odd photographs of tribal women looking like day-trippers from the Garden of Eden. There was only one photograph of the men of the tribe. It made me question the motivation for why certain men decide to enter the field."

"I best go get dressed," said Surrender-not.

"That's the spirit," I said, patting him on the shoulder.

I closed the door behind him and considered another drink. In the end I decided against. There were a lot of questions about Sambalpore that I wanted to ask over dinner and it was best to keep a clear head. The clock was ticking, after all. Unless we could find out who really was responsible for Adhir's murder, I feared Miss Bidika's fate could well be worse than the picture I'd painted for Surrender-not.

# CHAPTER
# SEVENTEEN

Emily Carmichael was a good-looking woman. Tall, blonde and with a flighty air that made me wonder how she'd ended up the wife of a diplomat.

She took charge at the dining table, personally showing her guests to their respective positions, and we sat down to dinner as a clock on the mantelpiece chimed seven. Other than the ornate fireplace, the room was simply and incongruously furnished — was there anywhere in the world less in need of a hearth? — and dominated by a mahogany dining table large enough to seat a regimental band and polished to a shine. On the wall hung the obligatory portrait of George V, and from the ceiling, a gently swaying wooden *punkah*. The only light came from a dozen candles placed in three candelabras situated at intervals along the table, which cast flickering shadows and gave the room an intimate air.

Two servants entered, both dressed in plain white *kurtas* and both barefoot. One carried a large silver tureen which he placed in the middle of the table, before ladling soup into bowls, while the other uncorked a bottle of white wine.

**150**

There were six of us in all, seated at liberal distances from one another: Carmichael at the head, his wife at the opposite end, Surrender-not and myself on one side, with the accountant, Golding, and the anthropologist, Portelli, on the other.

The accountant looked to be in his early forties, a thin man with short dark hair, neatly parted and flecked grey at the temples. Round, tortoiseshell glasses framed eyes that looked shaped by a lifetime of peering at ledgers. He picked at a tiny speck of something on the lapel of his dinner jacket before placing it on the table and wiping his hands on his napkin.

The anthropologist, by contrast, was a tanned, handsome fellow with short sandy hair and the look of a professor on sabbatical. He leaned forward and stuck a hand across the table for me to shake. "Portelli," he said by way of introduction.

"Italian?" I asked, as a servant filled my wine glass.

"Good Lord, no," he replied in impeccable English. "Maltese."

"Fascinating," said Mrs Carmichael. "I can't imagine there are many Maltese running around India."

I noticed her flawless complexion for the first time. As pale as milk, it suggested the most rigorous of efforts to stay out of the sun — no small miracle in these parts.

"You would be surprised, madam," replied Portelli. "There are a number of Maltese trading families in both Bombay and Calcutta. And it may also surprise you to learn that there is similarly a small but vibrant community of Indian traders, mostly from Sindh province, who have made their home in Malta."

It may indeed have come as a surprise to Mrs Carmichael, but judging by the speed at which she changed the subject, she didn't seem particularly interested by it. Instead, she took a sip of her wine and turned to me.

"So tell me, Captain Wyndham, what news of Calcutta? What are the ladies wearing these days?"

As far as I could tell, the women in Calcutta were wearing pretty much the same as they'd worn last year, and probably the year before that. The whole mass of petticoats, corsets, ankle-length dresses and flannel underwear that our women insisted on wearing, even in the stupefying heat of summer, in temperatures that left men dumbstruck, seemed like madness to me. They could have learned a thing or two from the native women, but of course, that was out of the question. We were British after all. We had standards. And so, our women, like the rest of us, went half-mad in the heat while wearing enough layers to allow one to comfortably take tea halfway up the Himalayas.

"Much the same as last season, I would imagine," I replied.

"I simply adore Calcutta," she gushed. "The theatre, the parties — not to mention the shopping. We are so cut off out here that sometimes I feel that if it were not for the rare visits from travellers such as yourselves, I should die of boredom. We receive the Calcutta and Delhi papers, of course, but they're generally four or

152

five days old by the time they reach here, and it's hardly the same thing as being there."

"Talking of Delhi," interjected her husband, "I sent off a telegram to the India Office informing them of your safe arrival." He seemed in ebullient mood.

Surrender-not and I exchanged glances.

"And was there any reply?" I enquired.

He shrugged. "I wasn't expecting any."

Mrs Carmichael turned to me. "Derek tells me you're investigating the crown prince's murder, Captain. How exciting," she beamed. "You must tell us all about it. Sambalpore is usually such a sleepy little place. Nothing interesting ever happens here. Derek says they've arrested the schoolmistress, that Bidika woman who always seems to have a bee in her bonnet about something or other. I can't imagine she's responsible, though."

"Why not?" I asked.

"Well," she said, stirring her soup, "for a start, I've met the woman. She may be many things, but she's not a murderess. As for the Yuvraj, I'm almost glad he's gone. Insufferable little man. He never had a good word to say about Derek — or many other people, for that matter. I wouldn't be surprised if his wife had him killed."

"His wife?" asked Surrender-not.

"Now, Emily," said Carmichael sternly, "let's not cast aspersions."

"Please," I said, "I'd be interested to hear Mrs Carmichael's thoughts on the matter."

Carmichael shot his wife a look which, if it was meant to cow her, failed miserably. I got the impression she wasn't the type of woman who was easily cowed by anyone, least of all her husband.

"Oh, come on now, Derek," she said brusquely, "it's hardly a secret. You told me the whole court knows about it."

"About what?" I asked.

"Why, his affair, of course."

"The Yuvraj was having an affair?"

"Absolutely," she said with more conviction than anyone should when making such accusations without first-hand proof. "Right here in Sambalpore, too."

"Forgive me, Mrs Carmichael," said Surrender-not, looking at her as though she was postulating differential calculus and he was having trouble following, "I don't understand how the Yuvraj *could* have an affair. His father has a harem. Surely any woman he takes a shine to simply becomes a bride or a concubine?"

Mrs Carmichael took a decent sip of wine and warmed to her theme. "Things aren't quite so simple." She grinned. "You see the lady in question isn't some local village girl, or even a high-caste princess. No, our Yuvraj found himself a *white* woman, and a *mem-sahib* no less." She laughed conspiratorially. "She goes by the name of Katherine Pemberley and they say he's besotted with her, that he was going to take her as his second wife. Can you *imagine* it, Captain? I could understand it if she was some common, working-class girl, like a waitress or that trapeze artist from Tooting that the Maharaja once bought a Daimler for, but this is a respectable woman from a good family. Derek says her father's an officer in the Admiralty. The notion that such a woman would have an affair with a native . . . Well, it beggars belief."

"He was a prince, though, madam," interjected Portelli.

"Oh, of course," she replied, "but still . . ."

"I doubt the royal family were particularly thrilled either," said Surrender-not drily.

"What?" said Mrs Carmichael, shooting Surrender-not a glance that seemed part irritation and part incomprehension.

"It's just that I'd imagine they'd find it hard to maintain the purity of their divine bloodline when the Yuvraj was involved with a white woman," he said defensively.

Mrs Carmichael seemed mollified somewhat. "I suppose that's possible. The Maharaja *can* be funny that way, especially given the curse."

"Curse?" I asked.

"It's nothing but stuff and nonsense," said Carmichael. "You shouldn't trouble our guests with these ridiculous superstitions, Emily."

"The natives believe it," Mrs Carmichael fired back. "And it's held true for as long as anyone can remember."

"What exactly is it?" I asked.

The Carmichaels exchanged a glance, but neither said anything further. It was the accountant, Golding, who filled the silence.

"They say there is a curse upon the royal household," he said. "The Curse of Sambalpore. It dates back several centuries to a time when the Maharaja's forebears were warrior kings. The details, though, are sketchy."

"Maybe I can help," said Portelli the anthropologist. "The story goes that the then raja became besotted with the wife of the ruler of a neighbouring kingdom. There was an alliance between the two, and the raja invited his fellow ruler to a banquet at the old fort, but then drugged him and slew him, before invading his kingdom and bringing the man's widow forcibly back to Sambalpore, where she was compelled to marry him. It is said that as the priest intoned the words of the marriage ceremony, the widowed rani cried out, calling down a curse upon the Sambalpori line for eternity."

"What sort of curse?" asked Surrender-not.

"That the wife of the ruler of Sambalpore shall be barren," he replied. "And so, bizarrely, it has proved."

"The current maharaja only inherited the throne because the wife of the previous ruler was barren. In turn, his own first wife, the First Maharani, has borne him no children. That is why he instituted the official practice of polygamy. Before him, the rulers of Sambalpore may have had concubines, but they did not take more than one wife. Both the late Yuvraj and his brother, Prince Punit, were born of the late Second Maharani, and little Prince Alok is the child of the Third Maharani, Devika. What's more, the Maharaja has not only increased the number of wives, he has also vastly inflated the number of concubines in the royal harem."

"That much is true," scoffed Golding. "Our esteemed maharaja certainly has an eye for the ladies."

"And the curse lives on," added Mrs Carmichael for good measure. "The Yuvraj's wife hasn't given him an heir either."

The servants entered and began clearing the detritus of the first course. I reflected on Mrs Carmichael's words. Curse or no curse, her accusations, however glibly made, deserved to be investigated. A white woman, a lady no less, engaged in an affair with a native prince. It was the stuff of fiction, the tawdry, titillating staple of those penny romance novels sold on station platforms back home. Surely such things didn't happen in real life?

I took a sip of wine as the ramifications of such a relationship sunk in. As Surrender-not had pointed out, it would be as objectionable to Indian sentiments as it was to ours, and it would go a long way to explaining why religious fanatics might want to assassinate the prince. I'd have to speak to this Miss Pemberley. And soon.

Dinner continued with more wine and more small talk. Mrs Carmichael had turned her attentions to Surrender-not, peppering him with questions ranging from the latest showings at the Rex cinema house to the domestic arrangements of the Lieutenant Governor and his wife. I felt sorry for the poor boy, but to his credit, he was making a decent fist of it, responding with monosyllabic replies to most of her questions, then really going for it when he got an easy one. It was the same technique he employed against off-spin bowling.

"So what brings you to Sambalpore, Mr Portelli?" I asked the anthropologist.

"I'm researching the local tribal customs on behalf of the Royal Anthropological Institute," he replied. "I was on my way to Puri for the *Rath Yatra*, the seven-day festival of Lord Jagannath, but when I heard of the unfortunate demise of the Yuvraj, the opportunity to witness the funeral rites of a member of the royal family was too good to pass up. So I made my way here."

"Well, you will certainly have your fill of the Juggernaut cult here in Sambalpore," Mrs Carmichael interjected. "The First Maharani's a devotee of that funny little heathen idol. She's even consecrated a temple to him on the banks of the river. Very superstitious she is. Goodness knows why the Maharaja married her. I once heard someone at court say she was the daughter of a sweeper, if you can believe such a thing."

Portelli smiled to himself. "The kingdom of Sambalpore is intricately linked to the legend of Lord Jagannath. The oldest known image of him is carved into the rock in a cave near Sonepur, not far from here."

"So why do people associate Lord Jagannath with the town of Puri?" asked Surrender-not.

"For one thing, the largest temple dedicated to him is there," replied the anthropologist, "and the king of Puri is venerated as the keeper of the sacred temple. But Sambalpore is also central to Jagannath worship. As you may know, he is said to have passed through the kingdom, in the form of a pillar of wood along the Mahanadi River."

Portelli was warming to his subject, and it seemed worthwhile indulging him. After all, anything was better than having to listen to Mrs Carmichael droning on about the hardships of being a diplomat's wife in an era of budget cuts.

"Can you tell us more about the deity?" I asked.

"Of course!" He beamed. "Jagannath — the name means 'Lord of the Universe' — is considered to be an avatar of Vishnu the Protector, the second deity in the Hindu trinity of gods who are responsible for the creation, upkeep and destruction of the world.

"And Mrs Carmichael is correct: Jagannath does look rather odd compared to most other Hindu deities. For a start, his idol is made of wood, while nearly all the others are fashioned from stone or metal. He is depicted as having overly large, round eyes, with stumps as hands and no legs. What's more interesting is that there is no clear reference to him in the *Vedas*, the oldest of the Hindu scriptures, and he doesn't appear in the classical Hindu pantheon. Indeed, it has been suggested that Lord Jagannath was originally a god of the forests, worshipped by the indigenous tribes of Orissa."

"What do you make of that, Surrender-not?" I asked.

"It's not a theory I've heard before, sir."

"I'm not surprised." Portelli grinned. "I am actively researching the idea that he was the god of the tribals and only became incorporated into Hindu mythology when your ancestors, the invading Aryans, arrived in Orissa."

He went on to tell the tale of the *Rath Yatra*, the story of how the strange wooden god, with stumps for arms and even less for legs, was each year transported in a giant chariot pulled by thousands of devotees to his aunt's house and then back again after a week.

Mrs Carmichael couldn't disguise her incredulity at the story, though what she thought more incredible: that a god would have no legs or that he would visit his aunt once a year was unclear. I too was sceptical, but if a god could appear as a burning bush then why not as a wooden stump? That, though, was the least of my concerns. The talk of Lord Jagannath had raised the spectre of something darker. Could it be that there really was a religious connection to the prince's murder?

"I wonder, Mr Portelli," I said, "if you may be able to help me with something else. Do you have an idea as to the significance of a certain marking that a holy man might wear on his forehead? Two white lines, joined at the nose, on either side of a thinner, red line?"

His face brightened. "You're speaking of the *Sricharanam*," he said. "The mark of the followers of the god Vishnu."

My mind raced. The markings the assassin had worn on his forehead was the mark of the followers of Vishnu. The man had disappeared into the crowd of the *Rath Yatra*, the procession of Lord Jagannath, whom Portelli had just told us was an avatar of Vishnu. He'd also signed into the Hotel Yes Please under the name of

Bala Bhadra, a play on the name of the deity's brother, and now it seemed that Sambalpore was central to Jagannath mythology. That was a lot of coincidences — and I don't believe in coincidences.

We were on the fifth or sixth bottle of wine by the time dessert arrived. Mrs Carmichael had settled into a state of happy inebriation, and the rest of us weren't far behind. From Carmichael's calm acceptance of his wife's condition, I took it that such an occurrence was probably not uncommon. In any case, who was I to judge? I imagined there was precious little for a young white woman who found herself marooned in Sambalpore to do of an evening other than to enjoy a drink or three. In her position I'd probably have done the same, and to be honest, I wouldn't have stopped at the drink. Not if there was opium available.

Golding and Portelli were discussing the arrangements for the Yuvraj's funeral, which was scheduled for the following day.

"Normally," said the anthropologist, "his eldest son would perform the funeral rites, but as he died childless, I imagine the duty will fall to his brother, Prince Punit."

"Not his father?" I asked.

"It's possible." Portelli shrugged.

His words pierced through Mrs Carmichael's drunken haze. She suddenly looked up. "I think that's highly unlikely. The word is that the old man's dying."

I turned to Carmichael for confirmation. "Is that true?"

By now, he'd given up any attempt to prevent his wife from saying things that the India Office might not approve of. "There have been some rumours," he said quietly.

"Oh come now, Derek," she continued. "Everyone knows he's off to Switzerland next month to see his doctors. The question is, will he come back?"

I had to hand it to Mrs Carmichael; she seemed to have more inside knowledge of the goings-on in the Sambalpore court than anyone else I'd met so far. If she ever tired of being a diplomat's wife, she could try for a career in intelligence. I'd happily introduce her to Section H myself.

"No father should have to bury his son," she continued, "especially after losing the boy's mother too . . ."

She let the sentence hang in the air, obviously keen to tell the story. I guessed it was salacious — three parts gossip to one part fact — and I wanted to hear it.

"What happened to her?"

A smile spread across Emily Carmichael's face, like the sun coming out from behind the clouds.

By the flickering candlelight she began to tell the story of the Yuvraj's mother — the Second Maharani — a beautiful princess, the brightest jewel in all of Sambalpore. Of a woman who had cemented her position at court by giving the monarch the male heirs he so craved. But she became bored: stifled by the world of the *durbar*, trapped in the confines of the *zenana*, while her husband lived it up in Paris and London. Mrs Carmichael told lurid tales of swimming pools filled with Dom Perignon and dalliances with telephonists and typists all mesmerised by the gifts lavished upon them and with thoughts of becoming a princess. Concubines were one thing, but affairs with European girls were quite another. Then came the tale of Miss Norma Hatty, a chiropodist's assistant from Bolton whom the Maharaja had met one night outside the Ritz.

"The Maharaja became besotted with her," said Mrs Carmichael, "and within the space of a month, had asked her to be his third wife. Of course, the little adventuress was overjoyed. She thought she'd hit the jackpot."

I could understand that. It isn't every day that a girl from Bolton gets the chance to become a princess.

"The Dewan and the Cabinet were panic-stricken," she continued. "The idea of such a common girl marrying into the royal family was anathema. A chiropodist's assistant as Maharani? Obscene."

"I imagine the situation wasn't helped by the fact that 'Hatty' sounds an awful lot like *hathee*," mused Surrender-not. "It means 'elephant' in Hindi."

Mrs Carmichael ignored the interruption. "What was surprising, though," she continued, "was that the only person who didn't seem to mind was the Second Maharani. Better, I expect she thought, to have Norma as a princess in the zenana where she could be kept an eye on, than to have the Maharaja's lover in the outside world. And she may have hoped that Norma would be a breath of fresh air in the stuffy world of the court.

"But it was not to be. In the end, the First Maharani prevailed on the Maharaja and convinced him that Miss Hatty was *unsuitable*, and the wedding was called off. Norma came out to Sambalpore anyway; they say she parked herself at the Beaumont Hotel and refused to leave until the Maharaja agreed to pay her half a million pounds." Her eyes widened as she marvelled at the sum. "I'm sure Mr Golding could confirm the amount."

The accountant coughed and took a sip of wine.

"You were telling us about the death of the Second Maharani?" I said.

"Oh yes. Anyway, the story goes that about a year after the whole Norma business, the Second Maharani decided she couldn't stand living in the harem any longer. She threatened to leave the palace and return to Calcutta. You can imagine the scandal. The wife of a maharaja leaves him and runs off to Calcutta. Of course, they tried to convince her to stay, offered her all sorts of inducements, but she was having none of it. In the end they threatened her. Told her she'd never see her two sons again. That's what made her reconsider.

"And then, within three months, she was dead. The doctors said it was typhoid fever but no one believes that. They say she was making plans to leave once again, and that she was murdered. Poisoned, probably."

Portelli let out an audible gasp, which caused the candles on the table in front of him to flicker. Golding's reaction was hidden behind the wine glass that he raised to his lips.

"By the Maharaja?" asked Surrender-not.

**164**

"That's the funny thing," said Mrs Carmichael. "By all accounts he was distraught at her death. He cancelled his trip to Europe for the season and remained cloistered in the palace. For a year he cut himself off from everything, including the running of the kingdom. They say that when he came out again, he was a different man."

The atmosphere seemed to die with the talk of the Second Maharani's possible murder. Golding had turned ashen-faced. He took another sip of wine while the conversation broke down into several small groups. Ignoring Surrender-not, Mrs Carmichael whispered quietly to the accountant while her husband discussed something with Portelli.

"Well," said Golding eventually, checking his watch, "if you will excuse me, I shall take my leave. It's getting late."

"Of course," said Carmichael, who seemed quite eager to call an end to proceedings himself. "Maybe we should call it a night."

That suited me well enough. It would give me a chance to have a chat with Surrender-not, assuming he still had his wits about him. Not that mine were as sharp as they might have been. It was now almost forty-eight hours since my trip to Tangra, and the aching in my sinews was getting worse. As the pain had grown, so had my enthusiasm for trying out the contents of my travelling case. My concerns over the foolhardiness of such a course of action, so concrete before, evaporated like the *afeem* above the flame of the opium lamp. I had an almost visceral urge to get to my room and the sooner I finished with the sergeant, the sooner I'd be able to assuage the hunger.

As the guests made their way to the drawing room, Golding pulled me to one side. He seemed somewhat the worse for drink. Sweating, he removed his bow tie and loosened his collar.

"Captain Wyndham," he said, in a hushed, wine-coated tone, "I need to speak to you." He pulled nervously at the signet ring on his little finger. "A most troubling matter."

"Of course," I said.

He looked around and spotted Emily Carmichael approaching with more drinks.

"Has it anything to do with the prince's assassination?"

He continued to fiddle with the ring. It was a curious thing, with the image of a swan etched on it. "I'd rather not say here. It's possible, I suppose. But I would urge you to tread cautiously."

"Shall we go outside?" I asked.

He shook his head resolutely. "No, no. Tomorrow. Early."

"Tomorrow then," I said. "I'll be at the Rose Building by nine."

"No, not there. I'll meet you here, at the Residency gates at eight."

# CHAPTER
# EIGHTEEN

I sat on a chair in Surrender-not's room, mulling over Golding's words. Something had spooked him. What exactly, I didn't know, but he'd seemed perfectly fine at the start of the evening. Was it something that had been mentioned over dinner, maybe one of Emily Carmichael's revelations, or was it just a case of the alcohol affecting his judgement? Either way, I'd find out at eight the next morning.

I glanced at my watch. The Germans had lobbed a shell at it, and me, during the war, and it had been a bit eccentric about keeping time ever since. It read a quarter after eleven. I took that to be a fair approximation, given that the second hand was still moving.

Surrender-not's room was smaller than mine, and less well furnished. The view was probably worse too but you couldn't tell in the dark.

"Well, that was interesting," beamed the sergeant. There was an alcohol-fuelled radiance to his face, as though he'd been out in the sun too long.

I didn't disagree with him. "I can't help feeling," I said, "that if Emily Carmichael was investigating this case, it would be solved within twenty-four hours. At

**167**

the very least she'd have rounded up a decent number of suspects."

He grinned. "Maybe we *should* interview the Yuvraj's widow, sir?"

"That's what I plan to do," I said.

That wiped the smile from his face. "Seriously?"

"She's got a motive. Or do you think that Indian women never murder their husbands?"

"To be honest, I'd be surprised, sir," he replied.

"I assure you, Sergeant, Indian women are just as capable of mariticide as their English counterparts."

He shook his head slowly. "Not Bengali women, sir. They just browbeat their husbands into submission. I doubt the need for murder would arise."

I couldn't tell if he was joking.

"Still," I said, "we *will* need to interview her, as well as the Englishwoman, Miss Pemberley, that the Yuvraj was apparently seeing."

"Fair enough, sir, but interviewing the princess?" He puffed out his cheeks. "Might that not prove somewhat tricky?"

"Why, because she's a princess?"

"Yes, but also . . ." he stammered, "because she'll be in the zenana. I would imagine that the only men allowed near her would have to be . . . you know . . ."

"You mean eunuchs?"

"Yes, sir." He blushed.

"Well, Sergeant," I said, "if we were forced to go down that route, it would at least solve the problem of your mother trying to marry you off."

After apprising Surrender-not about the scheduled meeting with Golding, I made my way along the corridor to my own room.

I locked the door behind me, pulled my suitcase from the wardrobe and placed it on the bed. My hands went to the locks, thumbs pressing down on cold, speckled metal. The clasps clicked open. I lifted the lid, threw the clothes that camouflaged my prize to one side, and paused.

My head spun.

I breathed out slowly and stared at the polished box with its silver decoration. In the quivering flame of the hurricane lamp, the dragon that formed the case's handle seemed to dance.

I felt as though I was at the edge of a clifftop. In front of me, a sheer drop into . . . I did not know what.

It was suicidally foolish to try smoking opium here. For one thing, the risks of being discovered were ridiculously high. One of the Carmichaels, or more likely one of their servants, might smell the telltale aroma. Given Carmichael's seeming fondness for cabling Delhi at the drop of a hat, if exposed, I didn't doubt that news of my habit would be hitting the wires before sunrise.

For another, I'd never prepared my own pipe before and my hands were hardly steady.

But as I stood there, it seemed that the very thought of lighting a pipe was putting steel in my nerves and ideas into my head. My doubts felt inconsequential. I reached into my trouser pockets and pulled out the packet of Capstans and a box of matches. The packet was half empty, but I figured only five or six cigarettes were necessary for what I had in mind. I took out half a dozen, lit them and placed them carefully in a tin ashtray which sat on the desk. Within minutes, a cloud of grey smoke began to fill the room. I looked on with satisfaction and for the first time felt I truly understood the meaning of the phrase, *necessity is the mother of invention*.

Leaving the cigarettes to burn, I turned to the travelling kit, lifting it gently from the suitcase and placing it on the bed. As I'd done on the train the previous night, I took the small silver key from my pocket, placed it in the dragon's mouth and turned it.

I don't remember emptying the box, but before I knew it, the red velvet case was bare and I'd laid out the items neatly on the floor in front of me. The pipe and its porcelain end pieces, the saddle and the pipe bowl, the opium lamp and glass cover, a wick, a small brass container I'd filled with coconut oil for the lamp, a selection of thin tools — some used in the rolling process, others for scraping the burned dross from the inside of the pipe bowl, and finally, the opium needle, without which the process of cooking the resin was futile.

I filled the lamp's reservoir with the oil, trimmed the wick and placed it into the lamp. I lit it and placed the glass shade over it. From a small compartment in my suitcase, I removed the ball of opium resin I'd liberated from the assassin's possessions and skewered it onto the needle. Settling onto my knees, I brought it above the flame, and began to try to emulate the actions that I'd witnessed in Chinatown a hundred times before.

The O softened as I turned and pulled it delicately over the flame, becoming viscous. A wave of elation passed over me. I was doing it; I was cooking the O, altering it from inert to magical. Like an alchemist transforming base metal into gold, I felt the secrets of the universe opening up to me.

And then it changed.

Something was wrong. The O began to smoulder, then char. I racked my brain. Had I forgotten something? Some crucial step in the process? Was I holding the O too close to the flame? I tried altering my technique, but even as I did so, I realised it was futile. The O was burning, not evaporating. I quickly transferred it to the pipe bowl and placed it in the saddle, in the hope that maybe some of the precious vapours were salvageable. I held the pipe to my lips and inhaled.

Bitter, charred smoke.

My heart sank.

I placed the pipe on the ground, then slumped to the floor beside it holding my head in my hands. A moment later, my body convulsed in a spasm of pain.

I don't know how long I lay there, but the opium lamp had gone out by the time I stirred. The pain had been replaced by a dull ache and a pounding in my head.

I stood up, and in the dim light of the hurricane lamp, wearily picked up the pipe. Removing the bowl, I stared at the remains of the blackened, brittle ball of O.

I picked it up and crushing it in my palm, I walked over to the window and threw the dust out into the windless night.

# CHAPTER
# NINETEEN

## *Monday 21 June 1920*

I fell asleep just before dawn. During the war, I'd learned to function on two or three hours' shut-eye, and it had been a habit I'd been forced to maintain ever since. In Calcutta, waking up wasn't exactly a problem. Anyone who's spent a night there could tell you that the city likes to wake you by attacking all of your senses at once: the cries of the cockerels and pariah dogs, the stench of the drains, the bed bugs feasting on your flesh. They all combined to render your alarm clock an irrelevance.

Sambalpore was different. It was quieter and it smelled better too, but that had its drawbacks. The silence meant I awoke with the suspicion that the sun was already far too high in the sky.

The flu-like symptoms had returned with a vengeance: pounding head, watering eyes. I'd gladly have paid a month's wages just to be able to turn over and lie there for another hour, but then I remembered Golding. I'd agreed to meet him at eight o'clock. I checked my watch. It had stopped at a quarter to three.

I wrenched myself out of bed, threw on a shirt and trousers and ran out of the door and down the stairs.

The clock in the hallway read ten to eight. Breathing a sigh of relief, I walked out into the compound in search of the accountant.

The sky was overcast, the air heavy. A native in white shirt and turban was busy raking gravel near the compound gates.

"Have you seen Mr Golding?"

"*Ji, sahib*." He smiled. "Golding *sahib* very nice man. He is coming yesterday only."

"Have you seen him this morning?" I asked.

"No, *sahib*," he replied with a regretful shake of the head.

I walked up to the gates, lit a cigarette and waited. After twenty minutes, the humidity and my headache became too much to bear and I headed back inside. There'd been no sign of the man. It was possible he was running late, but he didn't strike me as the sort of person who was ever late. If anything, I expected him to be early, especially as last night he seemed anxious to unburden himself of something. But then he'd had a skinful to drink. Maybe he'd sobered up and thought better of it. Or maybe he was sleeping off a hangover. Whatever the reason, he wasn't going to get off that easily. I would question him today whether he liked it or not.

Back at the Residency, Surrender-not was in the dining room having breakfast.

"Have you seen Golding?" I asked.

"I'm afraid not, sir," said Surrender-not. "Hasn't he shown up?"

"It would appear that he hasn't," I said.

"He did have rather a lot to drink last night. Maybe it slipped his mind?"

"Maybe," I said. I helped myself to a cup of black coffee from a porcelain pot on the table and pulled out a chair opposite him.

We heard a car pull into the compound and minutes later, Colonel Arora walked in.

"Would you care to join us for breakfast, Colonel?" I asked.

The colonel shook his head. "Thank you, no."

"You didn't pass Mr Golding on your way here, did you?" I asked. "We were supposed to meet at eight. Maybe people have a more liberal interpretation of time out here in the sticks," I added hopefully.

The colonel gave a short, bitter laugh. "Not our Mr Golding. He's always most punctual."

"And what are you doing here so early?" I asked. "I thought you'd be here at nine?"

"Maybe I have been learning from you English?" He grinned. "Anyway," he said, changing the subject, "I come bearing invitations. There is to be a small wake held this evening. His Highness the Maharaja has requested your presence. I'll send a car at seven to pick you up."

"Very well," I said. I checked my watch. Golding was now half an hour late. It didn't look like the man was coming. "Where's Golding's office?" I asked.

"In the *Gulaab Bhavan*," replied Arora. "The floor beneath yours."

"In that case, we should get going. Maybe we'll track him down there. Either way, there's plenty to do and we need your assistance."

A thin smile appeared on his lips. "I'm at your service."

Forty minutes later, we were back in our temporary office overlooking the gardens. We'd stopped by Golding's office on the first floor but it was locked. Now I took in the view as Surrender-not and the colonel discussed the list of people we wanted to interview.

"Out of the question," said the colonel vehemently. He rose to his feet, towering over Surrender-not. "Prince Punit — fine, that can be arranged; but Adhir's widow, the Princess Gitanjali, that flies in the face of all protocol. The maharanis and princesses, even the royal concubines, cannot be approached, and especially not by you, Wyndham."

"Me?" I replied.

The colonel sat back down and clasped his hands together.

"In two hundred years of our dealings with the British we have had to accept many things, but the one thing that has always remained inviolable is the sanctity of the zenana. Not just in Sambalpore, but throughout the princely states. The royal women must remain untainted. The late prince was not only my master but also my friend. Nevertheless, I would not request the Maharaja's permission for you to interrogate a princess of the royal household, even if I thought she'd murdered him herself."

"What about Sergeant Banerjee?" I asked.

Both he and the colonel stared at me.

"He's not an Englishman," I said, "even if he does sound like one. Maybe he could interview the princess? With you in attendance, of course."

The colonel shook his head. "No. It would be impossible without the Maharaja's express permission, and *he* would never accept it."

Surrender-not squirmed in his seat. "If I may, sir. It would be inadvisable to ruffle —"

I cut him off.

"At least ask him."

"Why do you want to question her anyway?" asked the colonel.

Given his rather fervent opposition to the idea, it seemed unwise to tell him that our request was based on the gossip of a rather tipsy Mrs Carmichael, so I did what any good detective would do. I lied.

"The Yuvraj received two notes, both of which were left in his apartments in the palace. Someone in the royal court was trying to warn him. Maybe his wife knows something about that. We wouldn't be doing our jobs if we didn't speak to her."

The colonel sighed, but didn't protest. That at least seemed like progress. "In the meantime, I'd like to examine the prince's rooms," I said. "I want to see exactly where the notes were left."

"Very well," he replied. "I'll organise it. Anything else?"

"There is a rather delicate matter," I said. "It's come to our attention that the prince was having a relationship with a *memsahib*, a Miss Pemberley. Were you aware of that?"

Arora's expression darkened. He stared at me and for a moment he had that cold look in his eye, the one I'd seen when I'd first met him on the steps of Government House in Calcutta.

"Of course I was aware of it. Whom do you think he charged with paying her bills at the Beaumont?"

"You didn't think to mention it to us?" I asked.

"It was irrelevant to your investigation. And the whole subject is frankly distasteful."

"You disapproved of the relationship?"

He paused.

"You can speak frankly," I said.

"His Highness's actions were not in the interests of the kingdom," he said finally. It was the answer of a diplomat. "Now if that's all," he said, rising to his feet.

"There's one more thing, Colonel," said Surrender-not, hastily retrieving a slim file from his satchel. He opened it, removed the photograph of the assassin's gun, which was now in an evidence locker at Lal Bazar, and handed it to Arora.

"Have you seen a revolver like this before, sir? It's five chambered with a folding trigger that only appears when you cock the pistol. It's quite distinctive."

The colonel gave the photograph a cursory glance, then handed it back. "It's a Colt," he replied. "A Colt Paterson. Obsolete, but effective."

"You've come across it before, then?" I said.

He gave a short laugh. "I should think so. I used to carry one. For many years they were standard issue to all Sambalpori officers. They were only replaced when we received modern weaponry from the India Office in 1915.

"Prior to that, your military wasn't too fond of providing the native states with arms, so we had to procure our weapons from other sources. The United States was one of them.

"I believe a stock of a hundred of these were purchased in the last century from the Americans. I understand that they once belonged to the Army of Texas, before that state became part of the union. Thereafter, they were used in the American Civil War, before becoming surplus to requirements and eventually being sold to Sambalpore.

"When the Great War broke out and the maharajas began raising regiments for the British war effort, your government naturally reconsidered its previous policy vis-à-vis arming the native states and replaced all our antiquated firearms with up-to-date weaponry. The Colts were supposed to be handed in, but a significant number went astray."

"The smoking gun," said Surrender-not quietly.

"What?" asked the colonel.

"This weapon was found on the assassin," I said. "We think it was the weapon used to murder the prince. That ties the killer back here to Sambalpore."

It also suggested that either the assassin or whoever had recruited him had some connection to the

Sambalpori militia, or had acquired the murder weapon from someone who had.

"Do you have any idea how many went missing?" I asked.

"I can't say, but there is one man who could tell you."

"Let me guess," I said. "Mr Golding."

The colonel smiled. "He's quite fastidious about stock takes."

"See if you can find him," I said. "Even if he's changed his mind about speaking to me, I still want to speak to him."

There was little else we required of the colonel for the present. He made some notes, then left, agreeing to inform us as soon as he'd set up the relevant interviews and arranged for access to the Yuvraj's quarters.

A few moments later there was a knock on the door. I assumed the colonel had forgotten something. Instead, in stumbled Carmichael.

He was sweating, which wasn't abnormal given the humidity, but it was the look on his face that worried me.

Surrender-not offered him a chair but he seemed in no hurry to sit down.

"What can we do for you, Mr Carmichael?" I asked.

"I'm afraid there's a problem," he stammered. "It really is most distressing."

He took a handkerchief from his trouser pocket and began to mop his brow. "I've received a cable from Delhi," he panted. "You have been ordered to leave

**180**

Sambalpore and return to Calcutta immediately after the cremation today."

I'd been fearing just such a development ever since Carmichael had informed us of the cable he'd sent. The fact that it had arrived from Delhi, however, and not from Calcutta, offered a glimmer of hope.

"And does it relate to both of us," I asked, gesturing towards Surrender-not, "or just me?"

"It simply says that Captain Wyndham is to be considered *persona non grata* in Sambalpore and is to return to Calcutta forthwith."

"But the Maharaja has asked for the captain's help," Surrender-not protested.

"I'm only telling you what it says," replied the Resident.

"From whom?" I asked.

"What?" he asked, flustered.

"Who sent it?"

"The secretary for native states, of course."

"I see," I said.

The telegram's wording, and its source, seemed damning. But I saw a possible way out. The cable had come from the secretary for native states, a man who was part of the Viceroy's inner circle. He was one of the top men in the Indian Civil Service. However, neither I nor Carmichael reported to the ICS. As an officer of the Imperial Police Force, I reported to my superiors in Calcutta, and he, as British Resident to Sambalpore, reported to the India Office in London.

"Well," I sighed, "it certainly looks like *you've* got a problem there."

He stared at me as though I'd just suggested he run through the palace grounds naked. "*I* have a problem?" he exclaimed.

"As I see it, what you've got is a cable from someone in the ICS, someone neither you nor I report to. I'm here on holiday and, as you know, the Maharaja himself has invited me to indulge my professional curiosity during my stay and observe Sambalpori policing methods.

"My leaving now would be construed as a gross insult to His Highness, the Sambalpori royal court and possibly the whole Sambalpori nation, especially when I have received no orders from *my* superiors to do so."

Carmichael's shoulders sagged and he finally slumped into the chair that Surrender-not had placed behind him. He looked queasy, as the true nature of the situation dawned on him. I didn't blame him. He was a career diplomat, a man used to a lifetime of following orders from faceless men on the other end of a telegraph machine. What was he supposed to do when those orders came from someone outside his chain of command and were actively questioned? Carmichael fell back on his training and, like any good diplomat, fudged the issue.

"I'll seek clarification," he said, "but in the meantime, I must insist that you vacate the Residency."

That was fine by me. Assuming they had any available, the rooms at the Beaumont Hotel were probably a damn sight more comfortable, not to mention the fact that they had electricity.

"Fair enough," I said. "If you're agreeable, we'll move our possessions out this afternoon, after the Yuvraj's cremation."

"Yes, well," he blustered, "I suppose that's acceptable."

"Now, if there's nothing further, the sergeant and I have work to do. I'm sure that you must be quite busy yourself. I imagine you'll be keeping up the British end at the funeral."

"Yes, of course," he replied, rising from the chair. "As you say, I best be getting on. I'll bid you both good day and see you there."

"It seems someone on high isn't keen on you being here," said Surrender-not, once Carmichael had left.

He was right, and there were two obvious candidates: the Viceroy, who had never really trusted me after the Sen affair the previous year, and the spies of Section H, who to be fair, never trusted anyone. But which of the two — and why — was a mystery. Once again, it suggested that there might be more to this case than religion or local Sambalpori politics. And that was troublesome.

"Well," I replied, "we've bought ourselves a reprieve, but it won't take Carmichael long to report back and get the matter clarified. If it's the Viceroy who's behind it, I doubt it'll take even a few hours for him to send the requisite orders to Lord Taggart ordering me back."

In truth, part of me was almost relieved at the prospect. My failure with cooking the O the previous night had left my nerves rather fraught. The thought of spending a prolonged period in Sambalpore, away from a secure supply of opium, was something I found myself shying away from contemplating.

Surrender-not, though, had other ideas. "There might be a way of forestalling him, sir . . ."

# CHAPTER
# TWENTY

"It'll never work," I said as we ran down the corridor.

"We've nothing to lose by trying," replied Surrender-not.

"We'll have to hurry," I said. "Carmichael's probably on his way over there now."

We were looking for Colonel Arora's office. I flung open the first door we came to and barged in, only to find it empty. Cursing, I turned around, just in time for Surrender-not to run smack into me.

"No one here," I said, as I manhandled him back out.

We continued our search, opening the doors of yet more unoccupied offices. It seemed as though the entire floor might be empty. Just as I was beginning to get exasperated, Surrender-not gestured for me to stop.

"Wait," he panted.

"Come on," I said. "You can rest when we reach Arora's office. And make sure you enrol for the officers' physical when we get back to Calcutta."

"No," he said. "There may be a smarter way of doing this, sir." He went into one of the empty offices, picked up a telephone and spoke to the switchboard operator.

"I need to speak to Colonel Arora urgently," he said. "Please put me through to his office."

I could hear the line ringing on the other end. Then he turned to me and smiled. "Colonel Arora," he said, "Sergeant Banerjee here. I have an urgent request, sir."

A few minutes later, we were standing in the colonel's office as he finished a telephone call. He replaced the receiver and stared up at us from behind his desk.

"It's done," he said. "There are two telegraph offices in town: one here at the palace, and the other at the station. Both shall be experiencing *technical difficulties* for the next hour."

"Thank you," said Surrender-not.

"Now, would you mind explaining to me the need for such action?"

Surrender-not looked at me and I nodded for him to continue. There was no good reason to keep the truth from Colonel Arora. More importantly, we hadn't had time to come up with a plausible lie.

"Mr Carmichael has received orders from Delhi for Captain Wyndham to return to Calcutta forthwith. Fortunately, due to an administrative error, the orders were received from the civil service and not the police. Mr Carmichael has gone to seek clarification from his superiors. Obviously, until such clarification is received, the captain is at liberty to remain here in Sambalpore . . ."

The colonel turned to me. "And why do they want you back in Calcutta, Captain?"

**186**

"They don't," I said. "If they did, the cable would have come from police headquarters in Calcutta, not from some pen-pusher in Delhi. They just want me out of Sambalpore."

"And why might that be?"

I didn't know, but I had my suspicions, all of them unhealthy and none of which I particularly wanted to share with the colonel.

"Your guess is as good as mine." I shrugged.

"So, you don't want Carmichael speaking to Delhi? Why can't he simply telephone them? There is, I believe, a telephone connection at the Residency?"

"Official orders need to come in writing, but now that you mention it, it might be nice if his telephone were to be affected too," I replied. "The monsoon rains might not have reached Sambalpore yet, but I understand that a lot of places between here and the capital are giving Atlantis a run for its money. It stands to reason that the telephone lines somewhere along the way might be down."

A smile broke out on the colonel's face. "I'll need authorisation. The Dewan might not approve, but I think His Highness the Maharaja may be agreeable. He enjoys cocking a snook at the British now and again. Indeed, he once presented Mr Carmichael with a golf bag and clubs as a token of Sambalpore's esteem for its noble Resident. Carmichael seems inordinately proud of it. What he doesn't know is that the bag is made from the skin of an elephant's penis. His Highness had it made especially."

"Interesting," I said. "If you manage to delay my recall by a few days, I'll make sure to challenge him to a game."

"You play?" asked the colonel.

"No," I replied. "I've never had the incentive till now."

The colonel let out a laugh, which was good in that it proved that he actually could.

"How long would you like Mr Carmichael's communications issues to continue?" he asked finally. "I can't cut him off indefinitely. Wars have started on lesser provocations, and I don't have permission to start a conflict this week. Besides, I would hate to be the man responsible for the end of British rule in India."

It was my turn to smile. "Of course," I said. "Mr Gandhi might never forgive you for beating him to it. But please, as long as possible. Ideally a week."

"Three days, maximum," he replied. "But there is a condition."

"Name it."

"You can never disclose to Mr Carmichael the provenance of his beloved golf bag."

"I think we can manage that," I said.

"In that case," he smiled, "you may rest assured that for the next seventy-two hours, Mr Carmichael will find it quicker to walk to Delhi than telephone or send a telegram there."

We were about to return to our office when there was a knock on the colonel's door. *Knock* probably wasn't the right word, though, as it sounded more like someone was taking a hammer to it. The door opened and in stepped a dark-eyed man with a beard as thick as an Axminster carpet. He was dressed in a flowing emerald-green silk tunic, belted at the waist, and carried an envelope which he handed to the colonel.

At a nod from Arora, he turned and stood beside Surrender-not, throwing the sergeant into shade as effectively as if he'd been standing under a tree.

The colonel tore open the envelope and extracted a single sheet of paper which he quickly unfolded and read.

"Well," he said, as though unsurprised by the contents. "Regarding the meetings you requested, His Highness has refused your request to interview the Princess Gitanjali."

Beside me, Surrender-not breathed a sigh of relief.

"What about Prince Punit?" I asked.

"His Highness has voiced no objections to that."

"Well, that's a start, I suppose."

Arora pursed his lips. "Not really," he replied. "The Yuvraj is leaving on a hunting expedition tomorrow. He has his brother's cremation to attend today. I doubt he'll make the time to see you."

"He's going hunting straight after his own brother's funeral?"

The colonel nodded. "It seems the hunt was scheduled to commence yesterday. The prince has been forced to delay his departure by over a day and is in no mood to extend it any further."

That was interesting. When my own half-brother, Charlie, had been killed during the war, I fell into a black slough of despondency for weeks, and I'd hardly known the boy. Hunting wouldn't have been high on my list of priorities.

"So where does that leave us?" I asked.

"You can still examine Prince Adhir's bedchamber; and interview the Englishwoman."

"That's not much to go on," I replied.

"Let me see what I can do regarding a meeting with Prince Punit. In the meantime, he'll also be attending his brother's wake tonight. Maybe you could ask him a few questions then?"

# CHAPTER
# TWENTY-ONE

The Yuvraj's apartments were located somewhere near the end of one of the wings of the *Surya Mahal*. It was difficult to be any more precise on account of the place being, well, the size of a palace, and because my mind was on other things.

We were following the man who'd delivered the note to Colonel Arora, with Surrender-not almost running to keep up. Eventually, we stopped at an arched doorway set into an alcove, ornately carved to resemble the feathers of a peacock and inlaid with jade and blue topaz tiles. The door itself was guarded by another bearded warrior of similar stature to our guide.

The two had a brief exchange of words. From the look of them, theirs was probably a language from somewhere near the North West Frontier. The sentry gave a stiff nod of acknowledgement, then opened the door and stood to one side.

Our guide turned to me. "His Highness the Yuvraj's quarters," he said and gestured for us to enter, before closing the door behind us.

We entered a small antechamber that led through to a larger sitting room furnished in a style that *House & Garden* magazine might have described as *oriental opulence*. The room was cool, despite there being no sign of a fan or *punkah*, and the smell of jasmine and attar of roses hung in the air.

"Nice place," mused Surrender-not.

"Mmm." I nodded. "We're certainly not in Premchand Boral Street any more."

"So what are we looking for exactly?" he asked as he walked through to an adjoining room which I presumed was the Yuvraj's bedchamber.

"I want to get a feel for the place," I replied. "There are few better ways of gaining an insight into a man than examining his living quarters."

"Even when the man's a prince?" asked Surrender-not sceptically.

He was toying with a few bejewelled trinkets that sat on a shelf recessed into the wall beside a large four-poster bed with gold silken sheets and a headboard inlaid with marble. He may have had a point.

I sat down on the bed. It was hard, probably packed with wadded cotton rather than sprung like a European mattress. This was a surprise. I'd assumed the prince's bed would be soft and westernised, like so much else in the palace.

I turned over one of the pillows. This too was hard in the Indian style. I remembered something the prince had said in the car journey across the *Maidan* before he was killed. He'd mentioned that he'd found one note under his pillow and the other in a suit pocket. It set me thinking.

Across the room from the bed stood an elegant writing desk. I walked over to it, pulled open the drawers and began to search through the contents: some official papers bearing the state seal, a few jewel-encrusted writing implements, but nothing of interest to me.

Closing the drawers, I walked into a small chamber replete with large wardrobes. I opened one and stared at a rack of thirty or so suits.

When I returned to the main bedchamber, Surrender-not was examining one of two silken tapestries that hung on either side of a gilded full-length mirror.

"Why?" I asked.

"Why what, sir?"

"Why were the notes left where they were?"

He looked at me blankly. "You mean in his quarters?"

"Why under the pillow? And why in the suit? Why not on his desk?"

"It's obvious, isn't it?" he replied. "Whoever left them there wanted to make sure that the prince, and only the prince, found them."

I got up, crossed the room and opened the one remaining door to find the prince's private bathroom. On a blue-tiled shelf sat over a dozen neatly folded white towels. I shook each one out, then dropped them in a pile on the floor.

"What are you doing, sir?" asked Surrender-not.

"Why leave two notes saying the same thing?" I asked.

The sergeant pondered the question. "I don't know, sir."

"Maybe because the first note wasn't found?" I suggested. "The prince said he'd found the first one under his pillow, and the second one in a suit pocket. But he's a prince, he probably has a hundred suits. What if the first one was left in his suit pocket and he simply didn't find it till later?"

I shook open the penultimate towel. A small white sheet of paper fell out and fluttered to the ground. I picked it up, opened it and looked over at Surrender-not.

"I think this might be the second warning note the prince was sent," I said. "It was a risk, leaving a note in a towel, especially when the prince seems to have enough of them to stock a Turkish bath, but it would be something that he and only he would be likely to use, and the chances of him finding it were probably greater than of him wearing one particular suit. When it wasn't discovered either, I'm guessing the third note was placed under the pillow, where he was almost guaranteed to find it."

"Their positioning implies a degree of secrecy," said Surrender-not. "If there was a plot to kill the prince, why didn't the informant simply tell him directly?"

"Think about it," I said. "The notes were written in the local language. That suggests they were written by a local. And someone with a very specific degree of education: enough to read and write, but only in the local language — a language that the prince himself didn't speak. Who would have access to the prince's bedchamber, but lack the stature or status to talk to the prince directly?"

The answer was obvious.

"A maidservant," said Surrender-not. "We should get back to Colonel Arora's office and request interviews with whichever maids would have serviced the prince's apartments." He walked back through to the sitting room and headed for the door.

"Wait," I said. "I've a better idea."

I crossed over to a table beside the prince's bed and picked up the telephone.

"You want to interrogate the maids now?"

Colonel Arora sounded somewhat exasperated.

"Who else would have left the notes in those particular places?" I asked.

"But how would a maid be aware of a plot to assassinate the Yuvraj?"

"We won't know that till we've talked to them," I replied.

"Very well," he sighed, "I'll see what I can do. I trust you've seen all you need to in the Yuvraj's apartments?"

"I think we're done here," I replied.

"In that case, I'd be grateful if you would meet me outside the Rose Building in ten minutes. A car will be waiting."

"Are we going somewhere nice?"

"That depends on your opinion of the lodgings of accountants," he said tersely.

"Has something happened to Golding?"

The colonel was silent. "I tried to locate him as you requested," he said finally. "He's not been seen this morning and he's not answering his telephone at home."

I felt a rising sense of dread.

"Is it possible he's gone off somewhere?"

"I doubt it," replied the colonel. "Even in an emergency, he'd never have left without informing someone."

The Mercedes drew to a halt outside a neat, mock-Tudor bungalow that wouldn't have looked out of place in Kent. A green-painted iron gate, set between high hedgerows, opened onto a path bisecting trimmed lawns and neat beds full of English flowers. The cottage itself appeared newly whitewashed, with its half-timbered frame painted the same shade of green as the gate.

The air was still, the silence punctured only by the calls of a mynah bird.

The driver waited by the car while Surrender-not and I made for the front door. Colonel Arora hadn't come with us. He'd left a note with the driver saying he'd been called off to deal with last-minute arrangements for the prince's funeral.

I reached for a large black door knocker and rapped it several times. We waited. There was no sound from inside the house.

"That should have been loud enough to waken the dead," said Surrender-not.

"Let's hope it hasn't come to that, Sergeant," I replied. "Make a circuit of the cottage. See if you can find any open windows or doors."

"Yes, sir," he said and moved off to scour the side of the house.

In the meantime, I walked around to the other side and tried to peer in through what I assumed were the living-room windows. The interior was dark and the window shrouded by net curtains, so it was impossible to make anything out. Returning to the front door, I gave it a hefty shove. It was solid, and locked, and I really didn't fancy shoulder charging it. The last time we'd tried to break down a door, we'd been met with a hail of bullets. Moreover, I was technically on holiday. Then I recalled that the owner was an accountant, and took a step back to lift the door mat at my feet.

I swore quietly to myself. No spare key.

Surrender-not returned from his circumnavigation. The look on his face told me all I needed to know.

"The rear door has been forced."

The garden at the back was larger, though just as neat as the one in front. A row of rose bushes with pink and red blooms ran close to the house and a table and two cane chairs sat under a jacaranda tree. It would have been a picture-postcard scene had it not been for the state of the rear door. Surrender-not had been conservative in his description when he said it had been "forced". It looked like someone had taken an axe to it. Half of it lay splintered on the ground, while the rest hung limply from one hinge. One thing was certain: Golding hadn't just decided to take the day off.

I pushed aside the remains of the door and stepped warily into the rear porch, shattered wood beneath my feet. The house was wreathed in silence. On the tiled floor stood a pair of brown riding boots.

With Surrender-not behind me, I opened the door to the next room, a kitchen which looked as if it had been hit by a bomb. Drawers pulled out, cupboards upended and crockery smashed on the floor.

I looked at Surrender-not. "Do you have your revolver, Sergeant?"

"I'm afraid not, sir," whispered Surrender-not. "It's back at the Residency."

I could hardly chastise him, not when mine was a few hundred miles further away in Calcutta.

"In that case, we'd better hope that whoever did this is long gone or is as complacent as we are."

We moved cautiously towards another door at the far end. I inched it open and viewed what would have been the living room. It was now just a chaos of overturned furniture. Books lay strewn on the floor, and the sofa looked like it had been disembowelled with a knife, a mass of grey cotton stuffing spilling from it. Thick velvet curtains had been pulled to the ground, their linings slashed.

From somewhere behind us came a crash. Startled, we turned and headed back towards the kitchen. Before I could warn him, Surrender-not threw open the door: a reckless act, given that neither of us was armed. Half expecting a volley of gunfire, I dived after him and

**198**

pulled him to the ground, but no shots rang out. Instead, on the floor in front of us stood a brown and black tabby cat, rather nonplussed by our entrance.

Surrender-not got up and brushed himself off. The cat meanwhile jumped onto a sideboard, sending more crockery crashing to the floor. I turned and went back to continue the search.

There was only one bedroom: a decent-sized room which had housed a bed, a wardrobe, a chest of drawers and a desk, but which now resembled a rubbish dump covered by a blizzard of feathers from a savagely hacked mattress. Drawers had been pulled out and their contents hurled liberally into the maelstrom.

I looked for signs of a struggle, but found none. The carnage in the room might have suggested one, but to me it looked like the results of someone searching for something. There were no traces of blood, though whoever had done this obviously had a knife. It appeared that Golding had been absent when the place was ransacked.

Surrender-not entered the room. He had the cat in his arms.

"You seem to have made a friend," I said.

"According to the tag on his collar, his name is Mordecai," he replied. "He must belong to Mr Golding."

It felt like the sergeant was jumping to conclusions. The back door wasn't exactly secure and the damn thing could have just wandered in behind us.

"How can you be so sure?" I asked.

The sergeant looked slightly taken aback at the question. "Because no Indian would ever give a cat such a ridiculous name."

The sergeant had a point. I knelt down and picked two framed photographs off the floor. The glass in one had shattered and fallen out. Both showed Golding, perhaps ten or fifteen years younger, standing beside a seated elderly woman. I searched the floor for other photographs but found none.

"What do you make of these?" I asked, passing the photographs to Surrender-not.

"Golding's mother?" he suggested.

It looked like the man was a bachelor, and I figured that a bachelor was more likely to own a cat than a married man was. Everyone needs some form of companionship, even an accountant.

I walked through to the bathroom and knelt down to examine the contents of a medicine cabinet that had been thrown into a zinc bathtub.

"What should we do with the cat?" asked Surrender-not from behind me.

"Just leave it," I said. "Cats can take care of themselves."

"It looks like an English cat, sir," he replied. "I'm not sure it would last five minutes on the streets in India."

I reminded him that our priority was finding Golding rather than worrying about his pet.

"Yes, sir. Sorry, sir," he said, abashed. "Do you think Golding was kidnapped?"

"If he was," I said, "I don't think it was from here."

"So where is he?"

"I don't know," I replied, picking up a small blue bottle that was half full of round white tablets.

"Maybe he's found himself in some kind of trouble and gone into hiding?" Surrender-not suggested. "He didn't seem particularly comfortable last night."

"Possibly," I said, though I doubted it. And as I examined the bottle of pills, I got the feeling that Golding hadn't intended on going anywhere for very long.

"His cottage has been ransacked." I said.

We were standing in Colonel Arora's office. He was sitting behind his desk drinking tea.

"You think he's been kidnapped?" he said, taking a sip.

"He might have been. Or he may have become embroiled in something and disappeared before they could get to him. It's hard to say one way or the other. But I don't think they took him when they upended the place."

"It is possible, though?"

The colonel set down the teacup and extracted a silver case from his pocket. Opening it, he offered us each a cigarette, then took one for himself.

"Whoever ransacked his cottage was looking for something," I said. "If they've kidnapped Golding, he doesn't seem to have told them where to find it."

"That's not to say they *didn't* find it," interjected Surrender-not. "From what we observed, they seem to have executed quite a thorough search."

"True enough," I agreed, "but I doubt it."

"Why?" asked the colonel.

"Every room in the house was turned upside down, even the bathroom. It would be odd for them to keep searching the place once they'd found what they wanted. So either they found it in the last room of the house or they didn't find it at all. My money's on the latter."

"And do you know what they were looking for?" asked Arora.

"I was hoping *you* might tell me."

He said nothing; just fixed me with a firm, expressionless stare. It was hard to tell what he was thinking, but from what I'd learned of the man over the last few days, I'd have wagered a sizeable amount that he was working out just how much to share with me. I was pretty sure that he was keeping something from us. After all, he had voiced his concerns about Golding's whereabouts within an hour of us asking him to find the man. In my experience, no one was ever *that* concerned with the well-being of an accountant out of mere goodness of heart.

"Do you know what he was working on?" I persisted.

This time the colonel was more forthcoming.

"He was preparing a report on the value of the kingdom's diamond mines. As you've probably surmised, Sir Ernest Fitzmaurice isn't just here to take the air. Anglo-Indian Diamond are once again sniffing around. This time, though, His Highness had instructed the Dewan to open a dialogue with regard to the potential sale of the mines. The Dewan was to report to Prince Adhir on the discussions. Golding was tasked

202

with preparing a report on the potential price that the kingdom might seek to obtain for the sale of the mineral rights."

"And now the prince has been assassinated and your accountant has disappeared," I said. "Do you suspect a connection?"

The colonel fixed me with his green eyes.

"Golding's a good man, Captain," he replied. "Scrupulously honest. Sambalpore needs men like him."

It wasn't an answer to my question, but it told me a lot. I took a pull on my cigarette. "I'd like to search his office," I said. "Maybe we'll find something there that will shed some light on his disappearance."

"Very well," said the colonel. "I'll arrange it immediately after the cremation."

"There's one other thing," I added. "Were you able to organise a list of the maids who would have had access to Adhir's chambers in the weeks before he was killed?"

The colonel picked up a sheet of paper. "I have the list here."

"Good," I said and turned to Surrender-not. "After the funeral, Sergeant, I want you to interview the women on this list. Hopefully you'll be able to find the one who left those notes for Adhir."

Surrender-not nodded slowly and took the list from the colonel.

"Very well," said the colonel, "I'll arrange for these girls to come to your office, one by one. I expect you'll also need a translator. Most of them won't speak anything other than Oriya."

"That's what we're counting on," I said.

# CHAPTER
# TWENTY-TWO

An hour later, Surrender-not and I were seated in a gilded, open-topped carriage pulled by half a dozen horses, each of whom looked like a potential Derby winner. They were held tightly in check by a turbaned coachman decked out in emerald and gold. It would have been an impressive sight by itself, but it was only one of twenty or more, a convoy of carriages relaying the members of the royal court.

Ahead of the procession walked a garlanded elephant, its tusks sheathed in silver. On its back, in a golden *howdah*, sat two natives blowing *kombus*, the large trumpets that produce an odd, high-pitched wail. Behind it came a phalanx of warriors in full ceremonial dress. They pulled a gun carriage, on which lay the mortal remains of the Yuvraj Adhir Singh Sai. There was no coffin, just his body wrapped to the neck in cloth and draped in the Sambalpori flag and myriad garlands of yellow and orange marigolds.

The procession wound its way through lanes choked with mourners. The streets were packed with men and boys, while small children perched in the branches of trees and women thronged the balconies and windows of the houses that lined the route. Flowers rained down from the rooftops.

Colonel Arora sat across from me.

"I have some good news for you," he said, leaning forward to make himself heard over the noise of the crowd.

"Good news isn't something we're used to," I replied, "I suppose it'll make an interesting change."

"I mentioned to His Highness your request to cut Carmichael off from the outside world. I'm pleased to say he found the idea most droll. He's agreed to the temporary severing of the telephone and telegraph lines for the next few days. In fact, he's considering implementing it more often. He says just seeing the look on the face of our dear Resident would be worth the inconvenience."

"That's a relief," I said. "It just leaves us with the problem of Carmichael kicking us out of the Residency."

"So you're homeless?"

"Unless you can secure us accommodation at the Beaumont?"

The colonel grinned. "Oh, I think I can do better than that."

The procession reached the edge of town and began crossing the bridge over the Mahanadi. The far bank of the river was less built up and the flowers no longer fell from above. With the crowds at the roadside stood a platoon of elephants, their ears painted and their flanks adorned in silks. As the gun carriage passed, a command rang out from a mahout and the elephants knelt in unison.

"Look, sir!" Surrender-not exclaimed, pointing. "I swear that elephant is crying."

I was about to laugh, but sure enough, the big grey beast did seem to have a tear in its eye.

"You are surprised?" asked Colonel Arora. "When a Son of Heaven returns home, why should the animals not also mourn?"

The cortège wound its way south along the riverbank. In the distance, the temple I'd spied from Shreya Bidika's prison cell came into view, its white marble tower rising high above.

As we drew closer, I saw that the edifice was embellished with the most graphic of carvings, gods and mortals intertwined in the sort of positions that your local vicar would probably never have imagined, let alone countenanced plastering all over the front of his church. And yet a vicar would be perfectly happy with gargoyles or stained-glass depictions of the damned burning in hellfire. It made me think. Why was it that we Christians seemed so squeamish about portraying scenes of love? What were our cardinals and archbishops so afraid of?

The procession came to rest at the gates of the temple compound. There, a guard of honour stood to attention like an exotic row of tin soldiers, their rifles held in front of them, and their golden turbans glinting in the sun. Beside them . . . the funeral pyre. It was larger than I'd expected, a pile of wood that could probably have been reassembled in the form of the *Cutty Sark*.

The dignitaries began descending from their carriages. Old men in white caps and white *kurtas* sombrely removed the garlands from the Yuvraj's body, placing them to one side with the reverence that priests show to holy relics. Then the soldiers lifted him from the gun carriage and gently carried him to the funeral pyre.

The Maharaja was helped down from the lead carriage by two attendants, while another held a large black parasol above his head. A throne of sorts — a raised dais, finished in red velvet and covered with cushions — had been placed before the pyre. Beside it stood a shaven-headed priest in a coarse saffron robe. His forehead was marked with two white lines, joined at the bottom, around a thinner red stripe: the mark of the followers of Vishnu.

The attendants held the Maharaja's hand and carefully assisted him to the dais, while the man with the parasol ensured no shaft of sunlight fell upon the royal head. The old man sat down, and another attendant with a large feathered fan began to wave a breeze for him.

The priest knelt and spoke a few words with the Maharaja. His Highness looked around, then pointed to a man dressed in white, who bore a striking resemblance to the dead prince. I guessed this was Punit, Adhir's younger brother, and that he would be performing his brother's funeral rites.

208

The congregation stood as the priest led Prince Punit over to one side, where a wood fire burned. Next to it was a small sack-cloth bag. The prince sat cross-legged before the fire as the priest lifted the bag and removed a silver vessel, into which he poured water from an earthen jug. I looked to Surrender-not for enlightenment.

"Do you know what's going on?"

"Vaguely."

"You're a Brahmin, for God's sake. Shouldn't your understanding be a bit more than just *vague*? What would your father say?"

"Not much, sir. He's an atheist. My mother, on the other hand —"

"Forget it." I sighed. "Just explain as best you can."

"Very well," he continued. "We don't believe in the resurrection of the body. It is but the earthly shell for the soul, which must be released to continue its journey. For that to happen, the soul requires to be fed. They are preparing the meal — a mixture of rice and sesame seeds."

The prince held the steel pot above the flames while the priest prodded at the fire with a bamboo stick. A thick white smoke curled from the end it. The priest took the pot from Punit then whispered something to him. The prince stood and began to walk slowly around the funeral pyre while the priest chanted a mantra, stopping every so often and waiting for Punit to repeat the words. The prayer complete, Punit returned to the priest's side. He took a handful of rice and sesame from the pot, fashioned it into a small ball and placed it on his dead brother's lips. The priest then passed him a sprig of wood. Punit dipped it in a pot of water and, reciting another prayer, he began to sprinkle water onto Adhir's body.

Taking a pot of *ghee*, the priest dipped his finger and drew three lines on Adhir's forehead. *Three lines*, I thought: just like the man who'd killed him, and the one who now administered his last rites.

The priest returned to the fire and began chanting, then lit a wooden torch and handed it to Punit, who walked over and held it to the funeral pyre. The pyre caught quickly, presumably brushed with something flammable beforehand, and as the flames spread, the priest's chants grew louder. I looked over at the dais. Tears glistened on the face of the Maharaja. Punit, though, betrayed no emotion. Chanting in a low murmur, he processed around the flames, soon followed by a procession of other mourners.

The scent of charred sandalwood filled my nostrils, as black smoke stung my eyes and the chants reverberated around my fragile head. I turned away and caught sight of a white woman in the crowd. She wasn't the only one in attendance: there were cooks, nannies, engineers and other staff from the palace, all dressed in sombre black. But this woman was different. She stood apart from the others, among the Indians, and she wore a white sari. The crowds parted. Momentarily I caught a glimpse of her face and my heart stopped. She looked so much like Sarah, my wife, that for a moment I thought I was looking at a ghost. She'd died back in 1918, but in that instant, the loss felt raw, as though it had only been weeks and not years. I tried to catch my breath.

"Who's that woman?" I asked Colonel Arora, pointing her out.

Arora nodded solemnly. "That, Captain," he replied, "is the Yuvraj's mistress, Miss Katherine Pemberley."

The priest's chants grew louder and a great sigh went up from the crowd. They surged forward and I lost sight of her.

I turned back in time to see Punit strike his dead brother's head with a stave. The colonel caught my surprise.

"He's piercing Adhir's skull," he said.

"Why?"

"So that his soul can be released."

The flames began to ebb. The mourners continued to circle the pyre with Punit at their head. The priest approached and sprinkled water onto the dying embers. Then he pored over the charred remains, sifting them with his bamboo staff. Suddenly, he bent over and with thumb and forefinger picked a small, blackened object out of the ashes.

"The *nabhi*," explained Surrender-not. "The navel. We believe it has a special significance. In the womb it connects us to the umbilical cord and to our mothers, and at death, at temperatures hot enough to turn flesh and bone to ash, for some reason the navel doesn't burn. It really is quite curious. We believe it contains our essence and must be returned to the earth."

I watched as the priest took the navel, packed it in clay and placed it in an earthenware pot. He handed it to Punit, who took it and walked from the pyre to the river. The prince waded in till the waters reached his midriff and submerged the pot in the waters. A cry went up from the mourners. When he returned to the shore, he made for the dais, then joined a number of dignitaries, taking a vacant chair next to Fitzmaurice. If that came as a surprise, it was nothing compared to what I saw next.

In the row immediately behind, next to Emily Carmichael, sat Annie.

# CHAPTER
# TWENTY-THREE

I left Surrender-not and began to run through the crowd towards her. The service over, the dignitaries had started to make their way to the waiting carriages, sharing in the muted small talk that follows a funeral no matter where in the world or what religion.

Punit was still talking to Fitzmaurice. I searched desperately for Annie's face, but there was no sign of her.

A trickle of sweat ran down to my collar. I stopped and cursed myself as a black fear enveloped me, a realisation that I might be seeing things that weren't there. First, mistaking Adhir's lover for my dead wife and now seeing Annie when I knew her to be in Calcutta.

But then I spotted her walking towards a car.

I breathed a sigh of relief and ran again without thinking. The car door was held open by a uniformed chauffeur.

I shouted after her. "Miss Grant!"

She turned, saw me and half-smiled. There was a spark in her eyes, and that defiance in her demeanour that had always fascinated me.

"Captain Wyndham."

"What are you doing here?" I asked.

"The same thing as you, I'd imagine. Paying my respects."

"When you didn't show up at Howrah station, I assumed . . ."

She seemed to bridle. "You assumed what, Captain?"

"That you weren't coming."

"Why? Because I didn't simply drop everything and come here with you? Did you honestly think I would?"

"And yet here you are."

It was a stupid remark, born of frustration and relief and of who knew what else, and I regretted it as soon as I'd said it.

"I'm here because I was invited by the family, not because of you. Now if you'll excuse me."

She turned.

"Wait," I said, reaching for her arm. "I hadn't meant . . . It was just a surprise to see you. A pleasant surprise."

Her eyes softened a little.

"How's your investigation going?" she asked, quietly.

"Badly. The Viceroy's trying to order me back to Calcutta and the Maharaja won't let me interview a key witness."

"Why not?"

"Because she's a lady of the royal court and I'm a man. The trouble is, I'm convinced the plot to murder Adhir was hatched here in Sambalpore."

She pondered my words, her expression suggesting she was unsure whether or not to offer me her sympathies, as though my investigation was as dead as Adhir.

"Maybe I can help?" she said.

I almost laughed.

"How?"

"You might not be able to question this woman, but I could. And I've met the Maharaja before. He might see things differently if it were me asking the questions."

"Are you serious?" I asked.

The look on her face answered the question.

"Do you want my help or not?"

Ten minutes later, I was in the back of a car with her, en route to the Beaumont Hotel. In the meantime, I'd tasked Surrender-not to return to the palace with the colonel and start interviewing the maids.

It turned out that by the time I'd telephoned her, Annie had already sent a telegram to the royal family, expressing her condolences. And they in turn had invited her to attend Adhir's funeral. Her arrival in Sambalpore had been even more noteworthy than my own, for if there was one thing that trumped the royal train, it was probably the royal plane. She'd flown in at the behest of Prince Punit, and had arrived that morning from Calcutta.

Annie applied powder to her face from a small, mirrored compact. "So, Sam, what have you discovered?"

"Precious little."

She snapped it shut. "Come now, if you want my help, you're going to have to be slightly more forthcoming than that."

I decided to be honest with her. Not just because she'd asked me to, but because a part of me wanted to tell her, and wanted her to be impressed. Though there wasn't anything particularly impressive in what I'd managed to piece together so far.

"Someone at court sent Adhir at least three notes warning him his life was in danger. And the local authorities have arrested a woman who's about as guilty of the crime as you are."

"Have you any leads?"

"I thought I had, but a man I needed to speak to seems to have disappeared and his house looks like it was visited by a couple of angry Japanese samurai."

For a moment she was lost in her own thoughts.

"So who do you need me to speak to?"

"If you get permission from the Maharaja, you mean?"

"Let me worry about that, Captain Wyndham," she said. "Besides, I can hardly get permission if you don't tell me who it is we need to interview."

"Princess Gitanjali," I said. "Adhir's widow."

The whitewashed Beaumont Hotel was an ocean liner of a building that seemed to have beached itself a hundred miles inland. I helped Annie from the car and walked into the lobby. Tiled floor, bare walls, and in one corner a table and chairs that had seen better days. On the table slept a rather neglected-looking cat.

"Thank you for the company, Sam," she said. "I should be seeing the Maharaja this evening. I'll try to have a quiet word with him. Is there somewhere I can contact you?"

"What?"

"Where are you staying?"

"To be honest," I replied, "I'm not sure. It's best if you leave a message for me care of Colonel Arora at the palace."

We said goodbye and I watched as she walked up the stairs. Then a thought struck me.

The reception was unattended so I rang the small brass bell on the desk. A native in a white shirt and bow tie appeared and flashed me a lopsided smile.

"May I be of assistance, *sahib*?"

"I've an appointment to see Miss Pemberley," I lied.

"Of course," he said. "If you don't mind, I'll send up a boy to inform her of your arrival."

I slipped a five-rupee note over the counter. "Just tell me which room she's in and I'll make my own way up."

The man looked around. The lobby was empty save for the pair of us and the cat.

"Room fifteen," he said, pocketing the note. "First floor."

I thanked him and headed for the stairs.

I knocked on a thin wooden door, rattling it on its hinges. A moment later it was opened and Miss Pemberley stood there, still dressed in her white sari. I took a sharp breath: the resemblance with Sarah was uncanny. Miss Pemberley's eyes were red rimmed and her blonde hair, so neatly tied back at the funeral, now hung loose.

"Miss Pemberley?" I asked.

"Yes?"

She seemed somewhat distracted. It was understandable, given the circumstances.

"My name's Captain Wyndham. I'm from the Imperial Police Force in Calcutta. Would you mind if I asked you a few questions?"

"Why do you want to talk to me?" There was a defensiveness to her tone. But then many people were unnerved by the thought of being questioned by a policeman.

"I'm assisting with the investigation into the late Prince Adhir's assassination. I understand that you and he were close. I was hoping you might be able to help me."

She hesitated for a moment, uncertain. I guessed she was still in shock. The cremation was probably the first time she'd seen the prince's body since he'd been murdered and doubtless the magnitude of it all was only now beginning to sink in.

"May I come in, Miss Pemberley?"

Her attention snapped back to the present.

"Of course," she said, standing to one side.

The room was a mess. Half-filled suitcases sat on the bed, and garments and other belongings spilled from a trunk which sat open on the floor. She must have noticed my reaction.

"Please excuse the state of the place," she said apologetically.

"You're leaving?" I asked.

"There's no reason to stay here any longer," she replied. Then she shook her head. "That's not true, but at any rate, I can't."

I directed her to a small sofa in the corner of the room beside French doors leading to the veranda. I took the chair beside her.

She sat down and composed herself. "So, Captain," she said, "what would you like to know?"

"Maybe you could tell me how you first met the prince?"

She nodded. "I met Adi about three years ago."

"In Sambalpore?"

"No, in London. It was at a function at the Oriental Club — a reception honouring the contribution of the princely states to the war effort. I accompanied my father who was there representing the Admiralty. Adi was there, along with the Maharaja. They were being feted for raising a regiment of Sambalpore volunteers, and for their financial contribution, of course.

"I ended up seated across from him at dinner. We hardly said a word to each other, but I could tell he liked me. More than once I caught him staring. In fact, he was quite brazen about it. At the time I remember thinking how rude it was, that this Indian should presume to stare at me without being in the least embarrassed.

"Two days later, a letter arrived, stating that the prince would like to meet me for tea at the Ritz that afternoon. Well, I was young and silly in those days and I couldn't believe the man's impertinence. At the same time, I was flattered. The thought of a liaison with a prince . . . well, it's every girl's dream, isn't it? In the end, I decided to go along and meet him.

**219**

"I turned up, half expecting him to be dressed like a character out of the *Arabian Nights*, but there he was, in a Turnbull and Asser shirt and a Savile Row suit; he might have been an English gentleman but for the colour of his skin —"

She broke off and looked out of the window, seeing, I guessed, not Sambalpore but maybe the Palm Court at the Ritz.

"Miss Pemberley?" I nudged.

She pulled a handkerchief from inside the cuff of her blouse and gently dabbed one cheek.

"I'm sorry," she said.

"Of course," I said, worrying that she was going to break down. In such a situation, there are only two reliable measures to ward off the water works. The first of course was tea, but there was no telephone to call down to reception and order a pot, so I was forced to try the second. I pulled out the packet of Capstans from my pocket and offered her one of the few cigarettes I had left.

She shook her head. "Thank you, no. I don't smoke," she said apologetically.

I was out of ideas. It meant that if the tears started, I'd be forced to pat her on the shoulder, and that wouldn't be pleasant for either of us. I'd misjudged her, however. She didn't break down. Instead, she dabbed her eyes and refolded her handkerchief.

"You went to meet Prince Adhir at the Ritz," I prompted.

"Oh yes. There and then he asked me to marry him. Told me we'd run off to India and I'd become a princess. Promised me a life I could only dream of."

"And?"

"Oh, it was tempting for about ten seconds. I'd read the stories about girls who had gone off and married Indian princes. It's all wine and roses in London, but then they take you home to their little bit of India, which is generally some two-bullock town in the middle of nowhere, where time hasn't moved on since the seventeen hundreds, and suddenly you're stuck in the harem, just one of ten wives and God knows how many concubines, wondering what the hell happened.

"That, Captain, was not the life for me. I told him I was flattered, but that no, I wouldn't be running off to India with him."

"And yet here you are." The phrase was an echo of the words I'd spoken to Annie less than an hour before.

She shrugged. "I don't think Adi was used to being rejected. It only made him try harder. He sent me flowers, then jewellery: small things — earrings, a necklace. I didn't really think much about it until Mama took them to Hatton Garden and had them valued. Anyway, I agreed to meet him again. He told me then he'd extended his stay in London, just to be near me. Well, something stirred in me. I saw a different side to him — a vulnerability.

"In the weeks that followed, he courted me most assiduously, and I began to appreciate him more. He wasn't just some spoiled princeling; he really *did* want to better the lives of his people. In the end, I agreed to come out here, not as his wife, but as his friend, and only if I could do some good." She smiled to herself. "I remember how happy that made him — like a puppy with a new toy. He organised a position for me at the local school here and a month later, we flew out together. I started work at the school, teaching English, and Adi . . . Well, out here he was a different man. He showed me the kingdom, its people and its wildlife. He wasn't much of a hunter, unlike his father and his brother.

"It was an idyllic time. We'd go for picnics in the jungle, and fly to Bombay for the weekend. I was falling in love with him. And I felt I was making a *real* life for myself here, not just with the children, but with some of the mothers, too. India's a conservative place, but in some ways the people can be surprisingly open minded . . . the women, at least.

"Then, about six months ago, things began to change. Adi's father took a turn for the worse. The onus fell on Adi to take up the reins. He became caught up in the affairs of state, but he still tried to make time to see me."

"What sort of things took up his time?" I asked.

"Sambalpore's proposed accession to the Viceroy's Chamber of Princes for a start," she replied. "Adi was dead set against it, despite the pressure from the India Office and from his own ministers. He doesn't really like the British."

"Other than you, of course?"

She smiled. "Sometimes I think Adi's courting of me might just have been another way for him to take a potshot at the British. Not that I could blame him. You know we were followed by Scotland Yard?"

"Really?"

"Oh yes. We were passing through Paris on our way to St Moritz last year. Adi spoke perfect French. He'd arranged to meet some Indians from Berlin there. They wanted his support for their campaign for Indian independence. All the time we were there, Adi was sure we were being followed. He even pointed out one particular man who turned up in at least two restaurants we visited. Adi said it was the man's suit that gave him away. He said no one but an English policeman would be seen dead wearing a suit from Moss Bros in the French Alps."

Now that was interesting — not so much the suit, but Adhir's suspicions. Of course, they weren't proof that they'd actually been followed, and it wouldn't have been Scotland Yard men but agents of the Secret Intelligence Service who'd have watched them, but it was definitely possible. Indian political agitators were a key target of the security services. If the intelligence services were tailing Adhir in Europe, it stood to reason they'd be liaising with Section H here in India, and it might go some way to explaining Major Dawson's presence at Howrah station a few nights earlier.

"Is there anything else he was involved in?"

"There's the business with the diamond mines, of course. The Anglo-Indian Diamond Corporation have been sniffing around. One of their directors has been virtually camped out in this hotel for most of the past six months. Adi said they would be making an offer soon."

"Do you know if he was minded to sell?"

"Only if the price was right."

"Did His Highness have any involvement in religious matters?" I asked.

"Not that I'm aware of." She shrugged. "He wasn't really one for religion. He was happy enough for the people to see him as divine, but he didn't believe any of that stuff himself. It's his stepmother, the First Maharani, who deals with the kingdom's religious issues. She's very pious. It's hard to believe the Maharaja would have married someone like that."

There was one question I'd been avoiding. It was a difficult thing to ask a grieving woman but I had no choice. I braced myself.

"Do you have any idea who might have wanted the Yuvraj murdered?"

She fixed me with a stare. "Isn't it obvious?"

"Please humour me, Miss Pemberley."

"His brother Punit of course. With Adhir out of the way, that leaves just him and the infant Prince Alok as the Maharaja's legitimate heirs. Punit's next in line to the throne. And with the Maharaja so poorly, he will likely be ruler by Christmas."

Punit was high on the list of suspects, especially since Colonel Arora had told me of his reluctance to cancel his hunting expedition after his brother's murder. And, as Surrender-not had also suggested, he did have the greatest motive of all. Still, it was important not to jump to conclusions.

"What about Adhir's wife?" I asked. "How did she react to him spending so much time with you?"

She raised one hand and tugged distractedly at her earlobe.

"I really don't know," she replied. "From what Adhir told me, she and Adi were married when they were little more than children. He said that she accepted the role of a princess of the royal house of Sambalpore and all that came with it — the *purdah*, the concubines, even the curse. I take it you've heard about the curse?"

I nodded. "So you don't think she'd have reason to murder her husband?"

"Maybe if she were English, Captain. But as far as I know, she was content with her situation."

"Do you know a woman called Shreya Bidika?" I asked.

"Of course," she replied. "I worked with her at the school. And I can assure you, she is in no way connected to Adi's death."

"You're sure, Miss Pemberley?" I asked. "By her own admission, Miss Bidika is not an admirer of the royal family. Indeed, she'd be happy to see the back of them."

She considered this for a moment. When she replied, it was in slow and measured tones. "I've known Miss Bidika for over a year now. It's true, we disagree on the royal family, but . . ." She fell silent.

"What exactly did you disagree about?"

"The value of the Maharaja and his family to the people of Sambalpore. Shreya would point out their extravagance: the concubines; the jewels; the sheer waste; while their subjects, the farmers and the villagers subsisted on close to nothing, each day a balance between life and death.

"But she failed to see the good that the family has done. The irrigation projects, the electricity, the schools . . . You seem surprised, Captain. I can tell you that the royal family has a complex and deep-rooted relationship with their subjects. They may be pampered, but they have obligations to their people too; obligations they take very seriously. As for Shreya, she may be many things, but she's not a killer. Besides . . ." Her voice trailed off.

"Besides what, Miss Pemberley?" I asked.

She hesitated, taking the handkerchief from its resting place, but this time, holding it gently to her mouth. Something in her eyes changed. The look of pain was replaced by something else: a determination of sorts.

"Shreya knew of my relationship with Adi."

"You'd discussed it with her?"

She nodded. "Sambalpore's a small place. I needed someone to talk to and Shreya was a sympathetic ear. She advised me to follow my heart.

"So you see, Captain. I can't believe she has anything to do with Adi's murder. Does that shock you? That I should confide in a native woman, especially when there are quite so many other Englishwomen at court?"

There wasn't much that shocked me these days. She was testing me, trying to see what sort of an Englishman I was: the type who believed that consorting with the natives as equals in some way

226

denigrated our whole race; or the other type. The type who realised that such attitudes were all sham and pretence and hypocrisy rooted in guilt. But I had no reason to let this woman know which of the two I was.

"I suppose," I said, "that sometimes it's easier to confide in a total stranger than among one's own."

She smiled weakly. "I can tell you, Captain, that Shreya was more of my *own* than those Englishwomen will ever be."

# CHAPTER
# TWENTY-FOUR

It was mid-afternoon by the time I returned to the office in the Rose Building. Surrender-not bolted upright as I walked in.

"So Miss Grant decided to follow you here after all, sir?"

"In a manner of speaking," I replied, taking a seat at the other desk. "Any luck with the maids?"

"Yes, sir," he said gravely. "We've found the one who placed the notes in Adhir's bedchamber. She's in Colonel Arora's office now."

"Well?"

"Well what?"

"Did she write the notes?"

He shook his head. "No, sir. She's illiterate."

My spirits sank faster than a depth-charged U-boat.

"So we're back to square one."

Surrender-not broke into a thin smile.

"Not necessarily, sir," he replied. "You see, she was handed the notes by one of the women in the zenana. You were right, sir. The plan was hatched *inside* the palace."

"So who gave them to her? Adhir's wife?"

"No."

"Then who?"

"That's the problem, sir. It's another woman of the harem, a concubine named Rupali. I asked Colonel Arora to set up an interview, but in light of the Maharaja's rejection of our request to speak to the Princess Gitanjali, he refused point-blank."

The frustration was etched on his face. My reaction was similar. There were now two women I needed to speak to, and the only hope I had was that Annie somehow convinced the Maharaja to let her interview them on our behalf. In the meantime, there was something else we urgently needed to do.

Golding's office was on the same floor as Colonel Arora's. It was small and stuffy and crammed with boxes of indexed files: almost every flat surface piled high with papers and folders, and all weighed down by paperweights, little glass worlds with pieces of coral or coins at their heart. The walls too were covered in paper, charts filled with numbers competing for acreage with maps of the kingdom of Sambalpore, each marked with a myriad symbols and crosses. The ceiling fan was switched off and hung impotently.

"Judging by the state of his office," said Surrendernot, "are we sure the mess in his house was the result of a break-in?"

I ignored the remark. "Let's just see if we can't find the report he was working on for the Yuvraj," I said. "The one to do with the sale of the mines to Anglo-Indian Diamond."

I instructed Surrender-not to go through the avalanche of papers. He had a head for these things which I lacked even at the best of times. In my present state, the whole room felt impenetrable, like being trapped inside a telephone directory. I turned to the charts on the walls. One in particular caught my attention. At the top, "MINES" had been written in black ink and beneath was the outline of the kingdom of Sambalpore, a shape I was becoming familiar with: the Mahanadi River running north to south, with Sambalpore town on its right bank. Upriver from it, a dozen crosses had been marked in red. Then, to the south-west, one more solitary cross, this time marked in black.

"What do you make of this?" I asked.

Surrender-not turned away from his papers and walked over.

"The location of diamond mines, I'd imagine, sir."

"What about this black cross down to the south-west?"

Surrender-not shrugged. "Maybe a disused one?"

There was a knock on the door and in walked Colonel Arora.

"Making progress?" he asked.

"It's hard to say."

"Well, maybe this will help," he said. "I've arranged rooms for you at the guest lodge in the palace grounds. Your belongings are being taken there as we speak."

A cold shiver ran down my spine. After my failed attempt to smoke last night, I'd packed away the opium travelling kit in my suitcase, but in my hurry to make the meeting with Golding this morning, I couldn't recall whether I'd locked the bag.

The colonel noticed my hesitation.

"I trust that is in order, Captain?"

"It's fine," I said. "Thank you."

When he left, I tipped the contents of one of Golding's desk drawers onto the floor. My mind continued to race, consumed with fear that the travelling case would be discovered. At that moment I could have stumbled upon Golding's suicide note without noticing it; I may actually have been on holiday, for all the good I was doing. Luckily, Surrender-not was still on the clock.

"You might want to have a look at this, sir," he said, from under a pile of documents.

"What is it?"

"It looks like Golding's diary."

He passed it to me and I flicked through the pages: business meetings, deadlines for submissions of documents, the usual schedule of a bureaucrat.

There was only one entry for today — a time and a place but no name — *6.30p.m. New Temple.*

# CHAPTER
# TWENTY-FIVE

I checked my watch. It was just after six p.m.

Once more I flicked through the diary. Almost every other appointment had a name next to it. Just who was Golding supposed to meet with at half past six, and why at the temple?

"Come on," I said, grabbing my jacket off the back of the chair and making for the door.

We ran down the stairs, out into the courtyard and over to the garages at the rear of the building.

"That one'll do," I said, heading for the old Mercedes Simplex.

The car's black bodywork glinted in the dull light.

"Have you got the key?" asked Surrender-not.

"We don't need one." I pointed to the slot under the car's radiator grille. "You have to crank start it. Now get in," I said as I retrieved the crankshaft from its home. "The engine has a tendency to kick when it starts and I don't want you getting injured."

Sure enough, there was a clatter as I turned the crank, then the glorious noise of the engine exploding into life as the car jerked back like a wild horse.

We were soon speeding through the palace gates, making for the bridge across the Mahanadi. The road was blessedly quiet. Other than a few sari-clad washerwomen returning from the river, the route was the preserve of cows and the occasional bullock cart. I couldn't help feeling that whoever Golding was supposed to meet, they were somehow connected to what he'd wanted to tell me. Would his contact show? Or would they know of his disappearance and decide to hightail it too? A little part of me even held out the faint hope that Golding might turn up himself; that he'd avoided his abductors and lain low in order to have this meeting. The adrenalin coursed as I accelerated along the dusty road, hoping to reach the temple before six thirty.

The light had died by the time we arrived and I pulled the car off the road a few hundred yards from the compound and parked behind a grove of trees. From there we quietly covered the distance to the temple gates on foot. I sent Surrender-not to scour the perimeter while I took up station under the canopy of a sprawling banyan tree.

The scene seemed tranquil enough. Several old men and women sat cross-legged and quiet outside the entrance. None of them looked like the sort whom Golding would have a meeting with.

Surrender-not, fresh from his circumnavigation of the compound walls, came over.

"Anything to report?"

"Nothing, sir. There are no other entrances."

It meant we would only need to maintain watch on one location.

"Good," I said. "In that case, all we have to do is stay here and see who shows up."

As we waited, others joined the small group at the entrance and within twenty minutes the crowd had swelled to almost fifty people.

Then, on the stroke of seven, a bell sounded. The gates opened and out walked several saffron-clad priests who proceeded to distribute alms. Shortly, the crowd began to disperse and the priests returned to the compound.

"It doesn't look like anyone's coming," I said.

"Should we wait?" asked Surrender-not.

I checked my watch. It looked like our dash to the temple had been a wild-goose chase. Whoever Golding was supposed to meet seemed to know he'd disappeared. There was little point in hanging around. Besides, Colonel Arora would be expecting us.

"We don't have time," I said. "Let's go."

# CHAPTER
# TWENTY-SIX

I gripped the steering wheel tightly as we drove back towards town. It had been a long shot, admittedly, but in my gut I had expected something to happen at the temple.

Beside me, Surrender-not was silent and sullen. His expression irked me more than it should have. I put that down to frustration and the dull ache inside my skull.

Arora was still in his office at the Rose Building.

"Anything?" he asked.

I kept my responses vague, but in any case he seemed too anxious that we not be late for the Yuvraj's wake to pick up on any deficiency in my answers.

"We should leave for the guest lodge," he said. "No doubt you will wish to change for dinner."

The guest lodge was a handsome villa nestling just out of sight of the main palace. We were left in the care of a liveried manservant who led us inside and up a flight of stairs, explaining the history of the building as he went. I paid him scant attention. The only history I was interested in was what had happened to my suitcase during the previous twelve hours.

"Your room, sir."

I thanked him as perfunctorily as possible without seeming rude, entered and locked the door behind me. The room was on the tasteful side of opulent, furnished with the obligatory suite of French furniture and a four-poster bed as big as a tennis court. I ignored it all and headed straight for the large teak wardrobe, almost tripping on the tiger-skin rug on the floor. The thing had a mouth the size of my head. I pulled the handle of the wardrobe and flung open the door.

My bowels turned to ice.

My clothes lay neatly folded on a shelf. There was no sign of the suitcase. Turning, I frantically scanned the room, finally spotting it on a foldable table in one corner.

I all but ran over and pressed the buttons releasing the clasps. They snapped back, and with a degree of trepidation I hadn't felt since the war, lifted the lid.

I breathed a sigh of relief.

The opium kit was still in there, and it was still locked. I fished out the key from a small silk pocket in the suitcase's lining and opened it. All the pieces were snuggly in place. My secret was still safe. Nevertheless, I cursed myself for the idiocy I'd displayed in deciding to bring it to Sambalpore in the first place.

After taking a shower, I was surprised to discover a starched white shirt and black tuxedo and tie hanging beside my own shirts in the wardrobe. As I dressed, I tried to make sense of what I'd learned.

Adhir was turning out to be a more complicated man than I had perhaps expected. Katherine Pemberley had only corroborated what Shreya Bidika had told me the day before. Adhir wasn't just some dilettante. He was loved by his people, and, it seemed, also by an Englishwoman. That last thought was bitter. It triggered something in me, something that I instinctively recoiled from.

I forced myself to focus. Plenty of white men had native mistresses; hell, the woman I'd been keen on for the last twelve months was hardly lily-white, so why should it be different when an Indian man fell in love with a white woman? But it was different. It was something that every Englishman knew — or rather felt — because it was never taught to you explicitly. You just absorbed it, along with the rest of the rubbish about the superiority of the white man. And while I could discount most of that nonsense, it seemed that love between an Indian and an Englishwoman was something I couldn't quite accept.

And then it struck me. I realised that what I found truly distasteful was not that an Indian should be attracted to a white woman — that, though undesirable, was at least understandable — but the idea that she might return his love. It wasn't, I found, something I wished to dwell on, though whether that was from an aversion towards Miss Pemberley's feelings or my own, I couldn't say.

Instead, I turned my energies to more productive ends. The number of potential suspects was growing and now included, as well as Punit, the dead prince's wife, the British security forces, and Anglo-Indian Diamond. The only person I felt I could discount was the woman whom the authorities had actually arrested for the crime.

Then there was the pressing issue of the missing accountant. Was there a link between Adhir's assassination and the disappearance of Mr Golding?

My train of thought was interrupted by a knock at the door.

"Captain Wyndham, *sahib*?" came a voice from the hall outside. "Colonel Arora is waiting for you."

I thanked the voice, finished tying the bow tie and slipped on the tuxedo jacket. It was a pretty decent fit, almost as good as the one hanging in my *almirah* back in Calcutta. I switched off the ceiling fan and made my way out of the room.

We pulled up outside the entrance to the *Surya Mahal*. Several other motor cars were parked already, the palace lights reflecting off their polished chrome and paintwork.

Arora led the way, past a line of guards and eventually to a set of doors, which, at a word from the colonel, were flung open to reveal a smoke-filled sitting room, large enough to swing the proverbial elephant. To one side stood Sir Ernest Fitzmaurice, holding forth to Carmichael with a whisky in one hand and a cigar in the other. The Resident appeared to be agreeing

**238**

wholeheartedly with him; indeed, Carmichael seemed the type to agree wholeheartedly with most things the businessman might say.

On a sofa in the centre of the room sat Mrs Carmichael and an attractive young Indian woman in a green sari. The Resident's wife was cooing over the woman's sapphire-studded necklace, and her companion seemed somewhat embarrassed by the attention.

In a far corner, removed from the other guests, the Dewan and Major Bhardwaj stood huddled, their conversation kept to a whisper. The Dewan was dressed in a cream, knee-length *kurta*, while the major wore his militia uniform, his chest plastered with enough medals to make you think he might have robbed the royal mint.

"Who's that?" I asked, gesturing towards the young Indian woman, as an attendant came over with a bevy of champagne flutes on a silver tray.

"That, my dear fellow," replied Colonel Arora, "is the Maharani Devika, His Highness the Maharaja's third wife."

That came as a surprise, not just because she looked young enough to be the king's granddaughter, but more particularly because I'd assumed the royal women weren't at liberty to wander around attending palace functions. I knew they took trips out in the *purdah* car, but I'd assumed it was only to places where there were no men present.

"She's not restricted to the zenana?" I asked.

The colonel shot me a look that suggested the question was either ridiculous or insulting.

"Captain," he sighed, "the zenana is not a prison. Just because men are not allowed inside, it does not therefore follow that the women are not allowed out. Its occupants are free to come and go as they please."

"Then why can't I interview Princess Gitanjali?" I asked.

The young maharani glanced over. She really was very beautiful.

The colonel took a sip of champagne, then read the look of confusion on my face.

"We've been through this, Captain. There are protocols to consider."

Before I could protest further, the doors opened and this time, Annie walked in, dressed in a black silk sari, its border embroidered with golden flowers. Her dark hair was tied back, and at her neck was the diamond-studded choker she'd worn in Calcutta. It was the first time I'd seen her in native dress and she glided into the room like some goddess made flesh.

Colonel Arora's face lit up.

"Miss Grant," he said, "it is a pleasure to see you again."

Annie returned his smile and walked over. Arora took her hand and kissed it.

"And may I say how radiant you look tonight."

It seemed he and Annie were already acquainted. It stood to reason, I supposed. She was a friend of Adhir's and Arora was the dead prince's ADC. Still, it irritated me slightly.

240

Arora turned to me, "May I introduce Captain Wyndham and Sergeant Banerjee of the Calcutta Police."

"Oh, these gentlemen and I are old friends," she replied, extending her hand for me to kiss. I was happy to oblige.

"Really?" exclaimed Arora.

"It's a small world," I said.

"That it is," added Annie. She had a mischievous look in her eye. "In fact, we all have a mutual acquaintance. The industrialist, James Buchan," she explained. "It was at one of his receptions in Calcutta that I was first introduced to Adhir and Colonel Arora." She turned to the colonel. "You must forgive Captain Wyndham, Colonel," she said. "He's not a great fan of Mr Buchan. But then the captain tends to view most men with at least a degree of suspicion."

The colonel looked to me, then back to Annie, and seemed unsure of how to respond. "Well, I'm sure the captain agrees with me that you look most elegant tonight," he said finally.

"I'll admit she scrubs up rather well," I replied.

"Why, thank you, Captain," said Annie with a smile. "And may I return the compliment. It's been so long since I've seen you in a tuxedo I was beginning to fear you'd forgotten how to tie a bow tie."

I felt my hand reach for the bow tie at my throat. She wasn't far wrong.

Sensing my discomfort, Arora attempted to diffuse the tension.

"Come, Miss Grant," he said, taking her arm. "Let me introduce you to some of the other ladies."

I took a sip of champagne and looked on as he led her over to Mrs Carmichael and the Maharani Devika.

I heard Surrender-not sigh beside me.

"What's wrong, Sergeant?" I asked.

"Nothing, sir."

"Spit it out," I said. "I'll be damned if on top of everything I'm going to have to worry about what's upsetting you all evening."

"I was just thinking that Colonel Arora seemed quite taken with Miss Grant, sir."

"Absolute nonsense," I said, pointing him in the direction of the bar. "I honestly have no idea where you pick up such ridiculous notions. Let's get a proper drink before your imagination gets any more carried away."

Sir Ernest Fitzmaurice broke off from his conversation with Carmichael and smiled as we walked over. Carmichael, however, seemed less happy to see us.

"Two double whiskies," I said to the barman, before turning my attention to the Englishmen.

"Any news from Delhi, Mr Carmichael?" I asked innocently.

"The telegraph lines are down." He frowned. "Apparently, the monsoon's washed away the lines to the north of Sambalpore. There's no way of getting a message out."

"That's a pity," I said, picking up one of the crystal tumblers that the barman had placed on the bar. "Have you tried the telephone?"

"Telephone lines are down too."

"Well, in that case, I suppose I should stay on until communications are restored. It wouldn't do to insult the Maharaja by upping sticks and leaving, especially after his gracious invitation to stay."

Carmichael downed his gin.

"And you, Sir Ernest?" I asked. "Are you planning on staying long?"

The businessman cast a sour look in the direction of the Dewan and Major Bhardwaj.

"I'll be glad to get back to Calcutta as soon as possible," he replied. "Assuming the city hasn't been washed away. I've heard the rains are coming down something fierce back there."

"You don't like Sambalpore?" I asked.

He took a pull on his cigar. "It's a bit too far from civilisation for my liking."

I surveyed the room and its well-heeled guests drinking cocktails and champagne.

"What did you make of the funeral today?" I asked.

"Quite a spectacle," he snorted, "and rather melodramatic for my tastes. I mean, crying elephants, for Christ's sake."

"Did you know Prince Adhir well?"

He took a sip of whisky. "Not well. We had business dealings, but he wasn't really my cup of tea."

"That's interesting," I said. "From what I'd heard, he seems to have been quite the man of vision. Brilliant even. People have told me that he would have made an excellent ruler."

"Yes, well," interjected Carmichael. "He was definitely intelligent. Maybe a bit too intelligent."

"A rather slippery fellow." Fitzmaurice nodded. "Difficult to pin down in negotiations."

"And you think it will be easier to deal with his brother?"

"Let's hope so." He smiled, raising his glass.

Before I had a chance to press him further, the door opened and in strode Prince Punit. All eyes turned towards him while his eyes turned towards the ladies. He was dressed in a tuxedo that had been tailored in a style sharp enough to slice your hand off. He walked into the centre of the room, his patent leather shoes reflecting light like a mirror, and gave a cursory nod to Carmichael before coming over to Fitzmaurice, who transferred his drink to join the cigar in his left hand, then proffered the right one to the prince.

"My dear Sir Ernest," said Punit, ignoring the outstretched hand, "I hope you're being well looked after?" The man might have been educated in India but his accent was as English as his deceased brother's.

"Of course, Your Highness," replied Fitzmaurice, managing, in one fluid gesture, to turn the rejected handshake into the first flourish of a bow. "Your father's hospitality is, as ever, impeccable."

"Wait till you try the food!" replied the prince. "We've a new chef in our employ since your last visit: a Frenchman, no less. He was head chef for the Romanovs until the damn Bolshies shot them. Still, it worked out nicely for us." He grinned. "We're fortunate to have obtained his services. They say both the George

244

Cinque Hotel and the King of Sweden wanted him, but naturally our budget stretched further than theirs."

The prince's eyes strayed back towards the ladies gathered around the sofa.

"Will His Highness the Maharaja be joining us?" asked Carmichael.

"What? Oh, I expect so." The prince gestured towards the young Maharani. "Otherwise I doubt Devika would be here." He turned his attention to Surrender-not and me. "You must be Messrs Wyndham and Banerjee," he said.

"Your Highness," I said.

"I understand you've both done sterling work tracking down my brother's killer," he said. "My family is in your debt, gentlemen."

I thanked him for that. "Is there a time when we could talk to you about your brother?" I asked.

"Talk?" he asked. "I'm afraid it'll have to wait a few days. I've a hunt planned for Sir Ernest for tomorrow. It's already been cut short by this terrible business and I'm determined he gets to shoot something."

"A pity," I said. "His Highness your father was most keen that we speak to you." It was a lie, but I felt it to be in a good cause.

"We'll try to fit something in later this week. Now, if you'll excuse me, gentlemen," he said, gesturing towards the ladies, "I really should tend to our other guests."

I watched as the prince sauntered over to them. Carmichael turned to Sir Ernest. "You think you can do business with him?"

Sir Ernest puffed on his cigar. "Oh, I'm sure of it," he said, a faint smile forming at the corners of his mouth.

The prince exchanged a few words with the Maharani Devika, who kept her replies short, never looking directly at him.

Next, Punit gave Mrs Carmichael significantly more attention than he had her husband, and she burst into sudden laughter. If she hoped that was a prelude to a longer conversation, she was to be disappointed: immediately, the prince turned his gaze on Annie. His actions became just that bit more animated, as men's often do in the presence of beautiful women, and I realised that, from the moment he'd entered the room, it was she who'd captured his attention. It's not as though I hadn't seen it happen before; it's just that it had never previously been a prince that she'd captivated, at least not while I'd been watching. She smiled as he took her hand and kissed it, and I felt something turn over in the pit of my stomach. The prince gave a bow, and for a moment I was sure Annie glanced in my direction. Then she was smiling and talking to Punit once again.

I caught Surrender-not looking at me.

"What is it, Sergeant?"

He gestured at the still half-full glass from my hand. "Would you like a top-up, sir?"

A gong sounded announcing the arrival of the Maharaja. He was leaning on a cane and aided by a grey-haired woman in a dark blue sari and a simple golden necklace. Beside them was a toddler dressed in an ivory silk *kurta* with emeralds for buttons. The Maharaja looked ashen faced, his dinner jacket hanging off his thin frame.

"Who's that with the Maharaja?" I asked Carmichael.

"The boy is His Highness Prince Alok, the Maharaja's third son. Devika is his mother."

"And the woman?"

"That, dear boy, is the Maharani Shubhadra, the Maharaja's first wife and our illustrious First Maharani."

She was a petite woman, a head shorter than her husband, with a kind, intelligent face, like that of a favourite aunt. She looked over at me and smiled.

The Third Maharani, Devika, had risen from the sofa when the Maharaja entered the room; now she went over to him. She kissed the little boy and spoke a few words to the First Maharani, then took the Maharaja's hand. If there was any animosity between the wives, I didn't see it. Instead, there seemed to be a tenderness, a squeeze of the fingers and a glance between them that spoke volumes. The First Maharani, her job done, turned and smiled at the assembled guests, then left the room, taking the infant prince with her.

Meanwhile, I caught the look on the Maharaja's face as his third wife whispered to him. He smiled as he looked at her. There was no doubt he was in love with her, but what was more interesting was the look the Maharani gave *him*. I was no expert, but it seemed that the young woman loved him back.

With the Dewan and Major Bhardwaj in tow, the Maharaja and his third wife slowly began a circuit of

247

the assembled guests, starting with Sir Ernest Fitzmaurice. Before they had made much progress, however, an attendant entered. The Maharaja eyed him expectantly.

"Dinner is served."

The dining room was dominated by a long mahogany table beneath a brilliant chandelier, flanked by large *punkahs* covered in green baize. On the table itself sat a golden locomotive modelled on the royal train we'd boarded in Calcutta. The miniature engine hauled wagons loaded with bottles of champagne and spirits along silver tracks that ran the length of the table.

We were shown to our seats by liveried waiters. The Maharaja took his place at the head, with Carmichael to his left and the Dewan to his right. Beside the Dewan sat Fitzmaurice with Annie next to him. Any hope I'd harboured that the call to dinner might draw to a close the conversation between Prince Punit and Annie lasted about as long as a cold spell in Calcutta, as I noticed the card with his name next to hers at the table.

The Third Maharani took the seat at the far end of the table, opposite the Maharaja, and I took the one to her right.

The waiters set to work, unfolding napkins and filling glasses. The Maharani Devika was fussing over something with the servants, while Mrs Carmichael talked at her husband. That left me with little to do but try to ignore the smiles and witticisms that seemed to be passing between Punit and Annie on the other side of the table. This shouldn't have proved too difficult given the quality of the 1907 Montrachet, but it took a few glasses before I truly started to appreciate the stuff.

When the young Maharani eventually turned to me, our fleeting conversation was the only bright spot of my evening.

"The food is not to your taste, Captain?" she asked in an accent somewhere between British public school and Swiss finishing school. She really was beautiful, not that you'd expect any less from the young wife of a maharaja. Large, brown almond-shaped eyes and a certain enigmatic air.

"On the contrary," I replied. "I just seem to have lost my appetite."

She caught me glancing in Annie and Prince Punit's direction. "Yes," she said, delicately touching her napkin to her lips, "I can understand that, given the circumstances."

That gave me a jolt. Were my feelings that obvious?

"It seems wrong to enjoy such things at a time like this," she continued, directing a hard, disdainful glance at the prince.

As if on cue, the prince's voice drifted over. "My dear Miss Grant," he said, "you simply must come to see the Côte D'Azur. There really is nowhere else like it." He turned towards Fitzmaurice. "I say, Sir Ernest. You have a yacht, don't you? You'll lend me it for a few weeks?"

"Of course, Your Highness," said the old Englishman. "It would be my pleasure."

The Maharani certainly had a point. My dislike for the prince was growing, and though it might have been rooted in his attempts to woo Annie, equally I wondered what sort of man could plan a Mediterranean cruise mere hours after lighting his own brother's funeral pyre.

The meal ended abruptly, which came as a relief. The Maharaja whispered something to an attendant, who then helped him slowly to his feet. He winced with the effort and the Third Maharani, noticing her husband's distress, rose and quickly made her way to his side. With cursory apologies, the royal couple then left the room.

The only one who seemed genuinely put out by this turn of events was Punit, and before long he had corralled the rest of us back into the salon. At a bark from the prince, an attendant cranked up the gramophone and the room soon filled with the strains of Charles Harrison singing some sickly sweet tripe about apple blossom.

I needed a proper drink. "Fancy a nightcap?" I asked Surrender-not.

He shook his head, and to be honest, he looked like he'd already had more than was good for him.

"Join me for one at least," I said.

"Very well, sir." He sighed. "I'll have a whisky, but only a small one."

"That's the spirit," I said, and headed for the bar to request two doubles.

"So, what did you make of the papers in Golding's office?" I asked a couple of minutes later as I handed him his glass. He weighed it dubiously before taking a sip.

"The man was certainly thorough. He had costings for everything from concubines' allowances to diamond processing fees. I'm going to need more time to go through it all, sir. I was hoping to start afresh tomorrow morning."

"Did you find the document he was working on for Prince Adhir — the valuation report on the mines?"

"Not yet . . ." He paused. "The funny thing is, I've found a lot of working papers — calculations of extraction rates, geological surveys and the like — but I couldn't find the actual report. Not even a draft."

"Maybe he had them destroyed?"

Surrender-not shook his head. "The man had kept records of nannies' salaries from twelve years ago. I got the impression he wasn't the sort to destroy anything."

"You think someone might have taken the report?" I asked.

"It's possible, sir."

"Who'd benefit from stealing it?"

"Someone trying to derail the sale of the mines to Anglo-Indian Diamond?" He shrugged.

"But surely that would merely cause a delay? I'd imagine a new report could be drawn up in short order, especially as you say the working notes are all still there."

"Then who?"

"Maybe someone who wants to know what the report says before it becomes public knowledge?" I looked over at Sir Ernest Fitzmaurice who was in conversation with the Dewan over a couple of cigars.

"But that doesn't explain Mr Golding's disappearance," replied Surrender-not.

"It doesn't explain very much of anything," I said. "Now drink up before your whisky evaporates."

He took a gulp, then winced.

I looked over at Annie. She was busy indulging Punit.

"Miss Grant seems to be fitting in well," said Surrender-not. "One could almost imagine her as a princess of the House of Sambalpore."

In hindsight, forcing that double whisky on him might have been a mistake.

"That's perceptive," I said. "I'd forgotten about your encyclopaedic knowledge of the ways of women."

He laughed. "Thank you, sir. I owe it all to you, my mentor. How is the pursuit of Miss Grant progressing?"

I took a sip. "Sometimes, Surrender-not, the thrill is in the chase."

"In which case," he chuckled, "you may be the most excited man in India . . . sir."

"You know, Sergeant," I said, "maybe leave the rest of the whisky. You've a lot more of Golding's papers to inspect tomorrow and I won't have time to play nursemaid to your hangover."

"Very sensible, sir," he said. With that he made his excuses, said goodnight to the others and headed for the guest lodge.

I stood at the bar with my back to the room and tried to ignore the murmur of conversation behind me. The aroma of cigar smoke drifted over as I slowly sipped the malt and thought of Prince Adhir. I considered the possibility that Punit had murdered his brother. If he felt any grief at the loss of his sibling, he was doing a damn good job of hiding it. I downed the whisky and ordered another.

As I waited, I caught the scent of Annie's perfume. I always felt a tightening in the pit of my stomach when I smelled it. I felt a touch on my arm.

"Enjoying yourself, Sam?"

"Not particularly," I replied, "but then, I don't often enjoy myself at a wake."

"Is that what you think this is?" She smiled. "I'd expected a tad more prescience from you."

The barman returned with my drink and Annie ordered a pink gin.

"I suppose you think it's a coronation for your new friend."

"Hardly."

"So tell me," I said. "If this isn't a wake or a coronation, what is it?"

"Isn't it obvious?" she said, lifting the glass proffered by the barman and taking a sip. "It's a puppet show."

"What?"

"Think about it, Sam. Have a look around the room. See who's here, and see who's pulling the strings."

"I have no idea what you're talking about," I said. And it was true. But that didn't mean I didn't appreciate the fact that she was talking to me and not to Punit.

"Captain Wyndham," she said, "you've drunk too much for your own good. Maybe you'll see more clearly in the morning."

Not without a hit of O, I wouldn't. I changed the subject.

"Did you get a chance to speak to the Maharaja about interviewing Adhir's widow?"

"No," she replied, "but I did mention it to his wife."

"Which one?"

"The young one, Devika."

"And?"

"She asked if you suspected Gitanjali of involvement in her husband's murder. I told her I didn't know, but that I'd be asking your questions for you and, if she secured the Maharaja's permission, that I'd tell her everything afterwards. That seemed to appeal to her. Can you imagine what good gossip it'll make? She said she'd do what she could."

I thanked her for her help, then told her I needed more of it.

"There's another woman in the zenana whom we need to speak to," I said. "A concubine. Do you think you might prevail upon your friend the Maharani Devika once more?"

"You don't ask for much, do you, Sam?"

"I'm involving you in an investigation, Miss Grant," I said. "Now don't tell me you'd be having that sort of fun with Charlie Peal back in Calcutta."

"I admit, it's more fun being an investigator than a suspect," she said pointedly.

The music ended and the prince came sauntering over. "I say, Miss Grant, what's that you're drinking? Pink gin? I'm minded to have one myself." He gestured to the barman who set to work preparing the drink with a tad more alacrity than he'd done with mine.

"So, Miss Grant," he continued, "have you considered my offer?"

"I'd love to, Your Highness." She smiled, as my heart sank through the floor. "But I was wondering: would you mind awfully if Captain Wyndham accompanied us? I don't believe he's been before."

"I've no wish to see the Côte D'Azur," I said sourly. "I saw enough of France during the war to last me a lifetime."

"I think you've got rather the wrong end of the stick, dear fellow," scoffed the prince. "We're talking about tomorrow's tiger hunt. I suppose you're welcome to tag along if you wish."

I had the impression that me tagging along was the last thing the prince wanted. That's why I immediately accepted.

"I'd be honoured," I said.

"Very well." He nodded. "We're heading out around lunchtime. I trust you'll be on time."

The music started up again. An Al Jolson record. I liked Al Jolson.

"Come, Miss Grant," said the prince. "How about a dance? We mustn't let the night go to waste."

She accepted and I looked on as the two of them headed back towards the centre of the room. It turned out that the prince was quite a proficient dancer, which just reinforced my dislike of him. There's something inherently untrustworthy about a man who knows how to dance.

I took of a sip of whisky and brooded as Colonel Arora walked over.

"You look troubled, Captain," he said.

It was a fair observation.

"Let's just say that this place is rather different to what I'd expected."

"Ah," he said, "you're not the first Englishman to have said that. Let me guess. You were expecting some uncivilised little backwater?"

"No, not at all . . ." I mumbled, but he was right. I'd anticipated something akin to the Dark Ages: a feckless despot with his diamonds, his harem and his people under his yoke. The truth was more complicated. There was, of course, the ridiculous wealth and the stories of the Maharaja's antics, but there was also the sophistication: the English nannies, the Italian chauffeurs, the French cook, and the dedication to the duties the royal family felt they owed to their subjects. But the greatest revelation was the zenana. I tried, through an alcohol-induced haze, to explain my thoughts to the colonel.

"You need to stop believing the things that your English writers are so fond of penning," he replied. "What do they know of the women they write about? What do they know of the eunuchs they are so fond of caricaturing? Open your eyes, Captain. Leave your prejudices in Calcutta. Better still, leave them in London. Some of the most astute businesspeople in Sambalpore are ladies of the zenana."

He read my expression.

"What? It shocks you to learn that a woman should have business interests?" He pointed in the direction of Annie. "I understand that Miss Grant there is quite the businesswoman. Why should it be any different for the women of the harem? You think just because you cannot see them, that *they* are the ones at a disadvantage? Do you not realise that they see and hear everything? And when it comes to business dealings, to see and not be seen can often confer a great benefit."

"And the eunuchs?" I asked. "Next you'll be telling me they appreciate being castrated."

"I would not go *that* far," he ruminated. "Still, their *disability* does confer upon them some real influence. The eunuchs are like counsellors to the ladies of the zenana. And they pride themselves on maintaining the secrets they are entrusted with. Many eunuchs have grown wealthy and powerful alongside the women they serve. And they do so without any issues of the heart or the flesh."

The last phrase struck me hard. "I suppose that would simplify things somewhat."

"This is India, Captain," he continued. "See it for what it really is, not for what your imperial apologists and your professors of Orientalism would have you believe. Until you do that, you will never understand us."

His words were like a door opening in my mind, letting in the light. For a moment, the certainties disappeared and new ideas, new possibilities, took their place. It was disorientating, exhilarating. I began to see Adhir's murder from a fresh perspective. And then I spotted a look pass between Annie and Punit on the dance floor and the door slammed shut. I drained my glass and set it down on the bar.

"You are leaving?" asked the colonel.

"I think the evening's pretty much run its course." I sighed.

"What you need is a tonic."

"Forget the tonic," I said. "Just give me the gin."

The colonel smiled. "I think, maybe, you might prefer a different sort of pick-me-up?"

I felt the hairs on the back of my neck stand on end.

"You know, Captain," Arora continued, "Sambalpore's wealth was built on more than just diamonds . . ."

I knew what he was talking about, but I wasn't about to admit it.

There was a certain sparkle in his eye. "Would it interest you to know, Captain, that a hundred years ago, we produced some of the finest opium in India?"

A cold sweat beaded my forehead. Could he know? He'd ordered the transfer of our luggage from the Residency to the guest lodge. My suitcase had been unpacked. It was entirely possible that whoever had done this had recognised the opium travelling case for what it was and reported the fact to the colonel.

He was still speaking. "For a long time," he continued, "we earned more revenue from it than we did from the mines. Of course, demand these days has decreased substantially, but we still produce a little. And very fine it is too."

"You've sampled it?" I asked.

"Of course," he said definitively. "Does that shock you?"

"No," I replied.

He laughed softly. "I didn't think so."

# CHAPTER
# TWENTY-SEVEN

I walked with Colonel Arora out into the courtyard and in the direction of the Rose Building.

"Isn't it a touch late for the office?" I asked.

"It is." He smiled. "But we are going across town, and for that we need a car, preferably a fast one."

From inside the royal garage came the sound of an engine being revved.

"Conscientious fellows, your engineers," I said.

"It's a busy time for them," he replied, pushing open one of the doors. "The cars need to be readied for the coming monsoon. Then there's the tiger *shikar* tomorrow. The camouflaged Rolls-Royces will be required for that. They spend most of their time being driven around the jungle and need regular maintenance."

Sure enough, two mechanics had their heads bent under a camouflaged bonnet. The colonel scanned the gleaming rows of vehicles.

"There she is!" he exclaimed, pointing to a red car at the far end of the second row. "She's always hiding!"

"We're not taking the Mercedes?" I asked.

"Good Lord, no! We're taking something much more interesting," he replied, striding off. He stopped in front of a flame-red coupe and gazed at it lovingly.

**260**

"What is it?"

"What is it?" he exclaimed. "My good fellow, this is an Alfa Romeo 20/80. She'll do over eighty miles per hour on a race track. I had her up to fifty on one occasion. Very nearly landed upside down in a ditch."

"You won't mind if we stick to twenty-five tonight?"

"Very well, Captain," he said, running his hand along the bonnet, "but it's your loss."

We were on an empty road, heading south out of town. Arora was going considerably faster than twenty-five and the rush of air delivered the coolest breeze I'd felt since England. I was keeping my own counsel, content just to watch the world fly past.

"So what do you make of our new Yuvraj?" asked Arora.

I wasn't sure exactly what to say.

"You're not an admirer?" He smiled.

"I think I preferred his brother."

"You seem to have reached your conclusion rather quickly."

"Do you disagree with it?" I asked.

"I did not say that," he laughed, "I'm simply curious as to what might have led you to form such a rapid judgement."

"Instinct," I said. "I'm a policeman, remember. I trust my gut."

"And it has nothing to do with his apparent interest in your friend, Miss Grant?"

"Miss Grant's an intelligent woman," I replied. "She can look after herself."

"I admire your confidence, Captain," he said. "I only wonder if it is well founded. After all, you'd be surprised at just how much sway a title and a hundred crore rupees can confer on a man."

He had a point. What woman wouldn't find the attentions of a millionaire, soon-to-be maharaja, appealing?

"Even if he's suspected of murder?" I asked.

Arora turned towards me. He suddenly had that steel in his eyes. "You think he was responsible for his brother's assassination?"

"Well, it wasn't Shreya Bidika," I replied. "And Punit's got the best motive of all."

"Have you any proof?"

"No. Not yet, anyway."

"And what if the proof is hard to come by?"

"I still have to try."

The colonel smiled grimly. "Of course — *innocent until proven guilty* — that's the British way, isn't it?"

"It's the law of the land," I said.

"Except this isn't your land," he replied, "and I'm glad to say such ideas take their time reaching Sambalpore."

We drove on in silence, till the colonel eventually spoke.

"Any progress in finding Golding?"

"A little."

He glanced over. I decided to elaborate, if only so he'd turn his attention back to the road.

"We think that whatever's happened to him may be linked to the report he was writing for Adhir.

Surrender-not says that Golding's working papers are in his office, but there's no sign of a report, not even a first draft. I'm thinking someone wanted sight of it before it became public knowledge. To what end, though, I'm not sure."

The colonel shook his head. "There's no mystery regarding the whereabouts of the report," he said. "The Dewan's got it. I overheard him mention it to Fitzmaurice this evening."

Now it was my turn to stare. "How did he get it?"

"No idea." The colonel shrugged. "I'll ask him tomorrow, if you wish?"

"That would be useful," I said, "but it would be better if you could get your hands on it. I'd like Surrender-not to go through it."

"And how am I supposed to do that?" he asked.

"You're a resourceful man, Colonel," I said as the car slowed and turned into an alleyway. "I'm sure you'll come up with something."

Arora brought the car to a halt outside a nondescript, two-storey house with shuttered windows and a balcony running along the upper level. I was still focused on Golding. If the Dewan had his report, what did that mean for the missing accountant? I was sure he hadn't left Sambalpore of his own free will. Indeed, I'd discounted that idea as soon as I'd searched his house.

I ran through the possibilities: Golding had given the report to the Dewan, then been accosted. Or he'd been kidnapped on the Dewan's orders and forced to hand it over. But that made little sense. The Dewan would always have been one of the first to receive a copy of the report. Maybe Golding had been accosted by Sir Ernest Fitzmaurice's men? Anglo-Indian Diamond had the most to gain from an early sight of the figures. But would they kidnap an Englishman simply for an advantage at the negotiating table?

Colonel Arora knocked on the front door. Almost immediately it was opened by a short man with oiled-back black hair, a pencil moustache and white *kurta*, who received the colonel like an old friend. Arora turned and beckoned me forward. I tried to get Golding out of my mind. Whatever had happened to him, the answers could wait until tomorrow.

The smell of opium hung in the air. The short man led the way, through an open courtyard and on to a large, dimly lit room dotted with silken beds, several of which were occupied. On the bed nearest the door lay a European, a man of some means judging by his clothes, an opium pipe beside him on a small brass table, wisps of smoke rising gently. In one corner, two women in saris were engrossed in whispered conversation.

As opium dens went, this was, if not the Ritz, then most definitely the Waldorf, and about as far removed from what I was used to as London is from the moon.

Still, when in Rome . . .

A pretty girl in a pink sari came over and showed us to two beds either side of a squat table on which I presumed the opium lamp would rest. I followed Arora's lead and took off my dinner jacket and handed it to her, then lay down on one of the beds while the

264

colonel took the other. She departed, taking our jackets with her.

In her absence, I lay on my side and tried to make myself comfortable. It should have been easy — the bed was far more comfortable than the wood and string *charpoys* favoured by the sort of dives I frequented in Calcutta, and yet the expectancy of a new hit, of cravings close to fulfilment, meant my body ached in anticipation.

The girl returned, having swapped our coats for a silver opium tray and two long-stemmed pipes. It was when she placed the tray on the table that I noticed the oddness of the layout. The lamp and the pipes were there, as were the usual plethora of instruments for cleaning them, but the balls of opium resin and the needle used to cook them over the flame were missing. In their place stood a small pipette similar to an eye dropper, a miniature silver pan with an area smaller than a rupee coin, and a lacquered bottle on which was inlaid a golden image of the Lord Jagannath.

"I thought we were here to smoke opium?" I asked.

Arora and the girl shared a look.

"We are," the colonel laughed.

The girl unscrewed the lid and the earthy scent of O filled the air. Taking the pipette, she dipped it into the bottle, then delicately placed four drops onto the silver pan.

"But that's —"

"Correct," said Arora, "a liquid. That, my friend, is the legendary candū, the highest quality, distilled from

**265**

the purest raw opium. Once perfected, it is bottled and aged like a fine wine."

The girl began to warm the pan over the flame of the opium lamp.

"Liquid opium? I never knew there was such a thing."

"You have been sorely abused, Captain," he said with a sparkle in his eye. "It's only to be expected, I suppose. Not much of it is to be found in the open market these days. True candū, taken in moderation, of course, is a wondrous thing, conducive to the creative and inspirational processes. And because it is pure, unlike the rubbish you get in Calcutta, it won't leave you in a stupor."

Above the flame, the candu began to sizzle, releasing an aroma like that of roasting peanuts.

"In the olden days," Arora continued, "Chinese mandarins, artists and high society all used it. But that was before your East India Company launched its opium wars."

"Wars which I understand the kingdom of Sambalpore did quite nicely out of," I added.

The colonel smiled. "True enough," he said.

The girl apportioned the smoking liquid between the two pipes. She handed one to each of us, and I leaned over, closed my eyes and inhaled.

Within minutes, it became obvious that Arora was right. The effects of the candū were starkly different from the dross I smoked in Calcutta. My skin began to tingle, the sensation travelling from my arms to my torso to my skull. The girl prepared and passed me a second pipe, and as I smoked the tingling transformed into an explosion of firing synapses and a sudden blinding white light inside my head. The light faded, replaced by a sense of deep calm and well-being.

# CHAPTER
# TWENTY-EIGHT

## *Tuesday 22 June 1920*

First light entered through French doors left open to the heat. I watched as the sky brightened over blue hills. There was no sunrise to speak of, just a gradual change of hue from black to gunmetal grey.

The clouds outside might have crowded low, but my mental fog had lifted. I had to hand it to Arora — he'd been right about the candū. I'd never experienced an opium hit like it. There'd been no coma-like stupor the previous night, and the usual lethargy of the morning had been supplanted by a crystal-clear lucidity.

We'd left the establishment after four or five pipes, Arora depositing me outside the guest lodge at around one in the morning. I'd made it to my room and fell asleep almost immediately.

Feeling better than I had done for a long time, I lay back under the canopy of a maharaja-sized bed and thought of Annie. It seemed a waste to be in such a bed all alone. And then I fervently hoped that Annie too was alone, in her bed at the Beaumont and not — I stopped myself. It was best not to imagine such things.

Instead, I turned my mind to Adhir and the dead assassin with the mark of Vishnu on his forehead. If

**268**

there was indeed a religious angle to the killing, there was one place where the answers might lie. I got up, dressed quickly and headed out of the room.

I considered waking Surrender-not, but there was no point. It was better to let him sleep: he'd need to be at his best later in the day. Instead, I made my way downstairs and out of the front door.

At the Rose Building I commandeered the Mercedes, guiding it along the gravel driveway and out of the palace gates. I headed south towards the bridge. But as I approached the fork, I had a different idea. Instead of making for the river, I took the left fork and headed into town.

The road outside the Beaumont was busy with passing traffic, but the hotel itself seemed sleepy. I parked close by and walked into the lobby. My new friend the receptionist was again on duty, though his face betrayed no sign that we might have met the previous day.

"I need the room number of one of your guests," I said. "A Miss Grant."

It was the second time I'd asked him for the room of an unaccompanied woman. He knew better than to question the motives of a *sahib*, especially one as willing to grease his palm as I was, but we still had to go through the formalities.

"We cannot give out such infor —"

I passed a five-rupee note over the counter before he could finish.

"Room twelve, sir," he said, "but you won't find the lady in question there."

My stomach lurched. Visions of Annie with Punit passed through my head. Had he slipped something funny into her drink and forced her to stay at the palace? Wasn't that the sort of thing one expected of an oriental despot?

"She's breakfasting in the dining room," he continued, pointing to a door.

I almost laughed in relief and passed him another five rupees.

The dining room hummed to the conversation of half a dozen round tables. Annie was close to the window; a little further along sat Katherine Pemberley. Silhouetted against the light, she looked so much like Sarah that I felt a renewed pang of anguish. Both women glanced over, and for a split second I had trouble remembering which of the two I'd come to see.

Then Annie smiled and I walked over and asked if I could join her.

"Be my guest, Captain," she said, taking a sip from a porcelain cup. "You disappeared rather quickly last night."

"Colonel Arora wanted to discuss something," I lied. "Did you stay long?"

"Not really." She dabbed delicately at her mouth with a starched napkin. "The whole evening was rather off colour, to be honest. So are you going to tell me why you're here?"

"I came to thank you for persuading Punit to invite me on his tiger-shooting jaunt this afternoon," I said. "And as a token of appreciation, I thought I might

**270**

invite you for a little drive in the country this morning, before it gets too hot."

She eyed me suspiciously, then took another sip of tea.

Annie lit a cigarette as the car flew across the bridge.

"Where are we going?"

"I thought we might have a look at that temple."

She took a pull. "The old ruin?"

"No, the new one. Next to where Adhir was cremated."

She threw me a look like a slap to the side of the head. "I'd have thought you'd be more interested in the relic than the new one, Sam. You always seem happier living in the past."

Ahead, the temple emerged out of the haze.

I pulled off the road and, amidst a cloud of dust, brought the car to a stop not far from the compound wall. In front of us the temple's marble carvings shone in stark relief. Annie took the images in her stride, not that I expected anything less. She might be an Anglo-Indian, but when it came to these sorts of things, she was far more *Indian* than *Anglo*. She walked towards the doors, touching her hand to her forehead, then her chest. I'd seen Surrender-not do something similar in the presence of the divine.

"What's that?"

"What?"

"That thing you did with your hand," I said, mimicking the action.

271

"Oh that. It's a Hindu thing. A mark of respect for the deities within."

"I didn't know you were religious."

"I'm not, but it can't hurt to be in with the gods, can it?"

I followed her up marble steps into the temple porch. The wooden doors were solid and closed. I was about to push on them when Annie put her hand on my arm.

"Wait a moment. We can't just barge in."

"Why not? It's a house of god. Surely they welcome all comers?"

"It's not a church, Sam," she replied tersely. "Some temples don't even admit lower caste Hindus. How do you think they're going to react to an Englishman and a half-caste?"

"Well, they'll never make converts with an attitude like that," I said.

"Hindus don't go in much for converting," she replied, "and if they did, I very much doubt they'd start with you."

"I'm hurt, Miss Grant," I said, as a low rumble came from the doors, which had begun to swing slowly open. "Maybe we should ask the priest?"

But it wasn't a priest who exited first amid a blast of incense. At the head of a small procession came an elderly woman dressed in a plain blue sari with a few golden bangles on her wrists. Her feet were bare. She emerged from the gloom and I realised I recognised her. The Maharani Shubhadra, the Maharaja's first wife. The one who'd accompanied him to dinner the previous evening before leaving him in the care of the young Third Maharani.

A few paces behind her walked Davé, the Dewan. My presence seemed to come as a shock to him, and not a pleasant one, judging by his reaction. He shot forward like an angry terrier and attempted to screen the Maharani from view.

"This is holy ground, Captain Wyndham. You cannot be here!"

I caught the Maharani's eye. A look passed between us, the suggestion of a shared thought contained within it. Perhaps she felt as amused by her minister's reaction as I did. I decided to take a chance.

"My apologies, Mr Prime Minister," I said. "Miss Grant has a love of religious architecture and I offered to bring her out to have a closer look at the temple. Of course, if we are causing offence to Her Highness, we shall go immediately."

I took Annie by the arm and made to leave.

"Captain Wyndham," said a soft voice behind me, "please wait. The Lord Jagannath, in his temple, recognises no distinction between the castes. And I have often thought that the matter should not stop there. Please. You and your companion are welcome to stay."

She spoke to the Dewan in her own tongue and the prime minister's face fell. Nevertheless, he swallowed down his instructions, nodded, then headed into the temple.

Fortune favours the bold, or so they say, but in India, there was no such thing as fortune. What we called *luck*, Hindus ascribed as an attribute of the goddess Lakshmi. And it seemed that she was smiling on me. I hadn't anticipated asking any questions of the Maharani Shubhadra, but here she was, out of *purdah* and unchaperoned, at least for the moment. All I needed was an excuse to keep her here for a few minutes. To my surprise, however, it was the old maharani who took the initiative.

"My dear Miss Grant," she said, "why don't you explore the temple while I keep the captain company?"

Annie smiled, uttered a few indistinguishable words and gave me a look that seemed to reach into my soul, before wandering inside. The Maharani waited, then turned to me.

"Shall we, Captain?"

I accompanied her down the steps and out into the temple compound. She gazed up at the grey sky.

"My husband tells me that you are investigating Adhir's murder. Have you made much progress?"

"A little," I replied. "I can tell you who *isn't* responsible: the woman that Colonel Bhardwaj has arrested — the schoolmistress, Miss Bidika."

The Maharani pondered this for a moment but said nothing.

"Do you know Miss Bidika?" I asked.

"I've had several dealings with her," she replied, "some more productive than others. She is a fine teacher, but . . . outspoken. I knew that her ideas would land her in trouble one day. But tell me, Captain, what makes you think there is a connection to Sambalpore?"

I considered how much to say.

274

"Three notes were left for the prince in his chambers warning him his life was in danger. That suggests at least one person at court had knowledge of the plot to kill him."

"And you have found that person?"

"I haven't been able to track them down yet."

Our conversation died as we passed two priests. Then, once out of earshot, the Maharani continued.

"Have you any suspects?"

"One or two," I replied, "but you will forgive me if I keep my own counsel for the moment."

"I understand," she said, "but please know this, Captain: the court of Sambalpore is a curious place. In my time I have come to learn how to chart its changing waters. With that said, if it is helpful to you, anything you wish to inform my husband of, perhaps without going through the usual channels," she turned to look back, "you can pass through me."

Having a path to the Maharaja that didn't pass through the Dewan or Colonel Arora could prove useful. It was probably the next best thing to speaking to him directly.

"Thank you," I said.

From behind me came Annie's voice. She was talking to the Dewan. I hadn't much time left.

"May I ask you a few questions, Your Highness?"

She paused. "Why don't you accompany me to my car?" she said. "As you can see, I'm hardly a fast walker. You may ask what you wish while we walk."

In the distance, a troop of black-faced monkeys sat sharing the spoils of offerings stolen from the temple.

They watched us warily from their perch atop the compound wall.

I was unsure how or where to start, and in the end decided it best to just dive straight in.

"I understand that Adhir had a mistress, an Englishwoman. Was that common knowledge in Sambalpore?"

The Maharani sighed. "Unfortunately it was; at least, among a certain section of Sambalpori society."

"And what did people think?"

Her expression darkened. "What do you expect they thought, Captain? The son and heir to the throne cavorting with a white woman. They were horrified. It's one thing to indulge in such things in London, but having her here, in residence at the Beaumont Hotel? It was a provocation, and a calculated insult to tradition."

"And what did *you* make of it?"

She paused.

"The woman is nothing more than an adventuress. Not that she's the first. Over the years, quite a few Englishwomen have made their way to Sambalpore, hoping to inveigle themselves into the favours of my husband. He knew that such things wouldn't be tolerated here and gave them short shrift. It appears, though, that Adhir indulged this particular woman, and in so doing he was storing up trouble for himself."

Something seemed to startle the monkeys. With a shriek they scattered, leaping for the safety of a nearby tree and sending a rustle of dead leaves to the ground.

"Trouble?" I asked.

"Sambalpore is a small state, Captain, and these are turbulent times. The Maharaja rules only with the consensus of the people and the royal family needs to be seen as a rock of certainty by them. One cannot offer that certainty by flaunting one's English mistress in people's faces."

"Did you ever mention it to Adhir?"

She seemed to stiffen. "It was not my place."

"What about the Maharaja? Did you discuss it with him?"

We turned the corner. The sun broke through a gap in the clouds and for a few moments, threw shadows over the courtyard.

"Ah, but there is the car," she said as the chauffeur quickly ran round and opened the rear door for her. "We shall have to continue this conversation another time."

"If I may, Your Highness, there is one other thing you might be able to help me with. It has nothing to do with Adhir."

She looked at me thoughtfully. "Very well, Captain."

"Did you come to the temple yesterday?"

"I come here most days, sometimes several times a day."

"And did you come yesterday?"

"Yes."

"Did you happen to catch sight of an Englishman, Mr Golding?"

She hesitated. "The accountant? Yes. I believe I *did* see him."

"And when was this?"

"Around this time," she replied, "just after my morning prayers."

"Morning? You're sure it wasn't the evening?"

"Absolutely, Captain."

"Did you see what he was doing here?"

"I'm sorry, I didn't pay him much attention. Maybe he was here for the same reason as your friend, Miss Grant — to look at the carvings?"

"And was he with anyone?"

She shook her head, "I don't believe so. Though I may be mistaken."

I heard footsteps behind me and turned to see the Dewan approach.

"Your Highness," he said to the Maharani, "we really must be going."

"Of course," she replied. "And Captain," she said, turning to me, "it's been a pleasure. Just remember what I told you."

I watched as the Dewan and the chauffeur helped her into the car. Without a further word to me, Davé made his way to the front passenger seat and got in.

As the car sped off, I contemplated the Maharani's words. Golding *had* been here at the temple, but at around six thirty *a.m.*, not six thirty *p.m.* Ninety minutes later, he'd failed to show up at the Residency to meet me. It seemed the old maharani may have been the last person to have seen him before he disappeared.

I ran through the possibilities. Might he have had two meetings scheduled here at the temple on the same day, one in the morning and one in the evening? But if so, why hadn't there been any entry for the earlier meeting in his diary?

Then it hit me. I almost laughed as I realised I had not only the answer to this, but also the name of who he was meeting.

# CHAPTER
# TWENTY-NINE

I collected Annie and headed for the car with purpose in my step.

"You look happy," she said.

"I am," I replied, opening the door for her. "It's amazing what a morning walk in the fresh air will do for you. How'd you enjoy the architecture?"

"Fascinating," she said as she got in. "Still, if you want to see the real thing, you should go to Khajuraho in the United Provinces."

"You've been?"

"Oh yes." She smiled. "A German archaeologist by the name of Brandt invited me earlier this year."

"A German?" I said, shutting her door with a little more force than was required, and headed round to the side of the car to retrieve the crank. Under those circumstances, starting the car proved no trouble.

"What's a German doing running round India?" I asked, getting in beside her.

She looked over. "There're more of them here than you'd think. They've been coming ever since a professor called Max Müller translated the Hindu scriptures into English."

"And this chap, Brandt, is he here translating Hindu scriptures too?"

"Hardly." She laughed. "He has this notion that Indians and Germans are descended from the same tribe."

"Sounds like a bit of an idiot, if you ask me. The old man is probably senile."

"Oh, he's not old," she replied. "He's younger than you."

The car skidded as I threw it round a corner and onto the road back into town. The route was busy with groups of natives on foot, their tools in hand or slung over their shoulders, heading out to the dry fields. There seemed little benefit in dwelling on Brandt and his crackpot theories, so I kept quiet.

Annie eventually broke the silence.

"You seemed to be having quite a nice chat with the Maharani."

"It was fascinating," I replied.

"What did she want to talk about?"

"Adhir's murder. She wanted to know whether we'd made any progress."

"What did you tell her?"

"The truth. I don't know who did it, but I know it wasn't Shreya Bidika."

"How did she take that?"

"I'm not sure. She didn't seem wholly convinced of her innocence. On the plus side, she offered me a direct channel through her to the Maharaja."

"Is that useful?"

"It might be." I shrugged. "It would avoid having to go through Colonel Arora, or, God forbid, that bloody Dewan, Davé. What did you make of him?"

She pondered the question. "He's a funny sort of chap. I think he considered our wandering round the temple sacrilegious."

"He should be getting used to it," I said. "According to the Maharani, Golding was here yesterday morning, also examining the carvings."

She turned to me in surprise. "Really?"

"Apparently."

"That's strange," she replied. "When we were inside, Davé made a big song and dance about how you and I were the first non-Hindus to be allowed access to the temple."

"You're sure?" I asked.

"Trust me, Sam. He wasn't at all happy about it."

"Then why would the Maharani say she'd seen Golding there?"

"Any possibility Golding might have been a Hindu?"

"Judging by the way he was tucking into his roast beef at the Carmichaels' the other night," I replied, "I think we can discount that particular theory."

"Maybe she saw him outside the temple grounds?"

I shook my head. "She said he was looking at the carvings. To do that, he'd have to be inside the compound."

"In that case, maybe the Dewan wasn't there when she saw Golding."

"No," I said, "I think he was."

Surrender-not was in the dining room of the guest lodge, polishing off an omelette. He looked up and almost choked at seeing Annie and me wander in together.

"Something wrong with your breakfast?" I asked.

He stifled a cough. "No, sir," he said, shaking his head. "Just a piece of green chilli that caught me unawares."

I patted him hard on the back and took the seat next to him. "Guess where we've been."

"Out for a walk?"

"Of sorts," I said. "Miss Grant wanted to see the carvings at the temple."

He blushed. "The erotic ones?"

"Absolutely. It turns out she's quite the aficionado."

"Stop teasing the poor boy, Sam," said Annie, as she sat down opposite us.

"Very well," I said as a waiter approached. "I wanted to have a look round the temple. Golding had a meeting there pencilled in his diary. Turns out the First Maharani, Shubhadra, saw him there."

Surrender-not looked at me, puzzled. "But that was scheduled for half past six last night, sir. He never showed up."

"We were wrong about the time," I said. I turned to the waiter and ordered an omelette.

"But the diary entry read '6.30p.m. New Temple'," protested Surrender-not.

"True," I said, "but I think that was a reference to something else. Suppose it actually meant a meeting at six thirty *with* the PM, the Prime Minister?"

Surrender-not leaned forward. "You mean the Dewan?"

"Exactly."

"Was the Dewan there yesterday morning?"

"He was there with the Maharani *this* morning. She was there yesterday and I'm willing to bet he accompanied her there yesterday too."

"But why would Golding meet the Dewan there? Why not at his office? And why so early in the morning?"

"I don't know." I shrugged. "I'm guessing it has something to do with that damned report he was writing. Colonel Arora overheard Davé tell Sir Ernest that he'd received a copy."

Surrender-not mulled it over. "So Golding meets with the Dewan, hands over the report, then disappears?"

"That's just it," I said. "I don't think he *did* hand over the report. If he had, there'd be no need to ransack his cottage. I think Golding wanted to hand the report over to us, not the Dewan. That's why he wanted to meet me yesterday morning. Maybe Golding's report is the key to the whole thing?"

"You mean Adhir's murder, sir?"

"It's possible. Let's assume there's something going on at the mines that the royal family isn't aware of. Maybe the Dewan is skimming off profits on the side. Suddenly, as part of the negotiations with Anglo-Indian Diamond, Golding is asked by Prince Adhir to prepare his report, and as part of his work, he stumbles across whatever the Dewan is up to. Davé, knowing he's going to be discovered, orchestrates the killing of Adhir in the hope of covering his tracks. But he still needs to get hold of Golding's report; and he also needs to ensure Golding's silence.

"So he meets Golding yesterday morning to try to buy him off, but Golding, fastidious accountant that he is, refuses to be bribed. Davé has him abducted, then organises the search of his house. Either he finds it there or, more likely, Golding cracks and tells him where it is."

I'd been thinking aloud and took a minute to fully digest it all. I suddenly had a suspect who fitted the facts — most of them, anyway — and who possibly had a motive, too.

"What does it mean for Golding?" asked Surrender-not.

"If we're right, it doesn't look good," I answered.

The conversation died as the waiter returned and placed a plate in front of me.

"They wouldn't kill an Englishman, would they?" whispered Annie as the waiter departed. "They'd never get away with it."

"It's a big step," I replied. "The Imperial Police would be all over this place if he's been murdered, but —"

Surrender-not finished my sentence: "But without a body, it's impossible to prove anything."

"And at present the Viceroy is keen to avoid any ructions that might stop Sambalpore joining his Chamber of Princes." I took a bite of omelette. Surrender-not was right. The chef hadn't spared the chillies. "Anyway," I continued, "this is all just speculation. We need to get our hands on Golding's report."

"And how do we do that, sir?" asked Surrender-not.

"I've asked Colonel Arora to get it for us," I said. As I spoke, a liveried bearer entered the room.

"Captain Wyndham, sir?" he asked. "I have a chitty for you from Colonel Arora."

"Talk of the devil," I said.

I thanked the man and took the note from him. It was simply a folded sheet of paper without an envelope. I unfolded it and read the handwritten note.

*Your request to interview Her Highness Princess Gitanjali has been reconsidered. Permission is granted upon the condition that all questions are put to Her Highness by Miss Annie Grant.*

*Arora*

I turned to Annie and Surrender-not and grinned.

"We need that report."

Colonel Arora was already at his desk. A cigarette stub burned slowly in a cut-glass ashtray, sending a wisp of blue smoke skywards only to be dissipated by the ceiling fan.

"I was going to ask Davé for it."

I'd left Annie and Surrender-not in Golding's office and now sat facing the colonel.

"I don't think he'll be keen on sharing it with us," I replied. I explained my suspicions to him — that the

Dewan had met with Golding early the previous morning and that he may have been responsible for the man's disappearance. "You'll need to come up with something else."

The colonel ran a hand across his beard.

"There might be a way," he said. "Palace security falls under my jurisdiction. As such, I have access to keys for all of the offices in this building, including his."

"Nevertheless," I ventured, "if the Dewan's willing to abduct an Englishman in order to get hold of the report, he's hardly likely to leave it lying around."

"He has a safe hidden somewhere in his office," said the colonel. He picked up his cigarette and took a pull.

"Have you got a safe-cracker among the royal retinue?"

"I have something better." He smiled. "His Highness the Maharaja has a habit of shooting the messenger. Six years ago, when the previous Dewan incurred his displeasure, I was given the task of turfing him out of his office. There was an interregnum of a day or so before Davé was installed in his place. During that time, I had access to all the keys from that office and took the precaution of making copies of them, including those for a safe — just in case the originals ever went astray, you understand."

"Of course," I replied. "The question is when would be an opportune time to conduct our search. Will the Dewan be accompanying Prince Punit's party on the tiger hunt?"

"Fitzmaurice is going," replied the colonel, "so I would expect Davé to be there, but even in his absence, his secretary will be in his anteroom. It would be best to try some time in the evening, after the secretary has left for the day."

"Fine," I said. "We'll aim to get hold of the report tonight, go through it and return it before his secretary arrives in the morning. That's assuming it's in the office in the first place, of course."

"Very well," said the colonel. "And what are your intentions until then?"

"I'm going hunting," I said. "And before that, there are a couple of ladies I'd like some answers from."

# CHAPTER
# THIRTY

"What do you want me to ask her?"

In the heat of the morning, Annie and I followed Colonel Arora towards the Banyan Mahal. It was a palace within the palace, an ornate, terraced building of yellow sandstone, its facade dotted with latticework windows.

"I want to understand more about Adhir and about her relationship with him. And I want to know if she has any idea who might have been behind his assassination. I'll suggest more questions as we progress," I replied.

The entrance to the zenana was guarded by two bearded warriors who appeared to have been chiselled out of a quarry, probably somewhere in the deserts of Rajasthan. The Rajputs had a history of offering their military services to princes across India, like the Swiss in Europe.

Inside, the corridors were patrolled by a rather different sort. The only men who were allowed unrestricted access to the Banyan Mahal, other than the Maharaja and his sons, were the eunuchs.

"In distant times," Arora had explained, "they'd have been slaves captured in battle, or criminals, caught and castrated." These days, it seemed, their provenance was, if anything, more disconcerting. They tended to be boys, mutilated in adolescence, often by their families in search of monetary gain. And eunuchs commanded a price; after all, who better to guard a king's harem than men forcibly freed from the lures of the flesh?

"Wait," said Arora. He pulled sharply on a rope and somewhere a bell rang. "The chief of the zenana will take you from here."

The echo of footsteps on stone heralded the arrival of a slender, smooth-faced man dressed in a blue silk uniform.

He pressed his hands together in greeting. "I am Sayeed Ali," he said. His English sounded impeccable. "You must be Miss Grant and Captain Wyndham."

I nodded.

"If you would care to follow me. Her Highness the Princess Gitanjali is expecting you."

"I'll meet you here after the interview," said Arora.

"You're not coming?" I asked.

He arched an eyebrow. "It is best to avoid the Banyan Mahal unless one has specific business there," he replied. "Moreover, I have to organise the meeting you requested with the concubine."

We left him and followed Sayeed Ali along a corridor whose walls were lined with murals that wouldn't have looked out of place in the *Kama Sutra*, and into a cloistered courtyard dominated by a huge banyan tree, which I guessed gave the palace its name. We walked through another arched doorway into a stairwell, climbing two flights before entering a well-apportioned sun-lit apartment. The room was divided by a carved teak screen peppered with small holes. In front of the screen, the marble floor was covered with a black and gold Persian rug, strewn with silk cushions.

"Please be seated," said the eunuch. "Her Highness will be with us shortly."

With that, he stood back and we made ourselves comfortable on the floor.

Soon came a click and the sound of a door opening somewhere behind the screen. There was a rustle of fabric followed by bare feet on marble. Annie and I stood up, more out of courtesy than anything else, as a body clad in white moved behind the screen, intermittently blocking the pin-pricks of light that fell through its holes. It halted in front of us. Then a woman's voice: "Please, be seated."

The princess, it seemed, was doing likewise.

"Your Highness," said Annie softly, "thank you for taking the time to meet with us. My name is Annie Grant. I was an acquaintance of your late husband, and with me is Captain Sam Wyndham of the Calcutta Police. He is leading the investigation into your husband's assassination."

There was a slight movement behind the screen. Through the latticework I caught sight of uncovered, dark hair.

"I understand that you wish to ask some questions of me?"

The voice was strong, tremor-free, with no indication that she was a woman in mourning. And her accent and diction were those of an educated woman, no stranger to the English language.

"That's correct, Your Highness," said Annie.

It suddenly occurred to me that I'd never questioned a witness in quite this manner before. While I'd often relied on Surrender-not to translate my questions to natives who couldn't speak English, I'd never interrogated a witness whom I could not see. This presented a few problems. A person's face often tells a different story from their words. What's more, you can learn a lot from their physical reactions to your questions — tics, a loss of composure, perspiration, a whole gamut of clues that a smart investigator can pick up on.

In this case, it seemed the tables were turned. Annie and I were seated at a distance from the screen, unable to discern much of anything behind it. The princess, I realised, was up close: the latticework would offer her a clear view of us. Given the situation, my best bet was to try a line of questioning more forceful than I might otherwise have been inclined to use. But how exactly was I supposed to forcefully question a princess whose husband had been cremated only the day before?

"Tell her that we might have to ask her some difficult questions," I whispered to Annie, "but only in the interests of identifying whoever's behind her husband's assassination."

Annie nodded, then turned to the screen.

"Your Highness may find some of the questions rather direct in nature. I would ask that you keep in mind that our sole objective is to find the parties behind your husband's murder," she said.

"I understand," replied the princess. "I shall attempt to answer your questions to the best of my ability. Now please continue."

Before I could feed her a question, Annie had already started asking one.

"Could you begin by telling us how you came to be married to Prince Adhir?"

There was a rustling of silk from behind the screen.

"Adhir and I were betrothed to one another when I was six and he was nine, though the process had been set in motion many years prior to that. I was chosen for him by his father's priests, from the matching of our astrological charts based upon the moment and location of our births. I dare say I was one of many girls of the right caste whose charts were examined, and I cannot tell you on what grounds, other than *karma*, I was chosen over the others. However, I didn't meet him until I was thirteen. We were married shortly afterwards, at which time I left my family and moved into the palace."

"Ask her if she had any say in the matter," I whispered.

"Are you sure?" said Annie.

I nodded. "Please ask the question, Miss Grant."

"Did either of you have any say in the arrangement?" asked Annie.

"That is a strange question to ask," replied the princess. "How can a child be expected to have a say in such matters? From the age of six, I was groomed for the role. It is difficult to have expectations of a different life when the *durbar* and the zenana are your destiny. It is the way of things, the way it has always been; the same for king and commoner alike. Until recent times, was it not much the same in your own country?"

Annie gave me a hard stare. "Forgive me, your highness," she continued. "I meant no offence."

"Perhaps," said the princess, "the captain was wondering whether, having married so young, there was love between Adhir and me?"

I struggled to find the appropriate words, and settled instead for a slight nod of the head, which I hoped she could see through the holes in the screen.

"I can tell you, Captain, that from even before I met him, I loved him. And that my love for him never wavered."

"And what of his love for you?" I asked, momentarily forgetting my place. Behind me, the eunuch Sayeed Ali stirred. "Captain Wyndham, I would urge you to remember the terms on which this interview has been granted. Another breach of protocol and I will have to insist that it is terminated."

I apologised.

There was a pause from behind the screen. The question had been a provocation on my part. The princess's reply, when it came, was tinged with defiance.

"I am aware of the gossip, Captain. The stories of the Englishwoman at the Beaumont Hotel. Rest assured, there is very little that is not known in the zenana. I have even seen her. But believe me, whatever her relationship with Adhir, it was never any threat to his love for me. He always had his concubines, and *they* had no impact on our relationship. Why should the matter be any different just because the woman in question happens to be white? The love we had transcended whatever tawdry liaison she might have had with him."

There was bitterness in her voice.

"Tell me more about your husband. What sort of a man was he?" asked Annie promptly. It was a good question. I decided to just sit back and listen.

"A good man." There was no hesitation in the princess's reply. "A man who cared. He had plans to bring Sambalpore into the twentieth century."

"What sort of plans?"

"He believed that the days of British rule in India were numbered, and that the future belonged to the people. In such a world, the continued existence of princely states was, he believed, anachronistic. He saw it as his duty to prepare Sambalpore for the changes he knew were coming."

"And what did others make of his ideas?"

There was another pause.

"If I may, Miss Grant, let me answer that by first asking you a question. Do you consider yourself an Indian?"

Annie hesitated.

"I do, Your Highness," she replied finally.

Despite the screen between us, I could feel the princess smiling.

"Then you understand this land and its people. They say our history stretches back thousands of years, but in that time, how much has really changed? Our people worship the gods in the same way their forefathers have done for millennia, our farmers till the soil much as our ancestors did in the time of the *Mahabharata*. In our land, change comes slowly. Mountains are reduced to pebbles by the desert wind in less time. There will always be those who set their hearts and wills against it."

"Did your husband do anything to upset any such people? Priests, maybe?"

"Adhir was not a religious man," she replied. "In fact, he believed it to be the cause of superstition and backwardness in the country. But he knew what the religious practices and rituals meant to his people. He did his duty."

"His duty?" I whispered.

"I would be grateful if you would elaborate, Your Highness," said Annie.

There came a clinking of bangles from behind the screen.

"The people expect their rulers to lead their religious rituals. If the Maharaja cannot, it falls to his heir to conduct them. Adhir was supposed to have led the procession at the festival in a few days' time, when the Lord Jagannath and his chariot return to their own temple. With Adhir gone, I expect that his brother Punit will lead the ceremony."

"Tell me about Prince Punit," said Annie.

"What is there to tell?" she replied. "He is his father's son."

"Unlike his brother?"

"Adhir, I think, took more after his late mother. Punit is unlikely, let us say, to push the type of reform that Adhir had in mind. He is not the sort to take such steps."

"Was there anyone in particular at court who objected to your husband's ideas?"

"I would imagine there were many. He was often at loggerheads with his father. Adhir blamed Davé for this. He felt the Dewan had too much influence on his father; that he was putting ideas into the Maharaja's head. He believed that Davé was solely interested in maintaining his own position and that he saw any change as a threat to that."

As she spoke, something in her tone changed. It was so subtle that normally I might not have noticed it. But the inability to see her face had forced me to concentrate on her voice. The way she talked of her husband had altered ever so slightly. When she'd talked of her love for him, or of his intentions for the kingdom, her tone had been fulsome. She *believed* every word of what she said. Now, though, there was something different. Her husband may have felt that the Dewan was responsible for turning his father against him, but I got the feeling *she* didn't.

"Ask her if she agreed with her husband's opinion?" I whispered. "That the Dewan was putting ideas into the Maharaja's head."

Annie did as I asked.

There was a rustling from behind the screen. I had the impression she was looking round at something . . . or maybe someone. Then her attention seemed to return to the screen.

"You will understand," she began, "that there are some questions which —"

A noise came from behind the screen. There was the sound of footsteps on the marble floor as someone approached the princess. Through the holes I saw a flash of green silk, followed by whispers.

"Your Highness?" asked Annie.

"It seems I am required in the zenana," she replied. "I am afraid that we shall have to cut short our conversation. Before we end, though, let me add one final thing. I understand that the captain was with my husband at the moment of his death, and that he was responsible for tracking down his killer. For that, he has my gratitude."

"A last question, if I may, Your Highness?" said Annie.

There was a pause, as if the princess might be seeking permission.

"Very well."

"What will happen to you now?"

"You mean am I to be tossed aside now that my husband is no more?"

"Forgive me for any offence," said Annie. "I only meant, will you return to your family?"

"You must understand, Miss Grant," replied the princess, "the zenana *is* my family. It has been so since the day I married Adhir. That has not changed. I am a princess of the House of Sambalpore and I shall always eat off a golden plate."

Annie thanked her for her time, but even as she spoke, it was clear that the princess was already on her way out of the room and back into the sequestration of the zenana.

# CHAPTER
# THIRTY-ONE

Arora was waiting outside. He stood in the shade of a tree, smoking a cigarette which he stubbed out as we approached.

"I trust the interview went well," he asked.

"It was most enlightening," I replied. "Did you manage to arrange the next one?"

"Oh, yes. The concubine, Rupali." He smiled mischievously and brandished a sheet of paper with the royal seal affixed to the bottom. "I have the order right here. It would appear that His Highness cannot say no to a request from Miss Grant."

"She has that effect on a lot of men," I mused as he passed me the letter.

Annie ignored the remark. "Tell me about the concubines."

"His Highness has a large and very handsome assortment of women," said the colonel.

"How does he choose them?"

"All sorts of ways," he continued. "Sometimes His Highness will simply be passing through a village and a girl will catch his eye. Then there are those he meets on his royal tours. I'm told he once brought back a dozen or so from a tour of Kashmir. Their families are paid handsomely, of course. Most of the time, however, he leaves it to the discretion of his advisers; though there are rumours that one or two of them can be rather 'hands on' in their selection process."

"I presume there's a pecking order?" I said.

"Naturally. At the top are the maharanis, His Highness's official wives, Shubhadra, Devika and of course Adhir and Punit's mother — the late Second Maharani; then Adhir's widow, the Princess Gitanjali. After that there are about fifty favoured concubines, all from good families or with particular talents. Then come the others, the village girls, of whom there are significantly more."

"That's a lot of names to remember."

The colonel laughed. "It would be, but our Mr Golding has devised a system of classification. Only the maharanis and the princess are known by their names. The concubines are each known by an individual letter and number sequence, starting from A1 and ranging to D42. It apparently makes the tracking of their costs easier."

"Costs?" asked Annie.

"Everything from the clothes they wear and the food they eat to the jewels and other gifts that His Highness bestows upon them are meticulously recorded by Mr Golding."

"What about the girl we're going to meet?" I asked. "Where does she rank in the pecking order?"

The colonel retrieved a list from his pocket and consulted it. "C23," he replied, "a simple village girl.

Barely twenty years of age. She speaks Oriya and not much of anything else."

"You've met her?"

"No, but I've read her entry in Mr Golding's asset register."

"A resourceful man, Mr Golding," I said. "It would be a shame if we can't track him down."

"A veritable disaster," replied the colonel. "He was in the process of a much more complex task when he disappeared, that of classifying the royal offspring. There are even more of them and His Highness often needs to be reminded of their names, so you can imagine the difficulty."

Taking our leave of the colonel, we re-entered the zenana and retraced the path back to the anteroom where we'd first met Sayeed Ali. I pulled the cord to ring the bell and waited.

A few minutes later, the eunuch returned.

"Miss Grant, Captain Wyndham. Is there something you have forgotten?"

"No," I replied, brandishing the letter. "We're here to question another of your charges, a Miss Rupali."

I handed him the order, which he carefully scrutinised.

"This is most unorthodox," he said, looking up.

"I'd imagine the murder of the Crown Prince qualifies as unorthodox too," I said. "That may be why His Highness the Maharaja is keen for us to interview whomsoever we deem necessary."

"It may take a few minutes," he said, pocketing the letter. "I will have to locate her and . . . she may be at prayer or . . ." The sentence petered out. "If you wouldn't mind waiting; I shall return having made the arrangements."

He pressed his palms together.

"Mr Ali," I said, "may I have the letter back?"

The eunuch hesitated.

"If I may," he replied, "I shall return it to you once I have organised the meeting."

With that, he turned and left the room, closing the door behind him.

"Odd, don't you think?" I said once he'd gone.

"What?" asked Annie.

"Why would he want to keep hold of the letter?"

"I suppose he wants to show it to someone," she replied.

"Yes, but who?" I asked. "It's an order from the Maharaja. He's the chief of the zenana. Why would he need to show it to anyone?"

"You're the sleuth," she replied. "You tell me."

"Actions are better than words," I said, making for the door. "Come on."

"Where are we going?" she whispered, as she followed me out of the antechamber.

"We're going to see where Mr Ali's off to," I said.

The corridor with the frescos of cavorting couples on its walls was blessedly empty and we walked quickly along it, heading towards the interior of the zenana. We stopped at a door at the far end which opened on to the courtyard with the old banyan tree.

"Maybe you should go first," I said to Annie. "If there's anyone out there, they're less likely to be alarmed at the sight of a woman."

"Are you throwing me to the wolves, Sam?" she asked under her breath.

"Let's hope not."

She took a breath. "Very well, Captain. Here goes."

She inched open the door. I waited as she looked out.

"Well?" I whispered.

"Sayeed Ali's just gone through the arch at the far end. I think he's making for the stairs."

"Is there anyone out there?" I asked.

"In the courtyard?" She opened the door further and peered out. "Two women. Sitting by the tree. I expect they're concubines, judging by the jewellery round their wrists."

It didn't seem we'd be able to go much further.

"I can see Sayeed Ali," she said suddenly. "He's at a window on the first floor. At least, I think it's him — it's hard to tell through the latticework. He seems to be talking to someone — a woman, I think. Yes, definitely a woman — she's wearing a sari. The concubine, Rupali, I expect."

"Over a hundred and twenty women in there and the first one he meets is the one we're looking for? It's unlikely," I said.

"Well, you take a look then," she whispered forcefully.

We swapped places and I peered through the gap into the courtyard and across at the windows high in the wall opposite. It took me a moment to find the correct one, but sure enough, there was the eunuch, his back to us, in conversation with a woman. She was facing him, and partially obscured so that it was impossible to make out much more than the colour of her sari and her hair.

Somewhere behind us, a door opened. I spun around.

"I think someone's coming," said Annie.

"Go and see if you can stall them," I said.

"What? How?"

"I don't know. Use that legendary charm of yours. It seems to work on everyone from Charlie Peel to Prince Punit. Lead them back to the anteroom."

"What are you going to do?"

"Good question," I replied.

Annie ran back along the corridor.

I looked outside. The two concubines were still seated under the banyan tree. There was no escape in that direction. Behind me I heard voices. By the sound of it, Annie had run into a man coming the other way. For a moment I thought it might have been one of the mountainous Rajput guards. Then I remembered that they were stationed outside the main entrance, and that it was more likely that she'd instead come across a eunuch. It suddenly hit me that if there was one group of men impervious to her feminine wiles, it was probably eunuchs. I crossed my fingers and hoped for the best.

I looked back up at the window. Sayeed Ali was no longer there. But the woman was. She stood there, still, as though thinking of something. Then she walked up to the window and stared out, as though straight at me. Despite being shielded by the door, I stepped back instinctively.

"Sir!" came a voice behind me. "You cannot be here!"

I turned to find a boyish-looking eunuch coming down the corridor, with Annie a few paces behind.

"Sorry," I said, heading back towards him, "I must have taken a wrong turn."

As I followed him back to the anteroom, I thought of the woman who'd been speaking to Sayeed Ali. I knew she couldn't have seen me, but in that split second, I'd caught a glimpse of her face. She was young and pretty and I'd sat next to her at dinner the previous evening.

Ten minutes later, Sayeed Ali returned.

"It has been arranged," he said, brusquely handing me back the order. "Please follow me."

"Mr Ali," I said, "do you speak the local language?"

He stopped and turned. "Yes."

"In that case," I said, "would you be prepared to interpret for us?"

The eunuch thought it over. "That should not pose a problem."

We followed him, this time to a smaller, plainer room, though again split by a latticework screen. The woman we had come to see was already seated. Through the holes, I made out a gold sari and dark-skinned, bangle-adorned arms.

Sayeed Ali sat down on the rug beside us.

I took a pen and a sheet of paper from my pocket, then passed them to the eunuch.

"Please give them to Miss Rupali and ask her to write her name and those of her parents."

Through an aperture in the screen, he passed the instruments to the girl and duly translated the instructions. She asked him something in return, he nodded, and she wrote the details on the pad, then passed it and the pen back to him. Ali then passed it to me.

The writing was in the same script as that of the notes found in Adhir's bedchamber. Whether it was the same handwriting, though, I had no idea.

"Please ask her if she knows anything about notes that were left for Prince Adhir in his chambers about a fortnight ago."

The eunuch put the question to her.

Her reply was hesitant.

"She says she has no knowledge of such things."

I didn't need to see her face or speak the language to know it was a lie. It was laid bare in the tone of her voice.

"Please tell her it is vital that she responds truthfully to our questions and that if she does so, she will not be in any trouble."

Sayeed Ali translated. Rupali's tone changed. She was pleading.

"She maintains she knows nothing of the notes," said Ali, deadpan.

"Tell her that we know she wrote them and that she gave them to a maidservant to place in Adhir's quarters. Tell her the maid has identified her and that her handwriting matches that in the notes."

This time, the hesitation was longer.

"Ask her again," I said. "Did she write those notes?"

"Sam," whispered Annie, "you're frightening her."

The girl began to weep. But between the sobs came words.

"She admits she wrote the notes," said the eunuch. "She says she meant no harm."

"Tell her I believe her," I said. I shot Annie a look. "Tell her that what she did was commendable."

Sayeed Ali translated. His tone was gentle and the words seemed to act like balm, calming the girl somewhat.

"Ask her how she came to write them," I asked.

Her answer went on for several minutes, breaking now and again, to allow the eunuch to translate.

"She liked Prince Adhir," he said. "He had been kind to her and she hoped her own position would be improved once he became maharaja. She overheard whispers in the zenana. Rumours of a plot to harm the prince. She says at first she thought nothing of it, that there is always gossip of many kinds swirling around, but the rumours persisted."

"Can she tell us where these rumours originated?" asked Annie.

"She says she doesn't know. The zenana is a hierarchy. She was generally restricted to mixing with girls of the same level as herself. No one knew where it started."

"Did she tell anyone?"

The girl was sobbing once again. The eunuch seemed genuinely moved by her distress. He rubbed a hand across his cheek.

"Captain Wyndham," he said, "if I may make an observation, the girl is very young and not well educated. She says she did not know to whom she could turn without getting into trouble. She felt the only thing she could do was to write those notes and entrust them to the maid in the hope that the Yuvraj would see them."

"Did the rumours say who was behind the plot?"

The eunuch shook his head. "They did not."

I felt suddenly deflated. I'd hoped this girl's testimony would unlock the whole affair, but all she had done was confirm the link to Sambalpore and the palace. As for who was responsible, I was still none the wiser.

"She's sure she didn't hear any names mentioned?"

"She is positive."

"Mr Ali," said Annie, "can you ask her how such a rumour might have started?"

The eunuch translated the question and waited for her reply.

"She says that everything that happens in Sambalpore is known in the zenana. The news is carried here on the wind. She knows not from where the rumours start any more than she knows where the sun goes at night."

"And you, Sayeed Ali," I asked, "did you hear rumours of this plot?"

The eunuch looked towards the door, then set his lips in a thin smile. "There are so many rumours that swirl around this place. Over the years I have learned to become deaf to them."

"That's not an answer."

The eunuch paused for a moment, then replied.

"It is all that I am willing to say on the matter, but I take it you are a Christian, Captain?"

"Nominally," I said.

"In that case, you may wish to recall the words of your own Messiah: *He that hath ears to hear, let him hear.*"

It seemed I wasn't going to get much out of the eunuch. I turned my attention back to the concubine.

"Ask her what she thinks of the new Yuvraj, Prince Punit."

Instead of translating the question, the eunuch turned to me.

"What do you expect her to tell you, Captain?" He sighed. "She is a mere village girl and you are asking her to comment on the future ruler of this kingdom. She will tell you what they would *all* tell you — that the prince is a descendent of heaven and will one day make a fine ruler."

"And you, Sayeed Ali?" I asked. "What would you say of your future monarch?"

The eunuch stared impassively at the screen as dust motes danced in the shafts of light.

"I would tell you, Captain, that if you want to know about His Highness Prince Punit, you should ask the woman whom he courted so assiduously for the last six months. The woman they have arrested for his brother's murder."

# CHAPTER
# THIRTY-TWO

Surrender-not stared at me as I burst into the room, my shirt clinging to my back.

"Get your jacket on, Sergeant," I said. "We're off to visit your friend Miss Bidika again."

I'd left Annie at the steps of the Banyan Mahal and all but ran back to the Rose Building where Surrender-not was still going through Golding's papers. In hindsight the running had probably been a mistake; the day was far too hot for that sort of nonsense, but I wasn't exactly thinking rationally.

I'd asked Annie to come with me to the old fort to question Miss Bidika, but she'd demurred.

"I've been invited on a tour of the palace," she'd said, then told me she'd meet me for the drive out to the tiger hunt. In my haste I'd left it at that. Now I wondered who'd invited her, not that I had time to dwell on it. The eunuch's revelation had knocked me for six. At first I thought he might be joking: the idea that the new Yuvraj had been courting the woman arrested for Adhir's murder seemed preposterous. But the man had a certain sincerity to him and he'd stuck to his story.

"But why has no one else mentioned this to us?" asked Surrender-not as the car sped through the palace gates. He held one hand to his hair against the wind. Even in our hurry to leave, he'd taken out his comb and run it quickly across his scalp.

"The eunuch says it's not common knowledge," I replied. "He says he only knows because as head of the zenana, he was the one tasked by Punit to arrange the gifts he lavished on her."

"You must have questioned him quite superbly, sir. I am only sorry I was not there to witness the interview."

"There was nothing to see," I said. "He all but volunteered the information."

The sergeant was silent. He had that expression on his face again.

"What?"

"Sir?"

"What's troubling you this time?" I asked.

His forehead creased. "I'm sure it's nothing, sir. It's simply that I can't quite understand *why?*"

"Why what?"

"Why would the eunuch voluntarily tell you all this?"

It was a good question. Only the previous evening, Colonel Arora had told me that the eunuchs were prized for their secrecy. Why then would Sayeed Ali share such a thing? With my questioning of the concubine, was I getting close to something he didn't want me to know? Or was it because someone had told him to tell me?

"I don't know," I said, frustrated with myself for not thinking it through sooner.

The old fort loomed large, shimmering in the heat.

I decided to change the subject. "Did you find anything useful among Golding's papers?"

He shook his head. "Nothing. The report certainly isn't there."

The driver stopped the car in the courtyard of the fort and Surrender-not and I jumped out and headed for Major Bhardwaj's office.

We were shown in by a tall officer with a jaw like the prow of a ship. The major sat behind his desk with a sour expression on his face. If he'd been less than happy to see us previously, this time he was positively hostile.

"Orders," he spat, rising to his feet. "I've received no orders granting you access to the prisoner. Who are you that you should come marching into my office and expect me to jump at your command? This is not your Raj, Captain."

"No, but the man whose raj it is has asked me to investigate and that's what I intend to do. It has come to my attention that Miss Bidika may not have been quite as forthright in her answers as I had hoped. So either you can offer me some cooperation or we can telephone the palace and see what His Highness has to say about it."

For a moment we both stood staring at each other like a couple of bulls in a pen.

"If I may, sir," interjected Surrender-not behind me, "I'm sure the major would be as anxious as we are to hear what Miss Bidika might have to say. We are all rowing for the same team, so to speak."

I wasn't overly keen on Bhardwaj eavesdropping, but I'd take Surrender-not's compromise if it helped gain us access.

"I've no objections," I said. "What about you, Major?"

Bhardwaj considered it, then slowly nodded his assent.

We followed him out of the office and back towards the tower where Shreya Bidika was kept prisoner.

"Rowing for the same team?" I said to Surrender-not quietly as we rounded a corner. "You're not at Cambridge any more, Bunty."

"No, sir. It just seemed an expedient way to break the impasse."

Miss Bidika was lying on her bed reading a tired-looking book. Dog-eared pages hung loosely from a frayed and ragged binding. She put down the book and stood up.

"Mr Wyndham and his Bengali sergeant," she said drily. "To what do I owe the pleasure?"

"Prince Punit," I said.

She blinked.

"What about him?"

"Last time I was here, I rather went away with the impression that you detested the man."

This time there was no reply.

"You failed to mention your relationship with him."

Beside me, Bhardwaj let out a gasp. "What is this nonsense, Captain? You led me to believe —"

I cut him off, focusing on the woman. "Well, Miss Bidika?"

She walked over to the desk, pulled out the chair but made no attempt to sit. "There was no relationship," she said.

"No?" I said. "I'm told the prince courted you most assiduously."

"He took a fancy to me. Like he did so many other women. He thought he could buy me."

"But he couldn't?"

"If he could, I would be sitting in the zenana right now rather than in here."

That much was true, but there was something she wasn't telling me.

"And yet I'm informed that you met him secretly several times."

"Initially, the family sent him to sweet-talk me. To convince me to cease the agitation against their rule. He offered me a position of influence in the zenana. He told me it was a chance to make a difference."

"He wanted you to marry him?" I asked.

"No." She gave a short, bitter laugh. "Not at first, anyway. At first he simply wanted to make me his concubine.

"I, of course, declined and told him a few home truths."

"But you continued to meet him?"

She walked over to the window and looked out towards the temple across the river.

"He asked me to. It was too good an opportunity to turn down. He told me that no woman had spoken to him like that before and that he wanted to change things in the kingdom. That's when the gifts started. A month later he offered to make me his wife. He said he needed an intelligent woman by his side."

"And you said no?"

She turned to face me. "I had no intention of becoming part of that family. I said no, and then I tweaked his tail. I reminded him of the curse that afflicts the first wives of the sons of the Sai family."

"How did he react?"

"He certainly wasn't delighted. At first I think he was somewhat bemused. He seemed to treat it as something of a game — the thrill of the chase, as you English say. But when he realised I was not about to change my mind, his bemusement turned to anger. He is, after all, a man who is used to getting what he wants."

"What did he do?" I asked.

She glanced nervously at Major Bhardwaj. "First came the threats. Then came the assassination of his brother and suddenly I ended up in here."

"You think Prince Punit is responsible for your incarceration?" growled Major Bhardwaj. "The order to arrest you came with the Maharaja's personal seal affixed." He turned to me. "This is ridiculous, Captain. I'm minded to put an end to this farce."

"Even if Punit wasn't responsible for my arrest," replied Miss Bidika, "he knows that I'm here, and he knows that I'm innocent. Do you not think he could release me with a snap of his fingers? But it suits his purpose to keep me here."

"Why?" I asked. "What does he stand to gain by it?"

"He wishes to bend me to his will. Maybe he thinks I shall repent my earlier actions and fall at his feet begging for forgiveness and freedom? But what would that freedom cost?" She held me with a stare. "Do not underestimate him, *Captain* Wyndham. He may project the aura of an amiable buffoon but he is in actuality a very smart man."

"Smart enough to have engineered the murder of his own brother?"

"That's enough, Wyndham," said the major angrily.

He opened the door and shouted for the guard. I heard Bidika's voice behind me as we were frogmarched out of the room. "Rest assured he's smart enough, Captain Wyndham. I wouldn't have expected him to do it, but then I wouldn't have expected to be arrested for the crime."

Colonel Arora was waiting for us back at the Rose Building.

"Where have you been?" he asked anxiously, checking his watch. "We must hurry, or else we shall not reach Ushakothi in time."

"Ushakothi?" asked Surrender-not.

"The forest where the tiger *shikar* will take place. It's twenty-five miles from here — a two-hour drive."

"You'd better send someone to fetch Miss Grant," I said. "She planned to accompany us."

"No need," he replied. "She left with His Highness Prince Punit half an hour ago."

Surrender-not read my expression. "It looks like we don't have to waste any more time," he said hastily.

"Yes," I said. "Wonderful."

# CHAPTER
# THIRTY-THREE

Ushakothi was a nowhere in the middle of nothingness. A forest wilderness at the end of a two-hour journey across a purgatory of stunted scrub and blackened trees caked in dust.

The Cadillac 55 had its roof down, with Surrender-not and I seated in the rear, drinking in a blessedly cooling breeze. Up front sat Arora and a chauffeur who seemed either mute or indifferent. The motion and the monotony lulled me into reminiscence.

I thought back to the war. The Yanks, when they'd finally shown up, used the 55 as staff cars for their top brass, and you saw quite a few them on the streets of Paris in '17. There were a damn sight fewer of them on the mud-bog lanes near the Front. Not that our own staff cars were any less rare.

My reverie was broken by the colonel. "The best time for hunting is the early morning," he said, "before it gets too hot. But His Highness prefers the late afternoon. It is not quite as cool, but it's a better fit in terms of his waking hours."

The car eventually turned off the dirt road, passing between age-old rusted gates set in a high mud-brick wall, and onto a track that meandered for miles through a forest of desiccated trees until it stopped abruptly at a clearing. The chauffeur pulled up in front of two white tents, each the size of a wedding marquee, and killed the engine. The silence of the forest enveloped us, perforated only by the crickets and the ticking of the resting motor. The grey sky was low and constricting, as though the gods had placed a lid over the clearing.

We got down and stretched, then followed Arora towards one of the tents. As outdoor accommodation went it was not too shabby: I'd been in brick buildings that were less solid. Within its curtained walls the forest outside was suddenly a memory, banished by Persian rugs, French furniture and a dozen hampers from Harrods and Fortnum's.

Annie, in jodhpurs and hunting jacket, was seated in a wicker chair, sipping from a flute of pink champagne and reading a copy of *Tatler*. Next to her sat Emily Carmichael, a jade-green silk scarf tied loosely around her neck. The prince sat opposite, dressed in plus fours and a tweed jacket probably more suited to Orkney than Orissa.

Off to one side, Fitzmaurice, a stub of a cigar in his hand, stood in muttered conversation with Carmichael and Davé. The latter hadn't dressed for the hunt and had chosen London pinstripes and Oxford brogues that wouldn't have looked amiss in Carmichael's wardrobe.

"You made it then!" exclaimed the prince, clearly relieved that he could now start hunting. "Champagne for the gallant captain and the sergeant," he shouted, rising from his chair.

I took two glasses from the tray that appeared and handed one to Surrender-not. As I sipped, I got the feeling I was being watched. I turned in time to see Fitzmaurice drop his gaze and take a vigorous puff of his cigar. He looked like a man trying to steady his nerves. I decided it was time to have a talk with the fellow. But before I could think of a way to get him alone, he extricated himself from the others and began to walk over.

He seemed shrunken somehow, his natural superiority chastened, replaced by something else. Surrender-not noticed it too.

"It seems Sir Ernest may have something on his mind," he whispered. He gestured to the hampers. "If you don't mind, sir, I'll go and help myself to a sandwich."

It's a fact of nature that an Englishman abhors sharing his intimate thoughts. It's why we accepted the Reformation so readily: we find it difficult to confess, even to a priest. And if we are loath to unburden ourselves to a man of God, there isn't a cat in hell's chance of us unburdening ourselves in front of a native. It would be a sign of weakness.

"Good idea," I said. "Just keep your eyes on us."

The sergeant nodded an acknowledgement and wandered off just as Fitzmaurice arrived.

"Captain Wyndham."

I noticed the sweat glistening on his neck. His throat looked red raw.

"I wondered if I might have a word."

"Shall we take a walk outside?" I asked. "The air in here is rather close for comfort."

I lifted the tarpaulin door and held it up for him to exit. We walked slowly away from the camp towards the tree-line, the detritus of the forest floor crackling under our feet. Fitzmaurice sniffed ponderously at the air.

"Is something on your mind, Sir Ernest?" I asked.

"I think . . ." He paused, as though summoning up the courage to continue. "I think that my life may be in danger."

I tried not to betray my surprise.

"What makes you think that?" I asked, staring straight ahead.

The businessman took a shaky puff of his cigar. "There's a man in Sambalpore, an Englishman, name of Golding . . ."

His voice trailed off, willing me to fill the void. But I wasn't about to do that.

"He seems to have disappeared."

Behind us came a rustling. I looked back to see Surrender-not emerge from the tent, keeping an eye out as promised. What I hadn't expected was to see the Dewan, Davé, already out of the tent, watching us too.

I decided it was best to ignore him and continue my little chat with Fitzmaurice.

"I don't understand," I said. "Is Golding a friend of yours?"

"Of sorts." Fitzmaurice stopped at the edge of the clearing and stubbed his cigar out on the emaciated trunk of a neem tree, then dropped it on the ground. "He used to be an employee of Anglo-Indian Diamond.

I was supposed to meet him yesterday but he failed to show up. I've tried locating him but no one seems to know where he is."

I thought back to Golding's diary. There'd been no mention of any meeting with Fitzmaurice. That meant that Golding had either forgotten to enter it, something I doubted, or purposely not made a note of it. Or, it meant that Fitzmaurice was lying.

"And you think his disappearance puts your own life in danger?"

Fitzmaurice turned to look at me. What little colour there was had drained from his face.

"Golding was intimately involved in a transaction which Anglo-Indian is negotiating with the royal family. He was preparing a report, the contents of which are critical to the deal. I'd been trying to persuade him to give me first sight of the document —"

"And how were you doing that?" I asked.

"The specifics are irrelevant," he said, shaking his head. "What matters is that he's disappeared. Certain people in Sambalpore would not be pleased to learn that Golding was speaking to me."

"You think they'd kill him for it?"

"Him *and* me." He looked like he meant it.

"They'd be willing to kill Englishmen for something so trivial?"

Fitzmaurice nodded. "These people aren't like us, Captain. They're rather keen on vengeance."

That might have been true, but I wasn't sure I quite believed him.

"In that case," I said, "I'd have thought the last place you'd want to be was a tiger hunt. Loaded weapons and wild animals aren't particularly conducive to a safe environment. Why aren't you already on your way back to Calcutta?"

"Trust me, I've thought of that. Had it not been for your presence here, and a direct request from Prince Punit that I attend, I'd happily have given it a miss. As it is, I'm leaving tonight."

In the distance, Punit exited the tent. He called out to Fitzmaurice.

"I say, Sir Ernest, best not to tarry. I'm sure you're eager to crack on, no?"

"Of course," called the old Englishman. "Such good sport."

The prince clapped his hands and Fitzmaurice and I headed back towards the tents.

A bearer handed out the guns. Good ones, too. Made by *Purdey's of Mayfair* — gunmakers to the King, as well as to international aristocracy and any other rich bastard who felt a need to shoot things that didn't shoot back.

Punit made a show of examining his, taking aim at some imaginary beast to the left of my head.

"Ever hunted before, Captain?" he asked.

"I can't say I have," I replied, "though I know my way around a gun."

"Excellent!" He smiled, then turned to a uniformed bearer and uttered a command.

**324**

A bugle sounded and from the edge of the clearing, four elephants lumbered into view, each resplendent in a green and golden sheet and a silver *howdah* — a seating platform of velvet cushions. Beside each beast walked its mahout.

"Now how shall we do this?" queried the prince. "Two per elephant, I suppose. Miss Grant shall ride with me, Sir Ernest and Captain Wyndham, Mr and Mrs Carmichael, and finally Sergeant Banerjee and Colonel Arora."

"What about Mr Davé?" I asked.

"He's not interested in hunting," said the prince blithely. "And he needs to get back to Sambalpore."

If the prince considered it odd that the Dewan would make the two-hour trip into the middle of nowhere simply to head straight back, he didn't show it. I didn't have time to dwell on the matter, though. I wasn't keen on the thought of Annie and Punit on the back of an elephant together. What was more, I had a reason to try to stop them. A good, professional reason — I wanted at last to get some answers out of Punit.

"Your Highness," I said, "I was hoping *I* might accompany you. I'm informed that Your Highness is quite the hunter."

The prince hesitated, torn between the appeal of imparting his wisdom to a *sahib* and that of being atop an elephant with Annie.

"That sounds like a good idea," interjected Annie. "Sam tells me he's a terrible shot. Maybe he could learn a thing or two from you?"

That settled it.

"Very well, Captain," said Punit. "You shall ride with me, and I shall teach you Britishers how to hunt tiger. Miss Grant shall accompany Sir Ernest."

People began making for their designated elephants. I caught Annie's arm.

"You seem to have a bit of sway with the prince," I whispered.

"You're not jealous, are you, Sam?" She smiled. "You should be thanking me. He wouldn't have agreed to your suggestion if I hadn't intervened."

Riding an elephant wasn't exactly the most comfortable of experiences, even when ensconced in the luxury of a well-padded *howdah*. The platform jerked constantly from side to side as the animal put one foot in front of the other, and the whole thing felt like being adrift in a rowing boat when the wind got up.

Nevertheless, the journey through the forest was almost pleasant, punctuated by the sounds of the birds in the trees and the heavy rhythmic footsteps of the elephants.

Then came voices.

We emerged into another clearing, larger this time, where stood close to a hundred natives, thin dark men with bare legs and white shirts, their heads wrapped in cotton turbans against the heat. A few carried drums; most had sticks and makeshift weapons.

"*Chalo!*" shouted the prince, and a roar went up from the assembly. The drums began and the men set off into head-high grass. The elephants, though, didn't follow.

"We must let the beaters get ahead of us," said the prince. "In your fox-hunting, you send your hounds to flush out your prey. Here we use men instead of dogs, but it's the same thing."

Maybe it was, but I'd never heard of a fox that could rip a hound to shreds.

"Are the beaters ever mauled?" I asked.

"Sometimes," he replied. "Not often, though, and if it happens, their families are well looked after."

That was reassuring.

"I tried fox-hunting in England once," he continued, "but I didn't much care for it." He made a face. "Riding around on a horse all day in the rain, chasing something resembling a large rat, and then watching as the dogs have all the fun. It was rather dull."

"Well, that's England for you," I replied. And I could see his point. It was hard for anyone to appreciate the subtle pleasures of a wet weekend chasing a fox round some sodden fields in Leicestershire, much less a prince used to shooting tigers from the back of an elephant.

The shouts and drums grew fainter until, finally, the prince gave the order and we lurched off into the undergrowth.

"Keep a lookout in the trees," urged the prince.

"What for?" I asked.

"Panthers. They're not averse to taking men from their *howdahs*."

I heeded the advice and cocked my rifle.

When the drumbeats grew louder once more, we saw the beaters splayed out in a wide semicircle, heading back towards us, beating the grass and shouting. I suddenly realised what that meant. They'd cornered a tiger and were driving it to us. I watched as the ring of men grew tighter, leaving no escape for the animal, hidden in the undergrowth.

Then I saw it, a flash of gold and black among the tall yellow grass.

"Here we go," said the prince, ordering the mahout to pursue.

We gave chase through the bush, until suddenly the tiger turned and stood snarling in front of us, its muscles quivering under its pelt. In my experience, no other creature bears comparison with a Royal Bengal tiger. It is grace, power and beauty made flesh.

Punit called over to Fitzmaurice. "Sir Ernest," he shouted, "may I offer you first shot?"

Ever the gentleman, Fitzmaurice demurred. "Maybe Miss Grant would care to shoot first?" he said.

I watched Annie raise her rifle, take aim, then fire.

The noise sent a flock of birds exploding from the trees. The tiger dived into the thicket.

"Women!" laughed the prince. "How did she miss from there?"

Fitzmaurice shouted something at the mahout and their elephant set off in pursuit. At the same time, the elephant of Colonel Arora and Surrender-not circled to one side, hoping to cut off the creature's escape.

The beaters, too, circled round, forcing the beast back, and suddenly it was cornered once again. This time, Fitzmaurice took the shot. The tiger roared. Then came another shot, this time from the prince, then a third from Colonel Arora, all hitting their mark. But the animal refused to fall. It took several more shots before its legs buckled and it collapsed to the ground. Still it roared its defiance. Finally, Punit took aim at the creature's head and fired one last time.

A gang of villagers set to work retrieving the beast. A native with a box camera began positioning his equipment, as Fitzmaurice harangued his mahout to let him down so that he could pose for a photograph with his prize.

"That didn't seem particularly sporting," I said, "what with the beaters and all. You might as well shoot fish in a barrel."

"It was for Fitzmaurice's benefit," said the prince tersely. "That man couldn't hit a moving target if his life depended on it. So we let him have a pop at some of the older, tired ones. We even have a special tape measure for him, so that whatever he shoots is recorded as being at least eight feet long. Me, though, I prefer a *real* hunt."

"Then call off the beaters, Your Highness," I said. "Let's do it properly."

He looked at me, then smiled. "I'd rather received the impression you didn't approve of this sort of thing, Captain. But I see you're a hunter after all." He reached for a silver hip flask, unscrewed the top and took a swig, then offered it to me.

"Of sorts," I replied, taking a nip.

Punit shouted down to one of the beaters and soon the message was passed along — *the prince wishes to*

**329**

*hunt* — and we were off, back into the tall, tinder-dry grass, this time without the shouts and drums.

We left the main party well behind. The Carmichaels had joined Annie and Fitzmaurice in stopping to admire Sir Ernest's kill, and that left only Surrender-not and Colonel Arora, and a solitary old tracker who walked ahead of us, looking for signs of tiger activity.

We travelled for what felt like hours, the sounds of the forest enveloping us: the strange, ghost-like bleating of the spotted deer, the crack and rustle of branches as the elephants passed by, and the calls of a dozen different birds. Here, in the midst of nowhere, everything began to seem simpler, as if Sambalpore and its courtly intrigues were a million miles away.

The prince broke the silence. "You know, in the old days, Father liked to come out here for weeks at a time. He'd get up early each morning, head out into the jungle with only his gun-bearer for company and shoot a tiger before breakfast. He was quite a prodigious hunter. I was seven the first time he allowed me to accompany him and Adhir. They brought out a tiger especially for me to shoot, obviously not a very good one, but to a child of seven it was impressive nonetheless."

"And did you shoot it?" I asked.

"Oh yes," he replied matter-of-factly. "Right between the eyes."

The light began to fade, yet still we continued. The tracker searched for signs — a pad print in the dirt, a tuft of fur caught on a thorn bush, even tiger excrement. Finally, he looked up and nodded: he'd caught the trail. We pressed on, keenly aware of something new in the still, sweltering air. It heightened our senses and imbued the forest noises with fresh significance, charging them with electricity.

Somewhere close by, a crow shrieked and flew skyward. I looked up. Even the monkeys in the pipal trees looked wary. I tasted dust on my tongue. Then abruptly, the tracker stopped and pointed. I saw a streak of something in the undergrowth disappear almost instantly, reappearing a moment later.

"We have him now," said the prince.

Except it wasn't a "him". The tiger was now only forty feet from us, but behind it were two more — small golden and black cubs.

"A mother," I said.

"Yes," he said and reached for rifle.

The tigress must have realised the danger. She could easily have run, yet she stood her ground, placing herself between us and her cubs, and bared her teeth.

Punit raised his rifle, took aim, and then everything seemed to stop, as it often does in that primal moment before the kill. Even the monkeys sensed it. From their positions in the trees, they began to shriek. I looked over at them and something else caught my eye.

A glint of metal in one of the trees.

Three years of sitting in a trench in wartime France might not have taught me much, but it had taught me to recognise a sniper when I saw one. I shouted to Punit to get down even as I leaped forwards to pull him to the base of the *howdah*.

I heard a shot, then what sounded like an echo. Above me the wooden canopy exploded in a hail of splinters.

"Stay down!" I shouted as I grabbed my own rifle. Another shot rang out, the bullet ricocheting off the silver lip of the *howdah*.

I raised my rifle. It took me a moment to pinpoint the attacker. I couldn't make out much at this distance save for the fact that the man was a native and clad in a grey-brown shawl. Then came the crack of another gunshot, not from the attacker, but from our left. It was Surrender-not. The other elephant had drawn level and the sergeant too had picked out the sniper. Surrender-not was pretty handy with a rifle, and his first shot was close enough to our assailant to panic the man. My training kicked in. I took aim and fired. My shot wasn't as accurate as Surrender-not's but it didn't have to be. All I had to do was keep the sniper off-balance. The sergeant could do the rest.

He followed up with another shot and this one found its mark. The gunman dropped his rifle and fell from the tree. Surrender-not trained his rifle on the spot where he should have landed, but, with the tall grass and the fading light, it was hard to make out very much.

The prince was still on the floor of the *howdah*. I leant over and tapped him on the shoulder. "The danger's passed, Your Highness."

He took my hand as I helped him up. Suddenly there was a shout from the other elephant. It was Colonel Arora.

"He's running for it!" he yelled, pointing to a movement in the grass. He turned back to me, "You're a military man, Captain. You know what to do!"

He ordered his mahout to circle out to the left and the elephant ploughed forward through the undergrowth.

"Your Highness," I said, pointing, "please order our driver to pursue our fleeing friend."

The prince uttered something. The mahout shouted "*Digar, digar!*" and we were off again.

"Where's Arora going?" asked the prince. "Why aren't they joining us?"

"Tactics, Your Highness," I replied. "It's just like tiger hunting. We're the beaters. Our job is to drive our prey into the path of the colonel and Sergeant Banerjee. They'll do the rest."

The light was dying but it was still just possible to follow him. I asked Punit to order the mahout to slow down: there was no point in pushing the attacker forward until Arora and Surrender-not were in position to head him off. It was a fine balance, and once darkness fell the odds would quickly turn in his favour.

Then a shot rang out.

"Faster!" I shouted and pointed towards the noise. The other elephant had stopped next to a river. Arora stood on the ground while Surrender-not was sat up in the *howdah* with his rifle trained on a figure lying prone in the grass.

"Is he all right?" I shouted down to the colonel.

Arora looked up. "He'll live."

"Did you shoot him?"

"No," he replied, brandishing the butt of his rifle. "I just gave him a tap on the head with this."

He knelt down and rolled the man over. The fellow was unconscious. His bare arms and face glistened with sweat, and on his temple, a purple bruise was blossoming where Arora's rifle butt had made contact. It had smeared the ash that was painted onto his forehead, but the original shape was unmistakable — the *Sricharanam*. The mark of the followers of Vishnu.

The mahout ordered the elephant to its knees and I jumped down.

"It looks like you gave him more than a *tap*," I said. "Do you recognise him?"

"I can't say I do," replied the colonel. "But Sambalpore is a small place. If he's from around here, someone will recognise him. And if he's not, we'll just have to get the truth out of him ourselves."

"In that case," said Prince Punit, "we should get him back to Sambalpore."

"You are unhurt, Your Highness?" asked Arora.

"I'm perfectly fine," replied the prince testily.

With the unconscious attacker hogtied and unceremoniously dumped atop the colonel's elephant, we groped our way slowly back through the darkness. It was over an hour before we spotted the flickering lights of the camp. The conversation had been muted since the attack. The prince didn't seem to want to talk, and I was happy with the silence as I had my own thoughts to organise.

**334**

I no longer saw much point in questioning Punit. Even if I did, asking him about his brother's assassination moments after someone had taken potshots at him seemed a trifle indelicate. As the camp drew near, though, the prince finally spoke.

"Thank you for your actions back there, Wyndham. I won't forget it."

"I did what anyone would have done in my position, Your Highness."

"Do you think you can get the bastard to talk?" he asked.

"We'll find out when we get him back to Sambalpore," I said.

"Be that as it may, I'm indebted to you. But, Captain, I'd be grateful for your discretion regarding what transpired today. I wouldn't want to spoil the mood for our other guests."

"Naturally, Your Highness," I said. "I won't mention it and I'll make sure Sergeant Banerjee doesn't either. I can't speak for Colonel Arora, though."

"You leave Colonel Arora to me," he replied.

Our approach triggered a buzz of activity in the camp. A half-dozen servants ran up to guide the elephants, help us dismount and pass round stiff shots of whisky. The prince knocked his back, then picked up another and headed for the tents, while Colonel Arora and his men dealt with the prisoner. I was about to join them when Surrender-not stopped me.

"I need to speak to you, sir," he urged. "In private."

He had that surly look about him that generally heralded bad news.

We walked close to where the elephants were being fed and watered, out of earshot of the tents. I took out a pack of Capstans and a box of matches, passed him a cigarette and took one for myself. I lit both, then took a long drag and exhaled.

"What's on your mind, Sergeant?"

"It's Colonel Arora, sir. I think he was in two minds about apprehending the attacker."

I almost choked on my cigarette.

"It looked to me like he did a pretty good job of clubbing the man over the head. Are you sure?"

"I think so, sir."

Surrender-not had to be mistaken. Arora would hardly have wanted the man to get away. "Tell me what happened," I said with a sigh.

The sergeant looked over his shoulder. Satisfied that no one could overhear, he continued. "As you saw, after the assailant jumped from the tree and started running, the colonel took us off to circle around —"

"Yes," I nodded impatiently, "to cut off the man's escape. It was a sound strategy."

"Yes. But it's what transpired *afterwards*, once we were in position, that's the issue." He took a nervous pull of his cigarette. "The colonel said he thought the man was making for a nearby river, the one place where the forest wasn't bounded by a wall. We headed for it and managed to reach the ridge above the river a few minutes before we spotted your elephant coming towards us.

"The colonel ordered our mahout to move directly into your path, in the expectation that you were driving the attacker that way. The light was growing faint and he thought there might be a chance that the assailant would slip past us, especially once he saw our elephant. So he decided to get down and conceal himself a little further along the ridge. He told me to remain in the *howdah* so that I'd have a clear shot if the man came towards me."

I was getting impatient. "That all seems quite sensible to me. What exactly is your point, Sergeant?"

"This, sir," he replied forcefully. "Despite the darkness, we caught sight of the attacker running towards the river. Sure enough, he saw the elephant and changed course; right into the path of where the colonel was waiting. The next thing I see is the colonel rising from the grass with his rifle. The attacker almost ran into him. Then the two of them stared at each other for a good few seconds. It was only after I'd let off a shot that the colonel hit him with his rifle butt."

"You're sure?"

"As certain as I could be given the failing light."

"And does the colonel know you saw him?"

"I don't think so. His attention was on the attacker."

I tried to make sense of it. If Surrender-not *were* correct, there were two possibilities. The first was that Arora had recognised the gunman, and for whatever reason had frozen — unlikely given his military background. The second was more disturbing — that Arora himself was somehow involved in the attack, and if he were part of such a conspiracy, did it mean he'd also been a party to the assassination of Prince Adhir?

I leaned against a tree and decided the most useful thing I could do was to finish my cigarette and think it through. It appeared that Punit, my prime suspect, was himself a target for assassination, and Arora, the only man in Sambalpore that I trusted, a man I'd smoked opium with hours earlier, might be a party to the plot. If that wasn't enough, there was the small matter of a missing Englishman whom I suspected of having been murdered by the kingdom's prime minister, and a second who believed his life was in danger.

I stubbed out the cigarette butt on the tree trunk.

"What now, sir?" asked Surrender-not.

"Now? We go back to Sambalpore and question our guest. But before that, I'm going to head back to the tent and help myself to a double of everything they've got."

# CHAPTER
# THIRTY-FOUR

The sudden possibility that Arora might be playing a double game cast doubt on almost everything.

I needed time to think, to try to figure out just what the hell was going on. I'd hoped the journey back to Sambalpore would give me that time, but Punit had other ideas.

I wasn't sure exactly when, but at some point after being shot at, he'd decided to appoint me his de facto bodyguard, at least till we got back to town. And so, in a black mood, I'd joined him and Annie for two of the longest hours of my life, sitting in the front of a ridiculously camouflaged Rolls-Royce, while the man whose life I'd just saved sat in the back and tried to flirt with the object of my affections. As experiences went, it rated slightly behind being subjected to a gas attack in a trench.

The prince's chatter was peppered with talk of high society, film stars and exotic locations, all dropped into conversation with the subtlety of a howitzer. But the thing is, a howitzer generally gets the job done. I didn't doubt that Annie possessed the intelligence to see right through Punit, but I'd imagine it takes an uncommonly strong woman to resist an invitation to Chamonix for

**339**

Christmas or Cannes in the spring. What was distinctly lacking from his conversation was any mention of the attack that had just taken place, or the fact that the gunman was now on his way to the palace in the back of one of the catering lorries. That felt like odd behaviour for a man who seemed to have a constant need to talk about himself. It was possible he was embarrassed by his role in the proceedings. Maybe had I not been in the car, he'd have recounted the tale for Annie's benefit, possibly portraying himself as the hero of the encounter. Or maybe the whole episode had put the fear of God into him.

I did my best to ignore the goings-on in the back and ran through the facts. Adhir was dead, shot by an attacker with the *Sricharanam* on his forehead. That man had later killed himself. Punit had just been attacked by a gunman with the same mark on his forehead. Portelli had identified it as the mark of the followers of the god Vishnu, of whom the Lord Jagannath was an avatar. And according to the anthropologist, Sambalpore was tied closely to the Jagannath cult.

That Punit had also been targeted for assassination suggested this might be a wider plot against the entire royal family, and, if so, would imply that he wasn't the instigator of his brother's murder. And yet there *had* to be some connection to the palace, or else how would the concubine, Rupali, have caught wind of it?

A plot to destroy the royal family, hatched from *within* the royal court. The two things were difficult to reconcile.

There was one other possibility that occurred to me, only because I was a suspicious bastard who really didn't like the prince very much. It struck me, as we jolted over a particularly deep pothole, that perhaps the whole attack on Punit had been a fake, stage-managed to throw me off the scent. Maybe the prince's life had never been in danger? Maybe the attacker was in the pay of the prince? Maybe that's why Arora had hesitated before clubbing the man.

But that would mean Arora was in league with the prince. Had he been Punit's man all along, charged with ensuring Adhir was murdered in Calcutta? He had, after all, been the one who'd chosen the circuitous route back to the prince's hotel that day. But it made no sense. It had been Arora who, over the objections of the Dewan, had convinced the Maharaja to allow Surrender-not and me to investigate. And it was Arora who'd organised for the telegraph and telephone lines to be cut to stop us being recalled to Calcutta. Why do any of that if he was responsible for the very crime we were investigating? I was tying myself in knots. There had to be something else, some other explanation for why he might have hesitated in apprehending the attacker.

Whatever the answers were, I hoped to get them soon enough from our prisoner.

"You'll join us for dinner, Captain?" asked Punit as the car drew up outside the guest lodge. "It'll only be a small affair. I was thinking me, Miss Grant, Fitzmaurice, Davé, Colonel Arora and you and your sergeant. It will give us a chance to have that chat you wanted."

I couldn't see any way of refusing.

"Of course, Your Highness," I replied, as a footman opened my door. "Though I have to attend to something first."

"Excellent," replied the prince, rubbing his hands together. "Shall we say nine o'clock?"

"I'll let Sergeant Banerjee know," I said, exiting the car.

"Nine o'clock then," the prince confirmed as the footmen closed the doors.

I turned to Annie as the car moved off towards the palace.

"You'll need to invest in some warm clothing," I said, "if you're planning to spend Christmas in the Alps with Prince Douglas Fairbanks there."

"Now now, Sam," she said as she took my arm. "That sort of talk really doesn't become you. Besides, I'm much more interested in what happened out there in the jungle after you'd left me behind with Fitzmaurice and the Carmichaels. You and Punit spend a few hours on an elephant and now you're his best friend?"

"I could ask you the same question," I said.

She smiled. "Did you manage to ask *him* what you wanted to?"

"Not really. I'm giving him the benefit of the doubt."

She took a breath.

"Adhir was murdered in Calcutta," she said patiently. "From what you've told me, it was a well-planned assassination, and when cornered, the assassin took his own life. Do you honestly think Punit is capable of that sort of planning or engendering that sort of loyalty?"

I said nothing and instead escorted her inside. The scent of attar of roses hung in the air. At the foot of the stairs she removed her arm from mine.

"Do you fancy a drink?" she asked.

Time alone with her — wasn't this what I'd hoped for when I'd invited her to come with me to Sambalpore? And yet right now I had a prisoner to question. I cursed myself.

"I can't," I said. "There's something I need to do."

"You're sure?"

"I'm afraid so."

Her face fell. "Well, in that case, I may as well have a rest before dinner. It's no fun drinking alone."

I watched as she made her way up to her room. She was probably right about Punit. The man was a fop, a good-time Charlie. Even if he possessed the inclination to murder his own brother, did he have the foresight to formulate such a plan and the discipline to see it through? And yet Shreya Bidika, who knew him far better than I did, couldn't discount the possibility. Who knew where the truth lay?

I walked back out into the evening air, just as the car containing Colonel Arora and Surrender-not drew up.

"Where's the prisoner?" I asked.

"He's being taken to the guardhouse in the barracks," replied the colonel.

"Is he *compos mentis*?"

"He's come round, but he's not making much sense," said Surrender-not. "He may have concussion."

That was less than ideal. I opened the rear door and got in beside Surrender-not. "Let's go and see, shall we?"

# CHAPTER
# THIRTY-FIVE

The guardhouse was a squat structure set close to the Rose Building. Entry was via an arched doorway into a corridor that smelled of boot polish and perspiration. At Arora's orders, we were shown through to the cells by two guards. The prisoner was at the far end lying on a cot bed. Arora nodded and the guards unlocked the cell door, then lifted the man up by his arms and onto his feet. His head hung limp. Arora walked forward, grabbed a fistful of his hair and yanked it back. The man's eyes opened, bloodshot and unfocused.

"You're going to answer some questions," said Arora. "Who sent you?"

The man said nothing.

"What is your name?" The man groaned as Arora yanked his head further. "We'll get what we need out of you."

Arora released his grip and the prisoner slumped forward again. He walked around behind him, muttered something in a foreign tongue, then punched him in the kidneys. The man writhed in pain as the two guards held him upright. The colonel raised his arm but I caught and held his fist before he could deliver another blow.

"Wait," I said.

He turned and stared at me. There was madness in his eyes.

"This is pointless. We want to ask him questions, not beat him to a pulp."

"You have a better way?" growled the colonel.

"Get a doctor in here. See to his head injury, then get him some food. We can question him in the morning."

Arora considered it. "Very well," he said. He issued some orders to the guards and then stalked out. The guards dropped their prisoner unceremoniously onto the cell floor, then guided us out and locked the door.

Surrender-not and I walked slowly back to the guest lodge.

"What do we do now, sir?" he asked.

"We stick to the plan," I said. "We have dinner with the prince, then get back to the Dewan's office and look for Golding's report."

"You think the Dewan might be involved in today's attack?" he asked.

"I don't know," I said, "but if he's a suspect in Adhir's assassination, that also makes him a suspect for the attack on Punit."

"There is another possibility, sir," he ventured. "What if the prince hadn't been the intended target? What if the victim was supposed to have been you?"

"Things are complicated enough without us indulging in conspiracies of that nature," I replied.

"I'm serious," he said. "And there's something else. What if the search of the Dewan's office is a trap?"

"Explain," I said.

"It's Colonel Arora, sir. I can't shake the thought of his hesitation before apprehending the assassin. Do you really think we can trust him?"

"He's the one who persuaded the Maharaja to allow us to investigate," I said. "Why would he do that if he didn't want to get to the bottom of it?"

He didn't look convinced. "But what about his actions this afternoon? You think there's an innocent explanation for that?"

I ran a hand through my hair. "I just can't believe he's involved in a plot to assassinate the Sambalpore princes."

Surrender-not thought for a moment. "Maybe he's only involved in a plot to assassinate the second prince?" he said quietly.

"What?"

"Maybe he believes that Punit murdered Prince Adhir. Perhaps this was his attempt at retribution?"

It was an interesting theory — it would explain why Arora might have wanted to let Punit's attacker escape but still wanted our help to solve the case of who was behind Adhir's murder. If Surrender-not was right, it meant that Punit was still a suspect with regard to Adhir's murder. And if Arora had hired the second assassin to kill Punit, it would explain the colonel's willingness to beat our prisoner to a pulp before we'd extracted any information from him.

"What do you think?" asked Surrender-not.

I sighed. "I think we need to keep an eye on Colonel Arora."

# CHAPTER
# THIRTY-SIX

Dinner was a low-key affair, at least by Sambalpori standards, and probably because Punit wasn't exactly in high spirits. I didn't blame him. Being a target for assassination was guaranteed to put a dampener on anyone's day; for a prince accustomed to adoration and obeisance, it must have been particularly troubling.

That was, of course, assuming he hadn't staged it himself. However unlikely that theory might be, I wasn't about to discount it just yet.

There had been the usual pre-prandial drinks, but Annie had turned up only minutes before the servants rang the gong and I suspected her tardiness hadn't helped the prince's mood. He'd barely said a word to Carmichael — not that I could fault him for that — nor to the Dewan; what he did say tended towards the monosyllabic. Fitzmaurice was missing from the ensemble, no doubt en route to the station to catch the train back to British India.

It was only when the conversation turned to hunting that the prince became animated. Carmichael began to retell the day's events for the benefit of the Dewan, who, to his credit, feigned interest remarkably well. Then came stories of Carmichael's previous hunts, where it sounded like he'd bagged pretty much every creature that had had the misfortune to cross his path, everything from antelope to water buffalo, like King Leopold of the Belgians shooting his way across the Congo. Bored, I spent a few pleasant moments imagining what his own head might look like mounted on a wall.

Annie's eventual arrival felt like a godsend. She was dressed in ivory silk and sported a golden necklace, intricately designed in the Indian style and studded with small diamonds. I'd never seen her wear it before, and the thought hit me that it might be a present from Punit. For my part, I'd once bought her flowers, so I felt we were pretty much even in the gift-giving stakes.

In the absence of his father, Punit sat at the head of the table, with Annie to his right. Colonel Arora made for the chair beside her, but I wasn't keen on that. In the nick of time I dispatched Surrender-not to beat him to it. Arora seemed rather put out, but there wasn't much he could do. Instead, he consoled himself by taking the seat next to me.

This all turned out to be a tactical error. Surrender-not said very little throughout dinner and Punit had Annie's undivided attention. I cursed myself. The colonel might at least have put up a conversational fight. Surrender-not just sat there chewing his vegetables.

Beside me, Arora sat with a face like Sisyphus behind his rock. He seemed to have as little time for Punit's stories as I did. As the meal ended, though, he became more animated. He murmured to me to wait.

As the others left the dining room, he reached into his jacket pocket and extracted a sealed envelope and passed it to me.

"Keys," he said. "To Davé's office and the safe. Happy hunting," he continued as I pocketed the envelope. "Now we should rejoin the others."

In the lounge, Punit was busy placing a record on the gramophone, and soon the syncopated rhythm of ragtime burst forth.

"Come on," shouted the prince, taking Annie by the arm, "let's dance!" She smiled and followed him into the middle of the room, and I looked on as Punit indulged in a series of physical jerks and gestures that reminded me of the actions of shell-shocked men in the trenches. Not that anyone else seemed to notice anything odd. Some of them even clapped.

"What's he doing?" I asked Carmichael.

"It's called the Turkey Trot," he replied, taking a sip of whisky, "an American dance that the prince is quite fond of."

"It looks like he's having a fit," I said.

"Don't let him hear you say that, old man," he replied. "He thinks it's the height of sophistication."

"Your Highness is quite the dancer," said Annie as the music ended and she and the prince walked over. "Wherever did you learn?"

"Right here," he replied, panting, "though my teacher was from Blackpool. It is a fact, my dear, that all the finest dancers hail from Blackpool."

350

He clicked his fingers and a liveried waiter appeared carrying a bottle of Dom Perignon and half a dozen champagne flutes on a silver tray. The prince took one and passed it to Annie, before helping himself to another.

He took a sip and laughed. "Tonight we shall party with gay abandon!"

I took two glasses from the waiter and headed over to where Davé stood watching the proceedings. He declined my offer politely.

"Thank you," he said, "but I don't drink."

"I thought everyone at court drank?" I said.

"Not all of us," he replied. "And someone must remain sober to ensure His Highness makes it safely to his bed."

"Babysitting the heir to the throne," I said. "That hardly sounds like a job for a prime minister."

"Well," he sighed, "let us say that my role is somewhat more *all-encompassing* than that of your Mr Lloyd George."

"You'd better make yourself comfortable," I said. "It doesn't look like the prince is in much of a hurry to get to his bed tonight."

I turned back to the revellers. The Carmichaels had joined the prince and Annie in the centre of the room, though from his face, it looked as though Mr Carmichael had not gone particularly willingly.

"You don't dance?" asked the Dewan.

I nodded towards Punit. "Not like that, at any rate."

I downed the champagne, made my excuses and headed for the exit, collecting Surrender-not on the way.

"Come on, Sergeant," I said, "we've got a report to find."

# CHAPTER
# THIRTY-SEVEN

The Rose Building was cosseted in darkness with only a solitary bulb shining in the garages below. Surrender-not and I felt our way through the gloom, up the stairs to the first floor and along the corridor to the Dewan's office. I slipped the larger of Arora's keys into the lock and turned it.

Entering the darkened room, I extracted a box of matches from my pocket and struck one. It flared into life, dimly illuminating a cavernous office split into two parts: an informal seating area, with sofas and a low table, and a step leading to a raised working area beyond, dominated by a large wooden desk. The walls were lined with paintings of rajas and ranis in regal pose, and the floor was covered with several rugs. Behind the desk stood a chair and not much more.

"Where's the safe?" asked Surrender-not.

"Check behind the desk," I replied.

The match burned down and I blew it out as the flame singed my fingers. On a corner of the desk sat a brass table lamp with a shade of emerald glass. Surrender-not closed the window shutters, then switched on the lamp, bathing the room in a dim aquamarine light. The desktop was clear of papers.

Surrender-not opened the desk drawers and began to search through them. Meanwhile, I scoured the room, looking for anything that might conceal the safe.

"Any luck?" I asked after several minutes.

He'd extracted some papers from one of the drawers and was busy leafing through them.

"Nothing so far," he said, his attention focused on the documents. "Any sign of the safe?"

"There's nothing behind any of the paintings," I said, "and there's precious little else in here to hide it behind."

"Maybe the colonel was mistaken?"

"It has to be here," I said.

"But if not under the desk or in the walls, then where?"

"I don't know," I said. Surrender-not was still poring over his pile of papers on the desk. I walked over.

"Anything?" I asked.

He looked up.

"Tell me you've found something."

"Geological reports, I think."

"Anything to do with the diamond mines?"

"I can't tell, sir."

"I suppose they're better than nothing. Grab them and let's go," I said, switching off the lamp.

He rose from his chair, and with the room plunged back into darkness we groped our way towards the door. Neither of us remembered the step between the raised area and the rest of the office. Things might have turned out rather differently if we had.

**354**

Being a few paces in front, it was I who missed the step first and took the fall. I landed awkwardly, and winced as a searing pain shot through my left ankle. A moment later, Surrender-not was sprawled beside me.

"Bloody hell," I whispered, rubbing my injured ankle. "Are you okay?"

"Yes, sir. You?"

I stood up slowly and cautiously put some weight on my left leg, then breathed a sigh of relief. "I think so," I said. "What sort of an idiot puts a step in the middle of the room?"

But the answer hit me before Surrender-not could reply. I hobbled back up to the desk and switched on the lamp.

"That rug," I said. "Help me move it."

Together, Surrender-not and I rolled up the rug that was behind the desk. I dropped to my knees for a closer look, then traced the outline of a rectangular panel, about one foot square, cut into the floorboard. At one end was a small hole, just large enough for a finger to pass through. I gently lifted out the wooden panel and placed it beside me on the floor. Beneath it was a grey metal box with a small brass plaque embossed with the words *FICHET, Paris*. I looked at Surrender-not.

"*Voilà*," I said, turning back to the hole in the floor. "One steel fire safe."

I reached into my pocket for the smaller of the two keys and placed it in the lock.

Inside the safe were a series of thin grey files, a small velvet pouch and a revolver, which, thanks to Colonel Arora, I now knew to be a Colt, identical to the one the assassin had used on Prince Adhir. Leaving the gun and the pouch in place, I lifted out the files and passed them to Surrender-not. Sitting back down at the desk, he began to leaf through the first one.

"Anything?" I asked.

"Just budget papers." He closed the file and put it to one side, then opened another. He looked up almost immediately. "This looks like it." He smiled. "Golding's report on the valuation of the Sambalpore diamond mines."

"Right," I said. "Replace the others and let's get out of here."

Ten minutes later, having repositioned the rug and locked the door, we were back in our own office. Surrender-not sat down and pulled the grey folder out from under his dinner jacket. As he did so, two thick documents slid out and onto the desk. He picked them up and examined the covers, then quickly leafed through both and frowned.

"What is it?" I asked.

"There are two reports here," he replied. "Both with the same title and both signed by Golding and dated the day before yesterday."

"Two copies of the same report?"

"I'm not sure. The signatures are different. Look, sir," he said, passing them to me.

He was right. The signatures were subtly different. I held both up to the light. There was something else peculiar. "The ink is different too," I said. "Both signatures are blue, but in different shades."

356

I passed the documents back to Surrender-not who opened both to the first page and began to compare them. He soon looked up.

"There's more, sir," he said, pointing to a paragraph in both documents. "The numbers are different."

"How different?"

"Quite substantially. It's as though they're describing two completely different sets of mines."

"How is that possible?"

"I'll have to go through them in detail, but from what I can tell from the summary, one report places a valuation on the diamond reserves hundreds of crores of rupees higher than the other."

Where we used *millions*, Indians talked in *lakhs* and *crores*. It was still confusing to me, but it didn't take a Ph.D. in mathematics to work out that hundreds of crores of rupees made for a damn big discrepancy.

"Which one has the higher figure?" I asked.

Surrender-not pointed to one. "This one," he said. "It looks as though you might have been right to suspect the Dewan, sir."

He continued reading. Suddenly his expression darkened.

"Could you just explain your theory to me, sir."

"It's simple," I said. "Davé has some illicit business going on with respect to the diamond mines. Maybe he's been dealing on the side or taking a cut on sales and covering his tracks by distorting the figures for the diamond reserves. Suddenly Anglo-Indian Diamond come sniffing around, wanting to buy the mines, and unlike in the past, this time the decision is taken to sell

**357**

them. As part of the process, Golding is tasked by Adhir with preparing a valuation report. That would have led to Davé's scam being uncovered, so he assassinates the prince and makes the accountant disappear. He then obtains the document and falsifies the figures."

Surrender-not's face fell.

"What?" I said. "Which part of it don't you like?"

"It's not that I don't like it, sir," he protested, "I just have some questions."

"How many questions?"

"Four."

"Four?"

"Yes, sir."

I stopped pacing and sat down in the chair opposite him.

"Prince Adhir was no fan of the British," he began. "I doubt he'd be happy with them having a hold over assets that are effectively Sambalpore's financial lifeblood."

"Very well," I said. "So someone else persuaded the Maharaja to sell the mines. It didn't necessarily have to be Adhir."

"Then why have Adhir assassinated? I would have thought that if the Dewan was trying to scupper the sale of the mines, Adhir would have been one of his closest allies."

It was a fair point, but as I thought it through, I realised it wasn't fatal to my theory.

"I guess he might have been at first," I said, "but when Adhir sanctioned the preparation of Golding's report, he would have sealed the Dewan's fate. He had Adhir killed so he could get his hands on the report, assuming that in Adhir's absence, it would automatically come to him. He must also have anticipated that he could then change the report and buy Golding's silence. I'm guessing Golding refused to be bought."

"Very well." Surrender-not blinked. "That leads to my second question: if the Dewan *is* responsible for Adhir's assassination, why would he also try to kill Prince Punit today?"

"You answered that one yourself earlier," I said. "The two assassination attempts aren't necessarily linked. Maybe Colonel Arora is behind the attempt on Punit because he suspects Punit had Adhir assassinated. The Dewan might have nothing to do with it."

The sergeant considered this, then nodded.

"Question three?" I asked.

"If Golding was such a fastidious accountant, why hadn't he discovered the fraud at the mines before? If, as Colonel Arora claims, he accounted for every penny spent by the royal household, it beggars belief that he wouldn't know what was going on at the diamond mines. They were the kingdom's chief source of revenue, and the size of the discrepancy suggests that any fraud must have been going on for years. How could he not have known?"

I didn't have an answer to that.

"Let's come back to that one." I sighed. "What's the fourth question?"

"As I mentioned," said Surrender-not, "the discrepancy is huge, hundreds of crores of rupees. That's millions of Pounds —"

"I know how much it is," I interjected, unwilling to admit I didn't know just how *many* millions.

"Well, I was wondering, sir . . . any man who had embezzled that much wealth would himself be almost as rich as a maharaja. If he realised the game was up, why not simply disappear and enjoy his wealth somewhere? Why bother staying on here as Dewan?"

I cursed. I had no plausible answer for this question either. The problem seemed intractable. I knew Davé was connected to Golding's disappearance. I just needed time to work out exactly how.

"Go through the two reports closely," I said, "then tell me what the differences are."

He placed the reports side by side.

"This could take some time, sir."

"You've got all night," I replied.

"You're not going to stay?"

"Would it help?"

"No."

I threw him the keys to the door and the safe and he caught them in one hand.

"Then I'll get back to the party," I said.

I headed back down the stairs and into the night. Across the gardens the palace, its lights blazing, shimmered like a mirage in the desert. Strains of American music floated over on the breeze, and the thought of having to go back in and watch Punit carrying on with Annie was suddenly more than I could stomach.

I leaned against a tree and lit a cigarette. The investigation was spiralling out of control. Punit, who'd had the clearest motive just twelve hours ago, had become the likely target of an assassination attempt and was now trying to woo Annie with the unwitting assistance of Al Jolson. Meanwhile, Colonel Arora, the closest thing I thought I had to an ally in this benighted place, looked like he might have been behind that particular plot. Then there was Surrender-not's theory that I, and not the prince, had been the intended victim, not to mention Fitzmaurice's fear that his life too was under threat. Maybe both were paranoia, but one Englishman was already missing, and Sambalpore, with its whispered plots and intrigue, seemed to be the sort of place where a healthy dose of paranoia might just help keep you alive.

I thought about Golding's disappearance and the role of the Dewan, Davé. I was sure the two had met on the morning the accountant vanished. Just how did Davé fit into the whole picture? At least we now had Golding's report. Indeed, we had not just one, but two versions of it.

In truth, all I had was a series of unending questions. I needed answers, and my best chance of getting them lay with questioning a man sitting in a cell a hundred yards away. I turned round and started walking in the direction of the guardhouse. It was time to end this.

# CHAPTER
# THIRTY-EIGHT

The barracks was busy with off-duty soldiers. They lounged outside in the warmth of the night, smoking *bidis* and playing cards, and eyed me as I walked past.

The dimly lit cell block was silent, save for the rustling of a newspaper that the duty officer was reading by a hurricane lamp.

"I want to see the prisoner," I said.

The man's face was pockmarked like a pineapple, his features dull.

He shook his head. "Not possible, *sahib*. Prisoner transferred."

"What?" I said. "To where? The infirmary?"

"No, *sahib*. To fort."

"When?" I asked. "And on whose orders?"

"Ten minutes only. Order is here." He brandished a chitty in front of me. It bore the Maharaja's personal seal and beside it a scrawl of a signature.

"Has Colonel Arora seen this?" I asked.

The man shook his head. "I don't know, *sahib*."

I left him sitting there and, taking his paperwork with me, ran out of the barracks and across the gardens, back towards the palace.

Punit's soirée was still in full swing, and Colonel Arora stood in one corner sipping a whisky.

I hurried over and grabbed his arm.

"I need to speak to you," I said. "Urgently."

Out in the hallway, I waved the transfer document at him.

"Did you order this?"

He looked at me in bewilderment. "What is it?"

"A letter authorising the transfer of the prisoner to Major Bhardwaj at the fort. It was delivered twenty minutes ago."

"What?" he said, snatching the paper from me. "On whose orders?"

"I was hoping you'd be able to tell me."

He stared at the chitty. "It's the Maharaja's seal, but I don't recognise the signature."

He crumpled the paper into a ball and stuffed it into a pocket. "Come with me," he said.

He led the way down the corridor to a study, where he picked up the telephone.

"Who are you calling?"

"Bhardwaj."

The colonel spoke rapidly to someone on the other end. The line went silent before the voice replied. The colonel's expression darkened as he listened.

He smashed the receiver back onto its cradle. "No prisoner has been transferred there this evening. What's more, they have received no orders instructing them to expect any. When was the prisoner taken?"

"About fifteen minutes ago now," I said.

The colonel picked up the telephone again. From his questions, I gathered he'd dialled through to the barracks.

"Who took custody of the prisoner?" he barked. "What?"

He hung up and looked at me.

"Who took him?" I asked.

"One of the eunuchs."

"A eunuch?"

My mind raced.

Suddenly I recalled the image of Sayeed Ali, silhouetted against the first-floor window above the courtyard within the zenana, in conversation with . . . But it couldn't be.

"Come on!" I said, making for the door. "We need to get to the Rose Building."

We ran back across the lawns, covering the distance in a matter of minutes. Arora instinctively headed for the front entrance.

"No!" I shouted. "We need the garages."

"Why?"

"Because I need to check something."

We ran round to the rear and pushed open the garage doors. The place was in darkness. The colonel switched on the lights and my stomach lurched.

"You need to set up roadblocks on all routes out of town," I said, "as quickly as possible."

"Why?" he asked.

I pointed to the one empty spot. "Because the *purdah* car is missing."

Arora stared at the space where the car should have been. He shook his head. "I don't understand."

I wasn't sure I did either. All I had was a theory.

"What if it's Devika?" I said. "The Third Maharani."

"What?"

"What if she's behind the attempt on Punit's life? What if she's trying to put her own son on the throne?"

Arora struggled to take in my words. "Prince Alok? She couldn't . . . And yet, why else would the eunuch be involved? She must have ordered him to hire the assassin, and now she's helping him escape. Who else could so easily get hold of the Maharaja's seal?"

Suddenly his expression changed. "But that would mean . . . she's responsible for Adhir's death, too."

There was a flash of something in his eyes. He turned and ran towards a telephone that hung on the far wall.

"Wait!" I shouted. "It's just a theory."

"Yes," he called back, "a theory that fits the facts." And a moment later he was shouting down the line in Hindi. He returned five minutes later.

"It's done, I've informed Punit," he said, making his way towards the Alfa. "Now I must go into town to coordinate the roadblocks."

"I'll come with you," I said.

"There's no need, Captain," he replied. "I'll inform you of developments."

"I want to be there," I said firmly.

He looked at me and considered it. "You don't want to inform Sergeant Banerjee?"

"He's busy with something else."

The colonel raised an eyebrow. "You found Golding's report?"

"Yes," I said. "We found two of them."

Colonel Arora hammered the Alfa down the road, headlights cutting through the gloom. His face was set hard, impassive as stone. He'd been all but mute since his exchange with Punit, replacing the conviviality of our previous night's journey with a determined silence. The brakes squealed as he threw the car energetically round a bend in the road, then on towards the centre of town.

"Something on your mind?" I asked.

He glanced at me. "You mean, other than the escape of our prisoner?"

"Yes."

He ignored the question and brought the car skidding to a halt outside the Beaumont Hotel.

"This is the tallest building in a central location," he said. "We should set up camp on the roof."

We rushed into the lobby, startling the receptionist. Arora growled at him in Hindi, then headed for the stairs. It seemed best to follow him. Four flights later, he flung open a door and walked out onto the roof. From the parapet I could see his men, silhouetted in the glow of the amber street lamps, moving into position.

The receptionist appeared behind us. He ran over and handed the colonel a note.

"Forgive me, Captain," said Arora as he read it, "I need to make a telephone call. I'll be back shortly."

As he headed down the stairs, I returned to the parapet and looked out over the sleeping city. Somewhere down there, our prisoner was being bundled out of town in the back of the *purdah* car, assisted in his escape by a eunuch from the royal court. Was it possible that a mere girl was responsible for it all? The notion still seemed fantastical.

To my surprise I heard the Alfa's engine burst into life and dashed over to the other side of the roof in time to see Arora speed off. Sprinting to the stairs, I ran down to the lobby and out into the street, but the car was long gone.

I hurried back inside and rushed up to the desk. The clerk had his head buried in a book. I knocked it out of his hand, grabbed him by his shirt and pulled him halfway across the counter.

"What was in the note you gave to Colonel Arora?" I asked.

The man's eyes darted from side to side like a cornered lizard. Jurisdiction or no jurisdiction, it was good to see I could still put the fear of God into someone.

"Nothing, *sahib*!" he pleaded. I felt his sour breath on my face.

"What do you mean, *nothing*?"

"When you entered, Colonel *sahib* told me to wait five minutes, then come up to roof and hand him paper."

I let go of his shirt and he stumbled backwards onto a chair. I cursed myself for my stupidity. Surrender-not had warned me not to trust the colonel but I hadn't listened, and as a result, I was stuck here, marooned at the Beaumont while Arora was off doing . . . Well, I had no idea what he was doing.

I considered my options. I could requisition some form of transport and make my way back to the palace or I could scour the streets in search of Arora. Neither seemed particularly fruitful. Instead, I settled on a third option.

"Is the bar open?" I asked.

"Yes, sir," the receptionist said, his face a confusion. He gestured with one arm. "That door."

I headed for it, then stopped and checked my watch. It was late but I had nothing to lose. I walked back to the reception desk.

"Please send a message up to Miss Pemberley in room fifteen. Tell her that Captain Wyndham apologises for disturbing her so late in the evening, but that he is in the bar and, if she's free, would request her company."

"Yes, *sahib*." He nodded as he scribbled the note onto a piece of paper.

The bar was empty save for a suited European slumped over a glass in a corner. I chose a table by the window and was nursing a Laphroaig when Miss Pemberley walked in, dressed in a white blouse and black skirt, her hair falling loosely over her shoulders. I stood up.

"I'm surprised to see you here, Captain."

"Miss Pemberley," I said, "I apologise for the lateness of the hour, but I was in the vicinity and I have a few more questions . . ." My voice trailed off.

"You're lucky to have caught me," she said. "I've been out saying my goodbyes. I'm leaving tomorrow."

"May I offer you a drink?"

"Tonic water."

I gestured to the barman and ordered her tonic and another whisky.

"How's your investigation coming along?" she asked.

"It's progressing."

The barman brought over the drinks. "So," she said, "you had some questions for me?"

"I wanted to ask your opinion of the Dewan."

"Mr Davé?" she asked, sipping softly at her tonic water. "I'm not sure I have one," she said, "though Adi didn't particularly like him."

"Do you think Adhir would have had him replaced, once he became Maharaja?"

"He mentioned it once or twice, but he'd no idea who to replace him with." She suddenly sat upright. "You don't think he had anything to do with Adi's murder, do you?"

"I'm considering all the options," I replied.

She shook her head in consternation. "You and I both know his brother Punit's responsible." Her tone had an edge to it. "Rather than considering all the options, Captain, I'd have thought your time would be better spent finding the evidence to prove it."

"Believe me, Miss Pemberley," I replied, "nothing would make me happier, but I'd be doing Adhir a disservice if I didn't investigate *all* avenues as thoroughly as possible."

She took another sip, then stared out of the window into the darkness. "I'm sorry," she said. "It's just that . . ."

"It's fine, Miss Pemberley," I said. "I understand your frustration, but I promise you this: I will find whoever is behind Adhir's murder."

Even as I said the words, I realised they were more in hope than conviction: words to assuage her concerns and salve my conscience. Things seemed to be spinning out of control. Before she could respond, the stillness of the night was shattered by staccato shouts and the sound of glass smashing. I looked out of the window. Men were running through the streets. Some carried torches, others makeshift weapons.

"What's going on?" asked Miss Pemberley.

As more men gathered, I was reminded of another crowd I'd witnessed running through the streets in the dead of night. That had been in Wapping, in 1914, and they were converging on a shop because they thought the owners were German. In some respects, it seemed East India was little different from East London. I downed my drink and stood up.

"I think you should get back to your room," I said. "And lock the door."

"Where are you going?" she asked.

I nodded to the window. "Out there."

I ran through streets and alleys that were bursting to life. Lights flickered in the houses and doors opened to disgorge more men — some bemused onlookers, others, like me, running towards the confusion. The news of a commotion was spreading. How many of these men knew what was happening? Very few, I suspected. They had got caught up in the maelstrom: wanting to be part of something bigger; to feel the excitement and the emancipation that comes from being part of the mob.

In the distance, half-obscured by a building, something was glowing. A burning car had ploughed headlong into a telegraph pole beside a makeshift roadblock of sandbags and barbed wire, its bonnet a shambles of contorted, mangled metal. I drew level with the wrecked vehicle. Its windows were shattered and a door, torn from twisted hinges, lay battered in the dirt. The stench of burning rubber and charred flesh caught at my throat.

The *purdah* car.

The driver lay dead, his head smashed against the wheel. Glass from the windows of the rear compartment crunched under my feet. Its curtains were torn down: blood was spattered on the leather seat and smeared against the inside door handle. More blood mottled the ground, a streak of it running away from the car. Someone had been dragged out.

I forced my way to the front of the crowd and stopped, dumbstruck by the horror of what was unfolding, illuminated by the flames from a dozen torches.

Two men, their faces wretched and bloodied, hands bound behind their backs, were being pushed towards a place where the road widened to form an open space. In front of them stood two short wooden stumps.

I recognised the men instantly. One was our prisoner, his head slumped forwards. The other — despite the blood and the bruising, there was no mistaking his tall, slender frame — was Sayeed Ali, the head of the zenana.

And then I saw Arora. He was standing next to the red Alfa, his face like a storm on a mountaintop. He snarled a command and soldiers forced the two men to kneel, then placed their heads on the stumps. They affixed each to the wooden blocks with what looked like strips of leather attached to hooks.

I shouted out to the colonel. He looked over at me and seemed momentarily to falter. Then his composure returned and he nodded with that glacial stare I'd seen the first time we met.

I fought my way over as the mob bayed for blood. Sayeed Ali seemed to be uttering a prayer. The other man knelt there without moving, almost as though he was in a trance.

"Captain Wyndham," said the colonel, his gaze fixed on the prisoners, "I was hoping to avoid your presence here."

"What's going on, Arora?" I asked.

"It's out of my hands," he replied.

"Are you going to flog these men?"

He turned and looked at me curiously.

"Flog them?" he said. "These men aren't being flogged. They're being executed."

I stared at him. Was this why he had hesitated in apprehending the assassin earlier in the day? He wasn't in league with the man — he was just deciding whether or not to kill him on the spot?

"You don't have the authority to execute them," I shouted.

He turned back to the scene before us. "I have my orders."

"From whom?"

"Punit."

"When?"

"When I telephoned him from the garage. I told him your suspicions."

"But the death penalty is expressly forbidden in the princely states."

"He's decreed them to be traitors."

"But we don't know that for sure."

This time he looked genuinely confused. "It was your suggestion, Captain. You made the link between the eunuch, the *purdah* car and the Maharani Devika. *You're* the one who has sealed their fates."

"But that was just a theory," I protested, "something that came to me in the heat of the moment."

"It appears your theory was enough to convince Punit. And if it helps to salve your conscience, you are probably correct." He gestured to the assassin lying prone on the ground. "We both know that's the man who shot at you and His Highness earlier today."

"We have to question him."

"There's no time."

He turned to one of his men and issued a command. The man saluted, then took a conch shell from his pocket, raised it to his lips and blew a long, sustained blast. A hush fell over the crowd, and soon only the crackle of their torches could be heard.

From behind a building, a bull elephant appeared. It was larger than the ones we'd ridden earlier in the day. On its neck sat a mahout, but there was no *howdah* on its back. Instead, it wore golden cuffs around its ankles, each studded with three short blades.

The colour must have drained from my face as I realised what was about to happen. The colonel looked at me closely.

"You may find it distasteful, but execution by elephant has been a traditional punishment here for millennia."

The elephant approached the two prone bodies. The assassin was now kicking wildly and the mahout decided to deal with him first. He led the beast behind the man and the animal raised one of its huge front legs. Instead of bringing its great weight down on its victim, though, with an almost delicate flick of its foot, it severed the man's legs from his body. His screams were drowned out by the roar of the crowd. I closed my eyes.

"You can't kill the eunuch," I insisted.

"He was helping the criminal to escape. He was in the *purdah* car with the assassin."

"Have you questioned him?"

"He admitted it all. Adhir was killed and his brother targeted, just so that the infant prince could be placed on the throne."

"He confessed?"

The colonel nodded. "Ten minutes ago."

"Where is the Maharani now?" I shouted.

"Word has been sent to the palace. Punit is having her dealt with as we speak."

"What will happen to her?"

"That is not for me to say."

I turned back to the macabre scene. The elephant was still toying with its first victim, slicing the remaining limbs but avoiding the torso.

"End it," I said.

"Very well."

The colonel barked something at the mahout. The elephant moved to face the prisoners and lifted one leg above the assassin's head. I could have sworn the beast looked over at the colonel, as though awaiting the final order. Arora nodded, and the animal brought down its full weight, crushing the man's skull as if it were no more than the shell of an egg.

The mob cheered.

I turned and began to walk back through the crowd, as the elephant moved on to Ali. I felt nothing, save for a gnawing hollowness. From behind me came another great roar as the eunuch was dispatched. I didn't turn round, just kept walking, all the way back to the Beaumont Hotel.

# CHAPTER
# THIRTY-NINE

## *Wednesday 23 June 1920*

Thirty hours after the last hit, my head was still clear.
No fog, no runny nose, no ache in my limbs. No
symptoms of any kind. At least not yet. Maybe Arora
was right. Maybe candū was a gift from the gods.
Somehow I doubted I'd be that lucky. Deep down I
knew this was no miracle and that the after-effects,
though delayed, would still come. I just hoped they
wouldn't arrive with a vengeance.

I'd returned to the Beaumont where Katherine
Pemberley was waiting in her room, and I'd
summarised for her what had transpired. She'd sat on
the corner of her bed and tried to comprehend it all,
and I wasn't much help, mainly because I wasn't
entirely sure myself.

I'd left her shortly after one in the morning and
returned to our office in the Rose Building to find
Surrender-not gone and a scribbled note left on the
desk. He'd reviewed both reports and returned them to
Davé's safe. He had no doubt that one was a replica of
the other, only with the numbers changed; his
conclusion was that the document with the lower
valuation was Golding's genuine report. It was good,

solid police work: the detailed, methodical analysis that formed the backbone of most inquiries. But after what I'd just witnessed, Golding's report seemed suddenly irrelevant.

I'd trudged back to the guest lodge and considered waking the sergeant to tell him what I'd witnessed, but there was no point. Two men were dead because I'd voiced a theory that I still couldn't quite believe, even if it *was* the only one that seemed to make sense. No, it was better to let the boy sleep. That sort of news could wait.

The grey morning clouds hung heavy as I walked down the steps of the villa and headed for the back of the Rose Building. The palace grounds were peaceful, as though the events of the previous night had never occurred. Somewhere nearby, a peacock called forlornly.

There was little activity in the garage. An oil stain marked the spot where the *purdah* car had sat. The old Mercedes Simplex was there, though, and I quickly cranked her up. The engine hummed to life and I set off, making for the bridge over the Mahanadi.

As I'd hoped, a car was parked outside the temple to Lord Jagannath. From the size and the shine, it was obviously one of the royal fleet.

I parked the Mercedes beside it, got out and walked into the compound. The temple doors were closed and from inside came the rhythmic chanting of scriptures. I sat on the steps and waited, watching a family of monkeys as they scrabbled down from the branches of a tree and entered the temple through an open window, reappearing moments later with pilfered fruits and devotional offerings in their small, black hands.

Eventually the doors opened, and, as on the previous morning, out stepped Shubhadra, the First Maharani. She was followed by Davé, a priest and the smell of incense. She looked tired.

I stood up to greet her.

"Captain Wyndham," she said. "If I had known you had such a fondness for our temples, I would have invited you to accompany the Dewan *sahib* and me this morning."

"Your Highness," I said, "I was hoping you might grant me a few moments of your time."

"Of course." She nodded, then turned to the Dewan and whispered a few words. Davé bowed low, before he and the priest retreated inside the temple. The Maharani gently touched my arm.

"Shall we take another walk?"

We set off down the steps and into the temple courtyard.

"I take it you are here on account of what took place last night," she said quietly, looking straight ahead.

"I wanted to enquire whether the Third Maharani was all right."

"Punit sent his men into the zenana in the middle of the night," she said with venom in her voice. "They have arrested her. It is an outrage."

"And Prince Alok?"

"The child is safe, for now. It was all I could do to protect him. Whatever the truth behind what has happened, he is innocent in all this."

"*You* protected him?" I asked.

"Who else would?"

"I thought maybe his father, the Maharaja?"

She stopped and turned to me. "What I am about to tell you must be in the strictest confidence. The Maharaja is gravely ill. When informed of Devika's arrest, he suffered a seizure. Otherwise I am sure he would have protected both the boy and his mother."

"You don't believe the Maharani Devika to be behind the plot to murder Adhir and Punit?"

She paused before answering.

"I *cannot* believe it. I fear that Punit is seeing conspiracies where none exist. Or worse, that he may be party to them himself."

"You think Devika is innocent and Punit is behind this?"

"Isn't Punit the more likely culprit? I tell you, Captain, I fear for the future. With the Maharaja incapacitated, Punit is already pushing to be announced as Prince regent instead of simply Yuvraj at his investiture at the Jagannath ceremony tomorrow. The people would no doubt see the timing as a sign that he has Lord Jagannath's blessing. With such divine backing, I've little doubt that he will become Maharaja in short order and then . . . who knows . . .?"

"What will you do?" I asked.

"What can I do? I am merely the wife of a dying man. I am not even Punit's mother. My influence is limited and diminishing by the day."

I felt as though I'd been punched in the gut. The manner with which everything had unravelled overnight was stupefying. And all of it set in train by my actions. Suddenly I found myself clinging to the old Maharani's suggestion that maybe Punit had staged the whole thing. Had he somehow engineered the prisoner's escape? But if so, why would the eunuch help him? And why would he give up his life for the prince? It made no sense.

"What about Miss Bidika?" I asked finally. "Will she be freed now that the Maharani Devika has been arrested?"

"I cannot say."

"But she had nothing to do with it."

The Maharani sighed. "If Punit has his way, and it is accepted that the Maharani Devika is behind the plot, then I should think he will have little to gain from Miss Bidika's incarceration."

"Were you aware that he sought to make her his wife?" I asked.

She nodded. "There are few such matters that are not known inside the zenana. Punit may wish to continue punishing her for her rejection of his marriage proposal, nevertheless I shall see what I can do to obtain her release, though it may require time and subtlety. If Punit realises that I am agitating for it, he may decide to hold her indefinitely."

**380**

The Maharani paused, then turned and took my hand. "May I make an observation, Captain?"

"Please."

"India is home to many faiths and they agree on very little, but one thing they all possess is a belief that the soul is the true essence of our being." She paused, adjusting the border of her sari before continuing. "Everyone's soul is unique, and different souls are driven by different passions, but certain souls, we believe, are driven by a higher calling, which they must follow no matter what the consequences. I believe your soul is that of a *satyanveshi*, a seeker of truth. Why else would you come to Sambalpore in the first place? As I understand it, you had tracked down the criminal who assassinated Adhir. Another officer would have closed the case there and then, but not you. Your soul would not let you rest. The urge to seek the truth was irrepressible, unstoppable as the chariot of Lord Jagannath. You had no choice but to come here. And I think you will also find a way to remain. That is why you are here this morning. To find the truth."

I shook my head. I had the odd feeling that the old woman was somehow toying with me. Mysticism made me uncomfortable and Indian mysticism was the worst of all. Indians had finessed it to such a degree that, even as you dismissed their nonsense, the look of serene superiority on their faces meant that a part of you always felt that maybe their mumbo-jumbo was right all along.

"Even if there were more to it," I said, "I wouldn't be able to do anything about it. Ultimately I have no jurisdiction here, and even if I did, I doubt the powers that be in Delhi would be much inclined to let me use it."

The corners of her mouth rose in a slight smile. "Come," she said, leading me towards the temple gates. In front of us, the Mahanadi River rushed past, engorged by monsoon rains that had fallen upcountry and which now passed through this parched land. She pointed to a large boulder that sat in the middle of the onrushing torrent.

"You see that rock?" she said. "One day, a thousand years from now, the waters of the river will have reduced that stone to nothing more than sand. It is hard to believe, but it will happen. You may not live to see it, still you know it to be true."

"I'm not sure I follow," I said.

"The truth and its consequences are two different things, Captain. Truth does not entail justice any more than high birth entails wisdom. I know that your soul hankers for the truth. If you live to see justice, all well and good, but if you do not, so be it. In any case, justice can take many forms. You may not even recognise it when you see it."

She turned back towards the temple. Davé and the priest stood watching us from its steps. "And now," she said, "I am afraid I must return to the palace. It would be inadvisable for me to remain here for too long on this of all mornings."

I thanked her for her time.

"And remember, Captain," she said as she turned to go, "at all times seek the truth, and do not concern yourself with its consequences."

# CHAPTER
# FORTY

I returned to the lodge to find Surrender-not in the dining room, finishing off an omelette. His eyes widened on seeing me and he almost toppled his chair in his hurry to stand.

"Have you heard the news, sir?" he said breathlessly. "They're saying the Maharani Devika's been arrested."

"It's true," I replied.

He stared at me with incomprehension. "But why?"

"Because Punit believes she was behind the plot to assassinate him and Adhir in order to place her son on the throne."

"But she's only a girl."

"The chief eunuch was helping her. He was caught aiding our prisoner to escape. Both he and the assassin were executed last night."

"But how do you know all this?"

"I was there," I said, gesturing for him to sit back down and finish his breakfast.

"Where?"

"Down in the town. I watched as they were killed. Who told *you* about Devika?"

"One of the maidservants. She speaks Hindi."

"So you can speak to women now, can you?"

He looked perplexed. "I've never felt uncomfortable talking to servants."

I sat down opposite him as a maid appeared to take my order. It was probably the same one who'd chronicled last night's events to Surrender-not.

"What happened?" he asked.

"It's a long story," I said, and it wasn't one I felt like recounting. However, the look on Surrender-not's face suggested he wasn't keen on waiting.

Leaving out my own involvement, I threw him a scrap. "All you need to know for now is that Punit is in control. And it seems our friend Colonel Arora wasn't in league with the plotters after all," I said. "He just felt that rather than giving them prison sentences, the interests of justice were better served by an elephant crushing their skulls."

"An elephant?"

I nodded. "Well trained too. Seemed to know its way around a human body."

"That's novel," he said.

"Apparently not. If the colonel's to be believed, they've been doing it here for centuries. How's the omelette?"

"What?"

"The omelette," I repeated. "Any good?"

He stared at me as though I was mad.

"Not enough chillies."

I turned to the maid and asked for an omelette and a pot of black coffee.

"Any sign of Miss Grant this morning?"

"I haven't seen her, sir. I expect she's at the Beaumont." He checked his watch.

"What time is it?" I asked.

"Almost eight." He took a sip of tea. "So what now, sir?"

I extracted a rather battered packet of cigarettes from my pocket and offered him one.

"Now we follow the only lead we have left," I said, taking one for myself. "Golding's report."

From outside came the growl of a car. I looked out of the window as the red Alfa pulled up.

The colonel and my omelette arrived at the same moment, though if the omelette had been as cold as the colonel's expression, I'd have sent it back.

"Captain Wyndham," he said.

"Colonel." I nodded. I didn't bother getting to my feet. Instead, I waved him to a chair. For a moment we sat in silence. I took a pull of my cigarette and exhaled slowly.

"I expect you disagree with my actions last night," he said eventually. "You must know that I couldn't disobey Punit's orders. If I had, it would have been my head on that block in place of theirs."

"It seems to me," I said, "that our interests might have been better served by questioning them before —"

"Before what, Captain? Before giving them a trial and allowing them to drag everything out into the open? Do you think the people want to hear of their young maharani's betrayal? And then what? A custodial sentence? As you so righteously pointed out, under

**386**

your laws we are not allowed to execute *anyone*, not even those guilty of the highest of crimes. As for questioning them, the men are fanatics. The one you confronted in Calcutta preferred to shoot himself rather than answer your questions. What makes you think these men would be any different?"

"They might have known something about Golding's disappearance," I said.

The colonel's face contorted. "You're clutching at straws, Wyndham. Our ways may be offensive to your sensibilities, but don't try to rationalise things by claiming that allowing them to live would have helped your investigation."

"You're sure yourself that the Third Maharani is behind this?" I asked.

He leaned forward and placed his hands on the table. "It's the only theory that fits. She knows that the Maharaja is not long for this world. As his favourite wife, she would have known for longer than almost anyone else. Once her husband had died, she would lose all influence. And what would become of her infant son?"

He picked up a spare napkin from the table and began absent-mindedly folding it. "She must have realised that the only way to secure Prince Alok's future was to murder the two princes in line to the throne ahead of him. She would have hatched her plot in the zenana with the aid of Sayeed Ali. But that is where her plan starts to go awry. They are overheard by the concubine, Rupali, who leaves notes warning Adhir. In spite of this, the attack on him is successful, and it is only thanks to your actions yesterday that the attack on Punit fails and the assailant is captured and brought back to Sambalpore. Word of his incarceration reaches Devika and she and the eunuch plot the man's escape. Who else would have such easy access to the Maharaja's seal or to the *purdah* car?"

"Maybe it's my turn to tell *you* something," I said. "Are you aware of the Maharaja's condition this morning?"

His brow furrowed. "No," he said. "What have you heard?"

"It seems when word of your little spectacle and the subsequent arrest of the Third Maharani reached the Maharaja, His Highness suffered some kind of seizure. He's not expected to survive much longer, which means Punit will be Maharaja rather sooner than expected."

"That truly is a tragedy." The colonel sighed, not bothering to clarify whether he meant the Maharaja's health or the prince's accession.

"So why are you here, Colonel?" I asked. "With all that's happened last night, don't tell me you came to see me just to salve my conscience."

"Golding," he said. "You told me last night that you'd found two reports in Davé's safe?"

I turned to Surrender-not. "Maybe it's best if the sergeant explains."

"Two versions, yes," said Surrender-not. "I went through both in detail last night. Much of the wording is identical, only the numbers and the conclusions are different. Both were signed in Golding's name, though the signatures are not the same."

"What does that mean?" Arora asked.

"One version paints a picture of large reserves of diamonds still *in situ*, the other shows a much diminished picture. As such, the overall valuations placed on the mines are also considerably different."

The colonel rubbed his beard. "I assume they can't both be genuine."

Surrender-not shrugged. "I don't see how."

"So which one is the real report and which the fake?"

"I can't say definitively until I've seen the geological report and Golding's back-up papers. They're still in his office. I was planning to examine them this morning."

"We've been working on a theory," I said. "It implicates the Dewan, but it has holes in it."

"Holes?" asked the colonel. "You think you can fill them?"

"We're going to try. Now that you've crushed our other enemies underfoot, there seems little else for us to do."

He grimaced. "That's the spirit, Captain."

There was a knock at the dining-room door and Carmichael entered, grinning like a mule.

"Mr Carmichael," said the colonel. "What brings you here?"

"I have a letter to deliver to Captain Wyndham," he said, handing me a rather damp envelope with my name typed on the front. I tore open the seal and extracted one sheet of paper with the crest of the India

Office at the top and the Viceroy's signature at the bottom. Carmichael mopped his brow with a handkerchief.

"The humidity's unbearable," he said by way of answer to a question no one had asked.

I quickly scanned the letter. One paragraph, typed, single spaced, ordering me and Surrender-not back to Calcutta.

"The telegraph lines are back up, then?" I asked.

"No," he replied. "They're still down, but I sent a message explaining the situation on Monday night's train to Jharsugudah. A telegram was sent to Delhi from there. The Viceroy himself has sent the letter recalling you. It was delivered by messenger less than an hour ago. I've taken the liberty of booking you a compartment on this evening's train."

"Decent of you," I said, passing the letter to Surrender-not. "Take a look at this, Sergeant, and tell me if it's in order."

"Of course it's in order," Carmichael exclaimed. His forehead was already dotted with perspiration again. "It's from the Viceroy himself. There's no higher authority in India."

"Still," I said, looking to Surrender-not, "best to be sure."

The sergeant looked up and nodded.

"Very well," I said. "If there's nothing further, Mr Carmichael, I'm sure you have a lot on your plate today . . . or haven't you heard?"

"Heard what?"

Colonel Arora and I looked at each other. "Mr Carmichael," said the colonel, "perhaps it would be best if you made your way to the palace and requested a meeting with the Dewan."

I watched Carmichael and the colonel depart, then stubbed my cigarette butt into a silver ashtray. A black mood descended. My time in Sambalpore was up. Two men mutilated; a maharani arrested; a maharaja struck down by a seizure, and a case ostensibly solved. For a moment, I fervently prayed that it *was* solved. Otherwise the blood spilt the previous night and that which might be spilt going forwards would be on my hands.

I stood up.

"Where are you going, sir?" asked Surrender-not.

"To pack," I replied. "I suggest you do the same."

He raised an eyebrow. "What about Golding? I thought you wished to find him."

"That was before we received the Viceroy's little note." I sighed.

"But the reports, sir?" said Surrender-not. "We *know* there's something untoward going on. You said yourself that finding Golding could be the key to everything."

I shook my head. "Golding's dead," I said.

Surrender-not looked as though I'd slapped him. "You don't know that for sure, sir."

"His pills," I said. "I found a bottle in his bathroom cabinet. They were sodium thiocyante, used for a heart condition. Whether he was abducted or he left of his own accord, he probably needed them to stay alive."

391

Surrender-not slumped back into his chair "But surely, sir . . ." His voice trailed off.

"All we have is a theory," I continued, "that Golding stumbled upon some fraud perpetrated by the Dewan. There's nothing linking his disappearance to the assassination of the Yuvraj. We've no proof of anything."

"So we give up?" he asked.

"You read the Viceroy's letter," I said. "He's ordered us back to Calcutta, probably on pain of deportation. At least he kept the damn thing brief."

Surrender-not took off his spectacles and wiped the lenses with a corner of his napkin.

"The next train doesn't leave until ten tonight," he said finally. "Do you propose we sit quietly in our rooms till then?"

"Well, Sergeant, what would you suggest we do?"

"You're the senior officer, of course, sir," he said tentatively, "but we could always stick to our initial plan of examining the back-up papers in Golding's office?"

The boy was right, damn him. Something did feel very wrong and Surrender-not knew it too. We had no choice but to keep digging.

# CHAPTER
# FORTY-ONE

I told Surrender-not to get started and that I'd meet him at Golding's office in an hour. Before that, there was somewhere I needed to be.

There was little to see in the deserted streets. Where the *purdah* car had crashed, there was nothing save a bent telegraph pole. I drove on and parked outside the Beaumont. There was a different clerk behind the reception desk. I ignored him, made my way up to room twelve and knocked on the door. I held my breath and waited for Annie to answer, but the seconds ticked by and a thousand thoughts, none of them good, ran through my head. I knocked again, this time louder.

"Just a minute," came a muffled voice and I breathed a sigh of relief.

"Who is it?" she asked, her voice clearer now.

"It's me. Sam."

The door opened and I was met with the scent of her perfume and the sight of her dressed in a silk bathrobe with her hair wrapped up in a towel. I found myself wishing that the sight was as familiar to me as the scent.

"Is everything okay, Sam?"

"Not really."

"Is this about last night?"

"You know about last night?" I said, trying hard to mask my surprise. "Punit told you what happened?"

"What's Punit got to do with it? I was talking about your little disappearing act. What are you talking about, Sam? Has something happened? Has it got something to do with Colonel Arora?"

"What?" I asked.

"Last night. I was there when the colonel telephoned Punit. We were still dancing when the call came through."

"What happened exactly?"

She stood back from the door. "You'd better come in."

I walked into the room. It was almost identical to Miss Pemberley's, except that this one contained five large bouquets of roses, each garlanded with a red silk ribbon and placed in vases the size of buckets.

"You're taking up horticulture?" I asked.

"They're from Punit," she said matter-of-factly.

"All five of them?"

"All five." She nodded. "One bouquet each morning, and one each afternoon."

"Seems rather excessive," I said. "Have you checked them for aphids?"

"Maybe I should have kept you waiting outside," she replied.

"Maybe you should have," I said, "I get terrible hay fever. You'd better tell me what happened before my eyes start watering."

I took a seat on the side of her bed, making a point of pushing a vase that had been placed on the bedside table as far away as possible.

"Well," she said, moving it back, "it must have been after midnight. We were still in the salon — Punit, Davé, the Carmichaels and me — when a guard burst in. It was the foxtrot and Punit wasn't best pleased at the interruption, but he went to the telephone. He returned a few minutes later and called an immediate end to the proceedings, saying he had something urgent to attend to. And that was it. He left the room. The party fizzled out after that. I went looking for you, but couldn't find you anywhere. Where did you run off to, anyway?"

"It doesn't matter," I said. "Now think carefully. What was Punit's reaction when he came back?"

"How do you mean?"

"Did he seem surprised or in shock?"

She thought for a moment, then slowly shook her head. "No. At least, I don't think so. Look, Sam, what's going on?"

"The Maharani Devika's been arrested," I said. "It's possible that she and her eunuch were trying to clear the path to the throne for Prince Alok."

She raised a hand to her mouth. "I can't believe it," she said. "Is it true?"

"She had a motive." I sighed. "The facts seem to fit."

Annie walked over to the window, then turned to face me. "There has to be some other explanation. Have they questioned the eunuch? What does he say?"

"Not much," I replied. "He's dead."

"How?"

I thought back to the previous night's execution. The cheer of the crowd as Sayeed Ali's skull was crushed. "It's best you don't know."

"What about the Maharaja? Didn't he stop them arresting his wife?"

"He's in no position to stop anything," I said. "When presented with the evidence of her involvement, he had a seizure. To all intents and purposes, Punit's in charge now."

That seemed to take her by surprise.

"Well, congratulations, Sam," she said definitively.

"For what?"

"I'd imagine Punit will be very grateful to you for saving his life yesterday. Maybe he'll offer you a position here."

I couldn't tell if she was joking.

"I doubt it," I said. "Besides, the Viceroy's ordered me back to Calcutta. The train leaves at ten tonight. I just thought I should let you know."

# CHAPTER
# FORTY-TWO

The drive back was hardly pleasant. The sun was still hidden behind a wall of grey clouds but the heat was stupefying. Every so often there came a low rolling growl, the rumble of thunder somewhere far off.

The Rose Building was in a state of animation. Harried-looking men armed with files and chitties ran along the corridors from one office to another. Fighting my way past them, I walked upstairs to the still-deserted corridor outside Golding's office and opened the door.

Surrender-not was seated at Golding's desk, his head buried in a sheaf of papers.

"Found anything?" I asked.

"Yes, sir," he said, looking up. "I came across these documents when we were in here the other day. They didn't mean an awful lot to me then, but having examined the two versions of the report, I'm quite sure I can now determine which one is genuine."

"How long?"

He looked up. "Five more minutes. If I'm not interrupted, sir."

I left him to it and wandered over to the window. It offered a view of the palace gardens and the *Surya*

*Mahal* in the distance. The flag above it still flew at full-mast. That was a relief: whatever his condition, the Maharaja was still alive.

With nothing better to do, I turned my attention to the map on the wall, the one marked with the crosses. I'd not paid it much attention the last time we'd been in here, mainly because I hadn't known what I was looking for. Now, however, it intrigued me: not so much the cluster of red "X"s to the north of town, but rather the solitary black "X" down to the south-west. I looked more closely. It was situated near a settlement, a town or a village of some sort, called Remunda. I walked over to the desk and dialled Colonel Arora's office. It was answered on the third ring.

"Arora."

"It's me, Wyndham."

"What can I do for you, Captain?" He sounded wary.

"Are there any diamond mines near Remunda?" I asked.

"Why do you want to know? You've been ordered back to Calcutta. You've no more business here."

He was correct, of course. But still.

"I've never been particularly keen on orders, Colonel," I replied. "And there's still the small matter of Golding's disappearance."

"Go on."

We're close to proving the link to the Dewan," I lied.

There was silence from the other end. I could hear him breathing.

"What do you want to know?"

398

"Remunda," I said. "Golding marked a spot near it on a map. Are there any mines there?"

"No," he said. "The only seam of diamonds in the entire area is in the north, in the plain between the Mahanadi and Brahmani rivers. Whatever you're looking for near Remunda, it's not a diamond mine."

"I'd like to head out there," I said, "find out exactly what it was that made Golding mark it on his map."

"Remunda is more than twenty miles from here," he said.

"I still want to go."

"On a wild-goose chase? Very well," he said abruptly, "I won't stop you. I'll even organise you a car. When will you need it?"

"We'll head off as soon as we're done here."

I replaced the receiver.

"What can you tell me, Sergeant?"

He laid a document down on the desk, took off his spectacles and leaned back. "The report with the lower figures ties in with Golding's papers, sir. It appears to be the real report."

"Good work," I said. "If I were a betting man, I'd wager a tidy sum that the Dewan intends to present the other one to the Maharaja and Anglo-Indian Diamond."

# CHAPTER
# FORTY-THREE

The journey took an age. Two hours into nowhere and two hundred years into the past. At points the dirt road was submerged under rivers of monsoon rainwater that had fallen upcountry. More than once, the driver was forced to detour around an unfordable stream that only yesterday had been dry river bed.

Remunda, when it came, was little more than a huddle of mud and thatch huts clustered around a temple and a tube-well. As in Bengal, the hut walls were covered in round cakes of cow-dung, baking dry in the heat of the day before being used as fuel in the evenings. But the similarity stopped there. Unlike the villages in Bengal, with their bountiful groves of palm and banana and their emerald-green bathing and fishing pools, this place was dust brown and bone dry.

Surrender-not ordered the driver to halt near the well. The engine died and a silence fell, broken only by the occasional cry of a mynah bird high up in a blackened tree. The village at first appeared abandoned to the heat. On closer inspection, though, you noticed the signs of life: a few scrawny chickens, their feathers coated in dust, pecking at the side of the road; a mongrel dog yawning lazily in the shade of a wall; a twitch at one of the darkened holes that passed for a window.

Soft tinkling was coming from the direction of the small whitewashed temple. A ragged saffron flag hung limply from a bamboo stick atop its spire. I nodded to Surrender-not and we headed towards it. The sound was that of a small bell, the kind used by Hindus in their religious ceremonies, and its ring mingled with sonorous murmurings of priestly incantations.

I waited at the threshold while Surrender-not entered to speak to the priest. Inside, three idols were visible, small and rough-hewn, but unmistakable: the over-large eyes, the stubby arms and the absence of legs that signified the Lord Jagannath and his siblings.

The chanting stopped. Surrender-not was speaking to the priest in what sounded like Hindi. I lit a cigarette and waited. When he came out, he turned to face the temple, touched his forehead and his chest with his right hand, just as Annie had done at the temple in Sambalpore a few days before.

I passed him a cigarette, which he gratefully accepted. "Any joy?" I asked, wiping perspiration from my forehead. He stuck the cigarette in a corner of his mouth and fished out a box of matches from his pocket.

"Arora was right," he said. "There are no mines around here." He struck a match and it flared into life. "But there is a cave."

"A cave?"

"Apparently so."

Inside, the bell began tinkling once again.

"The priest says it's about half a mile further up the road. There's a turning off to the right which leads to a hill. He says there's been a lot of activity up there recently. Outsiders. Men in lorries. It all stopped about a week ago, though."

"Any local men up there?"

Surrender-not shook his head. "It's unlikely, sir. This is farming country, if you can believe it," he said distastefully. "The village men would all be in the fields."

I stubbed my cigarette out on the side of a tree and began walking back towards the car. "Let's go."

Ten minutes up the road from Remunda, a dirt path split from the main track and snaked its way northwards. We followed it for a short distance before spotting the hill.

"That must be it," said Surrender-not, pointing to a rust-coloured mound of rock.

As we neared it, the entrance to the cave became visible: a dark slit amidst reddish stone. Surrender-not ordered the driver to stop. We got out and walked over, picking our way through the dry scrub. The place was deserted. You might even have believed it had been untouched by human hands, had it not been for the wooden beams and scaffolds that had been inserted to expand and reinforce the natural fissure that formed the cave entrance.

"What does this look like to you?" I asked.

"I'm no expert, sir," replied Surrender-not, "but it appears to be the entrance to a mine."

"Shall we see what's inside?"

Surrender-not shuddered.

"You're not scared of ghosts, are you, Sergeant?" I asked.

"Yes," he replied, "but that's not the problem, sir."

"What then?"

"Bats," he said. "That cave is bound to be teeming with them."

"It's the middle of the day. We'll need a torch, though. Check if there's one in the car."

Duly equipped, we continued, only to be hit by the acrid stench of ammonia within a few feet of the entrance. I pulled out a handkerchief and covered my nose and mouth, but it made little difference.

My eyes watered, but I pressed on, unsure of what I was looking for. The light from the entrance faded fast and behind me Surrender-not switched on the torch, illuminating a mound of what looked like brown rice grains, several feet high.

"I told you, sir," said Surrender-not. "Bat droppings. There must be thousands of the creatures in here."

He passed me the torch and I swept it across the walls, outlining a rectangular shaft cut into the rock.

"This way," I said and headed into a man-made tunnel.

A gentle slope ran downwards and after a few minutes there seemed to be a slight change in air pressure. As we walked, the smell of guano gradually receded. Whatever else was down this shaft, it didn't seem like there were bats.

Deeper inside, I stumbled over broken rock, almost losing my footing. Pointing the torch at the floor, I discovered shining black rubble. I knelt down, picked up a piece, examined it briefly then pocketed it.

"Exactly what are we looking for, sir?" asked Surrender-not.

"We'll know when we see it," I replied. But even as I said the words, the answer became apparent. Surrender-not noticed it too. The faintest of smells.

"Come on," I said, moving further into the tunnel. The odour grew stronger: that peculiar, putrid stench with a sickly sweet edge to it — unmistakable. There was a corpse nearby, and judging by the smell, it hadn't been here particularly long.

We hurried on over the uneven floor, and suddenly it was in front of us. A mangled heap of clothes and flesh that seemed to shimmer.

Surrender-not balked. "Maggots," he said. "Most unsavoury."

"Is it Golding?"

"It's hard to tell, sir."

I shone the torch at the decomposing corpse. The clothes and hair looked European.

Surrender-not bent down to take a closer look. It was brave of him. A year ago he'd have fainted at the sight of blood. Now he was poking around at a rotting body who knew how far underground. The torch beam reflected off something metallic. I knelt beside Surrender-not to better examine the object.

"What is it?" he asked.

"Golding's signet ring."

# CHAPTER
# FORTY-FOUR

The return to Sambalpore was an exercise in frustration. Two hours that felt as long as six. Each precious mile travelled felt like a journey in itself, purchased with the most valuable currency I had — time.

I felt a gnawing unease in my bones. Finding Golding had offered succour of sorts. I'd discovered not just his body, but also, I thought, the reason for his murder. The pieces slotted into place. The Dewan had been siphoning off diamonds, either for himself or for others. He'd killed Golding because the accountant had discovered the fraud and refused to be bought off. And where better to dump his body than in a mine shaft in the middle of nowhere?

Any exhilaration was tempered by cold reality: I may have worked it out, but there was damn all I could do about it. I thought I had the truth and, if the old Maharani, Shubhadra, was to be believed, I should be satisfied with that. It was all very high-minded, all very *Indian*. But I was British, and the thought of truth without justice rankled.

Through the afternoon the sky had grown black beneath the monsoon clouds and, as the lights of the town came into view, the first drops of rain began to fall.

Beside me Surrender-not smiled.

"What's so funny, Sergeant?"

"I was just thinking of the map in Golding's office, sir. It seems that sometimes 'X' does mark the spot."

"True," I said, "though it's rarely the final resting place of the man who drew it on the map in the first place."

What was more, having visited the site, I finally had some idea of what that "X" had meant. Colonel Arora had been adamant that there had never been diamond mines in that part of Sambalpore. It turned out he was right. I was no expert, but even I could recognise coal when I saw it.

"We need to contact the colonel as soon as we reach town," I said, suddenly straining at the leash of my own impatience. I had decided I had a Dewan to confront.

At the Rose Building, I jumped out into the rain before the car had even stopped and made for the stairs, taking them two at a time with Surrender-not close behind. I burst into Colonel Arora's office, startling his diminutive secretary.

"Where's the colonel?" I gasped.

"He's with His Highness, Prince Punit," said the man, rising from his chair.

"Find him," I ordered, catching my breath. "And tell him Captain Wyndham needs to speak to him immediately."

The man looked out of the window. The expression on his face soured as he saw the downpour.

"I'll call the prince's private secretary," he said, reaching for the telephone receiver on his desk. "That will be faster."

*And drier.*

The secretary dialled a single-digit number, asked the operator for the connection, then waited. With each passing ring, he became increasingly nervous, probably worried that should no one answer, he'd have to make the journey to the palace after all. Finally there came a click. He smiled, then spoke quickly in Hindi. The reply came just as quickly, the secretary nodding all the while. Seconds passed, then finally he passed me the receiver.

"What is it, Captain?" came the familiar voice.

"Just one moment, Colonel," I said.

I turned to the secretary and asked him to leave the room. The man was about to protest, but thought better of it once Surrender-not had grabbed him rather forcefully by the arm and begun to escort him out the door.

I turned back to the telephone. "We've found him."

"Golding?"

"What's left of him."

"Where?"

"In a mine shaft near Remunda."

"And you can link Davé to it?"

"Golding met with Davé the morning he disappeared, and his report was found in Davé's safe, along with a doctored version."

"It's not conclusive."

"Does it need to be?" I asked. "Even if we can't prove Davé's involvement in Golding's murder, we *can* prove his involvement in the fraud. You'll find all the evidence of that in Davé's safe and among the papers in Golding's office. As I see it, with the Maharaja incapacitated, it'll be Prince Punit who'll take the decisions round here in future. What with your little show last night, Punit obviously trusts you. I'm sure you could convince him to charge Davé on the latter point. And with him out of the way, the post of Dewan would be vacant. I think you'd be in line for a rather rapid promotion."

There was silence for a moment.

"And what would be in it for you, Captain?"

"I want to see Golding's remains retrieved and given a proper, Christian burial, and I want Davé to answer for his crimes," I replied. "If I can bring him down for the fraud he's perpetrated, I know that in Sambalpore he'd receive a fitting punishment for *all* his crimes. Especially if you were the new Dewan."

He gave a short laugh. "So, suddenly the concept of innocent till proven guilty no longer appeals to you? I can't say I'm surprised."

"I'm a believer in justice," I said.

He paused before replying.

"Meet me outside the Maharaja's office in an hour."

# CHAPTER
# FORTY-FIVE

I replaced the receiver.

"What now, sir?" asked Surrender-not.

"Now, Sergeant, you're going to pack your case."

"What about Davé? Is Arora going to arrest him?"

"We'll know in an hour. Whatever happens, we still have a train to catch."

He eyed me curiously. "You seem to be in a hurry to leave, sir."

He might have been right about that.

"Nonsense," I said.

We headed back down to the garages. The guest lodge was only a short walk away, but with the rain coming down in sheets, setting out on foot wasn't a practical option, unless we wanted to swim. Instead, we found a driver and commandeered the old Mercedes Simplex.

The car stopped under the lodge's portico and Surrender-not got out.

"You're not coming?" he asked.

"There's something I need to do first," I said.

He nodded and headed into the building, and I ordered the driver to make for town.

★ ★ ★

The lobby of the Beaumont was awash and a harassed-looking bellboy was on his hands and knees, mopping with a sodden rag. I made my way to the first floor and knocked on Annie's door.

This time the door opened almost immediately.

"Sam," she said, "you look like you've been for a swim."

"Don't worry," I replied, gesturing to the window behind her, "you'll get a chance too, soon enough. The train to Jharsugudah leaves at ten. Will you be joining us?"

"You'd better come in," she said.

The look on her face worried me, but as I entered the room, I still clung to the hope that I might be wrong.

The bouquets were still there, and another couple seemed to have arrived during the day.

"You're not bringing the flowers?" I asked.

She didn't reply. Instead, she walked towards the window and busied herself with closing it. I felt sick. I must have cut a ridiculous figure standing there, smelling like a wet dog and dripping on her floor. There was no point in waiting for her to say it. It was better if I said it. It might even leave me with a shred of dignity.

"You're not coming, are you?"

She turned around. "Punit's asked me to stay on," she said. "It's only for a few days. A week or so . . . There's the end of the Jagannath festival tomorrow, and his investiture. There might even be a coronation."

And that was it. One small sentence that stripped away all hope.

**410**

*A week or so.* It was good of her to try to sugar the pill, but her eyes betrayed her. She might actually return to Calcutta in a week but even if she did, the chances were she'd probably be back here soon afterwards. It looked like Punit had won. In truth, he was probably always going to win. He was a prince, after all, and one who was about to become a king. He only needed to raise his voice and the world bent to his whim. When I raised my voice all that happened was I grew hoarse. I should have realised I had no chance when I saw him do the Turkey Trot. Women can't help falling for men who can dance.

I thought about remonstrating, telling her that Punit was an unscrupulous, strutting peacock of a man; that he had given the order to execute two men in the most gruesome fashion last night. But there was no point. Anything I said would seem like jealousy, partly because it was. In any case, she was astute enough to make up her own mind, so I left it. Sometimes a man just has to admit defeat. There was no shame in losing, but losing to someone whose life I'd saved twenty-four hours earlier felt like a kick in the teeth.

"Well," I said, glancing at my watch, "I had better get going. Surrender-not will be waiting for me."

I left Annie and dragged myself down the corridor.

Twenty minutes later I was back in my room at the guest lodge. The wind was up and the shutters clattered noisily against the panes. A pool of water had gathered beneath the window. I locked the door, took off my wet shirt and lay face down on the bed. My limbs ached

**411**

and the fog was beginning to descend inside my skull. A drink would have been good, a hit of "O" would have been better, but I had neither. In my mind, I heard Annie's voice: *It's only for a few days*. But I was too old and too cynical to believe that.

I reflected on the absurdity of it all, then realised I was feeling sorry for myself; and that would never do for an Englishman in India. I heaved myself off the bed, stripped off the rest of my wet clothes, and put on fresh ones. I threw my belongings into my suitcase, then went into the bathroom and splashed tepid water on my face. Five minutes later I was out the door, off to meet Surrender-not at the foot of the stairs.

"Are you all right, sir?" he asked.

"I'm fine," I said. "Now let's go see if we can't arrest a Dewan."

# CHAPTER
# FORTY-SIX

The storm intensified. We were led through the palace to the study where we'd first been introduced to the Maharaja. This time it was his son Punit who sat behind the desk, with Arora at his right hand. The room was dimly lit, all the better to offer a view of the growing tempest beyond the French doors. A lightning flash illuminated the prince's face, highlighting an expression in keeping with the maelstrom outside. Beside him, Arora stood with his own face held firmly in neutral.

The prince looked over as we entered but made no effort to stand, nor to offer Surrender-not or me a seat.

"It is true?" he asked. "Has Davé been robbing us blind?"

"All I can tell you," I said, "is that we found two versions of the report Mr Golding produced into the value of the diamond mines in the Dewan's safe. We believe one is a fake, produced by Davé."

The reply seemed to irritate Punit. "Having two reports in his safe is hardly evidence of a conspiracy to defraud the kingdom," he snapped.

"In and of itself, no," I replied, "but Golding had a meeting with him pencilled in his diary, and he disappeared immediately afterwards. We found Golding's body at the bottom of a mine shaft a few hours ago."

The prince shook his head.

"If I may, Your Highness," interjected Surrender-not, "there is one way of ascertaining whether the Dewan is involved in some sort of plot. Ask to see him and request him to bring Golding's report with him. He's made no secret of the fact that the report is in his possession. If he brings the real one, the one that corresponds with Golding's papers, then he's in the clear. If, however, he brings the other . . ."

Punit mulled it over, then turned to Arora. "Where is he now?"

"In the Rose Building, Your Highness," replied the colonel. "Given the events of last night, the entire Cabinet is there."

From somewhere high up, as though from within the walls, came a faint drumming, like the beating of a bird's wings, and within seconds it had ceased. Punit looked up. His expression darkened further.

"Summon him," he ordered. "Immediately."

Arora picked up a telephone, and moments later he was speaking to Davé.

"Dewan *sahib*," he said, "His Highness the Yuvraj requests your immediate attendance in the Maharaja's study."

He'd referred to Punit as Yuvraj, even though Punit's investiture as the new crown prince wasn't till tomorrow. Arora had obviously decided who his new master was.

**414**

"He wishes to be apprised of the progress of the negotiations with Anglo-Indian Diamond," he continued, "and he requests that you bring Mr Golding's valuation report with you."

I heard Davé's voice on the other end, though his words were indistinguishable.

"Immediately," said Arora, then replaced the receiver and turned to Punit. "It is done, Your Highness."

The prince looked up and a thought seemed to strike him.

"Take two of your men," he said to Arora, "get over there and escort Davé back here. I don't want him getting lost or drowning between the Rose Building and the palace, not yet anyway."

Arora clicked his heels, turned and left the room.

The storm outside grew stronger, the wind rattling the window panes.

"Captain Wyndham," said Punit, "this is now an internal Sambalpori matter. Nevertheless, I wish you to remain. I suggest you and the sergeant stand as unobtrusively as possible to one side."

Surrender-not and I did as ordered and a few minutes later, the doors opened and in walked a rather wet-looking Davé, flanked by two sodden guards and with Arora bringing up the rear. In his hands, the Dewan clutched a document, its cover streaked with rain.

"You wished to see me, Your Highness," he said in that oleaginous, lap-dog tone he'd used with Adhir the first time I'd seen him.

Punit appraised him as though he were a bad smell.

"That is correct, Dewan *sahib*. I want to know the status of your negotiations with Anglo-Indian Diamond."

Davé wiped a trickle of water from his forehead. "They are progressing smoothly, Your Highness. There are some outstanding areas of disagreement, but I am confident that these can be resolved and that a position favourable to Sambalpore can be achieved."

"I am glad to hear that," said Punit. "I shall leave the details to you, but what I wish to know is: how much are the mines worth and what will the bastards pay for them?"

Davé became more animated. "There is good news on that front, Your Highness. The price should be a most favourable one." He held up the document. "I am pleased to say the report into the value of the mines is most reassuring."

Punit stretched out his hand. "May I see it?"

"Of course, Your Highness," said Davé. He bowed, approached the desk and handed the report to the prince.

Punit began to leaf through it. He nodded a couple of times, then passed the document to Arora. "Give it to the sergeant," he said, gesturing to Surrender-not.

Davé spun round towards us. His face clouded in confusion.

"Your Highness," he stammered, "that document is the basis of our negotiating position with Anglo-Indian Diamond. It is confi —"

Punit cut him off with a wave of his hand.

"Well?" he said. "Is it the real report?"

Surrender-not examined the document, then looked up and shook his head and suddenly things began to happen quickly.

Punit began roaring obscenities as Arora shouted at the guards, ordering them to arrest the Dewan. Davé began beseeching the prince as the soldiers took rough hold of his arms. He looked as though a mountain was collapsing on his head, and, given the way Arora had dealt with the traitors the previous night, being crushed by a mountain might have been more humane. He carried on pleading, invoking Lord Jagannath, the Maharaja and even the Maharani as those who would testify to his innocence. But the Maharaja was incapacitated, his young queen was under arrest and the god didn't seem to be listening.

The storm raged on. A flash of lightning rent the sky, throwing the room into sudden and stark relief. Davé's face was frozen in a rictus of fear. In that split second, though, something changed. He looked up at the tapestry and the latticework wall above Punit's head, and his features changed. From outside came an explosion of thunder. Davé stopped pleading and seemed to straighten.

"I am ready to answer any charges Your Highness may have," he said, "in the presence of an attorney."

Punit exchanged glances with Colonel Arora.

"Get him out of here," he ordered.

# CHAPTER
# FORTY-SEVEN

Sambalpore cut a sorry sight in the rain. Lamps lit drenched, desolate streets, the bunting that had adorned its buildings on the day of Adhir's funeral now hung tattered, in places torn down and washed into overflowing gutters.

The railway station looked no less forlorn as the car halted beneath its sagging awning. Surrender-not and I made our way inside and the driver went in search of a porter for our cases.

The half-deserted concourse was manned by a handful of attendants doing their damnedest to keep the waters at bay with as much success as King Canute.

Gone were the crowds, soldiers and pomp and circumstance that had greeted our arrival. Gone too was the royal train, replaced by a locomotive that looked like a child's toy, and carriages that might have belonged to one of those pretend trains that plied the promenade at Brighton.

There weren't many passengers tonight. A few native traders, some European salesmen with their sample cases, and farmers returning home from market with empty baskets and coops.

418

"I thought Carmichael was organising our tickets?" I said, scouring the concourse for the Resident.

"Perhaps he forgot?" suggested Surrender-not.

"So what do we do now?" I asked.

Surrender-not pointed to a fat man in a uniform and a peaked cap.

"He'll have some," he said.

I didn't question him. In India, it was often the case that the fattest man in the room was the one with the power. Sure enough, I watched as Surrender-not walked over and chatted to him, before handing over some rupees and returning with two squares of soggy brown cardboard. He passed me one. There were some illegible words printed on it.

"Tickets," he said. "First class."

Slipping a couple of *annas* to the porter, we took our cases and climbed the iron step onto the train.

The carriage smelled musty, its wooden benches ingrained with a musk acquired from years of contact with human bodies. Other than an Anglo-Indian who sat dozing at the far end, though, it was blessedly empty. Surrender-not pushed our cases onto the narrow rack above our heads while I sat down and tried to make myself comfortable, though that seemed like yet another battle I was destined to lose that night.

Surrender-not sat down opposite me, then stood up with a start.

A flicker of hope stirred inside me. Had he seen Annie on the station platform?

"What is it, Sergeant?" I asked eagerly.

"Tea!" he exclaimed.

"What?"

"The journey to Jharsugudah will take several hours. It would be wrong to start it without a cup of tea."

He hurried to the end of the carriage and descended on to the platform.

*Where there's tea, there's hope*, as some wag once said.

Surrender-not ran over to the old man in the red turban with his makeshift bicycle tea-stall. He returned a few minutes later with two small clay cups.

"Here," he said, handing me one. "It should make you feel better."

I looked at him, but said nothing.

The guard on the platform blew his whistle. There was a hiss of steam and the train moved gently off. I sat back, took a sip of tea and stared into the rain. I wasn't sorry to see the back of Sambalpore. *My* case — the murder of the Yuvraj, Prince Adhir of Sambalpore, was over the moment the assassin put a bullet through his own head on the roof of a seedy hotel in Howrah. It had been solved to the satisfaction of everyone including the Viceroy and if I'd had any sense, I'd have left it there. But I couldn't let it go. The Maharani Shubhadra had called me *a seeker of truth*. It was a fine phrase, but Sambalpore had taught me that I was no more a seeker of truth than I was a canary. The *truth*, when it challenged my perceptions, was just as unpalatable to me as it was to anyone else: that an Englishwoman might fall in love with an Indian; that a woman behind *purdah* in a harem might have the power to assassinate a prince; and that I might lose out to a fop. All of these things were true and I didn't particularly want to face any of them.

The train ploughed on into the night, towards the railway junction town where we would switch to the broad-gauge to take us back to Calcutta. The deluge drummed off the carriage roof and reminded me of the rain in the trenches, bouncing off tarpaulins and men's helmets.

Our progress seemed painfully slow, a combination of monsoon rains and a pitifully weak engine. Nevertheless, with every additional mile, I felt my spirits lift. Sambalpore was behind me. Annie was, too, and maybe that wasn't such a bad thing.

It was after one in the morning when we pulled into Jharsugudah station, not that you'd have believed it looking at the number of people milling around. Surrender-not and I retrieved our cases and alighted onto a platform swarming with pilgrims, porters and saffron-shirted *sadhus*. The calls of vendors touting their wares mingled with the chanted mantras of Hindu devotees.

"Any idea what's going on?" I asked Surrender-not.

"No, sir. I'll see if I can find a railway official."

He set off along the platform and I soon lost sight of him amidst a sea of bodies.

"Captain Wyndham?" came a voice from behind me. "This is an unexpected pleasure!"

I turned to find the anthropologist I'd met at the Carmichaels' dinner party standing in front of me.

"Mr Portelli," I said. "This is a surprise. What are you doing in the middle of nowhere at this hour?"

"The same as you, I imagine, Captain." He smiled. "Waiting for the arrival of a train to take me onwards."

"You're going to Calcutta?"

He shook his head. "No, sir. Like most of these people, I'm bound for Puri, to witness the final day of the Jagannath festival, assuming a train ever arrives to take us there. It appears the rains have washed away several sections of track to the east. No trains have come in from there for almost a day now. But the pilgrims keep arriving from the west, and without the trains to take them on to Puri, they're stuck here."

"You should have stayed in Sambalpore," I said. "I believe they have the same festival tomorrow."

"True enough," Portelli nodded, "but in Sambalpore there will only be one chariot. In Puri, there are *three*: one for the Lord Jagannath and one each for his brother, Balabhadra and his sister, Shubhadra." His eyes widened at the prospect.

"Puri might be politically insignificant compared to Sambalpore," he continued, "but it's the centre of the Jagannath cult and home to its most holy temple. In religious terms, it's by far the most important place in the region. So much so that the king of Puri has precedence over all of the local maharajas, even our friends in Sambalpore, and tomorrow is the highlight of his calendar. As the chariot of the Lord Jagannath returns to its temple, the king has the duty of sweeping the path before it with a golden broom. They call him the Sweeper King."

Those final words. They were an echo of something important, a whisper of something someone had told me not long ago. But what was it? Frantically, I searched my mind for the answer. I could feel it there, lodged in my skull, just out of reach. Then it hit me.

Emily Carmichael.

I recalled the Resident's wife's words that night at the dinner where I'd first met Portelli.

*I once heard someone at court say she was the daughter of a sweeper, if you can believe such a thing.*

She'd been talking about one of the Maharaja's wives. At the time, I'd dismissed it as drunken nonsense. A king would never marry a sweeper's daughter. But he *would* marry the daughter of another king. With a thudding clarity, everything dropped into place and my stomach lurched as I realised the error I'd made.

"Captain? Are you all right?"

I snapped out of my thoughts.

"I'm fine, Mr Portelli." I thanked him, hastily made my excuses, then turned and ran in Surrender-not's direction. Finally I spotted him coming towards me with a railway official in a cap and mutton-chops in tow.

"Surrender-not," I gasped as I reached him.

"This is Mr Cooper," he said, "stationmaster at Jharsugudah. He says the train to Cal —"

"Forget Calcutta," I interrupted, "Punit is still in danger." I turned to the stationmaster. "We need to get a message to Sambalpore, urgently."

The man's jowls wobbled as he shook his head. "I'm afraid that's not possible, sir. All lines to Sambalpore have been down for the last three days. Some sort of problem on their end."

I cursed. Of course the lines were down. I'd been the one to request them cut in the first place.

"In that case we need to get back to Sambalpore immediately," I said. "Do you have a car?"

The man stared at me as if I'd asked to borrow his wife.

"There are no cars in Jharsugudah. The local brickworks has a lorry, but it's two in the morning. The driver will be in his bed."

"I don't need the driver," I said. "Just the lorry."

"It's a five-minute cycle ride down the main street," he protested, "but I'll be damned if I'm going out there in this downpour!"

"Then give me two bicycles," I said.

Soaked to the skin, Surrender-not and I hurtled down the main street on bikes commandeered from the station staff. The brickworks weren't hard to spot. We just headed for the largest chimney in town.

A decrepit-looking lorry stood soaking in a yard that the rains had transformed into something resembling an Irish bog. A *durwan*, one of the ubiquitous nightwatchmen who appear indispensable to any organisation in India but who generally run for cover at the first sign of trouble, dozed in a hut nearby. Surrender-not shook him awake and hit him with the news that we were requisitioning his vehicle.

The man must have thought he was still dreaming. He was about to protest when he saw me. The sight of a white man, dripping from head to toe, gave him a shock and within seconds his objections melted away. I wrote and signed a note informing his bosses that their vehicle had been commandeered by the Imperial Police and that it could be retrieved from the royal palace in Sambalpore. In the meantime, Surrender-not waded through the mud, opened the driver's door and climbed in.

"Where are the keys?" he shouted.

"Try under the seat," I said, running over.

I reached the passenger door and hauled myself up just as the engine spluttered to life. Surrender-not checked his watch. In a few hours, the sun would rise, heralding the day that would see Punit crowned Yuvraj.

I only hoped we'd make it back in time to stop his murder.

"What are you waiting for, Sergeant?" I exclaimed. "Get moving!"

Surrender-not reversed the vehicle, then accelerated out of the exit and onto the main road heading south, back to Sambalpore.

# CHAPTER
# FORTY-EIGHT

## *Thursday 24 June 1920*

The sky turned from black to blue and finally to grey as we drove the fifty miles back to Sambalpore. On a good day and in a fast car, it might have taken two hours. On a monsoon night and in a lorry that moved at the pace of a bullock cart, it was over four before the walls of the town came into view.

That gave me plenty of time to explain my theory, and my fears, to Surrender-not.

"I should have spotted it myself, sir," he said as he drove, the hang-dog expression back on his face.

"Nonsense," I said. "I only figured it out myself after speaking to Portelli last night."

"Still," he said, "I am a Hindu. It should have occurred to me."

"The point is, we need to get back and warn Punit," I said, though even as I uttered the words, a dissenting voice spoke softly in my head. *Was there really any threat to Punit?*

Maybe there wasn't. Maybe I was wrong — Lord knows I'd been wrong about enough things to do with this case already, but something told me this was different.

I dismissed the thoughts, though not before registering a sharp pang of guilt.

The streets of Sambalpore were thronged with people despite the torrential rain.

"Head for the palace," I ordered.

"It may be better to head for the temple, sir," said Surrender-not. "The crowds are out for the procession of Lord Jagannath's chariot back to the temple." He frowned. "From the start, the whole case has been inextricably linked to Jagannath. Adhir was assassinated on the twenty-seventh day of Ashada, the start of the Jagannath festival. Now Punit is leading the procession back to the temple on its final day. If something is going to happen to him, it will probably happen there, while he is exposed to the crowd."

"Good point, Sergeant," I said. "Maybe you're not such a bad Hindu after all."

We inched our way through the hordes, finally reaching the bridge across the Mahanadi. On the other bank, the *Rath of Jagannath*, the Juggernaut, towered over thousands of the god's devotees. It lumbered forward, pulled along by a frenzied mass to a cacophony of drums and cymbals and chanting voices. Punit was down there, amid the mêlée, maybe with Annie close by. Time was running out.

"We'll never make it in this thing," I said, opening the cab door. "We need to go on foot."

Surrender-not parked the truck at the side of the road as best he could, then jumped down to join me as

I sprinted across the bridge then fought through the procession. Up ahead, the Juggernaut grew closer. It seemed to have stopped and a cheer went up from the crowd.

"Jagannath has reached the temple," shouted Surrender-not above the din.

Suddenly there was a bang, as of a pistol going off. Surrender-not and I stopped and looked at each other. A chill went up my spine. Then came several more explosions.

"Firecrackers!" cried Surrender-not.

"Come on," I shouted, "there's still time!"

We made it to the temple compound. The Juggernaut and a few hundred pilgrims had been allowed within its walls, with the rest of the throng held back by a line of soldiers. I spotted Major Bhardwaj under an umbrella near the entrance and ran up to him.

"I need to see Prince Punit immediately!"

He seemed shocked by my sodden, mud-spattered appearance. He shook his head. "His Highness is inside the temple for the prayers."

"Colonel Arora, then," I said. "Where is he?"

"The colonel is with him."

"I need to speak to Arora immediately!" I shouted. "If I don't, the consequences will be on your head."

He stared at me for a moment, then shook his head again. I didn't have the time to argue, so I pushed past him and ran forward with Surrender-not at my heels.

Inside the compound, on a raised dais under an awning stood members of the royal court, dressed to the nines despite the weather. Annie was among them, chatting to Emily Carmichael. She was as surprised to see me as Major Bhardwaj had been. Hurrying over to the railing, she called down.

"What are you doing here, Sam?"

I ignored her and ran towards the temple doors. As I reached them, I was grabbed by two guards, while another two accosted Surrender-not. I should have remonstrated, but instead opted to punch my way free. Ten hours in the monsoon rains has a tendency to cloud your judgement. I managed to throw a right hook before being coshed on the head by something hard, and then the wet ground rose up to greet me. Close by, I could hear Surrender-not shouting. He at least was still on his feet.

I was lifted unceremoniously back up, pushed against the side of the dais, in preparation for a blow to the face, when the temple doors opened. Out strode Punit. The priest I'd seen with the Maharani Shubhadra was at his left hand and Colonel Arora at his right. He was dressed in a silk *kurta* and turban, both encrusted in diamonds and emeralds, and it was fair to say he looked a bit better than I did. A conch shell rang out. Cymbals crashed and the crowds cheered, drowning out my shouts. The chief priest glanced over. He must have seen the guards restraining me. I hoped the sight of the struggle would cause him to pause. I hoped he'd realise something was dreadfully wrong and stop the coronation. But he looked straight through me.

Another saffron-clad priest walked over to him with a silver tray. The chief priest lifted a sweetmeat from it, blessed it and then placed it in the prince's mouth. The conch shell sounded once more. A line of priests exited the temple and began distributing sweet-meats to the assembled dignitaries on the dais.

I called out one last time and Colonel Arora finally caught sight of me. After the initial shock, he walked over, his head protected by a flunkey carrying an umbrella, and ordered the guards to release me.

"Wyndham?" he said. "What the devil are you doing here? You look like a drowned goat."

"You need to get the prince out of here and back to the palace," I shouted. "He's still in danger!"

"Nonsense," he said sharply. "We've arrested Devika, and Davé. What further threat can there be?"

"You need to trust me," I said urgently.

He stopped for a moment, then walked towards me. His neat, starched uniform darkened under the rain. He stopped inches from me. Water ran in rivulets down the crags of his face and into his beard. His expression hardened.

"Tell me this isn't some sort of joke."

"It's deadly serious."

He barked some orders at the guards who instantly surrounded a startled Punit. He began to argue, then suddenly stopped and clutched at his chest. His legs gave way. Arora ran towards him, still shouting orders. My captors released their grip and I sprinted forward.

Arora cradled the prince's head in his arms and shouted something at the soldiers. They lifted Punit and carried him to the shelter of the canopy. The prince writhed in pain, a crown of perspiration dotting his forehead.

"Get a doctor," I shouted to Major Bhardwaj. At the sound of my voice, Punit opened his eyes and looked straight at me. His silk tunic was mud-spattered and sodden. He seemed to want to tell me something. I knelt down and put my ear close to his face. But no sound came from his lips.

Suddenly I felt Annie beside me. She had her hand on Punit's neck, searching for a pulse.

"His heart's stopped."

I tore open his tunic and began to pound at his sternum. A pre-cordial thump they'd called it in the army. They said it offered a chance of resuscitation if applied appropriately and quickly enough. I'd never seen it work, but I had to try. Twenty seconds passed, then forty, then a minute. I kept pounding. I felt Annie's hand on my shoulder.

"Sam."

I looked up.

Tears ran down her face. Or maybe it was the rain. I looked back at Punit and hit his chest once more. A diamond studded button fell from his tunic. It skittered off the platform and landed in the mud at the foot of Lord Jagannath's chariot.

# Epilogue

The flames rose high into the air, orange tongues leaping from charred, cracked wood as though carrying the very soul of the dead man skywards. This was my third funeral in Sambalpore: it was almost becoming a habit. Still, in terms of spectacle, if there was one worth attending, it was probably this one. They'd pulled out all the stops this time. Princes were one thing, the old Maharaja was something else.

His body had been carried here to the sound of bagpipes and trumpets, atop a golden gun carriage, flanked by mounted lancers in emerald tunics and golden turbans. Ahead of them, the obligatory elephants — dozens of them adorned in gold and silken finery. They processed along roads strewn with rose petals and through a hail of flowers thrown from the rooftops, to the burning *ghat* on the river, just outside the temple to Lord Jagannath. It was the same spot where two of his sons had been cremated.

The funeral pyre had been lit by his third son, the infant Prince Alok, the new Maharaja of Sambalpore. The boy had to be helped by his prime minister, the

Dewan, Harish Chandra Davé. What is it the French say? *Plus ça change . . .*

Davé stood between the prince and the other dignitaries: princelings from the neighbouring kingdoms, British officers in plumed pith helmets, and Carmichael in his morning suit. But the person I wanted to see wasn't up there.

I turned away as the flames died down and walked back towards the temple compound. It was drier than the last time I'd been here, the mud baked hard again by the sun. I stared up at a blue sky. It was the first time I'd seen it that colour over Sambalpore. A new *purdah* car was parked to one side, in the same place that the old one had been that first morning, several months ago, when Annie and I had come here in the old Mercedes. That was good. It meant all I had to do was wait.

Sure enough, after fifteen minutes, the doors opened and into the sunshine stepped the old Maharani Shubhadra, accompanied by the priest who'd fed Punit his final meal.

"Your Highness," I said as I walked over.

"Captain Wyndham." She smiled. "It is a pleasure to see you again."

She betrayed no hint of surprise at seeing me. But why would she? From the start she'd known everything.

She joined me at the foot of the temple stairs. "It was good of you to come. My husband would have welcomed your presence."

"I seem to be attending quite a few funerals in Sambalpore," I said. "I sincerely hope this is the last one."

"As do I," she replied. "The new Maharaja is very young. I am confident he shall have a long and happy reign."

"With your guidance, Your Highness, I'm sure he will. In fact, that's why I'm here. I came to congratulate you on your appointment as regent."

The Maharani smiled graciously.

"And yet I feel there may be something more to your visit, Captain. Would you care to accompany me to my car?"

"Your Highness is perceptive," I replied as we set off slowly across the compound. "May I speak candidly?"

"I would expect nothing less from you, Captain."

I'd been building up to this moment for days, but now that the time had arrived, I fell mute, unsure of how to begin.

"Prince Adhir," I said finally.

"Yes?"

"By all accounts he would have made a good ruler . . ."

"Do you have a question, Captain?"

"Was it necessary for him to die? Punit I can perhaps understand — he was feckless, irresponsible — but Adhir was different."

"Why are you asking me, Captain? Do you think I was somehow responsible for their deaths? Adhir was killed in Calcutta, far from here, and Punit died of

434

heart failure from his exertions during the *Rath Yatra*. You saw him collapse. The post-mortem confirmed it."

"I've no doubt that's what the doctor's report would have said, but I saw him eat the offering given to him by your priest that day."

She stopped walking and turned to face me. "If you suspect foul play, Captain, you should report it. Indeed, you should have done so immediately. I take it you have some proof that the offering was tainted?"

"You know I've no proof, Your Highness, simply a craving for the truth."

Her lips turned up in a half-smile. "Perhaps the Lord Jagannath, in his wisdom, decided that neither Adhir nor Punit would be fit to rule Sambalpore?"

"Perhaps," I agreed, "but I suspect there was another power at work. On the night the monsoon rains came, I realised something. It struck me that you've always been the real ruler of Sambalpore. Your late husband might have been Maharaja, but by all accounts he was more interested in living the high life. I think he was content to leave the running of the kingdom to you."

She tapped my arm gently and we started walking, once more around the courtyard. The temple towered above us, imposing. In the bright sunlight, its marble carvings shone in a way they hadn't in the days before the monsoon. I should have paid them more attention. The answer had been up there all along, carved into the temple walls in explicit detail. The coupling of the divine and the mortal. Gods and women entwined.

"When your husband fell ill, you realised your days as de facto ruler were numbered. Adhir was next in line to the throne, but he was his own man, with his own ideas of how to run the kingdom. You weren't his mother. If you were, you may have had some influence over him, but he was never likely to follow your counsel. Worse, he might even have followed that of his white mistress, Miss Pemberley."

The Maharani seemed to shrink at the mention of the Englishwoman.

"So you had him assassinated. For the longest time, I couldn't understand why the assassin would kill himself rather than submit to arrest and questioning. That sort of devotion comes only from political or religious zeal. The man was obviously a devotee — he had the mark of the *Sricharanam* on his forehead and he carried out his assassination on the first day of the festival of Lord Jagannath. But I couldn't understand why? By all accounts Adhir had never upset any religious orders. Why would they want to kill him?

"It was on the night that the rains came that I realised. The assassin wasn't just a devotee of Lord Jagannath, he was also a devotee of his high priestess. *You.* You're the daughter of the King of Puri, the Sweeper King, the keeper of Jagannath's most holy shrine. Your very name — *Shubhadra* — is the name of Lord Jagannath's own sister! And of course, let's not forget poor Punit, who died on the steps of *this* temple — a temple that you had built. If all this truly was Lord Jagannath's will, then you were the more-than-willing vessel doing his bidding.

"I think you convinced the young maharani, Devika to go along with your plan. She's not much more than

**436**

a child and I'd imagine quite impressionable. You told her that with her help, you'd place her son on the throne. All you wanted in return was to be appointed regent until the boy reached majority."

The Maharani brushed back a stray strand of grey hair which the breeze had blown across her face. "That's quite a story, Captain. Let me ask you this: do *you* think Adhir would have made a good ruler?"

"I couldn't say. I only met him on the day you had him killed."

"Let me tell you about Prince Adhir," she continued. "In his own way, he was as arrogant and foolish as his brother. Refusing to accede to the Chamber of Princes on a matter of principle — what presumptuous nonsense. Sambalpore needs a voice and friends in high places if it is to survive. He dabbled in socialism, held discussions with the Congress and those ridiculous Bengali radicals. Adhir would have sidelined us, destroyed our credibility with the British and with it our sway over our neighbours."

"He would have had advisers," I said. "Colonel Arora for one." I wondered what had happened to the colonel. He'd disappeared shortly after Punit's death. The rumour was that he'd been arrested. Maybe he'd had his skull crushed.

"Advisers?" she spat. "The only person he ever listened to was that English mistress of his. She had him wrapped around her finger. And once he was Maharaja, I have no doubt she would have convinced him to marry her. And then? What message do you think that would send to the people? Sambalpore is a conservative place. The bond between the ruling family and our subjects is one built on more than simple loyalty. It is built on faith and devotion, *theirs* and *ours*. The people would never have accepted a white maharani. God forbid they should have had a child. Believe me, Captain, the kingdom most certainly would not have been safe in his hands."

"But it is safe in yours?"

She stopped and looked at me like a mother at a stubborn child.

"Do you think a woman cannot lead a nation? Would you believe me if I told you that the opposite is true? For two hundred years, your people have wielded a malign power in India, corrupting our rulers till they are no more than your feckless lackeys. In such a world, it is us, the women of the zenana, safe in our sanctuary beyond the pernicious reach of your Residents and your *advisers*, who have been the guardians of our culture and our heritage. For fifty years I have given my life to Sambalpore and its people. I have cared for them, educated them, protected them. I won't abandon them now. I fear, though, that may be beyond your comprehension."

I shook my head. The way she told it, Adhir and Punit's deaths were necessary for the very survival of the kingdom and her actions almost noble. "And was it for the betterment of the people of Sambalpore that you reinstated Davé as Dewan? A man who stole millions of rupees' worth of revenue from this kingdom and had an Englishman murdered to cover it up?"

"Davé stole nothing," she said as if it was a matter of fact.

"I saw the two reports," I said. "Golding's original and the one Davé doctored, increasing the value of resources in the diamond mines. Golding discovered the discrepancy and confronted Davé. He paid for that with his life."

The Maharani paused. "You are aware that Sambalpore is the only kingdom in the whole of Orissa where diamonds are found. It is one of the blessings bestowed on this land by the Lord Jagannath, and we have been mining them for centuries. It is a closely guarded secret, but for years we have known that the reserves of diamonds in our mines were reaching exhaustion. And we knew because Mr Golding told us.

"Every year he employed geologists to produce an estimate of what was left. As you are aware, Sambalpore's influence lies chiefly in the economic power that our diamond production bestows upon us. Without that power, we are nothing.

"Fortuitously, the British came to our rescue. For a hundred and fifty years you have been trying to get your hands on our mines, and Sir Ernest Fitzmaurice is merely the latest in a long line of suitors. This time, however, it was deemed beneficial to accept his advances. But Fitzmaurice wouldn't want the mines if he knew their true position. Davé therefore suggested that we paint a rosier picture for him, but neither Adhir nor Mr Golding would countenance such a thing, Adhir because he was pig-headed and Golding because of his scruples. The plan was shelved, that is until

Adhir's unfortunate demise, at which point Davé resurrected it. Golding, of course, objected. He was not meant to be harmed but in the course of rather heated discussions, he suffered a heart attack."

"A bit like Punit," I said.

"It is the truth, Captain."

"But selling the mines, at whatever value, doesn't solve your problem," I said. "Without them, you lose your influence."

"The world is changing, Captain." She smiled. "These days there are other things that are almost as valuable as diamonds."

And then it hit me. "Coal," I said.

"The funds received from the sale to Anglo-Indian Diamond will be used to exploit Sambalpore's coal deposits. In fact, Mr Golding was the first to advocate their commercialisation. The coal mines shall be his legacy."

I felt the bile rising in my throat. "You can't simply murder an Englishman and expect there to be no consequences."

"There was no murder," she said. "He died of natural causes."

"I found his body at the bottom of a mine shaft," I said. "Was that natural, too? His death demands justice."

"You remember when we spoke last time, I cautioned you about the concept of justice. What matters is the truth. You have that."

"And if I seek to act on it? I doubt the India Office will take kindly to the fact that a British subject was murdered."

"They would do nothing, Captain. The days when the British could openly meddle in the affairs of a native state are long gone. With all that's happening in the rest of India, their only concern is that Sambalpore remain a stable and trusted ally, and that we join the Chamber of Princes. It would take the deaths of a thousand accountants before they would jeopardise that."

"Perhaps," I said. "But it would be wrong of me not to mention it in my report."

The old maharani sighed. "It would be a shame if such baseless allegations were allowed to tarnish Sambalpore's reputation. I would wish to avoid such things."

She fell silent for a moment. "There is a woman of your acquaintance," she continued, "a Miss Shreya Bidika. She has not been prosecuted for her seditious acts against the kingdom, despite the advice of the Dewan and the head of the militia. I would not wish to have to commence proceedings against her, after all."

The situation was clear. I could report Golding's death to the authorities in Calcutta, but, as the Maharani had stated, it was hardly likely they'd act upon it. And, just in case I decided to do something foolish, she still held Shreya Bidika as insurance. I was beginning to understand how she'd managed to control this country for fifty years. I had to hand it to her. She probably *was* a better choice of ruler than either Adhir or Punit.

"And now," she said as the *purdah* car drew up, "you must excuse me. There are affairs of state to which I

**441**

must attend." She took my hand. "I hope we meet again some day, Captain. In the meantime, remember what I told you. Your soul craves the truth. You have that now. Justice is a matter for the gods."

She released my hand and walked towards the car. The chauffeur opened the rear door and for a moment I caught sight of Davé on the back seat. He had three lines marked in ash on his forehead.

The car sped off, leaving me with the Maharani's words ringing in my ears. Slowly I walked out of the compound, towards the banyan tree by the riverbank, under which Annie stood waiting.

# Author's Note

This novel was inspired by the tale of the Begums of Bhopal, a dynasty of Muslim queens who ruled the Indian princely state of Bhopal for most of the period between 1819 and 1926. In today's climate of religious fundamentalism and reactionary politics, we would do well to remember that for a hundred years, an Indian kingdom was administered (and administered well) by a line of Muslim women.

The kingdom of Sambalpur (Sambalpore) did exist as a princely state, roughly within the borders set out in the book, though it was seized by the East India Company in 1849 under the doctrine of lapse, when its last ruler, Narayan Singh, died without a direct male heir.

It had a history stretching back several thousand years and is mentioned in the book of Ptolemy as Sambalaka on the left bank of the river "Manada", the present-day Mahanadi. It is also mentioned in Chinese historical records, including those of Xuanzang, and in the writings of the celebrated King Indrabhuti of Sambalaka of Odra Desha, the oldest known king of Sambalpur and the founder of Vajrayana Buddhism and Lamaism.

Sambalpur has always been a centre for the worship of Lord Jagannath, with tenth-century records mentioning an idol of the deity in a cave near Sonepur within the kingdom. It would appear too that the Lord Jagannath bestowed his blessings upon the kingdom. It is the only location in Orissa where diamonds and coal were both prevalent. Indeed, the seventeenth-century French merchant Jean-Baptiste Tavernier in his travel account *Six Voyages en Turquie, en Perse et aux Indes* (1676–77) wrote about the numerous famous diamond mines of Sambalpur. He states that eight thousand people were at work in these mines at the time of his visit, though evidence suggests the diamonds were in alluvial deposits rather than deep mines. According to the English historian Edward Gibbon, Sambalpuri diamonds were exported as far afield as imperial Rome.

For those wishing to learn more about the Indian princely states and their flamboyant maharajas, the excellent *Highness: The Maharajahs of India* by Ann Morrow would make a fascinating and extremely readable place to start.

And for those interested in the lost world of opium smoking, *Opium Fiend* by Steven Martin is an eye-opening account of one man's fascination and descent into addiction with this most exotic of drugs.

# Acknowledgements

There are so many people who have helped take this book from an idea in my head to a fully formed novel, and I'm indebted to each and every one of them for their insight, advice, patience and good humour.

I'm indebted, in particular, to my wonderful team of editors, Alison Hennessey, Kate Harvey and Jade Chandler who have complemented each other's work so seamlessly and so excellently over the last eighteen months.

Thanks also to team Harvill Seeker, especially Anna Redman for her tireless work over the last two years travelling the length and breadth of the country publicising the book and visiting every Travelodge en route, September Withers for marketing the book so enthusiastically, Kris Potter for his wonderful artwork and Alison Tullet for her eagle eyes. Thanks too, to Liz Foley, Rachel Cugnoni, Richard Cable, Bethan Jones, Alex Russell, Tom Drake-Lee, Penny Liechti and the wider team at Vintage for believing in Sam and Surrender-not and for being so supportive.

I'm grateful to my agent, Sam Copeland, the handsomest man in publishing, for having faith in me, and to the team at Rogers Coleridge and White for all their hard work.

Thank you to my wife, Sonal, whose love and support makes everything possible, and to my boys, Milan and Aran, for bringing chaos to our lives.

A debt of gratitude is owed to Val McDermid, as well as to Vaseem Khan and the other members of Team Dishoom for their support, to the staff of the Idea Store in Canary Wharf for giving me a place to write, and to Yoana Karamitrova for keeping Sonal and me sane.

Thanks of course, to all those good friends who let me borrow their names without worrying about what I'd do with them: to my old art teacher, Mr Wilson, to Derek Carmichael, Nicholas Portelli, Vivek Arora, and Rajan Kumar, to my partners at Houghton Street Capital, Hash Davé, Neeraj Bhardwaj and Alok Gangola — you are like family to me and you owe me for not making any of you a eunuch.

And finally, a special thank you to Adhir Sahaye, Punit Bedi and Mark Golding — sorry for killing you.